North to Rabaul

North to

Rabaul

A novel by
Christopher Wood

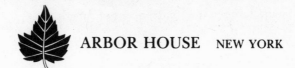 ARBOR HOUSE   NEW YORK

To my friends at the Port Morseby Squash Club

Prologue

The footsteps echoed hollowly down the long marble corridor of the Navy Department. It was ten past one and most of the outer offices were empty. Only the occasional secretary, enslaved by urgent business, pecked resentfully at her typewriter. The others were at lunch. The doors of the inner offices were usually closed, but here and there occupants could be seen sitting at their desks with chin cupped in hand or gazing pensively at wall maps. Certain people found the lunch hour a good time to put plans together.

"Mr. Knox."

Frank Knox looked up from his desk which bore a card carrying his name and the legend "U.S. Navy Secretary." "Hello, Tom." He took the buff folder from the cipher clerk and glanced at the Decoding Department classification. A green tag—it was not considered top priority. "Interesting?"

Tom Miles wobbled his head from side to side equivocally. He

showed no sign of going away so Knox opened the file and read
the sheet of paper that it contained.

RADIO INTERCEPT POST, DUTCH HARBOR, ALEUTIANS. SIGNAL
INTERCEPTED *0840* HOURS, 14 APRIL 1943. FROM FLAGSHIP
MUSASHI, TRUK. TO COMMANDERS JAPANESE GARRISONS RABAUL
AND BOUGAINVILLE. ADMIRAL YAMAMOTO ACCOMPANIED BY CHIEF
OF STAFF AND SEVEN GENERAL OFFICERS LEAVES TRUK FOR TROOP
INSPECTIONS *0800* HOURS 15 APRIL STOP ARRIVE RABAUL *1630*
HOURS STOP LEAVE *1400* HOURS 18 APRIL STOP ARRIVE
BOUGAINVILLE *1745* HOURS STOP ULTRA SECRET DOCUMENT
NOT TO BE COPIED OR FILED STOP TO BE DESTROYED AFTER
IMPLEMENTATION STOP.

Knox closed the file and looked up at Miles. "He flits around,
doesn't he?" he said. "I guess he's boosting the troops' morale."

"I'd like to boost his morale," Miles said vehemently. "Boost it
right up his little yellow ass."

"Sure, Tom," Knox said patiently. He wondered why those farthest from the front always seemed to hate the enemy the most. He
threw the file into the middle of the three trays in front of him.

"You know, in the old days that man wouldn't still be alive,"
Miles continued.

"They used to have single combat, didn't they? Where the commanders went out and fought each other in front of their men?"

"We don't do that any more," Knox said.

"I don't know why not," Miles scowled. "I can think of two
thousand men who'd like to have a crack at Yamamoto. They're
lying dead at the bottom of Pearl Harbor. The fact that he's still
alive is an insult to their memory."

"That's right," Knox said. He returned to his report and then,
his mind triggered by something Miles had said, reached out and
retrieved the buff folder.

"I'll be getting back," the clerk sighed. He paused at the door.
"You ought to eat something once in a while." His footsteps
started to echo away down the corridor.

Knox didn't hear him. His mind was on other things.

He reread the time on the signal with growing excitement: "AR-

RIVE BOUGAINVILLE 1745 HOURS." Allowing for the time change, there was over twenty-four hours before Admiral Yamamoto arrived at Kahali airstrip on the island of Bougainville. Knox leaned back in his chair and grinned. Yamamoto was renowned for his punctuality.

Crossing to the wall map, he sought the nearest U.S. air base to Bougainville. Henderson Field on the island of Guadalcanal, approximately four hundred miles away. Knox frowned. He asked the operator for a number and tapped his fingers impatiently while he waited. The telephone rang and a hard, flinty voice sounded on the end of the line.

"Charles Lindbergh."

Lindbergh, the first pilot to conquer the Atlantic solo, was adviser to the U.S. Air Force on long-distance flying.

"Frank Knox here, Chuck. I need your advice. It's urgent. Would a P-38 flying out of Henderson Field carry enough fuel to make an interception over Bougainville and get back to base?"

"Hang on." There was the sound of papers being shifted. Knox could imagine Lindbergh hurriedly making calculations on whatever surface was available to him. "No. Not without extra fuel tanks."

"How long would it take to fit them?"

Another pause. "If you had the tanks it would take about ten hours. What did you have in mind, Frank?"

Knox took a deep breath and found that he had underlined "Bougainville" so hard that his pen had gone through the paper. "I'm calling it Operation Vengeance," he said. "We're going to go after Yamamoto."

North to Rabaul

CHAPTER ONE

THE twin slopes fell steeply at first, and then swelled into gentle rises, climaxed by twin knolls. These stubby, brown peaks tilted forward over a sharp descent that culminated in an isolated thicket. Carter figured he'd place his machine gun teams on both knolls. After he burnt out the thicket.

The woman followed the sweep of Carter's eyes with drowsy interest. "What are you looking at?" she asked.

Carter raised his glance from her body. "Your pussy," he said.

The woman smiled and drew up her knees. She slowly parted her legs and let her head drop back against the pillow. "Look a little closer," she invited.

Carter smiled a conciliatory smile and changed his position so that his left arm stretched across her breasts and his nose nudged her cheek. The scarlet poinsettia outside the window stood out clearly as if in a picture frame. It tapped admonishingly against the

3

grille honeycombed with dead insects, and made him wish he was outside this tacky Port Moresby bedroom with a woman who did not even have the tact to put her husband's photograph in a drawer when she invited home a lover.

"I gotta get going," he said.

"I thought you said you had the whole afternoon?"

"I just remembered something." It sounded like a lie. He didn't care.

"You're a mean son of a bitch, aren't you?" She brushed her fingers through his short-cropped blond hair.

"If you like."

"I don't like." There was a pause while she reared up, her white breasts flapping. "Don't get me wrong. I don't want you to tell me you love me or any of that rubbish. I just don't want to be treated like a piece of dirt."

Carter sighed. "I'm sorry. But I have got to get back to camp. Swimming detail. I said I'd stand in for one of the other guys. They need an officer to go down to the beach." He made it up as he went along. "Believe me." He kissed her on the wrist.

She slumped down beside him, half-forgiving. "Can't they go by themselves?"

"Yeah, but they start brawling. You know what soldiers are like."

"Especially Yanks." Her right hand moved between his thighs hopefully as she looked into his slate-blue eyes.

"Yeah, we're the worst. You know why they call us that, don't you?" His fingers entwined themselves in her wet pubic hair. She giggled in nervous anticipation.

"Because they—?"

"That's right." He began to tug at the tight curls and drew himself up on one elbow, leaving a sweat patch on the pillow where his head had been. Grudgingly, his own body began to respond to his pulling and kneading of the flesh beneath it. It was a kind of once-removed masturbation. The woman thought he was growing because she was working him with her slippery fingers. He knew it was his own memories of other women and other times. Times when there was something new and exciting about it.

The woman opened her mouth to be kissed, and he pressed his face down against the pillow. He felt a sense of irritation and

4

despair. Why were they doing this? What were they looking for that either had the power to give? They should have known better. Why was he so depressed? The first post-orgasmic blues should be twenty minutes dead by now.

"Don't you want to?" Her voice was puzzled. Sad.

"Sure."

Carter looked at her. She was probably not having a very good time either. The difference was that she was trying. She knew that the only face-saving exit for both of them was the one he had already entered. He scrambled across her body and pushed himself forward, feeling nothing.

"That's good," she said.

He had a shower before he left, but by the time he was twenty-five yards from the bungalow the sweat had soaked through his shirt beneath the armpits. The heat had an almost tangible quality. It seemed to be packed into every hole in the body like oven-baked cotton wool. You could never forget it was there. Every sulky movement of the air brought it against you as if the door of a blast furnace had been opened. The glare hurt your eyes. A fine layer of dust infiltrated your nostrils and layered your tongue. Even the needle-sharp chirping of the insects in the grass seemed like some demonically orchestrated accompaniment to the shimmering heat.

The bungalow lay between the town and the airfield in what was once a residential area but was now mainly abandoned or destroyed by Japanese bombing and army and civilian looting. Gardens were reverting to jungle, the bougainvillea, hibiscus and oleander throttled by vines. Gutted shells of scorched plasterboard seemed held up by the greenery that overran them. Here and there was smashed crockery, broken shelves, a doll with its stuffing hanging out. A smell of decay hung in the air.

Far to the north were the mountains, blue-black, with their peaks lost in cloud like white fleece snagged on a fencetop. They stretched from left to right as far as the eye could see, menacing and aloof. The Owen Stanley range rose to over twelve thousand feet. There, troops of the 2nd Australian Force, and the Japanese trying to push their way down to Port Moresby from the north, were locked in combat. If Moresby fell, the Japs had secured

5

their last steppingstone to Australia . . .

Carter looked across to the airfield. It had been carved out of a valley covered with sun-browned grass and irregular clumps of gum trees, their leaves limp and thick with dust. Gun emplacements were notched into the hills, and areas of ground were burned black where fires had been started by bombs or crashing aircraft. The burned-out shell of a Mitsubishi 97 stood apart from a detritus of allied aircraft that had been hit on the ground and bulldozed to the side of the runway. On the runway itself three American B-25 bombers were waiting to take off. Sandbag-protected pits concealed scattered fuel dumps and the men who flew and serviced the planes. There was an all-pervading smell of gasoline and a fine cloud of gray dust that never had time to settle.

As Carter watched, a battered Lockheed transport taxied to a halt outside a corrugated iron shack, and three men and the pilot got out. One was a native, wearing a *lap-lap,* an ankle length twist of cotton material tied about his waist, and one of the white men had his arm in a sling, his legs covered with jungle sores. The other was tall and gnarled, with baggy shorts that flapped about his knees as he walked. His peaked officer's hat seemed to have settled onto his head like the roof of a long-abandoned house. Somebody saluted him, he returned the gesture awkwardly and several paces later, as if it was an afterthought, as if where he came from there was not a lot of saluting. In fact there was not . . . They had just returned from a mission they'd been on too many times before . . . watching on a near-by enemy-held island for movements of ships and planes indicating stepped up Japanese activity from Japanese-held Rabaul on New Britain to the north that might signal the long-feared major assault on Australia. They'd thought they'd been doing a job, but now had abruptly been pulled out by submarine—after a bloody exchange with a Japanese patrol.

His jeep was where Carter had left it, nose pressed into a clump of gum trees beside the strip. He could hear his driver slapping at mosquitoes when he was twenty yards away.

"Did you pick up the mail?" Carter demanded. There was an enforced briskness in his voice to conceal various feelings of guilt.

"Sure did." Jones rose lazily from behind the jeep, dusting down his uniform. "Did you get what you were looking for, sir?"

To Carter's ear, the "sir" came in a beat late. "Yes, thank you."

"Did you have a good time?"

"Same answer, Jones."

"What was she like?"

Carter paused for a moment. "She was like your mother." He let the remark sink in as he climbed into the jeep. "Now, do you want to hang around here and watch the hospital planes come in or can we get back to camp?"

As they drove Carter shielded his mouth and nose against the dust and looked at the face of Jones beside him. Three weeks in New Guinea. Nineteen years in the world. Bland, unformed, more innocent than he could ever realize, his skin only just beginning to turn yellow from the Atebrin anti-malaria tablets, his cheeks hardly pitted with insect bites. He had it all to come.

Carter's spirits rose with sight of the sea. It was a shimmering cobalt blue laced with green, and ran away like an enormous playing field to be bounded by the thin white line of the reef. When you were born and bred in the Midwest the sea meant something. Any sea. As they drew closer the water was shallow and transparent and he could see patches of wood and stony outcrops. The sand was a dirty brown, turned up as if by a plough, and littered with gnarls of driftwood. Two old women were wading in the water, looking for anything that the war would bring them, and they were the only people on the beach. Behind the sand a long line of stately casuarina trees stretched down toward the bluff, and on the other side of the road were coconut plantations and a few large houses, mostly abandoned.

It was before one of these houses that Jones slowed down while a sentry in a slouch hat surveyed the vehicle from the shade of the trees. A sign beside the double gates said REHABILITATION CENTER, QUIET PLEASE. The building did not look like a hospital and was protected by a double row of barbed-wire fencing rising to a height of twelve feet. Such locals who took any interest in the place believed it to be a center for treating allied servicemen who had suffered nervous breakdowns and other mental disturbances while on active service. This explained the large number of seemingly able-bodied Americans, Australians, New Zealanders, Dutch, British Filippinos, Indonesians and island natives who passed through the gates seldom to return again.

In fact, the building was the New Guinea Headquarters of the Allied Intelligence Unit, and its prime function was the recruitment and supply of units working behind enemy lines, plus the digestion and implementation of the information they sent or brought back.

The small town of tents behind the house was divided between members of the American and Australian forces, sometimes working together but mostly concentrating on projects within their own spheres of influence.

Carter acknowledged the sentry as the gates swung open and the jeep passed through and behind an avenue of frangipani trees. Here, among the coconut palms, began orderly lines of khaki tents with a dried-up streambed to divide the Australian and American lines. It was noticeable that the Australian side of the camp had smartened up considerably since the arrival of the Americans. A keen undercurrent of rivalry existed between the two groups of men.

Carter dismissed Jones and went to his tent, wondering whether it was worth taking a shower. His shirt was sticking to him, and he had a headache which might be the first symptom of some kind of fever. There was a message on his bed. "Report to me immediately. Dallas." "Immediately" was underlined twice. Carter sighed. That was the way to make something happen; go out and screw somebody. The note was written in Dallas's handwriting so no doubt the major had delivered it personally. What could be that urgent—or perhaps Dallas liked striding around camp seeing what everybody was up to and who was not where he ought to be. Dallas was the only man who *strode* in this heat. They said his shadow got tired trying to keep up with him.

"Major S. T. Dallas, USMC," was typed with visiting-card precision on the center of a rectangle of crisp white cardboard pinned to the door of an office on the second floor of the building looking out across the reef. Above it was another sign saying "Task Force 19." Carter could not remember having seen the second sign before. He knocked once and went in.

The room was dominated by a large wall map of Papua and New Guinea and the offshore islands spilling out to north and east. It

8

included Cairns and Townsville on the Queensland coast of Australia. There was a fan hanging down from the ceiling like an airplane propeller, but it was not working. Instead, a small table fan droned in a listless semicircle agitating the corners of the papers strewn across the desk. The two windows were covered by a fine metal grille to keep out insects, and further obscured by luminous green blinds that plunged the room into semidarkness. It looked cool but it felt hot and stuffy.

Major Dallas stood up impatiently as Carter came in. Sweat gleamed on his strained face. "Where the hell have you been?"

"I went to pick up the mail."

"The mail? It occurs to me that your talents are rather underemployed as a mailboy."

"I'm sorry. There didn't seem to be any other demand for them at the time."

"Not on the base."

"Not on the base," repeated Carter evenly. His activities with Jean must be more widely known than he had suspected. Jones shooting his mouth off, most probably.

"May I remind you that you officially need my permission before you go off base. Not to mention the question of basic courtesy. Discipline is lax enough in this outfit as it is."

Carter could agree there. He sometimes wondered why his transfer to the AIU from his old unit had happened. He guessed it was an unflattering judgment by his ex-commanding officer on both his own capabilities and those of the unit he was now serving. There was a body of opinion in the U.S. command that regarded the AIU as paying lip service to what was in reality an unworkable concept of Australian-American unity. Behind the scenes, each ally pursued his own projects in secret. Carter felt like a second-rater in a second-rate organization. "I'm sorry," he said. He was beginning to feel disagreeable again. First the bad sex, now Dallas needling him. It was a lousy afternoon.

Dallas took a deep breath and walked to the wall map. He turned dramatically and jabbed his finger at it.

"What do you know about Rabaul?"

"I know what I read in the coast-watchers' reports—"

"Exactly!" Now the finger jabbed at Carter. "You know it's five

9

hundred miles from Moresby on the northeast coast of the island of New Britain. You presumably know that it has a deep-water harbor, that it is surrounded by extinct volcanoes and that there are sixty thousand Japs dug in there. Japs who overran the island in January of '42 and have been building ever since."

"I knew that," said Carter. He sometimes wondered if Dallas had been an advertising executive in civilian life. He had a habit of leading off any address with a presentation of established facts so that you would accept them as a confirmation of any statement that came after. For the moment Carter pretended he was the client.

"From Rabaul the Japs have landed troops along the north coast of the island, and they're bombing shit out of us here. Every day they bring more men and material into Rabaul. Why? So they can stomp all over our faces when they step across to Australia."

Dallas looked at Carter accusingly, as if he suspected that his own face would be pushed forward to receive the first Japanese boot. Carter waited for him to get to the point.

"And what are we doing? We're lobbing thousands of tons of bombs on them and we're getting nowhere. They're dug into those pumice stone cliffs deeper than ticks on a sheep's back."

Carter nodded, thinking the sheep metaphor a peculiar one. Well, the major was peculiar.

Dallas retired behind his desk and sat down, gesturing for Carter to do the same. "You hit a sore point when you mentioned coast-watchers, Will."

Carter's voice showed genuine concern. "Why, have we lost somebody else?"

Dallas replied with a curt shake of the head. "No. But there's a feeling that we're relying on them too much."

"I don't know what you mean. They know the country . . . they know the natives. You were just talking about Rabaul. What information we can get is eighty percent from coast-watchers. Shipping movements, planes taking off—" He stopped as he realized that he was beginning to sound like Dallas.

"Yes, but that places us in a subsidiary role, Will. Whatever anyone else likes or doesn't like, we're in charge out here. The war in the Pacific is an American responsibility."

"Nobody's ever worried about that with coast-watchers before."

Dallas placed both his hands flat on the table. "Somebody is, now." He raised his eyes toward the ceiling.

Carter groaned. "MacArthur?"

"We are to take, and I quote, 'a more dynamic initiative.' "

"That must be MacArthur," Carter nodded.

" 'American prestige is at stake in this theater of war.' I'm quoting again. Our general, as you know, has a low opinion of the Australian fighting man."

"Has he ever seen one?"

"He was here in November."

"I understand he spent an hour at the beginning of the Kokoda trail." Carter laughed. "The nearest fighting was thirty miles away. I remember because my mother sent me a newspaper clipping from home. It said that General MacArthur was staying in a bungalow near the front line so he could be close to his men. You know what that bungalow was? Government House."

"The general is not responsible for his public-relations releases."

"You amaze me."

Dallas sat back in his chair. "Listen, Carter, I don't want you coming in here and bad-mouthing the general. He issues the orders."

"Right," Carter said. "What's he issued that affects me?"

"He wants a more pronounced American influence on all those activities currently undertaken by coast-watchers. He wants the people back home to know that we're playing a positive role and not just sitting around here on our butts or screwing the local talent. He wants us to get ashore on New Britain and find out what's happening in Rabaul. He wants commando raids on Jap-held islands—Don't look at everything on the basis of one personality. We need a morale boost right now. The British did the same thing when they were pushed out of France. They started making raids across the English channel."

"And lost a lot of good men."

"That's not the point, Carter. We're losing a lot of good men anyway. The General wants to try something different and beef up American leadership in this theater of war—"

"You forgot to say, 'And I quote.' Okay. Where do I come in?"

"You're going on a special training course to prepare you for your new assignment. You and a bunch of"—Dallas paused to choose his words carefully—"hand-picked troops."

"Americans?"

"Americans, Australians, natives. This is a joint operation. There'll be some coast-watchers, too. At least initially. I can introduce you to one of them."

He picked up the telephone without waiting for a reply. "Major Dallas here. Can you come down for a moment? I've got Lieutenant Carter with me."

He replaced the receiver and, for the first time in the interview, smiled at Carter. "Finally some excitement . . ."

"There's one thing I don't understand," Carter said. "This outfit is full of special details sneaking out all over the place. What's going to be different about us?"

Dallas's smile broadened. "You're going to be held in reserve for any special plan that the general cottons to. You're MacArthur's own." He let the news sink in. "I knew that would appeal to you."

There was a knock at the door and Dallas got to his feet.

"Come right on in, captain. This is Lieutenant Will Carter. Lieutenant Carter—Captain Andrew Hudson, Australian coast-watcher."

CHAPTER TWO

HUDSON sat on the beach and looked at the two men swimming a hundred yards from shore. The sea lifted and they disappeared into a trough. Only the black speck that was the forty-four-gallon oil drum further out was still clearly visible, bobbing on the crest of a wave.

"What do you think of this caper, Skip?" the radio operator of his seasoned coast-watcher's team, John "Jeremiah" Johnson, asked.

"It's too early to say."

He was lying. Being assigned to Dallas's Task Force 19 had made him feel that his worst fears about himself were being shared by others. Nobody knew what they were really supposed to be doing, and the unit was comprised of callow young American officers drawn from a variety of units and old-stager nationals like himself whose continuing presence behind enemy lines was now presumably thought to be a liability. Hudson sighed. Whatever happened, he didn't like a bit what he had got himself into. He looked at Johnson's yellow-brown frame beside him and started to fill his pipe. The scar from a Japanese bullet on Johnson's arm from the last operation was healed, as were most of the leg ulcers. He'd started to fill out too . . . the food was awful but at least it put some weight on you . . . But nothing could wash or wear away the sallow Atabrined skin or the memory of what had happened when his Australian garrison on Rabaul had been overrun by the Japanese, he'd escaped into the jungle, been captured and escaped again. He was a young man, already grown old.

"What do you make of the Yanks?"

Hudson sucked at his pipe. "Too early to say. They're friendly enough. They haven't had the experience, that's all."

Johnson brushed a fly. "I feel I'm wasting my bloody time. I mean, swimming out to stick limpet mines on an oil drum. Is that what we're going to do when we get back?"

Hudson's pipe started to draw and a thin wisp of smoke drifted across the beach like smoke from a distant stack. "What do you mean 'get back?' We don't even know where we're going, do we?"

"It's true that we're up for something special—"

"I don't know any more than you do." Hudson leaned back and pulled his hat over his eyes. He could hear the heavy murmur of the sea and the occasional pounding and retreating hiss of a wave. There was a ventilation hole in his jungle hat, and he could see through it like a peephole to the palm fronds above. They moved backward and forward across each other like myriad pairs of scissors, fuzzy and out of focus. The effect was soporific, and he closed his eyes and thought back to the thriving plantation he had been forced to abandon on the island of New Ireland. Twenty-five years' hard work gone to waste.

He remembered the small trading post he had started with. There was a track leading down to the wooden school, which had open latticework sides against the heat. The truant eyes of the children always rolled sideways as he rode past. Then there were the tulip trees in early summer. Eighty feet high, they looked as if they had burst into flames with their candelabras of fiery red

14

flowers at every branch tip. The giant pods lodged in the branches like nesting birds, and the soft water-filled buds were prized by the children because they could be used like miniature water pistols. He thought of the careful acquisitions of land, the extensions to the store, the house he had built by the beach with its crisp white nameplate: "Trade Winds," the boys who had helped him work the plantation—Nambu, Bosko, Kita—and the other settlers who had arrived—Jeff Sculley, "Ginger" Saunders, Ray and Doris White.

All dead now.

All killed.

"I don't ever want to see Rabaul again." Johnson's voice came unprompted and unexpected, like a radio set suddenly coming on.

Hudson pulled his hat from his face and sat up. The boy was staring out to sea but not seeing the horizon. His mind was somewhere else. Somewhere that caused a nervous twitch to run across the back of his hand.

Hudson took his arm and shook it as gently as he would have done if the boy was having a nightmare. "Do you want to talk about it?"

Johnson shook his head vehemently. "No, I don't even want to think about it."

"But you can't help it, can you?" Hudson nodded. "We all think about things we want to forget." He saw the Japs throwing Ray White through the window into his burning house. "Anyway"—he patted Johnson's arm—"anytime you want to give it a burl . . ."

"Thanks." The boy was still looking out across the Coral Sea.

Hudson was grateful for the silence. He did not want to talk. Words could never express what you felt . . . not his words, anyway. You made a gesture and that was it. You repeated things that people had said to you and you listened. That usually made people feel better. Doctors were great listeners . . . they could listen the breath right out of your body. "Well, don't worry," he said. "There's no talk about us trying to get to Rabaul."

"It doesn't really matter." Johnson snapped back his head and nodded out toward the swimming figures. "Is that joker ever going to get out of that drum?"

Hudson frowned. "They shouldn't even be trying. This is shark water."

Carter turned on his side and swam with his arm resting against the small float that supported the limpet mine. The drum was much further away than it had looked from the shore, and the sea rougher. There must be a current, too, because the slowness of his progress could not be only due to the swell that was running. The water buoyed him up so that he could see the drum twenty yards away, then he fell back into the trough. He hated those moments when the tops of the palm trees disappeared and he was buried in a hole in the ocean. He felt he was never going to come up again, that the water would close over his head. The thought made him panic momentarily and strike forward in a flurry of legs. His foot touched something. What was that? His mouth filled with water and he choked and gasped for air.

"Get it together, lieutenant. You're the slowest of the bunch."

The instructor was swimming beside him. A lazy crawl, probably perfected in some Pasadena pool. His mouth was an ever-open museum in which his perfect white teeth were the prize exhibit, and his stomach was hard and flat.

Carter had taken an instant dislike to him. It was now deepening into hatred. He cleared his nostrils and dog-paddled while he got his breathing working. A green mass of water surged past him and he found himself looking at the beach, where a sprinkling of men watched from the shade of the palms. It was an even bet that the old Australian with the baggy shorts and the pipe had his eye on him. He didn't miss much, that guy. And his radio operator, who never smiled, and only seemed to speak in monosyllables. Strange guys. Still, they must know their jobs. It was up to him to prove that he knew his.

"Do you think you can make it?" The voice was mocking, not sympathetic.

Carter bit back a go fuck yourself. "Sure."

"Let's go then, lieutenant."

The instructor flipped forward onto his stomach and flaunted the stirred honey of his shoulder muscles as he carved a passage toward the forty-four-gallon drum. Carter looked at it apprehen-

16

sively. It was straining against its weed-covered mooring and flopping through the water like a slowly turning top. It was not going to be easy to attach the limpet mine to either of the ends. One was almost below the surface, the other tilted in the air. And the mine was primed. Primed and packed with PLA, the newly developed plastic that exploded on contact with water and came with each unit packed in a heavy-duty polymeric protective bag.

Carter rested both hands against the back of the float and kicked out with his legs. When it came down to it, the ocean was something to be watched from the shade of the casuarinas on Ela Beach. He was scared of it, of what he could not see below its always changing surface. Something else brushed against his leg and he gritted his teeth, half expecting to feel the searing stab of pain that would tell him that it was a sea wasp or some other kind of jellyfish with a sting capable of causing death. He lunged forward and ordered himself to stay calm. He had enough problems with the mine without letting his imagination go out of control.

He rose to the crest of a wave and looked ahead. The drum was now less than fifty feet away, and the instructor had circled it and was coming back. Carter sank into the trough and came up again. The instructor had disappeared. Carter waited for him to surface and wondered what the crazy bastard was up to. Was he playing some kind of dumb game? Swimming underwater so he could grab Carter's leg and scare him shitless?

Then the blood hit Carter.

He saw it coming toward him down the wave like it was running down a gutter. The instructor rose out of the water, screaming. Carter could see all the beautiful white teeth and halfway down his throat. A white pointer shark had him around the thigh and the blood was washing back over one of its glassy eyeballs.

Carter clung to the float and drew his knees up in silent terror. He could almost feel the rows of teeth sawing and ripping through the flesh and muscle. Man and shark fell back into the sea, and a torrent of bloody water bore past Carter and toward the shore, as if escaping from the scene of a murder.

Carter abandoned the float and struck out blindly, trying to turn every stroke into a blow aimed at beating off attack. Behind him, the instructor was still screaming.

Carter heard a thumping noise and saw that the man was trying to scramble across the drum with the shark still coming at him. As he half hauled himself from the water one could see that his left leg had been nearly taken off at the thigh. It dangled, blood squirting from severed arteries, the firm brown flesh burst apart like a bale slashed with a bush knife. Carter choked as he saw white bone, trod water, felt he ought to try and help but *how,* in God's name . . . ?

The shark turned in a whirlpool and came in again. Its head broke the surface, and Carter glimpsed the teeth before they closed about the man. The tail thrashed and the drum spun slowly, unwinding its burden into the bloody, churning water.

Carter made for the shore. With every stroke he expected the shark's teeth to tear into him. Fear propelled him through the water. He could hear shouts from the men on the shore and caught a glimpse of palm as he fought to the crest of a wave. There was no feeling of exhaustion now, only a terror, fear that greased tired limbs and buoyed his body toward the safety of the beach. Other sharks would be attracted by the blood from the spouting carcass, their killer instincts primed to rip at anything that moved through the water.

Carter lashed out, and in his panic took in another mouthful of water that brought him to a choking halt. Desperately, he treaded water and tried to draw some air into his blocked lungs. A wave washed over him and spun him sideways, forcing him to look back toward the drum. It rose above the trough, then slipped back again. There was no sign of the instructor. Nor of the shark. Then, without warning, something moved past him below the surface. A white shape, like a bolt of light.

Carter twisted round, spluttering and kicking, trying to keep a watch on all sides. Seconds passed. He dared not swim because that meant he could not see what was coming up behind him. He was paralyzed with fear and uncertainty, circling in the water.

A dorsal fin cut the water twenty feet away and then disappeared. Carter drew up his legs almost to the surface and waited, watching every fleck and turbulence. Something white glinted in the corner of his eye, and he spun round as it closed with him. The float carrying the limpet mine. He felt sick.

The float skipped daintily over the crest of a wave and slid into the trough. It was ten feet away when the fin broke the surface beyond it. Carter could see it clearly, along with the twenty-foot shape of the shark beneath as it pointed back up a wave. Then it started to come in, the fin slicing through the water.

Carter could hear himself shouting at the top of his voice. He clenched his impotent fists and started to thrash the water. The shark veered to one side and he saw its mean pig-eye through the water and the jaw close about the bobbing float as if attempting to swallow it whole. There was a blinding flash and something stung his face. Then darkness.

CHAPTER THREE

WHEN Carter opened his eyes he thought he was looking at gray sky and one of the wind pumps that brought up the water on his father's farm in Wisconsin. But it was a sun-faded blind, and a slowly turning fan in a hospital ward crowded with men and flies. He began to remember what had happened and felt his legs to see if they were both there.

"Hi. How are you?"

The nurse was pert, not pretty. Her uniform damp under her armpits.

"I was hoping you were going to tell me."

The girl nodded and pulled at the sheet that covered his body.

"You're going to be fine. You swallowed a whole lot of sea water and you were concussed. You haven't got a problem compared to most of the guys around here."

Carter looked at the surrounding beds.

"When can I get out?"

"Depends on what the doctor says. Tomorrow. Today, maybe."

Carter continued to stare at the girl's face. There was something unusual about it. He was accustomed to the yellow complexion that resulted from Atebrin, the anti-malarial drug, but this was different.

The girl noticed his interest. "It's my lipstick," she said. "Compliments of the cosmetic people back home. Specially designed to go with yellow. Does it raise your morale?"

"My temperature's going up already," said Carter politely.

The girl laughed and patted his wrist. "I'll get you a drink. You must have a sore throat after swallowing all that sea water."

She came back with a glass of lemonade and a letter.

"This came for you." She lowered her voice to the level of a stage whisper. "I believe it was left by a lady."

"You don't say."

Carter took the letter. He could only think of one woman in New Guinea who would want to write to him. Somebody started dying noisily three beds away and the nurse left to help. Carter opened the letter.

As he had expected, it was from Jean. He crumpled it up and tossed it away. It was no doubt a rotten thing to do, but his prime emotion was relief. He did not want to see Jean again and this way it was going to be much easier.

"And now you have a visitor." The nurse's tone was a mother's trying to make her child appreciate the Christmas presents it was receiving.

Carter looked up to see Hudson approaching the bed. He appeared diffident, almost uncomfortable, holding his unlit pipe in his hand like a talisman. He glanced at the dying man and ducked warily as he approached the fan.

"Good day, Will."

"Andrew. Good to see you. Pull up a chair."

Despite the exchange of Christian names the tension between the two men did not relax. Hudson perched his tall, spindly frame on the edge of a chair and looked about him uneasily. "You're looking much better than I thought you would. You were blown clear out of the water, you know."

21

"Like the shark."

"Yes, but not in so many pieces. It was falling on the beach."

"I was lucky."

"You sure as hell were." Hudson studied Carter as if the reason for his good fortune was written across his face.

"Who got me out?"

"Corporal Johnson got to you first. Buy him a beer sometime. The others went off down the beach for the boat. Stalled the bastard, straight off. Beaut operation. Mind you, it was a crazy idea in the first place. I should have put my foot down. People do things in a war that would get them killed in peacetime." He smiled. "You know what I mean. Because there's a war, people start taking crazy risks—"

"You mean, like us," Carter said quietly.

Hudson's face clouded. "I didn't mean that. Anyway, I still don't know what we're supposed to be doing, but I'm told that at least training is officially over—"

"They must have got scared they were going to kill us before they could send us anywhere." Carter took a deep breath. "Listen, Andrew, I may be an American but I don't know any more than you do. I know the general wants a closer involvement in your kind of coast-watching operation and I know he wants to find a way of hitting at Rabaul. He's worried about the build-up of men and materials and our not doing anything about it. I guess he's right to be worried. One of these days they're going to come down out of there—"

"And we may have to wait until they come," Hudson said. "We haven't got a force that can take Rabaul. They've got a network of tunnels that goes back miles into the hills. They have hospitals there, workshops, munition dumps, fuel dumps—and all underground. No bomb can touch them."

"Have you been there?"

"Before the war, yes. Many times. My home was on New Ireland, to the north. I know the place like I know, say, Moresby."

"So you think MacArthur is wasting his time?"

Hudson paused before answering. "I think he may be inclined to underestimate the terrain. You don't walk in this country—you climb or you crawl. Most of the time you're fighting the climate rather than the Japs. Your finger can rot off before it gets the chance to pull a trigger. I mean, look around you. How many men in this ward are suffering from bullet wounds? Three out of ten? What about the rest? Bacillary dysentery, malaria and pneumonia, I'd guess. Hell, I'm not saying that MacArthur doesn't know what he's doing. He did a good job in the Philippines by all accounts and that's not the easiest country in the world. I just think that Rabaul is something else. To get the enemy out of those tunnels is going to be like getting maggots out of a cheese."

"So what do we do?"

"More or less what we're doing now . . . try and contain them. Keep listening posts open to report all air and sea movements so that we can hit them when they do come out in the open. Wait until *we* can stockpile enough men and supplies to go in and attack—"

"Hoping that they don't do it first."

Hudson shrugged. "You always hope that, don't you?" He tapped the stem of his pipe against his teeth as if eager to start smoking it. "Anyway, all this talk about Rabaul reminds me what I really came here for. Wasn't just to see how you were. The Yanks"—he broke off and held up a self-admonishing hand—"an American PT Boat picked up a Chinese drifting in a dugout in the Solomon Sea. He apparently escaped from Rabaul after killing a Jap. I came along to see if he could tell us anything."

"He's here, in the hospital?"

"Somewhere. Apparently he's in pretty bad shape."

"Do you mind if I come along?"

"Not if you can make it."

Carter swung his feet off the bed and winced as pain zigzagged through his back. It felt as if he had been beaten by rubber truncheons.

"Can you manage?"

"Sure, I'm just bruised, I guess."

He rose unsteadily to his feet and fended off the nurse's objections with a promise of speedy return. "That lipstick is really growing on me." Halfway down the ward, the man who had been dying now had a sheet over his face. Dark patches of sweat showed through it. There was a set circle which announced the position of his mouth. As Carter looked, a fly landed in the middle of it.

The ward was one of many that branched off bungalow style from a covered corridor opening onto a pleasant garden in which mangoes, red ginger and angel's trumpet predominated. The hospital had been barely large enough in peacetime and was now surrounded by a hinterland of hastily assembled tents and inadequate walkways of coconut matting which would be washed apart in the first downpour of the rainy season. The contented murmur of insects did not come only from the blossoms on the trees.

Hudson patiently showed a piece of paper to three orderlies in turn and eventually was directed to a row of tents set apart from the rest and guarded by two Australian soldiers in slouch hats armed with heavy Lee-Enfield rifles. One of them saluted grudgingly and led the way to the last tent in the line. He pulled back the flap and gestured inside.

At first sight, the man lying on the camp bed appeared to be dead. He was pitifully thin and his arms lay on the sheets like sticks. They were a fiery red. So was his face, which had eyelids swollen like partridge eggs. His nose was also swollen and the scarlet skin about it split like a fried tomato.

A large water blister puckered his chin. Carter wondered if this was the right man. There was nothing about the face on the pillow that looked Chinese.

"He must have been in that canoe for days," Hudson said. "The sun's nearly finished him."

Carter picked up the medical report sheet at the end of the bed. Clipped to it was a piece of paper torn from a log book and covered in neat writing.

"Hey, listen to this," he said. " '. . . 0500 hours. March 8, 1943. This man found drifting in a dugout canoe west of Vella Lavella Island—' "

Hudson whistled through his teeth. "He was drifting the wrong way if he was hoping to get to New Guinea. Bella Lavella is southeast of Bougainville."

Hudson continued reading. " 'When taken aboard he was semiconscious and badly sunburnt but recovered sufficiently to say that he had escaped from internment at Rabaul after killing a Japanese guard who had murdered his wife while raping her. All his per-

24

sonal effects accompany him when placed in care of Captain Henderson, RAAF. Signed this day, Lieutenant John F. Kennedy, U.S. Navy. Commander PT 109.' "

"They do a good job, those PT boats," said Hudson. "Got me out of a few tight spots in my time." He turned back to the figure in the bed and spoke softly. "Can you hear me?"

There was no reply. Carter looked down at the small, emaciated body and wondered how it could have found the strength to kill a Jap guard. Then he thought of the man's wife being raped and murdered before his eyes. "Maybe we'd better find a doctor," he said.

Hudson did not reply but levered himself awkwardly to his knees and placed his lips beside the man's ear. "Can you hear me? You're at Port Moresby. You're safe."

Again there was no reply, and Carter began to wonder if the man was dead. Then the swollen eyes opened slightly and the mouth peeled apart slowly, as if the lips had been held together by a zipper.

"Do you want some water?" Carter asked.

The man nodded.

"Easy with it," Hudson said. He watched as Carter guided a beaker to the man's lips. "We work for Allied Intelligence. If you feel up to it we'd like to ask you some questions."

The man moved his head in what seemed agreement. Carter removed the beaker and dabbed at the two small rivulets of water that ran from the corners of the man's mouth. He winced at each touch.

Hudson spoke. "You escaped from the internment camp at Rabaul, right?"

The man nodded.

"How many internees are there? Two hundred? Three hundred?"

The lips came apart, still joined by hinges of congealed saliva. "Four hundred." The voice was parched but showed little trace of accent.

"Many Australians and Americans?"

The head shook from side to side.

Hudson frowned and turned to Carter. "Most of the prisoners

25

the Japs captured went down with the *Montevideo Maru* when it was taking them back to Japan."

Carter gritted his teeth. By one of the lousy ironies of war the *Montevideo Maru* had been torpedoed by an American submarine off the Philippines. There had been hardly any survivors . . . "Is our bombing doing much damage?" he asked.

Again, a shake of the head. "Japs in tunnels." The man had managed to raise his head from the pillow and was looking around the tent as if searching for something.

"What do you want?" Carter asked.

The head fell back against the pillow and a scrawny arm pointed toward a bag lying on the floor in one corner. It was a *bilum,* a woven string bag used by the natives to carry their belongings.

Carter picked up the bag and noticed that it had attracted a column of small red ants. He removed a pair of worn sandals, a tattered khaki shirt and a pair of frayed drill shorts.

The man gestured at the shirt. Carter quickly went through the pockets and found nothing.

The man feebly moved his hand toward the shirt and raised himself on one elbow, his face contorted with pain. The liquid in his blister moved as if in a plastic container. He inserted skeletal fingers into one of the breast pockets to pry open the pleat. From this hiding place he withdrew a small white object and flopped back against the pillow, leaving it on his open palm.

Hudson took it and found that it was a twist of paper that had become sodden and then dried under the sun until it was brittle. He began carefully to force it open. There was something written on the paper.

"Where did you get this?" Carter asked.

The man spoke, every word an effort. "I was in a cell . . . chained with another man . . . slide my hands from the manacles . . . escaped. He gave me this."

Carter looked at the twiglike wrists and believed that they could slip any handcuff. Hudson looked at the piece of paper he had unfolded, handed it to Carter. It contained a crude, pencil scrawl. Immersion in sea water had almost obliterated the lettering: "HAVE VITAL INFO ABOUT JAPS, MAKE CONTACT, HARRY GREEN."

"Old Greeny. I thought he was dead," Hudson said. He turned back to the man and spoke with a hard edge to his voice. "Harry Green is in the prison camp at Rabaul?"

The man nodded.

"He gave you this?"

Another nod.

"What was he doing in the cells?"

The man shrugged. "Always in the cells."

Hudson gave a short laugh. "I can believe that." He got to his feet and carefully folded the piece of paper. "Right. Thanks for all this . . . when you're a bit stronger we'll be back to ask you to draw us some maps. Look after yourself." He nodded and jerked his head at Carter to signal that it was time to leave.

The Chinese said nothing but closed his eyes and turned his head slightly toward one of the walls.

"Do you know this guy, Green?" Carter asked as they came out into the droning heat.

Hudson pulled out his pipe and started to stab at the crust of used tobacco with a penknife. "I used to bump into him sometimes. Before the war. He was what you might call a character. Must be about fifty now, I suppose. Came out here for the Edie Creek gold rush but never struck it rich. Worked for the administration for a while—he was a nicely spoken fella—then got a job recruiting native labor. I think he picked up an arrow somewhere. Anyway, he didn't stick it for long. Then he came out to New Britain. Tried his hand at the copra business. He was making a fair disaster of that when the war came."

"Do you think it could be a trap?"

"I don't see why the Japs would bother. If we were actually on the island it might be different. I'd be suspicious of somebody handing me a note saying, 'Come down to the prison camp.' But from this distance?" He shrugged. "I can't see the Japs priming our Chinese friend to fry himself to death in an open boat just so they can trap a couple of coast-watchers."

"So what do you think his message means?"

"I've no idea. Maybe he's gone crazy. He always liked his booze." Hudson tilted his pipe to his lips as if it was a bottle. "But on the other hand, I think it's probably on the level. When it came down to it, Greeny was a pretty straight shooter. I think we ought to go and take a look."

"Are you serious?"

Hudson was trying to light his pipe and didn't answer immediately. "Sorry about this thing. I can't smoke on an operation so I try and fit in as much as I can when I'm back at base. The boys say I ought to take it with me. A couple of whiffs and we'd clean the Japs off any island." He puffed enthusiastically before realizing that he had not answered Carter's question. "Yes, sure I'm serious. If we keep the numbers down to the minimum we should get ashore without too much problem. I don't believe the Japs will think of us landing so near Rabaul. They're funny like that. We can get the Chinese to clue us in on the exact position of the camp—it can't be too far from the sea, from what he said. What I most like about the idea is that it's a good test operation for our set-up—what are we called, 'MacArthur's Own'?"

Carter shrugged.

"Well, it doesn't matter what it is. Sooner or later we've got to cut our teeth, and this could be a good exercise to get the logistics sorted out. Submarine drop, dinghy to shore, hide dinghy, get to prison camp, talk to Green, back to the shore, pick up. We could be in and out overnight."

"You make it sound simple." Carter shook his head.

"I want to. Everything is based on making things simple. And good team work." He looked at Carter. "I don't want to sound rude, Will, but I've already got a team. If I take you or any other American I'm working with an unknown quantity—"

"Are you thinking about what happened when I was swimming out to the drum? Do you think I'm going to crack up?" He was aware that it was his own fear that was putting him on the defensive. His voice grew louder. "I guess you figure we're all Johnny-come-lately fuck ups—"

Hudson's eyes were dark. "I don't think you are different from anyone else. If you were a Kiwi or a Pom I hadn't worked with I'd be talking to you exactly the same way. All I'm saying is that I want to make sure that we can walk before we run. Because, sure as hell, one day we're going to have to run."

He turned and walked away down the line of tents. He was a big man when he moved, and his head jutted forward angrily, as if it was going to butt the sun to pieces.

CHAPTER FOUR

"**F**IVE minutes." The executive officer looked at Hudson, who nodded to show that he heard. "Can I get you more coffee?" the man continued.

"No thanks." Hudson felt he had been drinking coffee ever since he'd come aboard the submarine. He looked at the window of dials along the hull and then to Joe, who was sitting with his back to a bulkhead, polishing the firing mechanism of his newly issued Sten gun. He had been taking the submachine gun apart and reassembling it, polishing each segment until Hudson worried that he would take off a precious thickness of metal and make it unfireable . . . Joe, the third member of Hudson's old coast-watching team, was a six foot six Tolar from near Rabaul on the island of New Britain, where the Japanese were amassing their men and armaments for what appeared the inevitable assault on Australia via the steppingstone of New Guinea. The flesh across Joe's shoulders

30

appeared to be mounted on a girder, the thick muscles in his chest glistened like a suit of armor. His not so distant forbears had been inveterate warriors and cannibals, and whatever of their traits he'd inherited had found welcome outlet during Hudson's coast-watching missions into the islands that overlooked the shipping approaches to Rabaul.

Carter, too, was checking his weapons and putting on his dark green combat uniform. Hudson watched him out of the corner of his eye. He had been at pains not to give any impression of riding the American, and Carter was making it easier for him. Relations between the two men had not deteriorated since the flare-up at Port Moresby Hospital. There was a wariness on both sides, but no more.

Johnson clipped the waterproof cover over his dry battery, an ATR4A transmitter, and slid his arms through the two straps that held it to his back. His face was thoughtful but there was no sign of strain. He had made no comment when he had been told that their mission was on New Britain, and Hudson had not pressed the matter.

Every item of equipment that was going ashore had been checked and rechecked. The rubber dinghy had been inflated and deflated, and disembarcation drill had been carried out with the submarine on the surface. Hudson needed no reminder of the problems of coming alongside a pitching submarine at night in a choppy sea. He also wanted to make sure that Carter knew as much as possible about every problem that might come up. Not only for efficiency. He didn't want to lose face if something went wrong . . . He was aware that there had been strong American pressure at Allied Intelligence to make the first leader of a joint landing party an American . . .

Hudson finished rubbing black antiglare cream on his cheeks and pulled down the infrared goggles that been resting on his forehead. Through the sunglass effect he could see the other members of the party doing the same. Wearing the goggles would ensure that they could see when coming out on deck at night.

"Nineteen-thirty hours," the exec said. "Dinghy ready for launching, sir."

"Right. Synchronize watches." Heads bent over wrists as

31

Hudson gave the countdown. He could see Joe looking at his blacked face in silent amusement. Rare for him . . . especially when in a "steel fish," which he hated. Joe had sweated patiently through the day as the submarine moved up and down the coast making periscope sightings and looking for Japanese positions. Any sign of new building at the outskirts of a village was immediately suspicious. It might be a watchtower or a "house iron," a corrugated-iron strong-post enclosing a Nambu 7.7-mm machine gun. By midday a landing spot had been chosen. It could be approached through a gap in the reef and was not near the cluster of native villages surrounding Rabaul. Occasional sightings had been taken through the day but there was no sign of movement in the jungle or on the narrow strip of beach. Joe had been certain that the nearest inland village was over two miles away.

As he came on deck, Hudson filled his nostrils with the hot, sweet smell that wafted off the shore a mile away, and listened to the slap of the water against the submarine's hull. He felt a sense of identity with his surroundings that was missing in the brightly lit interior of the submarine. There it was like being inside the mechanism of a giant watch. A phosphorescent fish slid by in the dark water and the shriek of a night bird told them where the shore was. The night was black, there were no stars.

Two sailors were securing the dinghy against the sloping side of the sub, ready to lower it into the water, as Hudson approached the looming outline of the conning tower. "Thank you, commander," he said.

"Good luck. We'll be waiting for you."

Hudson gave the order and the dinghy slid into the water and chafed against the hull. Then he joined Carter in their predetermined positions in the prow of the dinghy, and both men unstrapped their paddles. Joe and Johnson followed. The mooring lines were thrown aboard.

Four swift digs on the paddles and the submarine had melted into the night. There was only the whisper of the trade winds and the distant hollow drumming of the surf. Hudson studied the luminous face of his prismatic compass and gave orders that would keep them on their bearing for the shore. There was a swell of about fifteen feet running and a strong current pulling them off course.

Carter listened to Joe's rhythmic grunts behind him and tried to probe the darkness ahead. The sea seemed very choppy. He dug down with both arms and felt the muscle-stretching satisfaction of his paddle moving a solid weight of water. Thank God to be doing something physical after two days poring over charts, checking equipment and establishing signaling procedures.

"This cow of a current is taking us to starboard, skipper." Johnson spat angrily into the sea.

"I don't think it matters. The tide's running high enough for us to shoot the reef. Keep pulling."

Minutes passed, breathing grew heavier. There was a black outline before them, darker even than the night, and the sound of the surf was like native drums. Carter tried to control his fear as he thought of capsizing on the reef. The coral would cut them to pieces and their blood would bring the sharks in—

Suddenly there was white water ahead.

"Right, you jokers, dig in. We're going straight through," Hudson ordered as he dropped his shoulders and braced his knees against the side of the raft. He could feel it straining and trembling like a frightened animal as the mass of swirling water thudded against the rubber, trying to force a way in.

Four backs bent and the paddles flexed as the tide snatched at them. The dinghy surged forward and met wild water, the coral only inches below. A wave threw them forward again, they seemed to be sliding. There was a hideous rasping sound and the dinghy lurched sideways as if about to pitch them into the surf, then a wave washed over them and carried them clear into the lagoon.

Carter looked back at the white water rushing over the coral.

"Wait till we have to get out," Johnson said.

"Shut up and keep paddling," Hudson told him.

The sea inside the reef was calmer, and within five minutes they could clearly see the outline of the shore. The once angry water was now sucking docilely at the bottom of the dinghy. They paddled until they reached shallow water, then slipped over the side and guided the dinghy to the beach.

33

Carter felt the firm sand underneath his feet and looked back toward the sea. Nothing but darkness.

He helped carry the dinghy up the beach and went back with Joe to brush out their footprints. When he returned, Hudson and Johnson were dragging the raft into the twisted mass of roots of a giant callophyllum tree and covering it with foliage.

"We're about four hundred yards off course," Hudson said. "Nothing serious. We'll check the wireless and then get going." He turned to Joe. "Go for bush. Watch for Japs."

Joe nodded and disappeared.

Johnson slid the radio from his shoulders and unclipped the waterproof case. He deftly manipulated the controls to the operating frequency and slipped on the headset. "Alpha Bravo to Charlie Foxtrot . . . Alpha Bravo to Charlie Foxtrot. Report signal strength. Over."

Carter listened to the static and counted the seconds. Hudson knelt beside Johnson and looked at him inquiringly. He was about to speak when there was a sudden trough in the static.

"Charlie Foxtrot to Alpha Bravo. Signal strength four. Over."

"Little beaut," Johnson said approvingly.

Hudson took the mike. "Alpha Bravo to Charlie Foxtrot. Thank you. Good night. Out." He stood up and jerked his head toward the bush. "Okay let's go. We've got four hours' march ahead of us."

Johnson started to pack up the radio. Carter nodded and unsheathed his bush knife.

"Don't use that until you have to," Hudson said. "Nothing shows up easier than the marks of somebody hacking their way through undergrowth."

He gave a high birdlike whistle and Joe came out from the trees, reporting that he had found a track and that there were footprints showing a heavy tread on the sole. Almost certainly Japanese. The prints were not recent. Carter felt relieved that their own boots bore a specially molded sole that was the replica of a native's bare foot.

Joe led the way through palm trees and bamboo thickets to a narrow all but unrecognizable path. Once away from the open beach each member of the party switched on a small flashlight with a treated red glass filter that provided just enough light to reveal the immediate surroundings. It would be mistaken for a glowing insect by anybody seeing it from a distance.

Carter walked third in line behind Joe and Hudson. He soon felt his face burning with sandfly bites. Tall grass closed in about them and the track began to twist upward over ground broken by tree roots that looked like snakes or giant lizards in the feeble glow of the flashlight.

What followed was the nervous chirping of insects, a sudden explosion of sound as some unseen creature ran or slithered through the undergrowth, the touch of wet moss on a tree trunk, giving like rotting flesh . . . a prickly vine tearing at the sleeve, sharp razor nicks from cutting grass . . . Carter could see how the jungle could unhinge a man without any help from the enemy—

He felt a sharp pain at ankle level and reached down to touch something soft. Disgusted, he stopped and shined the flashlight. Clamped to his ankle between gaiter and boot were the repulsive, shiny black swellings of three leeches.

Johnson stopped behind him. "Don't touch them. When they're full they'll drop off. Start messing about with them and you've got a poisoned sore, then you've got an ulcer, then you've got a problem." He paused. "I know."

Carter said nothing. The glow of Hudson's flashlight in front of him had disappeared. He hurried forward, nearly falling over a root. There were bigger problems ahead than leeches.

They had been walking for nearly an hour when there was a strong smell of human excrement and a dog started to bark. Joe held up his hand. They were approaching a native village. The people were known to him and he did not trust them. "Bloody monkeys belong to Japanese."

It was agreed to skirt the village. Soon they came on fences of bamboo enclosing gardens of yam, sugar cane and sweet potato. On occasions there were the shadowy outlines of thatched huts, and once the embers of a still-smoking fire. Eventually they came to an open space and Joe paused.

"You know this place, Joe?" Hudson asked.

Joe nodded and pointed to what seemed like impenetrable jungle. "Road there."

"Is it good?" Johnson asked.

"Gets better—"

"Okay. Let's take the bastard. This is Joe's backyard. He ought to know what he's doing," Hudson broke in.

Joe led the way and they turned off the track and seemed to walk straight into the jungle.

"After ten yards we'll start cutting," Hudson said. He pulled out his bush knife and dug his shoulder into the undergrowth.

Carter felt something sting his cheek and touched sluglike slime and softness. The leeches must be dropping from the branches above their heads. A sense of terrible isolation took him over, combining with his fear. It seemed impossible that anybody could find their way in this jungle, in pitch darkness, and with seemingly no track to follow. "Andrew," he called out softly, "does this guy really know where he's taking us?"

"He knows," Hudson said. "His people have got a lot of tracks like this they use for hunting possum. They can tell the way by the feel of the earth under their feet. Be ready . . . we're going to start climbing soon." He strode on, the pattern of his breathing hardly changed since he was on the submarine.

Carter touched his cheek. Where the leech had been there was now a smudge of blood.

Hudson was right. The track suddenly made a sharp upward turn and lost its way among steep outcrops of rock and pit-pit grass. Sometimes it was necessary to claw their way upward, as if climbing a mountain. Mostly it was just a case of feeling the thigh muscles ache as the knee came up before the face and another vertical foot was achieved. There was no relief from the insect bites. Carter felt the back of his hands and they were an uneven mass of stinging lumps.

"When we get to the top we'll be able to see Rabaul. After that it's downhill," Hudson whispered.

Carter wanted to ask how much farther they had to go but his pride wouldn't let him. The fact that they were scheduled to make the return journey in a few hours was something he tried not to think about.

Approaching eleven o'clock, the moon came out and Carter could see the jungle stretching away on all sides, as if growing in

36

the bowl of an auditorium. There was no sign of the path they had taken, and no glimpse of a gap between the interweaving trees and creepers. There was only the sea, thousands of feet below, now looking no more menacing than a piece of black velvet. Carter grit his teeth and heard his sinews creak as he forced his legs forward and upward.

Twenty minutes later he was at the summit. Rivulets of sweat were running down beneath his armpits. His flesh was stinging from cuts and insect bites, and his sodden uniform chafed his raw skin.

Joe approached him solicitously and gestured toward the direction they were to take. "It is easy now."

Carter snorted. "I'll believe it when I see it." He drank greedily from his water bottle and crossed to Hudson who was looking through a gap in the trees.

"You can't see the town from here but that's one of the volcanoes, Matupi. It's on the far side overlooking the airstrip." He pointed to the outline of a stunted pyramid, barely visible against the dark sky. "The harbor was formed thousands of years ago when another volcano blew up. The sea rushed in to fill up the hole. Must be one of the deepest harbors in the world." He paused, and glanced at Carter. "How are you doing?"

"I'll be okay," Carter said.

"I hope we all will," Hudson nodded. "From now on we can expect Japanese patrols or gun posts at any time. Don't fire unless you have to. Even if somebody opens up they may be shooting at shadows. Don't give yourself away. We've got a river at the bottom, so watch it." He called to Joe and waved him on impatiently.

"We should be there within an hour," Johnson said, answering Carter's unasked question. "Provided the river isn't a problem."

"Why should it be?"

"Do you hear that noise?"

Carter listened hard and heard a noise like distant artillery fire. "What is it?"

"There's a storm in the mountains. Sometimes the water comes down like a flash flood. The river level can rise several feet in seconds." He nodded after Joe and Hudson. "Better stretch it out."

37

Carter drove his legs forward as the moon sulked behind a bank of clouds. The descent was even steeper than the way they had come, but Joe moved lightly from rock to rock, not causing the small landslides of earth and stones that the others set in motion. Occasionally he would stop to listen and sniff the air, and Carter would wait apprehensively during the long seconds before Joe's thick, gleaming black arm beckoned them on. The only thing Carter knew for certain was that the path was going downhill.

Another twenty minutes and the track broadened and led to a cluster of ragged huts thatched with palm fronds. They stood among overgrown gardens that seemed to be deserted. There was no sound or sign of life. Joe led the way through, almost on tiptoe. The moon appeared again and beams of light broke through the branches of a giant ficus tree, painting ghostly patterns on the walls of the huts.

Carter began to feel that he was being watched; that somewhere beyond the dark shadowy doorways a machine gun was mounted on a tripod, and an enemy soldier was waiting with moist fingers, ready to feed the ammunition band through the chattering breech. The image was so potent that it dulled all physical sensations. He was entering a nightmare. He could see the doorway and the spot fifty yards on where they would be shot down defenseless in the middle of the clearing. With every step he became more convinced that he was walking to his death. The feeling was so strong that he wanted to call out to the others. To tell them to dive for cover. But he was in the grip of the nightmare and could say nothing. He walked on, counting the paces as brilliant moonlight flooded the clearing. Forty-seven, forty-eight, forty-nine—

There was a crashing noise, he spun around and faced the doorway, heart pounding, carbine out before him.

A pig ran squealing from the hut and into the bush. Carter released the pressure on his trigger and stood where he was, the tension slowly ebbing out of his body in time with the drooping muzzle of the carbine.

Johnson nodded admiringly. "You got good reflexes, sir," he said.

It was the first time that Carter could remember Johnson addressing him as "sir."

After the settlement the pathway became a track and the going was much easier. Vegetation thinned out and cultivated gardens were more frequent. They were approaching the bottom of the valley. Soon after passing a thick grove of bamboo they heard the sound of rushing water and came to the edge of what appeared to be a wide, boulder-strewn ravine with a stream running down the middle of it.

Joe cocked his head upstream and listened intently. "Water comes."

"How soon—?" Carter began.

"Come on!" Hudson interrupted. Without waiting for a reply, he started to slither down the side of the ravine and pick his way through the boulders.

Johnson nudged Carter. "Step on it. You don't want to get caught in the middle." He hitched up the straps of his radio and launched himself forward into what Carter now realized was a broad riverbed.

Carter followed but fell awkwardly, striking the stock of his carbine against a granite boulder. The pain ricocheted through his arm and he fell back against more sharp, wet stones. The boulders about him had been worn smooth by the passage of water, and some were taller than a man. It was like picking a way through a maze. With every clumsy pace he strained his ears for sound of the approaching waters. If he was caught here he would be beaten to pieces.

Johnson was waiting, cursing quietly, by the central torrent of the stream. He was soaked to the skin and his arm was bleeding. "I slipped trying to ford the bastard . . . I think I might have buggered up the wireless."

Carter did not reply. Above the noise of rushing water could be heard a distant rumbling sound which came from upstream. The men looked at each other. The far bank was nearer and Hudson and Joe were already scrambling onto it, but then there was the stream to cross.

"Come on," Carter demanded. "Give me your rifle."

Johnson bystepped into the torrent, freeing a hook attachment that clipped itself to the muzzle of his carbine just below the sight. This he fixed to the same attachment on Carter's carbine so that

39

the two weapons were fastened together forming a flexible pole. Carter held his rifle by the butt and Johnson edged forward into the stream, the swiftly flowing water breaking over his knees, then his thighs. By the time he reached the stones on the far side he was holding his end of the supporting rifles at arm's length.

Once he'd found a foothold Carter stepped down into the stream. At any other moment the touch of the icy cold water would have been a balm, but now it had the feel of death about it. The rumble from upstream had become a roar. The flash flood must be seconds away.

Carter took a step, staggered. The stones beneath his feet were slippery and the force of the water was much stronger than he had anticipated. Without the support of the rifles he could have been swept downstream, racing the pursuing torrent to the sea.

He edged forward again, leaning against the force of the water and seeking a firm foothold. Johnson was gripping his rifle with tense hands, bracing his foot against a rock, trying to haul him in like a fish.

One more step and Carter's free hand touched rock. He launched himself forward and threw the weight of his shoulders toward Johnson's feet. A hand seized him under the armpit. As he hauled himself upward and scrambled to his feet, his rifle was thrust into his hand.

He followed Johnson's back toward the far bank. Two steps, and a foot of water surged around his ankles. He looked upstream and saw a crazy swirling of foam above the boulders. The noise was deafening. Four more paces and the water was above his knees and nearly knocking him over. The roar came up behind him like a breaking wave.

Joe was leaning down from the bank and Carter grabbed at his hand as the tide began to carry him away. The firm, dry grip dragged him to safety. He turned to see Johnson pulling himself onto the bank with Hudson's help.

Behind them a wall of boiling water hurled itself down the river-bed, breaking over the boulders like thunder. Tree trunks were swept along like twigs in a gutter as the first mad rush of water slopped over the bank to whip against the hanging foliage. Carter thought they were still going to be carried away. Then the tide slackened and the foaming vanguard of the flood crashed away around a bend in the river.

Johnson was already examining the radio set. He swore softly. "Sorry, skip. I've buggered it. The batteries are wet."

Hudson thought for a moment. "Bring it with you anyway. We can't afford to let anybody find it."

Carter looked at the fifty-yard-wide river now roaring and foaming behind them. "How are we going to get back?"

"In two hours the water level should have dropped several feet," Hudson said.

"If there are no more storms in the mountain," Johnson added gloomily.

"That's why I sometimes call him Jerry," Hudson said. "Short for Jeremiah. He's such a cheerful type. We haven't got far to go now. The camp is at the end of this valley. I don't think the Japs will have a post before we get there but you can't be sure." He looked at his watch. "Midnight. Everything should be quiet now. Keep in single file and we'll follow the river till we get near the camp."

He waved Joe forward and started to follow when Joe was ten yards away. Carter rubbed half a dozen mosquitoes to pieces against his cheek and looked up at the dark outline of the jungle-covered hills that surrounded them. Not far ahead was the impregnable fortress of Rabaul, with its grim bodyguard of volcanoes. A cockatoo shrieked from the top of a pandanus tree. He tightened his grip on his carbine.

After twenty minutes Joe held up his hand and pointed to the scrub on their left. Carter listened, heard what sounded like the hum of a generator.

"We're very close now," whispered Hudson. "You two stay here. Joe and I are going to have a look."

The two men disappeared into the bush and Carter sank to one knee beside Johnson, his ears straining into the darkness.

Five minutes later Joe materialized beside him as if sprung through a trap door in the ground. There was no sound to announce his arrival. Carter felt grateful that he was not a Japanese sentry.

Joe touched his arm, motioned him forward.

Carter followed close and found Hudson lying beside a clump of kunai grass.

"There it is," Hudson said. "Up there on the rise. It's the old prison. I've been here before. Strictly as a visitor."

Carter settled down beside Hudson and peered in the direction indicated. A broad swathe of jungle had been cleared, and in the center of it were upward of fifty thatched huts surrounded by barbed wire. Outside the barbed wire was a weatherbeaten bungalow and a corrugated iron hut that gleamed in the darkness like a shiny tin can. A dirt track led past the hut.

Hudson nodded, almost to himself. "The Japs will be in that lighted hut. Pity about the light. I hoped they'd all be asleep. How do you reckon this lines up with our Chinese friend's plan of the place?"

"Seems accurate enough." Carter shrugged. "Green should be in one of the middle huts."

"Right. Let's pay him a visit. Joe, you stay here. Give a signal if there's any movement from the hut—and keep your itchy finger off that trigger." Hudson rose to a semicrouch and moved swiftly from the grass to the shelter of the jungle. Carter followed him, and the two men skirted the trees until there was an open space of twenty yards between them and the barbed wire.

"Now we crawl," Hudson whispered. "Hope there isn't a death adder crawling the other way."

He threw himself down and started to edge forward, his head barely off the ground. Carter waited to take a last look around and followed, holding his weapon in front of him with two hands. Somebody inside one of the huts was moaning in pain but there was no other sound.

Hudson approached the wire and tested it with his hand. The strands were about five inches apart with the lowest almost at ground level. They were stretched tight and there was virtually no give. Hudson said nothing but turned on his back and unbuttoned a pocket at his thigh. He withdrew a slim system of metal rods little longer than a fountain pen and pressed it between the two bottom wires. Carter did the same. There were now two uprights of metal a shoulder's width apart. Taking their knives, both men activated a spike set in the middle of the handle and inserted it into the

42

center of the metal rods. As the knives turned, the two end pieces of metal were forced apart like the operation of a miniature car jack, taking the wires with them. Eventually there was an opening wide enough for a man to crawl through and one of the strands had been broken. Carter replaced his knife. MacArthur's special training program had not been a complete waste of time.

Hudson motioned him through and wondered whether to dismantle the system once they were inside. The Chinese survivor had told them that there was no regular system of sentry patrols but that the Japs would walk around the perimeter wire when the mood took them. Inspections of the wire itself were infrequent and always took place during daytime. Hudson decided to leave the rods in position. If a guard did make a sortie he would be unlikely to look down and see that anything had been tampered with. It would be more risky to take time to set up the system again from the inside of the fence. He wriggled through the hole and pulled grass against the wire before joining Carter, who had scurried to the shelter of the nearest hut and was standing with his back flat against the wall and his weapon across his chest. The moaning had stopped and there was now only the sound of snores and people stirring in their sleep.

Carter jerked his head over his shoulder. "What do we do now? Go and rout him out?"

Hudson held up a restraining hand and listened. From a nearby hut came a creaking sound and the noise of unsteady footsteps dragging across a rough palmwood floor. Hudson motioned Carter to follow.

The man emerged from the hut and opened his mouth in amazement as he saw Hudson standing in front of him. Before he could say anything, Carter's hand closed over his mouth from behind and forced him against the wall. The whites of the man's eyes widened as Hudson came close to his haggard, unshaven face.

"I'm sorry to frighten you, we're looking for Harry Green. Is he here?"

The man nodded vigorously and Carter decided it was safe to remove his hand.

"Where?"

"In there." The man indicated the hut behind him.

43

"Tell him some friends have come to see him—just him."

The man looked inquiringly from one face to the other and then decided that he did not have any questions. He retreated into the hut. Carter remained with his finger on the trigger and watched the shadows. A large rat moved unconcernedly from behind the next hut and began to climb the bamboo wall to the thatch of nipa leaves. There was a mumble of voices behind them and a figure appeared in the doorway. A man in tattered shorts and a torn shirt that finished short of his waist. Perhaps the shorts had once fitted, now they were barely able to make contact with the hip bones. The man's shoulders were stopped and he was wasted by disease and malnutrition. He was also shivering, due, Carter suspected, to a bout of malaria rather than the cold. It was difficult to tell his age but he was certainly over fifty. He looked older.

The man's eyes took on life when he saw Hudson, and he seized his hand and held it tight. Then, looking around to see that no one was watching, he drew him along the row of huts without saying a word. Carter followed until they came to a roofless, woven grass structure that his nostrils told him could only have one use. Hudson was led inside and Carter, unwillingly, went after him.

"Andrew Hudson. By God, it's good to see you." The man's eyes blazed with excitement and fever. "Sorry to have to bring you here, but it's amazing what people will do for a few extra grains of rice from our Nippon overlords." He turned to Carter whose hand was over his mouth. "I envy you, young man. I can't smell it anymore. If I smelled a pretty woman I'd probably throw up."

"Harry, this is Lieutenant Carter of the United States Army. He's working for Allied Intelligence with me."

Carter stuck out his hand. "Will Carter. Glad to know you, Harry."

"An American," said Green with real interest in his voice. "Do you know a chap called Flynn? I had words with him once."

Carter looked quickly at Hudson before replying. "No, I don't think I do.

"Do it . . . Errol Flynn? He's a famous Hollywood actor. Used to loaf around out here like me. Been rather more successful, though. I knocked him out once. Of course, I was in better shape then, weighed a bit more too."

44

"Harry," Hudson's voice was patient but firm. "We didn't come all this way to listen to your life history."

"No, by God. Forgive me. I imagine you're here because you got my message? Amazing. I never thought our little Hong Kong friend would get through."

"He nearly didn't," said Carter. "He was picked up by a PT boat after God knows how many days in an open canoe—"

Green shook his head. "Poor devil. I hate to think what the Nips would have done to him if he hadn't slipped those cuffs. He escaped through a hole I wouldn't have bet on a cat getting through. Little buggers took it out on me."

"What were you in for?" asked Hudson.

Green screwed up his eyes. "Damned if I can remember. They seem to think I owe them some kind of respect. Out of the question."

Carter found himself admiring the spirit of the bent little man. "There are about four hundred internees?"

"Probably less than that now. They brought in a lot of Indians after the fall of Singapore. They're digging the tunnels and dying like flies. The rest are mainly Chinese and a few civilian Aussies. They make us work in the docks."

"Is there much stuff coming in?"

"A hell of a lot after dark. Spare parts for planes, mortars, machine guns—even light tanks. A lot of men too."

"So they're building up?"

"Definitely. Our rations are suffering because of it. Hardly any rice. Salt stopped months ago."

"And our bombing?"

Green shrugged. "It feeds the little buggers. After every raid they come out of the tunnels and collect all the dead fish floating in the harbor."

Hudson swore under his breath. "Bloody marvelous. Okay, Greeny, what have you got to tell us?"

There was a long pause as Harry Green opened and closed his fleshless fingers nervously. "By God, I hope I haven't brought you fellows here for nothing. I was so positive, but now, faced with saying it . . ." His voice trailed away uncertainly.

"What is it, Harry? We've got five hours to get back to the sub."

45

Green raised his head and pulled back his shoulders. "What do the years 1874 and 1937 mean to you, Andrew?"

Hudson thought for a moment and shrugged. "My wife died in 1937; 1874 doesn't mean anything."

Green took a quick breath. "In both those years Rabaul was destroyed by a volcanic eruption." He searched their faces for reaction to the news. "In 1937 I was here. I saw it."

"Go on, Harry."

"By God, Andrew. I think it could happen again." There was a slight quiver in Green's voice.

Carter tried to digest the implications of what Green was saying.

Hudson leaned forward intently. "What makes you think so?"

The fervor in Green's eyes rekindled. "So many of the signs are the same. There have been more tremors lately."

"There have always been tremors at Rabaul," Hudson said.

"I've never known them so persistent or so strong. I remember suddenly thinking, 'This is exactly like '37.' And then there's the dead fish in the harbor—"

"Killed by our bombing," Carter interrupted. "You just told us."

Green shook his head vehemently. "No! These fish weren't stunned. I saw them when I was working in the docks. The flesh had been boiled off the bones! It was pulp. The same thing happened in '37. The sea was boiling near Vulvam Island before the eruption."

"What else?" Hudson asked.

"I talked to a fisherman who'd been round near Matupi. He said there was a great yellow stain in the water and that the fish were dying. You know what that is, don't you? Sulphur. Something's stirring down there at the bottom of that volcano. It's beginning to get angry."

Hudson tried to control his excitement. "Is that all?"

"No. I talked to a Tolai who'd been hunting up the other side of Matupi. He said he'd come across a stream running boiling sulphur. You understand what all this could mean, don't you? If we had another major eruption the harbor would be choked with pumice and the Japs would be running back up their tunnels with the lava scorching their backsides. In '37, the boats in the harbor were buried up to their smokestacks and half the town was destroyed. You couldn't move. I think that this time, everything points to an even bigger explosion. I know the positions of the Jap tunnels and I could guarantee that two-thirds of them would be sealed, perhaps even completely penetrated. You couldn't devise a better method of getting at them if you tried. And it's here, waiting right on the doorstep."

"Waiting for nature to press the button," Carter said.

Green looked at them. "Perhaps nature needs a little nudge. I've been thinking about this ever since the idea came to me. I'm certain that everything is primed for an eruption but I can't be absolutely positive that it's going to happen. Yet what an opportunity lost if it doesn't—"

"I agree with you," Hudson said. "What do you suggest we do?"

Green paused, swallowed hard. "Force Matupi to erupt."

"Start a volcanic explosion?" Carter said incredulously.

"Not start, *trigger off,*" Green said. "There's a great yellow boil throbbing up there. What we've got to do is lance it."

"How?" Hudson asked. "Bombing?"

Green shook his head. "I don't think you could ever guarantee the accuracy. Also, the run-in that gives you most chance of lobbing something into the crater takes you straight over the airfield. The strip is plastered with antiaircraft batteries. Coming in low, which you'd have to do, you'd be shot out of the sky. I have another idea. I got to know Matupi pretty well when I was hunting for butterflies—"

"Butterflies?" Hudson broke in.

Green looked slightly shamefaced. "One of my little schemes. I was going to mount them in glass boxes and sell them to dealers in New York and London. Bloody war put the kibosh on that, of course. Anyway, when I was up there swishing my net about I came on a tunnel going into the side of the mountain. Must have been an ancient blowout, I suppose. I went down it a few yards and turned back. Didn't have a torch, of course, and it was full of bats. The tunnel seemed to go on through. You see what I'm getting at?"

"Putting a charge inside the volcano," Carter said.

"Exactly. I don't know how much explosive you'd need but

47

I expect somebody could work it out."

"Is this tunnel easy to find?" Carter asked.

"No. I literally stumbled into it. There was a grass-yellow on a vine. I took a swing at it, slipped, and went straight through the vine. Must have fallen about ten feet. When I looked back it was as if I had gone through a bead curtain."

"So you can't see it from the outside?"

"Not a hope. I bet you the local natives don't even know it exists."

"Could you draw us a map of how to get there?"

Green shook his head. "Couldn't guarantee you'd ever find it. The backside of Matupi is thick bush going nearly to the rim of the crater. It's crisscrossed with hunters' trails. You'd lose your way in no time. I'd have to show you where it is."

Hudson looked at the frail, stooped figure in front of him and tried to remember the well-built six-footer he used to know. "Harry, you're not even in shape to walk to an ambulance."

Green pushed a matchstick arm against Hudson's chest. "Don't you believe it. You catch me at a bad moment. Twinge of malaria, always suffered from it. I'll be A-one when you next see me. I guarantee you I won't let you down. One thing about this place, I've kicked the booze." He laughed, a reedy treble that ended in a burst of coughing.

Hudson patted him on the shoulder. "Harry, you're incredible."

"I've got motivation, friend. It's worth a hundred thousand quid for me to get out of here."

"Come with us now," Hudson said.

Green shook his head. "Daren't do it, old boy. If I'm missing at roll call tomorrow morning they'll kill every woman and child in the camp. They said so after the Chinese fellow went."

"So how the hell would you ever be able to get out to lead anyone to the tunnel?"

"Have to do it in the course of a night," Green said. "Last roll call is at six. Then they leave us alone until eight in the morning —unless we're Asian women. You'd have to spring me and bring me back." He turned to Carter. "That's an American expression, isn't it?"

"Sort of," Carter said.

Hudson looked seriously at Green. "Harry, do you really think you're capable of walking from here to Matupi in a night? And what's going to happen to the people here if it goes off?"

"*When* it goes off. Let's have positive thinking. The people here will be all right. They'll be protected by the hill. Just a few boulders flying about, and some ash and smoke. They'll be cheering so loud their lungs will burst." He coughed again and turned it into the noise of someone clearing his throat.

Hudson's expression was grim. "But what about you, Harry? It's not just your health . . . if you don't survive the mission we could lose a lot of lives—"

"I know that," Green said. "And I repeat what I've said before. I know what I can do. You've got to be pretty tough to survive in this place." He held out his wrists to reveal the festering sores left by manacles. "I may look like a wreck. I may *be* a wreck. But I won't let you down on this . . . believe me."

"I'm not promising anything," Hudson said. "It's a fantastic idea, back at HQ they may think it's too fantastic, not worth the risk."

"Don't let them waffle," Green urged. "They'll talk, they'll make reports, they'll weigh up the pros and cons. In the end they'll decide to let nature take her course and nothing will happen. You *know* it's worth the risk."

Hudson took Green's arm. "Stay ready and keep out of trouble. Our wireless is crook so we've got to get back before we can put anyone in the picture—"

There was a shrill three-note bird call from the entrance to the camp. Both Hudson and Carter recognized Joe's warning signal.

Hudson quickly moved to the latrine entrance and looked beyond the wire. He beckoned to Green. "Somebody's coming. Get back to your hut. See that clump of rattan over there?"

"Yes."

"When we're coming for you, two of the stems will be broken across each other. We probably won't be able to give you much warning."

"Got it." Green quickly shook the two men's hands and hurried away.

A minute passed and there was silence except for the sound

49

of scavenger beetles rummaging among the excrement. Then Carter felt Hudson's fingers tighten on his arm. A guard was approaching outside the perimeter wire. His forage cap was pulled low over his eyes and his rifle with fixed bayonet was slung over his shoulder. He was a small fat man meandering close to the fence. Too close, thought Carter. He approached the spot where they had entered and stopped. Carter listened to his heart thumping and looked at Hudson, whose hand moved slowly down the barrel of his Sten gun to ease off the safety catch. The Japanese unslung his rifle and leaned against the wire. Carter felt certain he must have seen something. Then the guard pulled open the front of his baggy trousers and began to urinate noisily. Carter breathed more easily. The guard finished, reslung his rifle and moved on his way. He reached the corner and performed a small dance step as if thinking of happier times and another place.

Carter found himself almost liking the man and then wondering if he was one of the soldiers who had raped and murdered the Chinese man's wife.

The soldier moved out of sight and Carter looked at Hudson, who shook his head and cupped his hand to his ear. "Wait here till we get the signal from Joe," he was saying.

Twenty minutes passed accompanied by the hoarse, ratchetlike croaking of tree frogs, and then came Joe's two notes, signaling the all-clear. Hudson said nothing but moved immediately and swiftly to the entrance hole in the fence via the cover of the huts. Away from the open sewer of the latrine, Carter filled his lungs and breathed in the heavy scent of jungle gardenia. He felt tired but this was submerged by a sense of excitement and anticipation. This time he would know the route they were taking. He had a goal to look forward to. Even the eternal presence of marauding insects seemed less important.

Hudson slithered through the gap and waited. Carter followed, cutting his forearm on the wire but hardly noticing it. Together the two men dismantled the miniature steel jacks and pressed the undergrowth back into place. Satisfied that they had covered their tracks, they retraced their route along the trees and were joined by

Joe. There was now no light showing from the corrugated-iron hut. Hudson took a last long careful look at the camp and then led the way back to the riverbank.

Johnson was waiting with his finger on the trigger of his carbine. He asked no questions but jerked his head over his shoulder. "The river hasn't gone down a lot, skip. I reckon we'll have to cross native style. I rescued a couple of logs."

Hudson looked at his watch. "Only four hours left, we've got to move a leg." He turned to Carter. "I don't think we covered this one on the course, so Jerry and I will go first to show you the hang of it."

Johnson led the way to the water's edge, where two gleaming twelve-foot trunks had been half-hauled onto the bank. Quickly checking that all their equipment was securely fastened, he and Hudson took one trunk and their weapons under the left arm and stood poised at a point where the bank sloped gently into the fast-flowing water.

Hudson looked over his shoulder. "Right?"

"Right!" Johnson said.

The two men ran down the bank into the water and began to strike out with their right arms. The current snatched them away but it was clear that they were heading diagonally toward the far bank.

Joe stationed himself at the head of the second log and Carter took up a position behind him. The water looked dark and menacing. Long strips of snakelike liana drifted by, and Carter decided he'd rather not get mixed up with them. But Joe started forward without a word and the log was nearly wrenched from his grasp. He caught up just before Joe entered the water and was amazed how soon he felt nothing below his feet. Two strokes and the bank had disappeared. His cheek scraped against the log and he struggled to keep the breech of his carbine out of the water as he paddled with his right arm. It was easy to see why Joe had positioned himself at the head of the log. With every thrust of his powerful arm he seemed to jerk it a foot sideways. Carter looked out for the far bank and was relieved to see foliage reaching out over his head. His foot struck something and for a split second he saw the mangled leg of the instructor dangling by its ligaments as the man tried to claw himself onto the bobbing drum. The memory drove his arm and within seconds the bank loomed up and he felt shingle below his feet. He released the log and floundered toward the shore, pausing only when he felt himself safe from the current.

Hudson splashed through the shallows toward him as he sucked in mouthfuls of air. "Okay?"

"Fine," he gasped.

"Right. Let's go." He strode off, talking softly to Joe.

Carter decided that first impressions could be misleading. Hudson might wear baggy shorts and look like an arthritic basketball coach wondering where the next lousy job was coming from, but he was definitely worth having on your side during a war.

Joe found a track that would take them back to their approach road and the next hour passed with hardly a word being spoken. Insects glowed, crawled, chirped, whirred, and stung. By the time they reached the summit of the hills overlooking Rabaul, Carter felt numb with fatigue. The blisters had rubbed off his swollen feet and his toes were stuck together with blood and sweat. His ankles ached as if a tourniquet had been applied to them. He looked down at the dark, stunted mass of Matupi visible through the trees and felt nothing of his earlier excitement.

The volcano looked long dead. There was no soft, crucible glow at its crown to indicate that a ticking time-bomb lay inside. Could there be anything in what Green had said or was he just a cranky old man, his imagination inflamed by recurrent bouts of fever?

Fifty yards ahead the trees started to rustle as if shaken by a violent wind. There was the sharp crack of a branch breaking and the ground beneath Carter's feet started to shake. A tree beside him trembled and then rocked as if about to fall. A boulder groaned and there was a swift flurry of falling stones. Carter braced himself as the tremor became more severe and tried to understand what was happening. Then, as suddenly as it had come, the shaking died away and there was only the sound of a stone bounding away down the path.

He stood still, listening to the silence, unsure whether it was safe to move. Hudson came down the track toward him.

"That was a tremor, in case you didn't know." Hudson smiled.

"What our friend down there was talking about. I've never experienced one like it at this height." He looked down toward Matupi and put his hand on Carter's shoulder. "You know, I think old Greeny might really be on to something."

CHAPTER FIVE

AT three o'clock it started to rain. A continuous heavy downpour that drummed against the leaves and turned the track into a miniature waterfall. Burdened by his radio, Johnson fell heavily and there was a delay of thirty minutes while the party searched for his flashlight. It was vital that nothing was left to be found by the enemy.

Soaked to the skin, Carter scrambled in the mud on his hands and knees, with the undergrowth tearing at his exposed arms and face. He could see the leeches glistening on his flesh and briefly wondered if the mosquitoes fed on the leeches. Eventually the flashlight was found and the party slithered on for another half hour through a steady downpour before Hudson called a halt.

"We're not going to make it," he said. "To get to the beach on time for the sub we'd have to skirt the village, and there's a risk that some of the women will be out in the gardens by the time we get there. We'll take a long way round and lie up till nightfall. We'll be in better shape then anyway."

Carter felt relieved and disappointed. He was eager to get away but aware that he was becoming dangerously tired. It was not so much a question of physical strength—he would be capable of putting one foot in front of the other for hours—but of a diminishing sense of awareness. It was the one thing fatal for survival in the jungle. He was moving like an automaton, as if he were walking in his sleep.

By five o'clock the rain had stopped and the going was flatter. Hudson called a fifteen-minute halt and the party huddled together under a clump of lopsided tamarind trees.

Carter listened to the raindrops dripping from the leaves with the regular beat of a metronome and closed his eyes. When he opened them it was to find himself being shaken awake by Johnson.

"Okay, lieutenant. We're on our way."

Carter struggled to his feet, his sodden clothing working itself into knots against his flesh. His eyes were gummed together and their lids swollen with insect bites. The inside of his mouth tasted like charcoal. Every limb ached as if the sinews had shrunk, pulling the bones out of their sockets. He took his place behind a silent Hudson.

As they walked on the sky began to lighten and the cold give way to the thick, clammy heat of day. Pockets of mist hung above their heads and the vegetation steamed. Parrots shrilled from the tops of trees, and the paths became infested with large black slugs, some of them almost a foot long. Joe led the way through a variety of pathways and tracks and frequently told the others to wait while he went ahead to scout. After one such expedition he hurried back, looking worried.

"*Tabanda,* you come." He led the way to a track running across the trail they were traveling on. Clearly imprinted in the soft earth was the pattern of a Japanese boot.

"How long ago?" Hudson asked, looking down the trail.

"Little while," Joe murmured.

Carter was alert now . . . The Japanese had been here, recently, and it was barely daybreak.

"Where'd they go?" Johnson asked.

"Place that belongs to *kanaka* . . ." Joe stumbled, searching for the words.

"The village," Hudson said.

"Are they after us?" Carter asked.

"Pretty unlikely," Hudson said. "We can't take any chances though. How long to the beach, Joe?"

Joe pointed down the track with the Japanese footprint on it. "That way shortest, *Tabanda.*"

Hudson looked serious. "We'd better go around. The long way. Maybe the *kanakas* found the boat and tipped off the Nips."

"Bastards," Johnson said.

"If they did, they'll be waiting for us. We'll make a wide detour and take a look at the beach."

Joe led the way and the party moved slowly forward. Every fifty yards Joe scouted ahead and returned to give the all-clear. The sun was climbing in the sky, visible only as a pattern of rhinestones against the dense foliage above their heads. Even in daylight the jungle was a dark and somber place, illuminated by unexpected flashes of color as some plant or creeper burst into grotesque life.

After an hour's snail-like progress the jungle ended abruptly at the edge of an overgrown coconut plantation. Carter could see blue sky through the trees. Joe left his weapon and sauntered forward, just a native looking for a good tree to climb. He reached the far side of the grove unchallenged and disappeared for a few seconds before standing up in a half-crouched position and giving the signal for the others to move forward.

"Holy shit," Carter muttered as he sank to his knees behind Joe. Four hundred yards from where they crouched, a motorized barge was riding at anchor, a large Japanese flag flopping loosely at its stern. Carter recognized the barge from aerial photographs. It was one of a fleet used for ferrying troops along the coast and for unloading vessels that anchored outside Rabaul harbor at night. Half a dozen Jap soldiers were visible onboard, the same number on shore. They had been ferried by a small tender that was pulled up on the beach. Some smoke from further up the beach suggested that they had lit a fire. Within a hundred yards of the moored tug was the callophyllum tree where the rubber dinghy was hidden.

"I hope they're just beating the drum through the villages,"

Hudson said. "They've probably sent a party ashore to tell the head man that the rising sun shines out of the emperor's what'sit." He wondered what the commander of the sub would be thinking as he watched the scene through his periscope. If only the wireless was working.

"They'd better not find the boat." As Carter spoke, a Japanese appeared from the direction of the callophyllum tree carrying an armful of dry palm fronds.

Johnson whistled through his teeth. "If they start poking around for firewood, we're really up the creek."

Two more soldiers began sauntering along the beach looking for driftwood, slowly but surely closing in on the callophylum tree. All they could do was watch as a desultory gabble of Japanese floated toward them. The dinghy was concealed below a few layers of palm fronds and would immediately be found out by anyone entering the tangled root structure in search of firewood.

The first man now rejoined the others. After a few moments spent rearranging one of their loads, he stepped under the archway of roots.

A shrill cry.

For a moment Carter thought that it signaled discovery of the boat. Then a large party of men began to emerge from the jungle —half a dozen Japanese and upward of a hundred natives, men, women, and children. Most of the natives moved forward like frightened prisoners under guard, but there was a separate group wearing khaki and armbands who strutted along carrying long spears. Carter recognized the armbands from intelligence reports. They belonged to the *Kempei Tai,* a native police force recruited by the enemy and especially brutal.

The arrival of the party on the beach was galvanizing. Firewood was dropped and weapons sought at the double. More soldiers appeared from the shelter of the trees, and NCO's barked orders. Clearly responsible for the display of activity was the man at the head of the arriving party. Both by his uniform and the deference with which he was treated it was obvious that he was an officer of high rank. He carried a long, curved ceremonial sword and was followed by a soldier bearing a Japanese flag scarcely smaller than the one on the motorized barge. His breeches were of riding-

57

school quality and his green cap more precise than the khaki forage caps with neck flaps to protect against the sun worn by ordinary soldiers.

"What rank is he?" Hudson whispered.

"I think he's a goddamn lieutenant general," Carter said. "Could be Koji, commander of the Rabaul Garrison."

Hudson shook his head. "What's he doing here? It must be more than flag-waving."

"Looks as if we're going to get a chance to find out," Johnson said.

Down the beach, the general flourished his sword arm toward the coconut plantation and the natives fell over each other to stumble forward like frightened sheep. A lieutenant lashed at them with a stick while the common soldiers joined in with boots and rifle butts, assisted by the *Kempei Tai*. Carter winced as a spear was thrust into a man's haunches so that its oval tip disappeared into flesh. He eased back the safety catch on his carbine, figuring to kill the spearman with his second shot. The first would be for the general.

Hudson sank down nearer to the ground, raising and lowering his palm in a "keep calm" gesture.

Fifty feet from their position, the lieutenant snapped out an order. The natives stopped and stood still. A child started to cry and was immediately shaken into silence by its terrified mother. The general stationed himself in front of them. His standard-bearer stood close behind him so that the flag brushed against the general's shoulder. Seen from up close he was a ramrod-straight man of about fifty. His face was cadaverously thin and he wore a Hitlerian mustache beneath the exclamation mark of his nose.

The soldiers fell in menacingly close to the natives as the general began to speak, waiting after each sentence for one of the *Kempei Tai* to translate.

Carter looked at Hudson inquiringly until he relayed Joe's translation in a whisper. " 'The *kanakas* are a lot of lazy so and sos. . . . They were ordered to build a watchtower on the beach for the Emperor so he could help defend them against the corrupt Americans and Australians and they have done nothing. . . . The Emperor is very angry. . . . He says that they must be punished and

58

made to realize that this is time to do what they're told.' "

As the general's address reached its end, his voice became more and more angry and shrill and was only exceeded in intensity by that of his translator, who drove the helm of his spear into the sand to emphasize each point.

Carter hated his sense of impotence, but any intervention was out of the question if they were going to survive and get back with the information to Port Moresby. They had to lie still, and watch.

The general finished speaking, saluted the Japanese flag, then snapped out an order to the *Kempei Tai.* Like dogs that had been waiting for the order to retrieve, they sprang into the crowd and dragged out five men who were thrown to the ground at the general's feet. One pathetically tried to rise to his knees and was knocked half senseless by a blow from a spear shaft. The men's arms were secured behind their backs and they lay still, chickens trussed for the market. Not one of them struggled. It was as if they had no hope, were even reconciled to what was going to happen to them.

A middle-aged Japanese soldier built like a sumo wrestler waddled down the beach carrying something wrapped in a silk cloth. He saluted the general and the flag and began carefully to unroll the silk cloth, revealing the gleaming blade of a *katanga,* a samurai sword, its edge shining viciously in the sunlight.

The cloth was handed to a soldier, who folded it carefully. The squat man took practice swings, making the sword hiss through the still air. He wore no shirt, the sweat dripped off his fleshy shoulders and glistened in the rolls of fat around his waist. Satisfied that he was ready, he nodded to the *Kempei Tai,* who fell on the prisoners and set them up on their knees in a row, facing the band of silent natives. A child began to whimper. Like a snail tentatively leaving its shell, the first man put his head forward . . .

Carter felt sick, lowered his head. The way the man had meekly extended his head for the sword made him want to throw up. Five times he heard the swish of the falling blade, the gentle "chunk" that told of a head being separated from its neck. Five times, the dead-weight fall of a body toppling over like a sack of flour.

When he looked, the heads were scattered almost to the general's feet, the necks pouring dark blood into the sand. The *Kempei*

Tai ran forward and began to plunge their spears into the corpses.

Carter grunted, drew up his weapon, and Hudson rolled sideways and pinned him to the ground while Johnson clung to his weapon until his arms went limp. Slowly the others released him and he lay still, his face against the ground, breathing through his half-open mouth—

From the beach, a scream. Running from the jungle, a long-limbed girl, black hair streaming behind her, feet kicking up sand. She wore an old European dress that finished at her thigh, but she was clearly Melanesian.

On hands and knees she scrambled from one head to the other until she found what she was looking for. She plucked it up as a *Kempei Tai* attempted to grab her, was promptly bitten on the hand. Furious, he struck her with the shaft of his spear and she slumped sideways, unconscious, still clutching the head.

An angry murmur at last broke from the herded natives, immediately silenced by a rush of *Kempei Tai* and Japanese, who broke ranks and presented their weapons. The girl stirred and was seized by one of the *Kempei Tai,* who twisted her arm behind her back and held her, head pressed into the sand.

The general resumed his peroration, and Hudson shook his head. "They've got to build a watchtower by nightfall or the Emperor is really going to fix them." He looked to Joe for a further translation. "A watchtower capable of holding a searchlight. How the hell are we going to get to the boat with a searchlight playing all over the beach—?"

Joe abruptly started to wriggle away like a snake and the others followed. Guttural bellows from the beach suggested the natives were being unleashed to make up for their dilatoriness, and hardly had the party reached the comparative safety of the thick jungle than a group of natives poured into the coconut grove and headed for an adjacent clump of bamboo, which began to melt away as hefty canes were cut down and dragged back toward the beach. Four soldiers appeared to supervise the operation, but they soon became bored and moved away, leaving the field to the *Kempei Tai,* who lashed out at anyone in sight until they too became tired and squatted under the coconut palms.

Hudson left Joe on watch and retired deeper into the jungle with

60

Carter and Johnson. When they had found a hiding place in a clump of sago palm, he said, "Let's take stock . . . the sub will be lying offshore until midnight tonight. They might push off after what they've seen but I don't think so. Our wireless is crook and any other form of signal is out of the question at the moment. Without the searchlight there's a slight chance we might be able to get to the boat and launch it further down the coast. With the searchlight we're buggered, we'll never get near it."

"If it hasn't already been found by then," Johnson said.

Hudson gave him a look, went on . . . "Now, we can forget walking—"

"I agree with *that,*" Johnson said, face grim.

Carter looked at him. His face had turned ash gray beneath the blotchy tan.

"I walked from Rabaul in '42," Johnson said. "It's when the Japs got hold of me."

Hudson kept talking. "As I see it we have two alternatives. We can move downcoast, build a raft and hope there's an opening in the reef we can get through."

"Then find the sub," Johnson added.

"I already like the second alternative," Carter said. "What is it?"

"Wipe out the searchlight post and retrieve the boat. I know it puts the kibosh on the Japs not knowing we've been here," Hudson continued, "but if we don't get back nobody's going to know about Matupi either."

"Besides, they're on their guard already if they're bothering to put searchlight posts along the coast," Carter said.

"What bloody luck," Johnson said. "They must have looked at this place and thought just what we did. A nice quiet place to make a landing."

"You talk about wiping out the post like it's easy as going to the john," Carter said. "Any idea how we're going to do it?"

"Depends how many Japs there are," Hudson said. "My guess is they'll leave a section to set up the searchlight and show the *Kempei Tai* how to use it. Maybe they'll man it themselves. I reckon on about four Japs and the same number of *Kempei Tai*. Best thing we can do is rest up now and take another look when everything quiets down." He pulled open a pouch and took out a neatly folded

61

square of mosquito netting. "Jerry, take the first watch. Wake me in an hour."

He settled back against a stump and draped the netting over his head and shoulders. His eyes were closed before his chin touched his chest.

Carter envied him his ability to fall off so easily. His own mind was still full of what he'd seen on the beach . . . especially the girl, what would happen to her?

Johnson was getting to his feet to move off.

Carter touched his leg. "I'll take the first watch, Jerry."

Johnson looked toward the sleeping Hudson as if worried by the change of plan.

"It doesn't make any difference, does it?" Carter said.

"I guess not. I'm pretty beat at that." Johnson settled down opposite Hudson with his carbine across his lap and his finger on the trigger guard.

Carter picked his way carefully to Joe's position and guided him back to the sago palms. "I'm going to take a quick look at the beach," he said.

Joe looked unhappy. "I go with you."

Carter tried not to show his irritation at Joe's protectiveness. "No, you stay here," and moved back toward the coconut grove. Shafts of harsh sunlight broke among the trees. The clump of bamboos was decimated and deserted except for the insects greedily clustered on the sap that ran from the severed shoots. Carter rested on one knee, looked, listened. From the beach he could hear the hollow thumping of ax against bamboo and then, suddenly, the long continuous blare of a siren. He guessed that it was the barge preparing to leave.

Hoping that all eyes would be directed seaward, he crept swiftly through the palms toward a point where the ground began to rise and reunite with the jungle. Near the beach a tall rain tree protruded from the undergrowth, its branches craning over the sand. Carter saw the blood running down in fork marks on his arms as he pulled himself up into its lower branches. He rested for a moment, then propped his carbine among the foliage and worked his way out laterally, hearing the large tan-colored pods that hung

62

from the branches rattling like miniature castanets. Suddenly his head poked out into the dazzling sun and the bark beneath his fingers was almost too hot to touch. He looked sideways and could see along the beach.

Close to the spot where they had first lain hidden, the structure of the watchtower was already taking shape, bamboo framework lashed together with liana. Beyond, the barge was pulled away from the shore, the Japanese flag beginning to flow out as it gathered speed and left a V in the placid waters of the lagoon. The tender bobbed obediently behind, like a duckling fearing separation from its mother.

Carter noted that five men had been left behind, along with a searchlight and generator that had been uncrated and were standing among the crowd of sweating natives laboring on the tower. Nearby, the corpses lay where they had fallen, flesh glistening under a moving mantle of flies. Their heads had been mounted on *Kempei Tai* spears and faced the laborers as a grim reminder. The message appeared to have been received.

Carter looked for the girl, was relieved she was not lying among the dead men on the beach. He searched among the men and women trimming and lashing lengths of bamboo—no sign of her.

The Japanese started to move up the beach, and Carter studied their weapons—one Nambu 7.7-mm machine gun carried by two men, one of whom was swathed in ammunition belts, and four rifles. Two of the men had canister grenades hanging from their belts.

Carter noted that the Japanese were headed for the shade at the top of the beach, then began to wriggle back down the branch to return and report back on what he'd seen—as he looked back he saw dangling from a horizontal branch above the one he was on a bright yellow snake nearly a yard long. Its head swayed toward him, he froze . . . All right, probably a small tree python, not poisonous, but a deep-rooted fear of all reptiles made him damn unwilling to put theory to the test. He stayed where he was, watched the bulging gray eye with its bisecting pupil play steadily on him. He shook a foot at it, and the snake merely dropped onto the same branch as if attracted by the movement. Maybe it *was* poisonous tree snake—Suddenly from the beach came the sound of angry Japanese voices. And the shouts did not stay on the beach. They came nearer.

Carter quickly decided that he feared Japs more than snakes. He was barely twenty feet from the ground and easily visible to anyone looking up into the branches. He needed more protection . . .

He continued wriggling back toward the trunk, the snake twisted toward him, hissed a warning, then dropped to the ground, its tail flicking his leg on the way down. It had just slithered away when there was the sound of someone running through the undergrowth. Carter pressed himself flat against the branch, peered down through the fork . . .

The girl ran into the small clearing, one eye nearly closed, hands tied behind her back. A length of liana secured to one ankle suggested that she had either shaken free of her bonds or else had escaped when they were undone. She looked around for somewhere to hide, then up into the tree, and her eyes met Carter's. She started back, Carter opened his mouth to speak, then said nothing as two Japanese soldiers came through the undergrowth. The girl took two steps before her foot caught a root and she fell. The two soldiers were on her. She bit one, making him yell out, then hit her in the face, bundled her over, her face in the dust. The other soldier sat between her shoulder blades.

The first soldier squatted beside his companion, rubbing his hand. For a few seconds their heavy breathing was the only sound to be heard. Then three more soldiers arrived, talking excitedly. Carter prayed that nothing would make them look up.

They squatted around the girl. One pulled back the remnants of her skirt, groped between her legs. Carter felt powerless, humiliated. A set of dice was produced and as each man cast, Carter realized what they were throwing for—the order in which they would have the girl. He itched to use his carbine . . . none of the soldiers was carrying a weapon and they could have been mowed down in two bursts . . . but the noise would also attract the *Kempei Tai* . . . The shrill of the men's chatter reached a climax and the girl was dragged to her feet, still trying to bite at hands, kicking out with her long legs. A blow to her jaw half stunned her, she was

64

stripped and thrown down on her back right underneath Carter's hiding place.

A soldier sank down beside her, a bayonet in hand, and for a moment it seemed that her throat was to be cut. Then the bayonet was placed with its point just inside the girl's nostril. A second soldier took off his belt, pulled open the front of his trousers, let them slide toward his knees as he sank down and edged forward between her thighs.

The girl opened her eyes, looked up at Carter. Her nose was long and slightly arched. Her forehead was high. Her black hair was bunched forward onto her shoulders. There was no expression in her brown eyes . . . no reproach, no call for help, just a blank stare that told nothing to the animals looking down on her.

The soldier mounted her, the girl closed her eyes.

Carter pressed his mouth against the bark. In a way he felt as if he was one of the men waiting to void himself between the girl's thighs. She could have betrayed him to give herself a chance to get away . . . she said nothing.

The first man, done, changed places with the soldier holding the knife. The girl opened her eyes again. They showed nothing. She would not give them the satisfaction. The second soldier was followed by the third, and the others clustered around, smoking a shared cigarette. Not once did they raise their eyes a few feet from what was happening on the ground . . . The last man was finished, clamped his belt around his waist, pulled his sweat-rimmed cap onto his head. After a final kick, the girl's wrists were freed and she lay slumped on the ground as the soldiers walked away.

Carter waited until the beach was silent, quickly dragged himself down from the tree. The girl turned her head swiftly as he approached, drew away. He laid his rifle down beside her and went to his knees.

He took one of her hands, squeezed it gently. She looked at him in astonishment, allowed herself to cry. He put his arms around her shoulders and hugged her to him like a child who'd just awakened from a nightmare. The girl drew away and looked up at him. "Australian?"

"American. You speak English?"

The girl pulled her long wavy hair forward over her shoulders,

65

tried to smooth it over her naked breasts.

"A little. I was a children's nurse at Rabaul before Japanese come. You are pilot? Your plane is show down?"

Carter looked into the swollen but still lovely face. There seemed to be no alternative. "Yes. What's your name?"

"Sula."

"Will."

She repeated it with difficulty. "You are the only man left when plane crash?"

"No. I have friends close by—" Sula grabbed his arm.

"Men come," she whispered, picking up the remnants of her dress and pulling him by the hand.

Carter could hear nothing but didn't doubt her for an instant. He took up his rifle and followed her long, loping stride.

Thirty seconds later the first of the *Kempei Tai* came into the clearing, his spear raised expectantly. The Japanese had told them that they could do as they wanted with the girl.

They shouted their frustration when they found she was no longer there.

Chapter Six

BY six o'clock in the evening the tower was finished. It was forty feet high, with the searchlight mounted on a platform at the top and the machine gun on its own platform a few feet below. Positioned thirty feet from the jungle and fifty from the high-water mark, it had an uninterrupted view along the beach and out to the reef.

The tropical sun sank fast behind the jungle, and a chorus of insects began to chirp its requiem. No sooner had darkness fallen than the generator was started and the searchlight switched on to startle the flying foxes returning from their evening run on the village gardens. The light cut swathes along the beach and swept out like an admonishing finger to point at the opening in the reef.

The faces of the watching villagers borrowed a little of its light to show their fear, and awe. Only the fly-blown eyes of the severed

heads failed to observe the splendid edifice their deaths had con-
tributed to.

"*Raus.*" It was one word of German-borrowed pidgin that the
Japanese had learned. To accompany it the searchlight was tilted
downward so that it shone directly in the faces of the watching
natives. They scattered before the dazzling light and ran into the
jungle, pursued by the beam until it shattered into fragments
against the closely packed trees.

The Japanese soldiers laughed at the savages and began to eat
the roast pig and yams they had requisitioned, throwing their
leftovers down toward the swollen corpses still humming with
insects.

More sensitive nostrils would have found the aroma unsupporta-
ble, but these soldiers had been at war in the Pacific for nearly two
years and were well used to the sight and smell of rotting flesh.
Besides, the bodies were needed as a reminder that the Emperor's
word was to be obeyed; they would stay there until the first high
tide hissed among the bleached bones. . . .

Corporal Toyoda ordered the light cut and leaned against the
bamboo balustrade to look along the beach. Without the searchlight it was difficult to see more than thirty paces, and the darkness
began to play tricks. The bundles of unused bamboo seemed like
attackers crawling toward the tower, and even the corpses looked
as if they were stirring.

He gave the order and the light was switched on again, to play
against the twisted roots of the grotesquely shaped tree halfway
down the beach. As the light began to move on, something caught
Toyoda's eye and he ordered it swung back. He'd seen something
glinting among the roots and wondered if it was an animal . . . He
peered down the beam. It was difficult to see through the roots but
there appeared to be some kind of thatched, oblong structure with
something bright gleaming on its side. Some kind of trap set by the
natives? But for what? It was too high to be a fish trap, and wild
pigs were unlikely to come down to the beach. He debated with
himself and decided to go and look. It was going to be a long night
cooped up on top of the tower, the insects were beginning to bite
. . . He heard the ammunition belts stirring on the floor below and
the sliding noise as the gunner tested the traverse of the machine

gun on its tripod . . . The wireless set crackled and the signalman from Rabaul came up asking if there was anything to report. Situation reports were to be made every hour with an immediate call if anything unusual was seen or heard. The call was answered with the minimum of words and the set switched off. At beach level, the generator started to hum.

Temporarily distracted from the object among the roots, Toyoda searched for a flashlight and prepared to detail two men to accompany him. Just as he found the flashlight there was the sound of a voice from the edge of the jungle. The searchlight swung around, momentarily dazzling him, and the machine gun moved with it so that it was pointing down the center of the beam. A lone figure was picked out framed by two trees. Toyoda blinked, rubbed his eyes. It looked like the crazy girl they'd had earlier. She stepped out of the trees, talking the native language and gesticulating toward the bodies.

"She's mad, that one," said Private Tishoro. "What does she want?"

"She wants to buy the men we executed," said Toyoda.

"If we shoot her that will save her the trouble," said a voice from the platform below. The men laughed.

"Shall I shoot her?" asked the machine gunner.

"Not yet," another voice said. "I think I could use her again."

"If I shoot her in the right place you *can* use her again," the machine gunner said.

The girl continued to talk and wave toward the bodies.

"Raus," Toyoda shouted. He had a stomach-ache after eating too much undercooked pork, did not even want to have her again. He also didn't want the machine gunner to waste ammunition. Let the native police have her for their pleasure—

Suddenly the girl stopped gabbling and ran toward the jungle, the searchlight following her as if she was making a fast exit from a darkened stage. Toyoda was surprised. "Tishoro, Kob." Toyoda called the names of the men he wanted to go with him and moved toward the rough bamboo ladder. Strange. Was it the shadows playing tricks or had a figure just run into the jungle on the opposite side from the girl? He looked down and let out a shout. A small red flame was burning at the foot of the tower. A small red flame

69

that moved . . . Toyoda threw his leg over the side of the guardrail just as a blinding yellow flash and a violent explosion came and lifted him into the air like a handful of feathers. One corner of the tower was blown away and the whole structure keeled over and toppled toward the jungle. Fragments of bamboo penetrated Toyoda's stomach and spleen. He felt the sensation of clutching at nothing and hurtling downward. He hit the sand, bounced almost into the jungle. Behind him the machine gun lay on its side with one of the buckled legs of the tripod holding off a roof of collapsed bamboo. One man was dead beneath the gun; the others screamed in pain while those that could struggled to find their weapons.

Four figures burst then from the jungle, and a volley of automatic fire crashed into the shattered framework of the tower. Splinters of bamboo flew like chaff, and the four Japanese were shot down, trapped as if in a cage.

Toyoda saw the angry streaks of light and heard the machine guns paring the cries to silence. Instinctively his hand had gone to his wound, but now he withdrew the warm, sticky fingers and tried to crawl to the jungle a few feet away. A spasm of pain went through his stomach as if a knife had been plunged into it. He bit into the sand, realized now that the girl had been a decoy. While they'd occupied themselves with her, someone had stolen up to place a charge against the tower. He'd been guilty of negligence, stupidity. He knew that he was going to die, but before it happened he needed to make amends to the Emperor for his failure. His disgrace.

He felt something dragging against the sand, slid his hand under his belly. It was his own intestines, beginning to leak out. It was as if some divine agency had performed hara-kiri for him.

He wriggled on, sheltered by a slight dip, and dragged his body behind a sparse scrub of mangrove. Turning sideways, he lay on his shoulder and struggled to unhook the grenade at his waist. The pain was now almost unbearable and he bit another mouthful of sand and swallowed it. At the third try, the clip on his belt released and the grenade dropped from his fingers. He pulled himself up, peered toward the beach. The enemy were searching the bodies of his comrades, cutting the insignia from their uniforms. One man was pulling apart the shattered framework as if looking for something. He turned and spoke urgently to the others in English. At his words all the men stopped what they were doing and looked inquiringly toward the jungle. They must have discovered that he was not among the wreckage. Well, they would soon know where he was.

Toyoda rubbed one of his bloody hands in the sand and grasped the grenade securely. He prized up the firing device and put his finger in the loop. One last effort and his life could end with some honor. His finger tightened against the metal—something appeared beneath his chin. A knife . . .?

He looked up and saw the girl. Most of all he saw her eyes. He was still looking at them as the knife began to slit his throat.

Chapter Seven

"**W**ELL?" Carter asked.

Major Dallas walked across the room and paused before tossing his hat onto the desk. He arched in his swivel chair and spun it around before leaning forward and clasping his hands.

Ask a simple question and you get an Academy Award performance, Carter thought, slumping down in his chair.

"The colonel is not overly enamored of the concept." Dallas shrugged. "He wants the opinion of a second vulcanologist."

"Christ, you know how long it took to find the first one. And what did he say? He thought it was probably possible to blow up a volcano if it was ripe but he wasn't certain how much explosive without seeing the volcano and where it was going to be placed . . . I thought we were going to have to take him back with us."

"You're never going to get a definite answer," Hudson added. "The most important thing is that this guy thinks it can be done.

72

I'd be *worried* if he said it was plain bloody stupid."

"Why don't we go straight to MacArthur?" Carter asked. "He'd think it was worth a try—"

"The colonel doesn't want to put any proposal forward unless he thinks it has at least a fifty percent chance of success," Dallas said. "Don't knock it, Will. It's your goddamned hide he's thinking about. We can't rely on beautiful native girls to get you out of trouble on every mission."

Carter shook his head wearily. "I've told you, we had to bring her back with us."

"We couldn't leave her," Hudson backed him up. "It was odds on the Japs would find out she'd helped us. They'd already beheaded her father, raped her—"

"I'm not blaming you," Dallas said. "Besides, like I said, she's a beautiful girl."

"I think so," Carter said. "She saved my life."

"She saved all our lives." Hudson emptied his pipe into an ashtray. "Now, can we get back to the plan? It's nearly a week since we got back and everybody's looking around for another 'in' box to dump it in."

"Yeah, what about the 'dynamic initiative,' major?" Carter said.

"MacArthur is the dynamic initiative and he's in Pearl Harbor at the moment," Dallas said. "You've got to go through the colonel to get to him. I'm sorry it's taking so long but it's totally outside the scope of anything that's been tried before . . . Anyway, lieutenant, why don't you let me in on the details of your great plan? You're going to need me on your side too, you know."

Carter looked at Hudson, shrugged, and opened the buff file in his lap. "Okay, but don't take everything I say as gospel. We're still working on a few things . . . First of all, some basics. I've checked it out, and the most effective explosive for us to use would be PLA. The engineers tell me that a thousand pounds of that placed inside would blow the top of a small mountain."

Dallas whistled. "A thousand pounds? How are you going to get it there—by truck?"

"I'll come to that," Carter said. "Second basic. The Japs have gun emplacements and searchlights all around the entrance to Rabaul harbor and Matupi Bay. Sula tells me that a curfew has recently been announced and that it includes movement by water. Any native canoe out after dark is liable to be blown out of the water. Apparently the Japs are very jumpy about night attacks, and our little bust-up isn't going to make them feel any more relaxed.''

Dallas said nothing.

"Third basic. We have to get Green out of the prison camp after six o'clock in the evening and return him before eight the next morning.''

"Otherwise he turns into a pumpkin?'' Dallas said.

Carter bit his lip, trying not to explode.

Hudson sensed the danger, got into it. "It seemed to us that we were faced with two alternatives. Either to get ashore a safe distance from Rabaul and manhandle a thousand pounds of explosive through the jungle, or figure a way of getting as close to Matupi as possible. If we choose the first alternative and get ashore without being seen, it's virtually impossible to avoid bumping into some native on the way to the volcano. Once we do that the word will be all round the peninsula and the Japs will be on to us. It'd be impossible for us to give them the slip, weighed down with all that explosive.''

"You'd have to find some bearers to carry the explosive,'' Dallas said. "That's going to tip the Japs off too.''

"Right,'' Carter said. "The average weight a bearer carries is fifty pounds. A strong man can carry double that over a short distance. If we can land near Matupi we'd only need ten bearers compared with twenty further away. The shorter distance to cover would also lessen the risk of discovery—''

"Except that the whole of the shoreline is going to be crawling with Japs,'' Dallas said. "How are you going to get past the searchlights and the gun positions?''

"The searchlights are going to be no problem because we'll be landing by daylight,'' Carter said.

Dallas looked at him and shook his head. "It's impossible to land in daylight.''

"It depends what you're landing in,'' Hudson said.

Carter flicked through his file until he found an aerial photograph that he placed on the blotter in front of Dallas. A section of the photograph was circled in blue grease pencil. "That's a tiny little beach below Matupi," he said. "It's tucked away behind the Japanese gun emplacement at the mouth of the bay. The Japs can see out to sea and across the bay but they can't see back to the beach."

"I can see that," Dallas said shortly.

"Do you also see what's lined up on the beach?" Hudson asked.

Dallas picked up a magnifying glass and laid it on the photograph. "Looks like native canoes."

Carter nodded. "That's right. Native outriggers. They belong to the local fishermen. That's what we intend to use."

"How?"

Carter said, "Zero day minus two. A submarine drops Joe down-coast from Rabaul. He knows a bay with deep water right up to the reef. Joe swims ashore and makes his way around to Matupi, avoiding all villages. Here's where we get lucky."

"I was wondering when we were going to."

Carter ignored it. "Joe's home village is near Matupi. He'll spend a day checking out the land and recruiting local bearers. That'll take us up to the morning of zero day. Immediately after first light, when the curfew is lifted, he'll paddle out to sea with two outriggers as if he and another native were going fishing."

"Just before dawn, a submarine will have dropped us with the explosives at a point off the main shipping lanes outside the harbor," continued Hudson. "We'll rendezvous with the canoes and return to Matupi Bay. The Japs will think it's the same fishing canoes returning."

"They're not going to notice the extra people?"

"Not if they're lying in the bottom of the canoe covered with brushwood."

"And the explosive? You're not going to tell me you can store a thousand pounds of explosive in two dugouts? What kind of volume are we talking about?"

"Approximately five cubic feet," Carter said. "We're aware of the problem and we're working on it."

"I'm real glad to hear that. You haven't forgotten that you've chosen an explosive that's liable to detonate on contact with water?"

"I'm hardly likely to forget it," Carter muttered, remembering the whiplash sting of the shark's guts hitting his back as the explosion blew them both out of the sea.

"We've thought about that and decided it's a risk we'd have to take," Hudson said. "No other explosive packs the same punch for such a low weight and volume. If we wanted to get the equivalent blasting force with a conventional explosive we'd need to carry twice as much."

Dallas moved the fan so that what little air there was in the room became his own private property. "Do you know how many submarines we have operational in the Pacific at the moment? Less than fifty. And they're stretched from here to Salt Lake City. I can't see Admiral Halsey giving you one to play with for several days."

Hudson started to fill his pipe. "Mind if I continue with the plan, major? Let's say we land in the little bay below Matupi at around eleven hundred hours. Joe will take a look around and if everything is clear we'll hide up there until nightfall. As soon as it gets dark Will and Joe will go to the prison camp and get Harry Green. Jerry and me will stay with the bearers and start lugging the explosive round the backside of Matupi. We aim to rendezvous around ten o'clock."

"Green leads us to the tunnel and we place the explosive," Carter continued. "We've left three hours for that . . . the going is apparently tough as hell and we're doing it at night. Green's memory might be getting a little rusty too."

Dallas thought that might be the least of their problems.

"Let's say we're through by two o'clock with the charges set to go off at eight. That leaves us four hours to get Green back before sun-up." Carter sat back in his chair.

"Then what?"

"Then I hope we hear a bloody great bang and start breathing soot," Hudson said.

Dallas turned to Carter. "What happens then?"

"We'll lie low during the day and head for a pick-up point at dark. Andrew's got two lined up. The choice depends on whether the bastard blows its top or not."

"We don't want to have to wade through molten lava," Hudson said. "Our feet should be warm enough by then as it is."

Dallas stood up and walked across to the window. He pulled

76

aside the green shade and looked down to the frangipani trees and the stunted palms. "Do you guys really think this plan has any hope of success?"

Hudson looked at Carter. "We don't think we can afford not to try it."

Carter looked at the yellow, festering scratches on the back of his hands and turned them over. The lines that ran across his palms were now etched deep and black. One of them, he had heard somewhere, was his life line. He'd rather not know which one and start checking for a sudden break in it.

"It still seems to be that there are too many things that could go wrong—"

"I don't get you," Carter said. "When you first called me in here you were talking about commando raids on Rabaul. About really shaking things up. Now we come up with a real plan and you start having second thoughts—"

"Somebody has to see the broad picture. Put yourself in my position. Four guys are going to paddle into the middle of sixty thousand Japs, spring a guy from prison and blow up a volcano—"

"Four guys and a woman," Carter corrected.

Dallas turned around. "Now wait a minute—!"

Hudson held up a hand, turned to Carter. "I think it would be easier if we showed Major Dallas exactly what we're talking about, don't you, Will?"

"Definitely."

Hudson stood up, nodded at Dallas and extended a polite hand toward the door.

CHAPTER EIGHT

THE freighter had been hit by bombs from the Mitsubishi 97's, and now lay a rusting hulk at the entrance to Port Moresby harbor. When a heavy sea broke over the reef the ship twitched and groaned.

Carter braced himself against a section of its bomb-gouged deck plating and shouted through a loudspeaker, "Okay, are you ready inside?"

"No . . ." A muffled shout from the interior of the freighter.

Carter turned to Dallas, who was propped up beside him and looking down uneasily at the choppy water. "I figured if we could do it from this, it could hardly be worse with a sub."

"Provided you don't hit bad weather."

"If we hit bad weather we're in trouble anyway." Carter shrugged. "Come on, you guys, you're keeping the major waiting," he shouted through the loudspeaker.

There was an incoherent grumble from inside the hulk and then Hudson's voice. "Ready when you are."

Carter produced a stopwatch. Green weeds swirled like drowned hair against the submerged bulkheads, and from inside the wreck came the thwack of water slopping through its rusted metal innards. "Go!" he shouted.

As his finger went down on the stopwatch an inflated rubber dinghy attached to a line was tossed into the water from one of the deck housings. Following down the line came Johnson dressed in a combat suit and with a Sten gun strapped across his shoulders. He let himself fall into the bottom of the boat and scrambled to his knees in time to unstrap a paddle and cover the few feet that separated him from a second inflatable rubber dinghy that had been tossed into the sea. Joe slid down the second line and helped secure the two boats alongside each other by fastening their paddle straps. Then he scrambled into Johnson's boat and caught a third line, which was secured to the stern of the raft. Once Joe's giant fingers had fastened the knot a plump plastic bag slid down the rope. This was attached via a hole punched in the three-inch overlap of plastic that surrounded the bag and through which the rope was threaded. Joe swiftly slit the plastic to release the bag and passed it to Johnson, who stashed it in the bottom of the empty dinghy. Other bags arrived thick and fast, and were passed to Johnson as quickly as he could handle them. The rubber boats rode on the swell and the sea slapped against their bottoms.

Dallas nodded. "Not bad."

"We know we're asking a lot, bringing a sub to the surface during daylight. That's why we want to insure that it's a question of seconds rather than minutes before she can submerge again."

The first dinghy was filled fast and Johnson began to unfurl a rubberized cover that could be zipped over its cargo.

"It works out good," Carter said. "Two hundred and fifty bags each boat."

As he spoke the cover was zipped and clipped over the first load and a third dinghy was launched to be brought alongside the others. After it was secured, loading rope was lashed to its stern. Bags slid down immediately and were packed tight along the floor of the boat. Both men worked feverishly, the sweat dripped off their faces and soaked their shirts. At last there were no more bags waiting on the line and all three ropes were cast off.

Carter snapped down his finger and glanced at his watch. "Well done, you guys. That's the fastest yet." He turned to Dallas. "The moment the last bag is off, the sub can submerge."

Dallas looked skeptical. "Three rafts lashed together, two of them stuffed to the gunwales with plastic explosive. Do you really believe you're going to be able to tow that ashore without the Japs seeing it?"

"No . . ."

"I mean, even with the native canoes—" Dallas broke off. "What do you mean 'no'?"

Hudson appeared then, sweating from the inside of the hulk, and leaned back against the part of the sloping deck that was in the shade. He nodded toward the reef. "Watch."

Moving smoothly toward them with the blue horizon behind it was a slim outrigger canoe. A hollowed-out trunk with a framework of spars attached to a parallel log that gave extra stability. Paddling the canoe with practiced skill was Sula. She did not wear a flower in her hair, it was not a Hollywood set with beautiful South Sea maiden gliding up to do trade with handsome visiting merchantman. But Carter had to admit that for a moment it damn near could have been. Most females out here were as ruined and overripe as the vegetation, full of jungle rot and worse. Sula was a rarity, no question, but her job with them was hardly one for a movie queen. Her looks were as improbable as their mission. . . which in a way made her fit even more . . . She wore a plain, loose-fitting cotton smock, and the look she gave Carter was as undisguised and basic as all the rest of her.

Dallas shook his head in disbelief. "The girl—"

"The only thing you can have against her is that she's a woman," Carter said.

"Cut it out," Dallas said. "I know she played Pocahantas to your Captain John Smith, but that doesn't make her right for what you're trying to do—"

"Doesn't rule her out either," said Hudson. "Look at the pluses —she's a native and she knows the area and speaks the language. We're dividing into two parties but we've only got Joe if we need

80

an interpreter and somebody who knows their way around."

"If we send her in with Joe, she can bring one of the canoes out," Carter added. "She swims like a fish, she's got more guts in her little finger than most guys I know have in their whole bodies."

"And being a woman and native," Hudson said, "means that once we get ashore she's going to fade into the background much more easily—"

"Okay, okay," Dallas said, "but now answer me this. How does she get a thousand pounds of high explosives back to shore when there's a whole detachment of Japs within spitting distance?"

"She's only responsible for five hundred pounds." Carter smiled. "We're going to have two canoes, remember?" He extended a raised thumb toward the canoe. "Okay, Sula."

He watched as Sula made a few deft strokes and the canoe swung in toward the rafts. Her mood had changed dramatically since their return to Moresby. She had stopped watching everyone like a cornered animal, even smiled for the first time when Johnson slipped getting out of the Catalina flying boat and nearly fell in the sea.

Finding somewhere for her to stay had been a problem. The native compound only catered to male natives and it was thought, not unreasonably, that the introduction of Sula might be disruptive. Eventually she was billeted with the cook, a large black lady who stood for no nonsense from anyone and boiled taro until it looked as if it had been put through a liquidizer. This arrangement worked well, although she missed Carter . . . Carter missed her too. He found himself inventing military rationales so he could be with her and ask questions about the Japanese defenses around Rabaul. Sometimes he would forget to take notes. It didn't matter much because he had nearly always asked the question before . . . He had seen her physically exposed in a way that put him almost too close to her. When, if he touched her, they both would remember . . .

Sometimes, he found it difficult to look her in the eyes. He felt like one of the Japs . . . by being present he had taken part . . . by doing nothing he had collaborated . . . He had never mentioned the rape to the others, had told them that he'd found the girl running away from the Japs. She had given no sign that she understood his lie, or was grateful for it.

Sometimes he wondered how much she did understand. More than the others suspected, he felt. Perhaps when living with the planter's family in Rabaul she had realized that the more people talked, the less they said. She seemed to observe everything, and spoke infrequently. When he thought about it, she was the first woman that he had ever really respected. . . .

A young barracuda bullet-nosed through the clear water and Sula brought the canoe around so that the outrigger came within Joe's grasp. He clung to it while Johnson unstrapped one of the boats packed with explosive. Dallas watched.

When the boat was floating free Johnson pressed the air-intake valve and there was a loud hissing noise. After a few seconds the sides began to crinkle and the boat spread itself lower in the water, like a deflating balloon. Dallas glanced at Carter questioningly but could not catch his eye. Johnson waited a few more seconds and took his hand from the valve. The swell was now washing over the gunwales. Sula extended her body across the spars that held the outrigger to the canoe and started to pull the near-submerged boat beneath her so that it was enclosed between the two parallel timbers. Joe climbed into the dugout and began to untie some long bamboo poles that were lashed to its side. These he in turn fastened to the top of the raft while Johnson let out some more air. Like a grille, three canes pushed down on the raft and, when secured to the lower outrigger spars, held it securely just below the water, below hull and outrigger. No trace of the raft was now visible.

"Pretty neat," Dallas said grudgingly. "Can you move it okay?"

Carter nodded, called down, and Joe and Sula began to paddle away from the two remaining rafts. The canoe moved slower through the water but there was still no sign of the raft.

Six miles away in the foothills there was the crump-crump of antiaircraft fire, and puffs of smoke began to hang in the sky. Some Zeros must have sneaked in from Rabaul to strafe the airfield. Dallas was scrambling up the deck trying to find a higher vantage point.

"I think he's impressed," Hudson said.

"Yeah"—Carter grinned—"better not tell him it's the first time

82

we got it right." He clambered after Dallas, trying to avoid touching the sunbaked metal.

"I'm just trying to find a spot where I can see if it shows up under the water," Dallas said. "I've got to say it's good, it's damn good." He realized he was in danger of indicating approval for something that might be vetoed by higher command. "Of course, a rough sea is going to bitch you—"

"Sure," Carter said. "This method of carrying the explosive is very effective when it comes to landing. We can bring the canoes right in, a few feet offshore in shallow water, and nobody is going to notice anything. Then we unload them at night."

Hudson watched Carter explaining the procedure to Dallas and smiled to himself. The kid was shaping up well. The idea of semideflating the dinghy and concealing it under the outrigger had been his. Hudson had been skeptical at first but after trial and error it had begun to work. Now it was a question of whether they'd be allowed to use the technique in a real-life situation. Hudson felt for his pipe and pulled his slouch hat over his eyes.

The antiaircraft guns were still blasting away at Six-Mile Field, and there was the sullen rumble of exploding bombs. The Zeros must have been escorting a squadron of Kate bombers . . . Hudson turned his eyes away from the shore. Funny how he unconsciously described Carter to himself as "the kid." If Marjory had ever been able to have a child he would have been about Carter's age now. The thought had never occurred to him before. He cupped his hands around the bowl of the pipe and sucked in the flame.

All along the line, things were turning out better than Hudson had expected on first meeting up with Task Force 19. Dallas's manner set his teeth on edge, but at least the man showed signs of being maneuverable. Carter was a quick learner. The initial scratchiness had disappeared and he was showing that he could work on a team. The trek to the prison camp had been tough, and Hudson had seen the fear in the boy's eyes, but Carter had kept going. He would be better equipped next time.

And Sula? Hudson looked down at the slender figure standing in the prow of the canoe. Beautiful—beautiful and unspoiled. Unusual for a native girl who had lived among white people. She was something unique . . . if they got the chance to go for the

83

volcano he was confident she'd do her job.

And Joe, sitting on the side of the canoe chewing beetel nut. Joe was what he'd always been. A friend to count on.

Only Johnson worried him. Nothing he could point to specifically, just a feeling. There were moments when he thought the man was going to crack. A twitch of the mouth, a tremor in the voice . . . Things you only noticed if you had lived with a man when death was the sound of a snapped twig away. Maybe he shouldn't come on this mission. But how do you tell a man that? What excuse do you give? Once you started breaking up the team you had to play a different game. And Hudson reckoned he was too old to change. . . .

The banshee wail of an eleven-hundred-horsepower engine made him turn 'round and face the shore. Coming out of the sun was a fighter, a Jap Zero. It leveled out only feet above the sea and came toward them. The pilot must have been heading for home after strafing the airfield and seen the cluster of boats around the wreck. Hudson shouted a warning and jumped.

Further up the sloping deck Dallas felt as if he were pinned to the middle of a target. He slithered down the hot rust to a twisted deck housing and threw himself forward, hoping in midair that he was going to clear the submerged scuppers. The water closed over his head and he clawed his way to the surface to find himself behind Johnson and the two dinghies. Instinctively he flung an arm over the side of the first dinghy before he realized that it was resting on five hundred pounds of high explosive.

He let go of the side of the raft, then grabbed it again. Dallas could not swim.

Ahead, the Zero was coming in on a line straight toward him and so close to the sea that it seemed to be taxiing on it. Twenty-millimeter cannon shells hammered into the rusty deck plating behind him and a whiplash of machine-gun bullets cut up the water like a squall of rain. He could see the line of bullets coming toward him and ducked down behind the dinghy, waiting for the explosion that would spatter him over the deck of the freighter.

There was a bang loud enough to make itself heard above the screech of the Zero, and the dinghies disappeared. Dallas found himself clinging to a piece of sinking fabric in a sea turned white by the contents of the ripped white bags. The Zero sped toward the horizon pursued by a P-40 Kitty-hawk.

Dallas was so surprised to be alive that he nearly drowned. Carter swam to his side and pulled him to the outrigger. He clung, gasping for several seconds before nodding to the bulky outline of the punctured rubber raft below the surface. "What about that damned explosive?"

"I thought you knew." Carter fought to keep a straight face. "We were using dummy bags."

CHAPTER NINE

THE convoy was small but impressive, especially to the two small pigs tusking by the side of the road who butted each other back to the shelter of the gum trees. An armored car was in front, a jeep with a rear-mounted one-hundred-and-eighty-degree traverse machine gun behind. In the middle was a jeep carrying four helmeted and gaitered military policemen armed with submachine guns and an officer with a heavy filigree of oak-leaf cluster on the peak of his hat. He raised his arm in salute to a small boy who looked up inquiringly at his mother.

The convoy was moving fast, as it always did, and the vehicles huddled together as if joined by invisible couplings. The dirt road gave way to tarmac, and the convoy emerged as if from a cloud. It was now entering a residential area in which beautiful tropical shrubs pressed in on featureless houses.

A radio crackled from the armored car, and further down the

road a heavy iron gate started to swing open. Hardly slackening speed, the convoy passed through and stopped before a second gate between two concrete command posts. A sentry stepped forward and saluted smartly as he peered into the middle vehicle. He gave a signal and the second gate opened.

The convoy passed through and continued up a long drive flanked by English-style lawns that had been allowed to turn brown so that they did not attract attention from the sky. The house was wide and low with windows on the ground floor and a veranda that ran around three sides.

Outside the large front entrance two military policemen came to attention. "Here comes World War Three," murmured one of them.

No sooner had the vehicles stopped in front of the house than the officer stepped down briskly, acknowledged the salutes of the guards and went into the house. He was met by an ADC who told him that there were no important messages and that the party had been waiting for an hour. The officer nodded, said that he wanted to go to the john and returned to be conducted to large double doors guarded by a military policeman. The door was opened and he passed through.

Carter had only seen General MacArthur in the newsreels. He was impressed by how the man looked in the flesh, tall and rangy, with a Roman nose that made him look like a hunting eagle. The impression carried through to the all-seeing blue eyes and the lean, spare face. He could have been a Hollywood film star playing himself. Even the uniform seemed to have been specially tailored, the creases put in by a wardrobe mistress moments before the star entered the room.

The ADC made the introductions. "Gentlemen—I mean, lady and gentlemen—General MacArthur."

The general jutted out his chin and nodded agreeably.

"Major Dallas, Captain Hudson, Lieutenant Carter, Corporal Johnson, native orderlies Korachi and Teosin," the ADC continued.

"I must apologize for keeping you waiting," the general said. "However, I don't have to remind you that there's a war on."

Thin laughter led by Dallas. Sula looked puzzled.

"Let me offer you a drink and then I can quickly come to the point." He nodded to an orderly who stepped forward and started taking orders. "First of all I want to congratulate you"—he looked at Dallas as he spoke—"on the imagination and initiative shown in the development of this plan. It is very much what I had in mind when I asked that your group be formed."

Dallas avoided looking the others in the eye. "Thank you, sir."

"Furthermore, I have studied your proposals and I think, given the right circumstances in regard to the volcano, that they have an even chance of succeeding—" He broke off and turned to the ADC. "Did we get those photographs of the inside of the crater?"

"No, sir. The cloud cover was too low."

"Too bad." The general frowned and then turned back to the others. "Well, you're going to know what it's like soon enough. I only have one comment in relation to your plan. Do you think you are taking enough men?" He did not look at Sula, who clearly made him uneasy.

"I think, sir, that the only time we need more men is to get the explosive to the volcano," Hudson said. "And I doubt it's worth taking them just to use as pack animals. There's a slight risk involved in using native bearers but five of us in the bush are less likely to be seen than fifteen. If this mission succeeds, it will be because the Japs don't get wind of us until it's too late."

The orderly took Carter's drink order and nodded toward Joe. "What does he drink?"

"Human blood," Carter said. "With a beer chaser."

MacArthur nodded at Hudson. "I accept what you say, captain. I'm very aware of the work you've done in this area in the past. Aware and grateful. I speak for all American servicemen when I acknowledge the debt we owe to the coast-watchers."

"Thank you, sir."

MacArthur drew himself up and raised his glass. "I wish you all good fortune, and I look forward to welcoming you back here after a successful mission. I make no secret of my belief that with the recapture of Rabaul we push over the first in the line of dominoes that will fall back across the Pacific to crush Japan. When I see you standing here—Americans, Australians, Islanders—I have no doubt that we shall succeed. Your brave action will light a candle

88

of hope that will shine from Sydney to Washington."

Carter looked at the crossed American flags behind the desk. Hudson looked at his feet. Next, a few farewell words and the party was shown out by the ADC.

MacArthur went behind his desk and unclipped the dispatch case. He smoothed out the first piece of paper.

"One thing, sir?" the returning ADC asked.

"What is it?"

"It relates to the volcano operation, sir. The colonel's report cites the need for an assault group to be in readiness to take advantage of the situation should the volcano erupt, to take care of survivors . . . We haven't lined up anything yet."

MacArthur continued to smooth out the dispatch without looking up. "Newman," he said, "when you light a candle, you don't make plans to recover the melted wax."

In the depths of his concrete bunker Lieutenant General Mori Koji pushed the tray of decoded radio messages away and stroked the sides of his mustache.

Watching him from across the dimly lit room, his adjutant, Major Yukichi, knew that he was worried. He had served the general long enough to know the signs. At the same time he had served him long enough not to ask questions. He waited for the moment when the general would choose to speak.

Despite the thickness of the walls, the sound of falling bombs revealed itself as an intermittent thumping noise, sometimes accompanied by the lights flickering and dust falling from the roof.

"How many tonight?" Koji asked.

"Forty bombers," Yukichi said. "And a fighter escort. We've shot down three fighters, the antiaircraft batteries claim two bombers."

The general said nothing for a moment but reread the piece of paper in his hand.

"Let them squander their resources. They can drop bombs until the end of our lives and we will still die of old age. My only hope is that they do not kill all the fish in the harbor."

Yukichi smiled politely. It was true that the American attacks were building up, but that they also did little damage. Only a floating crane that had been towed to Rabaul after the fall of Singapore and a couple of barges caught on a wharf provided visible evidence of Allied success.

General Koji tapped the paper against his fingertips. "I have some information here that concerns me far more . . ."

"Yes, sir?"

"We are about to be visited. Admiral Yamamoto is making a tour of key battle stations. He will be with us for three days."

"Admiral Yamamoto!" It was impossible for Yukichi to keep the excitement from his voice. The architect of Japan's day of destiny: December 7, 1941, when the attack on Pearl Harbor had shattered the myth of American invincibility and initiated the most rapid territorial conquest in the history of the world.

"You have not met him?" Koji asked.

"I have seen him but I have not had the honor of exchanging words with him."

"A remarkable man," Koji said. "A man of vision, too valuable to lose."

Yukichi nodded. "His presence here will do much to raise morale. The men are getting bored. Living like rats in the tunnels saps their spirits."

"We have come far and we have come fast," Koji said. "It is wise to rest and build up our strength. Only a fool tries to outrun his feet."

Yukichi nodded quickly and waited for the general to continue. He had anticipated that Yamamoto was coming to Rabaul to direct an invasion of Port Moresby, something that he had often discussed with his commanding officer and which would provide the logical base for expansion into Australia.

But Koji said nothing and continued to draw his fingers down the thin brush of his mustache.

Yukichi decided that in the circumstances it would not be impolite to ask a question. "May I inquire the purpose of the esteemed admiral's visit?"

"He wishes to obtain firsthand information on the state of the war and show himself to the troops."

"There is nothing specific in terms of our position here at Rabaul?"

The moment that he had closed his mouth, Yukichi realized that his question had been unwise.

General Koji looked at his adjutant. "I am not privy to every one of the admiral's plans, and if I were I would think twice before discussing them with you."

The reaction was extreme, and both men knew it.

Yukichi bowed his head to show regret. "Sir, you said that you had information that concerns you?"

General Koji stood up and walked to the map of the Pacific that had been painted on one wall of the bunker. "I was referring to the admiral's visit. Since Pearl Harbor there have been three attempts on his life . . . a bomb in Bougainville, a sniper at Brunei and an amphibious assault on his headquarters on Luzon—luckily he was not there."

"I was not aware of this," Yukichi said.

"The attacks have not been made general knowledge for obvious reasons. What is clear is that the Americans are determined to revenge themselves for what they choose to call 'The Day of Infamy.' My immediate preoccupation is therefore with Admiral Yamamoto's safety while he is with us."

"Here?" Yukichi said. "We now have sixty-five thousand men inside the most impenetrable stronghold in the Pacific. The admiral could not be safer in the middle of Tokyo—"

"You really think so?" Koji said levelly. "Your complacency is alarming. What about the raid on the searchlight post?"

Yukichi said nothing.

"Five men wiped out by an American raiding party. I have a personal interest in the affair. I was standing on that same beach five hours before they died. Very probably in the sights of an American carbine. If me, why not the admiral?" He turned back to the wall map and with his finger traced a line around the area of the harbor and Matupi Bay. "I believe that if the Americans get wind of Admiral Yamamoto's presence here they could well put a party ashore to try and assassinate him. They could even be here now. We have no evidence that the group that destroyed the radar post did not escape into the jungle."

"No, sir."

General Koji struck a match and applied it to a corner of the message. He held it at arm's length, watching it burn.

"You and I, major, are going to devise a plan that will guarantee the admiral's safety while he is with us. It will cover every eventuality."

He dropped the message just before the flame reached his fingers, and the two men watched it burn to ashes on the stone floor.

Chapter Ten

THE night Sula left to fly to the submarine base Carter called for her at the cook's house and Jones drove them to the airfield. It was a strange, sad occasion; as usual, a mixture of the social and the military. She wore a khaki *lap-lap*—too large—and a WAC blouse —too small—which polarized the extremes. She sat in the front of the jeep beside Jones as they drove through the mostly abandoned suburbs of Port Moresby. Occasionally she turned to smile at Carter, as if encouraging him to talk to her. He concentrated on memorizing her face, in case he never saw it again.

Beside her was a small *bilum* of colored wool that contained all her belongings. Carter could see a grass skirt and small packets which contained salt and trade tobacco. The girl would have to live off the land. She carried no visible weapon. It had been decided that there was no time to instruct her in the use of a firearm and that if she fell into the hands of the Japs her chances of survival, and those of the arriving party, would be better if she were carrying nothing to distinguish her.

Carter thought of what they were asking of the girl—and how he had lobbied for her inclusion in the party—and felt guilty. She should have been a spectator in this war, not a participant. But for most of the natives, the war was a marauding ogre destroying their gardens and raping their women. To survive you had to kill the ogre.

The girl could fight. She had cut a man's throat as easily as one might slit open an envelope. Killing was in her people's blood. But then, on the evidence of the present war, killing was in all people's blood . . .

Dallas, Hudson, Johnson, and Joe were waiting at the airstrip. A heap of still-blazing metal was being bulldozed off the runway.

"The ack-ack guns just got a Kate," Johnson explained. "Bastard tried to crash it into the control tower."

Carter took Sula's hand and squeezed it. She returned the pressure. Anywhere else but in this war they would have put their arms around each other in case there was never another time. He released her hand, and she and Joe climbed into a Lockheed Tristar that already had its props turning. It dawdled down the runway, turned and took off over the dust-covered gum trees.

On the way back to camp, Carter got Jones to drive him down the street where Jean had lived. The house was empty and boarded up against looters.

"Everybody moving out of town," Jones said.

"Yes."

Jones had been unusually quiet that evening. He kept looking in front of him and chewing gum. "I'll probably be going soon, I've put in for a transfer to a combat division." He gestured toward the overgrown gardens and the tired weatherboard houses with names like "Dunrovin" and "Shangri La." "This place is a dump."

Carter thought of Jones getting his ass blown off on some island. "They're all dumps," he said.

Two nights later Carter was lying on a bunk staring at the bundle of cables inches above his head and wondering how a fly got onto a submarine. Wondering also how it could stand the heat. The fan

94

seemed to blow in hot air rather than take it out. He glanced at his watch for the third time in half an hour and was relieved when Hudson entered the cabin.

His face was grim. "I've just been talking to the captain. He's got the latest weather reports—high seas and near gale force winds."

Carter swore. "And we haven't had a chance to practice the launching drill."

"You can forget about it. If the weather doesn't improve, you can forget about the whole deal."

Carter swore again. It seemed weird being cramped up in this suffocating heat listening to the vibration of the engines when forty feet above their heads a full-blooded storm was blowing.

"How much longer have we got?" Hudson asked.

Carter did not need to look at his watch. "About three and a half hours."

"Maybe it'll die down. You want to sleep?"

Carter shook his head. "In this place? Who could sleep in it."

"Don't bet on it. When you come back you'll go off like a baby."

Carter nearly said "if I come back" but stopped himself, thought instead how Joe and Sula are doing, about how important their role was in this thing, rounding up the bearers, getting the canoes, finding the others . . .

At 0500 hours there was another weather report stating that the wind had dropped but that there was no telling how long this would last. Bad weather was still forecast for the launch area.

"We'll just have to take a look when we get there," the captain of the submarine said. "I hope you can go because I sure as hell can't wait to get that thousand pounds of explosive off my boat."

At 0545 hours Hudson was called to the control room. Carter went with him. The change in engine noise told him that they were hove to, presumably just below the surface.

The captain confirmed this. "We're in the launch area," he said. "I'm just going to take a look." He turned to the sailor beside him. "Stand by for observation. Up scope."

With a pneumatic hiss the periscope rose from the well and the sailor snapped down the handles. The captain dropped to his knees on the deck, seized the handles and pressed his eyes to the eyepiece. He rose to his feet with the ascending periscope.

Carter waited, feeling tense but relieved too. At last something was going to happen, he could stop worrying and start doing.

The captain stepped back. His face was solemn. "Take a look."

Hudson advanced and stooped awkwardly over the periscope. He swung it through a hundred and eighty degrees as the captain had done and stepped back.

"Apart from the fact that there's a heavy sea running, I can't see anything, sir."

"Neither can I," the captain said. "We've come up in the middle of a thick fog."

Carter looked at Hudson disbelievingly. If this was a sample of their luck, they might as well give up and go home.

"I know this coast, sir, and I think there's a good chance that the fog's localized," Hudson said. "If we can move on a few thousand yards we may be out of it."

The captain nodded, slapped up the handles and the periscope hissed back into its well. "Officer of the deck, come right to zero-zero-zero and tell maneuvering to make turns for eleven knots."

Hudson turned to Carter. "It's a bastard but it's not the end of the world. Might even give us some cover from the Japs. I'm more worried about the sea."

Ten minutes later the periscope went up again and the captain shook his head. "No change," he said.

Carter pressed his face against the rubber eyepiece and experienced the unreal sensation of looking across the surface of the sea as if he were swimming in it with goggles. All he could see was a broken swirl of water fragmenting against the periscope glass and affording glimpses of deep troughs and swells enclosed in a stygian gloom that reduced visibility to a matter of yards.

"I'll take her up and you can have a look," the captain said. "Stand by, the launch team."

The order echoed through the boat, and the area below the conning tower quickly filled with men wheeling trolleys containing the bags of explosive. The internal drill had been run through many times on the voyage from New Guinea and each member of the team knew his job once the hatches were opened.

The captain turned to Hudson and Carter. "All right, gentle-

96

men. I'd appreciate a quick decision when we surface."

"You'll get it," Hudson said.

Carter stood at the bottom of the ladder leading to the bridge. Was it possible that after the slog through the jungle and all their training, planning and testing, the operation was going to be called off because of the goddam weather before it had even begun? What he saw when he got to the bridge was even more depressing. The submarine was wallowing like a broaching whale as waves washed over the decks. The fog pressed in on all sides and seemed to be resting on their heads.

Hudson said, "I was hoping to load the dinghies on deck and float them off when you submerged. That's cooked." He turned to Carter. "What do you think? You're the launching expert. Shall we give it a go?" There was no question in it, really. More encouragement. It got through to Carter.

"Why not?" he said.

They informed the captain, and moments later the forward deck hatch opened and the first dinghy went over the side. Carter leapt into it. The sea threw it up nearly level with the deck, then troughed to almost swallow it. Hudson came with the second dinghy and the third arrived immediately so that the three lashed together would effect a better platform in the water. Carter, quickly soaked to the skin, gave up the idea of using a paddle to reach Hudson. Not with the sea in this mood. When Hudson came near enough, he would grab him.

Eventually the two rafts were thrown together and Carter lunged out across the gap to cling to the side until Hudson had secured the straps. Now the two dinghies bounced on the waves and threatened to accordion while the crew played the third within their reach. Finally it was hauled back on deck and released again almost on top of them. Hudson grabbed at the rope and clung to it until Carter could secure the straps. The two-hinged structure buckled over the waves, and Carter felt nausea as the sea swept past in front of his eyes.

On the bridge, Johnson waited for his moment and drew back his arm to throw down a rope with a weighted end. It spiraled out and was caught by Hudson. He swiftly lashed it to the center raft. As soon as it was in position, the first bag of explosive slid down, barely clearing the gray-topped rollers that slapped against the hull of the sub. Hudson snatched at it with cold, pinched fingers and nearly dropped it.

"Try and hold us steady!"

He thrust a paddle into Carter's hands and sprawled across the gunwale to stow the first bag. On the submarine, the crew manning the ropes hunched their heads into their shoulders and watched through narrowed eyes as the bags began to hang from rope like seed pods.

"Not so fast!" Hudson swore.

The rope suddenly dipped, and the platform of rafts swirled in toward the submarine. For a second it seemed that the explosive would be ground between the hull and the side of the rafts. Then Carter worked his paddle through the rudder mounting and took the full force of the swell on his blade. The boats quivered and swung away to a safe distance.

"Hold her there, for Christ's sake!" Hudson called as he worked feverishly. The rope stretched taut, and glistening bags began to cover the floor of one dinghy.

Carter started to count them, knowing that at any second he could reach the unlucky number that would blow them all to hell. "Sixty-five, sixty-six, sixty-seven . . ."

The mist still pressed in but the sea had lost some of its fury. The spiteful, wind-whipped claws of waves came now in a rhythm that could at least be learned and anticipated. Carter paddled till his arms ached in their sockets, and watched the dinghy fill. "Two hundred and one, two hundred and two . . ."

The first dinghy was filled and the cover unfurled—and then one of the zippers stuck. From the bridge, Johnson and the submarine commander watched anxiously. With every second that passed they were challenging the moment when the fog lifted and the submarine became a sitting target on the surface.

"Leave it!" Carter urged. He noticed the ominous strain that was being placed on the securing straps but said nothing.

Hudson changed sides and started to stow the bags. His face was gray with fatigue and tension. His knuckles white with cold. His fingers were beginning to fumble and he dropped the short-bladed knife he'd been freeing the bags with. The knife plunged downward into the bottom of the dinghy. Carter closed his eyes. When he opened them, Hudson was retrieving the knife from the plastic overlap of one of the bags and muttering something to himself that Carter couldn't hear.

Johnson was now holding up two hands from the bridge and starting to clamber down the outside ladder from the conning tower.

"Ten more!" Carter shouted. "I never thought we'd do it."

Hudson said nothing as he reached out for the remaining bags. The deck crew tightened their grip on the two ropes that held the dinghies and prepared to haul.

"Got you, you beaut." Hudson closed his hands around the last bag and triumphantly untied the loading rope.

The deck party pulled the rafts nearer to the submarine, and Johnson judged his moment and jumped into the waiting arms. Good-luck was shouted from deck and bridge, and suddenly the hatch was slamming down and the bridge was empty.

Carter looked up at the gaunt outline of the submarine and experienced a terrifying sensation of isolation. As the hull began to settle in the water he felt like a sailor watching his ship sinking. Point of no return—they were on their own. The water swept over the foredeck and the stern tilted. The conning tower made a bow wave of its own, then tilted forward, as if nodding a courteous farewell. It glided through the water, gathering speed and sinking fast until it slid below the surface in a small eruption of white bubbles. The waves rolled on. There was no hint that it had ever been there.

Alone.

Carter finished securing the cover of the second explosives dinghy and looked about him. The mist still closed in eerily without a break. The swell was running high.

"Got you, you cow." Hudson freed the stubborn zipper on the first explosive dinghy and locked it in the closed position. He slumped into the bottom of the dinghy, soaked and exhausted. "Right," he said. "I think this calls for a small celebration." He felt in the breast pocket of his tunic and fumbled with cold fingers to produce three brandy miniatures. "Captain's compliments. Keep you warm until the sun comes up."

99

Johnson lost no time in opening his bottle and downing it at a gulp.

Carter drank his gratefully. "Any idea where we are?"

Hudson had his compass in hand. He jerked a thumb over his shoulder. "If the captain knows his business, that's Rabaul."

Johnson asked, "Do we take her in toward shore?"

"Trouble is, we don't know our exact position," Hudson said. "If we go in, and the mist suddenly lifts, we could find ourselves staring at a beach full of Japs."

"And if we stay here the current could take us out to sea or miles down the coast," Johnson said.

"The weather's not getting any better," Carter added.

The sea swirled around them, the water slapping mournfully against the stretched fabric of the rafts. Once again, Carter noticed that one of the straps was parting with its mooring.

"A bit of a squall could blow this bloody mist away," Hudson said.

Suddenly there was a thumping noise, like a heartbeat, coming louder and nearer.

The three men looked at each other. Johnson reached for the Sten gun strapped across his shoulders. The thumping hammered at their eardrums. It seemed to be coming from all around them. Then, like the head of an attacking shark, the bows of a destroyer broke through the mist and bore down on them. Carter glimpsed the concave sweep of its prow towering above him, and then the bow wave tossed them contemptuously aside and he was hurled into the water.

Down, down, until it seemed that his eardrums must burst and the water invade his lungs. His eyes closed tight. He kicked as if on a hangman's rope, and felt at last that he was rising. His head broke the surface and he sucked in mouthfuls of air.

Around him was nothing but churning sea and fog. No sign of the destroyer, no sign of Hudson and Johnson. And no sign of the rafts.

The mist drifted above his head. He listened, heard nothing. He called out. Nothing.

The destroyer must have been standing out of Rabaul harbor and making about thirty knots. She would never have had time to see them, but it hardly seemed to matter. Not now.

He rose with the swell and called out again. Still no answer. Had the rafts blown up? Were Hudson and Johnson drowned? If the explosives had gone up, the destroyer would have gone with them but there was no sign of wreckage. The others must be in the fog somewhere. Should he try and find them or use his remaining resources of strength and swim to shore? Except where was the shore?

He pulled at the compass that hung around his neck and treaded water while he tried to read it. A wave swept over him, and he choked on a mouthful of water. His teeth were chattering and the Sten gun strapped across his back cut into his flesh. He shouted again and heard the echo of his voice across the water. At the back of his mind was always one thought—sharks. In each swirl of water he saw a dark shape closing.

Fifty feet away he saw a dark outline in the mist. A shark . . . ? Maybe the rafts . . . He shouted and struck out. The shape dipped into a trough, and disappeared again.

Carter panicked. Was the current taking them away from him? His arms lashed at the water, burning up his strength. If he did not catch up with them soon he would be done for. He raised his head and saw the bulky shape momentarily outlined on the crest of a wave. But there was no sign of Hudson and Johnson—they must have been swept overboard. He struggled on, expecting at each moment to feel banks of razor-sharp teeth paring his flesh to the bone. His arms were very tired, the cold was numbing. He looked again, and for a moment thought that his objective had disappeared, until it bobbed up out of a trough thirty feet away and he saw that there was only one raft. As it tilted he recognized the cover of one of the explosive dinghies. The stress generated by the destroyer must have finally forced them apart . . . He covered the distance in ten untidy strokes and clung to the rope that ran around the gunwale. For a few moments he sucked in breath, and then his fear of sharks made him try to haul himself from the water. His feet strayed under the raft, and it took several attempts before he could rest his elbow on the side and pull himself up and out, to sprawl across the mound of bags.

He lay face down, heart pounding, salt water stinging his face, and opened his legs and arms so that he had a better purchase on the raft. Five hundred pounds of plastic explosive. Some damn sanctuary he'd found for himself . . .

He was still drifting in fogbound open sea in the shipping lanes at the entrance to Rabaul harbor. He shouted as loud as he could, once, and then listened intently. It might have been his imagination but there seemed to be the sound of distant surf. He pulled out his compass and checked the direction of the noise. It was possible, but, if true, it meant that he was in a current moving along the face of the coast. He hoped that it was toward the pick-up area. Another shout and he sank down exhausted, his head on the side of the raft . . .

The air seemed lighter and a faint shadow fell on his hand. He looked up and saw blue sky through a gap in the fog, then a glimpse of distant jungle-covered coastline, clouds and mountains in the background.

"Kal-o-o."

The call echoed across the water like the noise of a reed instrument. He paused, tried to imitate the sound.

The call was repeated, but this time from further away.

Time was running out. He turned—and coming toward him was a dugout canoe skimming down the waves. Kneeling in its stern was Sula, who plied her paddle to come alongside.

It was unreal . . . she looked like a Gauguin painting, bare breasts, a single cowrie shell dangling between them, a pig's-tusk bracelet curved around her upper arm. Her khaki *lap-lap* had been replaced by a grass skirt. There was method in her get-up . . . to potentially curious eyes she was a native girl out on a fishing expedition, however unusually attractive she might be. To be more modest would be more risky. A fishing net was heaped in the prow as a further prop.

Carter looked at her and couldn't find words. Hers were to apologize . . . *apologize,* for God's sake . . . for taking so long to find him.

"Have you seen the others?"

She shook her head. "Joe is looking, what happened?"

Carter quickly told her. "And you?" he asked.

"Japs are very excited. Patrols and roadblocks are everywhere. Joe wonders if they found out we are coming."

"They couldn't have," Carter said, knowing that in fact anything was possible. It suddenly occurred to him that Green might have inadvertently blurted something that had got back to the Japs, or that they'd gotten on to him. He said none of this, indicated the raft. "First we have to handle this."

The sea was calmer now and the mist had vanished. The clouds were breaking up fast and great rifts of blue appeared. Only in the distant mountains did the clouds still loom, as if guarding dark secrets.

He started to let air out of the dinghy while keeping an eye open for sharks. A school of moon jellyfish drifted past, their slimy milk-white bodies glistening. He was grateful he was not still in the water. He worked his way onto the framework between the canoe and the outrigger and started to draw the semi-inflated dinghy underneath. When the canes were lashed in place to keep it steady and below the water line, he climbed into the dugout, facing Sula. The solid feel of sculpted wood was reassuring. He unharnessed his Sten gun and checked that the waterproof bag had done its job.

Now that he was back on schedule, he felt better. Two hours had been lost, but since they'd intended to rest during the day this was not so serious. His real worry, apart from Sula's report of increasing Japanese activity, was what had happened to Hudson and Johnson.

"Hungry?" Sula asked.

"Starving."

She produced a small bundle of fruit. Carter set to it greedily.

"We go to the beach?"

Carter nodded, his mouth full, and reached for a paddle. The fishing net he placed at his feet so that he could hide underneath it when they came within sight of land. At first they seemed to be making no impression on the distance, but slowly a line of beach separated from the trees and he could see the entrance to a bay. Rabaul and its harbor were around the point, and invisible.

The huge flat-topped mass of Matupi soon detached itself from its surroundings, rising out of thick jungle to the right of the bay. Its summit gleamed black in the sunlight. It was a

103

brooding, sinister presence, the dark shadows on its side showing where the jungle had poured in to fill subsidiary craters. To the right of the volcano, the ground leveled off swiftly to flat marshland that marked the delta of a large river flowing down from the mountains.

Carter squinted his eyes against the sunlight and looked into the sky beyond the volcano—where the main airfield should be.

As he watched, a biplane appeared, climbing to the left of the volcano, turned lazily and started to fly over the jungle.

A spotter plane . . . a complication they'd not thought of. They had never checked the visibility of the submerged dinghy from directly above. Carter wondered anxiously what would happen if the plane flew over them.

The spotter plane's appearance made him consider that he might be visible from the shore to anyone with a pair of powerful binoculars. He explained to Sula and lay down on the bottom of the canoe, his shoulders chafing the sides, his gun between his legs. He turned his head to talk to her and saw that she was wearing nothing beneath her grass skirt.

Sula saw his glance, made no effort to change her position. This was no damn Stateside tease . . . this was not even a woman at the moment. This was somebody who had just saved his life.

Her paddle dove in, and a latticework of muscle flickered beneath the smooth tan of her arm. Small drops of water annointed her breasts, glistening like jewels around the aureoles of her nipples. He took it back, this was a *woman* who had just saved his life.

"The plane." Sula gestured toward the shore.

Carter quickly pulled the net over his head, watched the sky through its chinks.

After a short while came a buzzing sound, and the biplane passed less than fifty feet above their heads. Carter glimpsed the goggles of the observer looking down, prayed that the dinghy would not be seen as the biplane passed out of his view.

He was beginning to breathe again when there was a change of engine note. The biplane was turning to make another sweep. Had they seen something? He pressed backward, his shoulders scraping the sides. The engine note quickly grew to a roar. This time it passed within twenty feet and a voice shouted something from

104

the cockpit. Was a radio message being flashed ashore to alert a patrol boat?

The sound of the plane diminished to a drone, then died away. Carter pulled the netting from his face. It smelt of fish, the least of his problems.

"What did he say?"

Sula paddled on. "I think he likes me."

Carter pulled the net over his head and raised himself up to peer over the side of the canoe. The entrance to Matupi Bay was now less than four hundred yards away, and he could see the first line of the defenses—two large, concrete blockhouses built in the water and providing uninterrupted fields of fire over the narrow strips of beach on either side. Somewhere behind those narrow slits, interested eyes would be watching.

Carter glanced toward the submerged dinghy and the spars and canes that held it in place. The system seemed to be working as well as it had during testing. He sank back and tried to wriggle into a more comfortable position.

Now came the worst part. Waiting.

The canoe was so close to the blockhouses that Sula could see the glint of a man's spectacles behind one of the slits. In the shallow water beside it four naked men were washing, one of them still wearing his cap. They looked up as she passed, made the expected comments.

Further along the shore was the rusting hulk of a landing barge knocked out by a direct hit from a mortar during the Japanese invasion of '42. She could see a wireless aerial rising from the deck and could hear the intermittent gabble of the signalman inside. Stretching away from the beach, the ground rose unevenly among palm trees with their tops blown off by bombs to sandbag emplacements which concealed the big guns. The area between was an untidy warren of trenches and foxholes covered by barbed wire.

"*Tomare!*"

She knew that the word meant "stop" and that it was directed at her, but she kept paddling.

"*Tomare!*"

This time the voice was angry and accompanied by the sound of a rifle bolt sliding back. She continued to paddle.

The rifle boomed, the shot splintered the top of the outrigger two feet above the explosive. A parakeet screamed in alarm and crashed away through the palms. Sula stopped paddling.

On the shore, half hidden by a clump of mangrove, was a dugout canoe. Two Japanese hurried toward it, one of them shouldering his rifle. Sula saw the netting stir as Carter fumbled for his gun.

One of the soldiers climbed into the canoe as the other pushed it off and scrambled aboard.

Sula stood up and prepared to greet them. There was no movement from the netting. When they were halfway to the canoe the man in the bow began to talk and gesture, and her heart sank. They wanted all the fish she had caught . . .

She must stop them from searching the canoe. She dragged the net up and shook it, indicating with her head that she had caught nothing. At her feet Carter lay vulnerable as a baby in its cradle. Some cradle . . .

The soldiers kept coming. Either they did not understand or they did not believe her. They were very thin, skin stretched tight across cheekbones, sun-bleached uniforms hanging like castoffs from bigger men. They came in until the prow of their canoe was resting against the outrigger. If they looked down they must see the raft. But they were looking at Sula. As a hungry man looks at a piece of meat. Sula had seen the look before.

The man in the prow reluctantly took his eyes from her breasts and craned forward to see what was in the canoe. He spoke to his companion and they started to paddle around the outrigger to take a closer look.

Sula held her breath and slowly looked down to her feet. The netting twitched in anticipation. The first man stretched out his hand to seize the side of the canoe above Carter's head—

The wail of the siren pierced the silence and fell across the water. The soldier pulled back his hand, looked around. Approaching fast across the bay, its prow out of the water, was a small launch flying a Japanese flag. The two men looked at each other apprehensively and allowed Sula's canoe to drift a few feet from them. The launch swung around, stopped abruptly, throwing out a wave that washed over both canoes and nearly capsized the Japanese. Its engine raced and an angry froth of water bubbled from its stern. No less angry was the voice of the major standing in the prow, surrounded by a lieutenant and half a dozen men. He shouted at the two soldiers in the dugout and waved toward the shore.

Sula waited for someone to see the outline of the raft now clearly visible beneath the limpid blue water, but all eyes were either on the major or the miscreants. The major's gabble ended and the launch sped on toward the shore. The two soldiers raised their heads from their chests and hurriedly paddled after it without a backward glance.

Sula noticed that the bathing men had disappeared and that there was activity in the foxholes. Men hurried into position, and a soldier was speedily removing some articles of clothing that had been laid out to dry on the wire. It looked like a surprise inspection —more disturbing evidence that the Japanese were expecting something special . . .

She settled down in the canoe and began to paddle, dug a toe into the netting until she could feel Carter's head. "They have gone, you can uncover your face."

Carter pulled back the netting and looked up at the sky through stinging eyes. Sweat lathered his forehead, the hair stuck close to his head. "What happened?"

The canoe moved along the shore past a torrent of tropical greenery that tumbled down steep slopes to the water's edge. Unseen birds called from the tops of trees, and there was the repeated shrill chatter of an angry monkey. Looming over all was the unstable mass of Matupi, menacing even in the sunshine. The jungle clung to its side like moss to a great boulder.

Sula looked down and saw a catfish swimming weakly, barely able to move below the surface, and then another, belly up and twitching. It was puzzling. There was no mark on them. Nothing to suggest that they had been attacked by another fish. She looked toward the end of the bay and then looked again, shading her eyes. No, she had not been mistaken. The water was stained with clouds of yellow. She veered toward it, and within the space of twenty strokes was confronted by thick yellow tide sprinkled with dead and dying fish. As she looked down she could see a stream of yellow bubbles rising to the surface. She sank to her knees, dipped in the water. It was hot.

107

"What is it?" Carter said.

Sula shrugged. "I do not know, the water is hot and yellow."

Carter lowered his head. "Good."

As yet untouched by the yellow tide and recessed inland from the Japanese position was the small beach of black volcanic sand that had shown itself on the aerial photographs. Half a dozen dugout canoes were drawn up on the sand, but there was no sign of the upright paddle wedged against the outrigger, which was the signal to say that the other party had arrived and landed safely.

Sula was more worried by the presence of several children splashing in the shallows. She knew Carter needed to get ashore and rest, but she knew also that it would be dangerous if the children saw him. They were of Joe's tribe, but the word would spread like wildfire if a white man was known to be in the area. Her presence had already excited comment among the villagers. She was known as "Joe's woman," a title that added luster to Joe's already impressive reputation. Sula waited until she was fifty yards from the beach, then started to beat the water with her paddle, shouting, "Shark!" The bathers fled for the beach and started to clamber over the surrounding rocks for a better sight of the mythical raider. Sula brought the canoe closer in and wedged it against a shelving rock a few yards from shore, which had been preselected for the purpose. The children were scrambling among the rocks.

"Wait."

She slipped into the water and waded ashore, checking the sands for any sign of fresh bootprints. There seemed to be nobody about. The sun was high in the sky and the sand almost too hot beneath the feet. The natives would be in their huts and hopefully the Japanese on the local post occupied with their inspection.

Sula waited at the edge of the beach for a few minutes to see if anyone appeared, then waded out to the canoe. She started to lift out the net and under its cover Carter slipped into the water and started to rub the feeling back into his cramped limbs. Sula returned to the beach to lay out the net on a framework of drying poles. Carter waited, then felt his way through shoals of minute fish to lie with his nose barely above water, his chest pressed against the sand. Sula looked about, gave the word. Carter got to his feet, ran beneath the net to throw himself into the shelter of

108

the bush. Seconds later Sula sauntered to his side and, without pausing, led him to the hideout she had prepared with Joe.

At first glance this seemed like an ordinary clump of thick rattan, but when Sula picked her way carefully through the undergrowth to pull back the outside canoe, Carter could see that a narrow tunnel had been made and the center of the clump hollowed out to make a cool open chamber. The severed canes provided a rough floor. Carter unslung his weapon and withdrew it from its waterproof bag before stretching out. He felt exhausted but grateful—and surprised—to be alive. Sula looked down at him for a moment, moved to take up a position at the mouth of the tunnel. When he next looked she had disappeared.

He lay back and tried to find promise in the glimpse of sunlight breaking through the dark foliage far above his head. Then he closed his eyes and fell asleep.

CHAPTER ELEVEN

WHEN Carter awoke it was to a hand over his mouth and another pressing against his shoulder. He opened his eyes, not certain if he was having a nightmare, and saw Hudson looking down at him. Behind were Johnson and Joe. There was no sign of Sula.

"Hey," Carter whispered when the hand was removed. "I thought I was going to have to blow up half a volcano all by myself. What happened to you guys?"

"Same as you, mate," Johnson said. "Bloody current took us halfway to New Ireland. I thought I was going to be in the States before you."

"Joe gets another medal for finding us," Hudson said.

Joe smirked.

"Order one for Sula while you're at it," Carter said. "Where is she?"

110

"Standing watch."

Carter looked at his watch. He doubted if he'd ever be able to master the jungle on his own. Half-past three. That meant that he'd been asleep for over three hours. The others would hardly have time to close their eyes before the night's operation. He looked at Hudson. "You going to be in shape for tonight?"

Hudson looked annoyed. "Yes, I'd rather keep moving than stay here. The sooner we get that explosive out of the water, the better."

"Too right," Johnson said. "Mind you, once or twice I thought it was going out of the water and taking us with it. We nearly lost our outrigger coming past the Japs."

"Was there a launch there?" Carter asked.

"No," Johnson said. "They all seemed to be tidying the place up."

"Tell me more about the launch," Hudson said.

Carter gave an edited version of his trip ashore, with emphasis on the spotter plane and the officious major.

Hudson said, "It bears out what Joe has been telling us. Our friends are definitely alert."

"Any idea why?"

Hudson shrugged. "Probably they're sore about what we did to the searchlight post. Too bad we were forced to let them know we were there." He looked at his watch. "Jerry and I will get our heads down for a couple of hours. Joe will make contact with his people. Will, wake me at sunset. I want us to have a scout round before it gets dark." He lay down and seemed instantly asleep. Johnson lay down opposite him.

Joe saluted and went out. Carter stripped and reassembled his Sten gun to make sure it was in good working order, moved to the mouth of the tunnel. Through the rattan he had a partial view of the clearing, could see the overgrown pathway leading to the beach. No sign of Sula.

He listened intently for several minutes, could detect only occasional bird cries, the throbbing of insects. He felt a familiar pricking sensation and stooped to find the first leech on his ankle. His arm was already red with mosquito bites. Where was Sula? Nearby, he assumed . . . He stepped forward from semidarkness into the twilight of the forest. Nearby a swallow-tailed Uranus moth, wing-span as wide as his spread hand, paused on a jungle blossom, then shadowed away among the creepers. Stepping carefully so as to leave no trail of crushed vegetation to the rattan, he joined the path and made his way back toward the beach, expecting to see Sula with every step. He was surprised when he suddenly reached the black volcanic sand with no sign of her. The children had disappeared and the beach was deserted. He looked across to the rock and saw that a second outrigger canoe had been moored against it. Several of the support spars were dangling in the water to bear out what Johnson had said about the damaged outrigger.

Carter turned his head and looked up toward Matupi. Its sliced top was just visible over the trees. As he tried to calculate how long it would take to reach the summit a flight of planes appeared flying directly over the crater—two Betty bombers escorted by six Zeke fighters.

Carter was curious. The Zeke was the latest and more maneuver-able version of the Zero, with tapering wings. Whoever was in the bombers must be important. As the Betties peeled off to land, the Zekes began to circle protectively until they in turn came down one by one to disappear behind the trees.

Carter waited to see if he could hear or see anything else of interest, then withdrew from the fringe of the beach. He had taken about a dozen paces when he heard somebody approaching down the path. There was no thick cover available, so he got down behind a tree with jungle ferns up to his shoulders. A large yellow grasshopper struck him on the chest like a missile and he jerked back in surprise before pressing forward until he was peering through the whorls of lichen-covered liana that encircled the trunk. Sula . . . ? It was not Sula approaching down the path. Something was brushing through the undergrowth below waist height. Before Carter could move, the ferns parted, and he was face to face with a large vicious-looking dog, its long pink tongue lolling from its mouth. The dog seemed about to spring at him. Carter stood up, raising his gun. Behind the dog loomed a native carrying a long hunting spear. At the sight of Carter he drew the spear back.

"No!" Carter pushed his weapon out in front of him, the native's

112

arm froze. Slowly, he lowered his arm and said something to the dog, which drew back from the crouched position, its eyes still on Carter's throat.

The tension was broken by Sula, who appeared silently from the foliage on the other side of the track. She looked at Carter.

"Ask him what he's doing here," Carter told her.

Sula spoke swiftly in Tolai, but the man shook his head. She resorted to pidgin.

The man paused for a moment, shifted uneasily before answering.

Sula didn't believe his story that he was hunting pig.

The man lapsed into a sullen silence and looked at his dog, and Carter thrust the machine gun forward a couple of inches to discourage any order to attack.

Sula turned to Carter. "He is lying. There are no pigs here."

The man looked anxiously toward Carter, as though sensing what was being said. Carter knew he had an ugly decision to make . . . The man did not speak the local language and was hunting pig where none existed. Carter knew enough about New Guinea to know that no man wanting to stay alive would hunt alone in another tribe's territory. He also knew that the Japs used native trackers and dogs to hunt down coast-watchers. Every indication was that the man in front of him was one of them. Weigh the success of the mission against the risk involved in letting this man live. Was it so difficult a decision? When the volcano blew many innocent natives would die along with the Japs. Green might not return and the inmates of the prison camp would be executed.

Except, damn it, to kill this man in cold blood . . . that was different. Somehow it turned his stomach. This was not a Jap, this was a native trying to survive in *his* country . . . Besides, he carried a hunting spear, maybe he *was* telling the truth . . . A shot was out of the question with the Japs less than a mile away. Was he up to cutting the man's throat . . . ? No, he'd take him back to the others. Hudson could play Solomon and high executioner if necessary . . .

Sula was moving up behind the man, her hand went to her thigh and parted her skirt to withdraw a slim dagger made of sharpened

113

cassowary bone. She started to raise her hand, the muscles in her arm tightened—

Carter told her "no," and as he did the man shouted at the dog, which leapt on Carter, and spun around to disembowel Sula with his spear. She twisted away just in time and the spear, thrown at Carter as he fed the dog his forearm, thumped into the dog's back. As it fell kicking to the ground, the man ran. Sula instantly threw the dagger, which lodged in the middle of the man's back. He staggered but didn't fall, and in moments was swallowed up by the bush.

Sula didn't need to say what was on her mind—and Carter's . . . why didn't he let her kill the man, who now might survive to tell the Japanese of their presence. There was no conflict for a woman who had been multiply raped . . . black or yellow, or white, an enemy was an enemy. Carter, still an amateur, worried too much about rules of another game. All very civilized . . . and an invitation to disaster, he told himself. He looked at his arm so as not to look at her. The dog's teeth had punched deep holes, the blood welled up and began to flow down his arm to his fingertips and drip onto the ground. Flecks of foam appeared around the dog's mouth and the first blowflies homed in gratefully. He held his hand over the wound to stop the blood dripping. "We've got to warn the others," was all he could say. She knew what he felt.

When he came through the rattan, Hudson's gun was pointing at him. "What's up?"

Carter quickly reported what had happened, and Hudson's face turned predictably grim. No recriminations, though . . . what was the point . . . ? He nodded to Johnson. "Bind his arm up. If they've got dogs and native trackers they'll be here in no time. We'll have to go deeper into the bush."

"What about the explosive?" asked Carter quietly.

"We'll have to take a chance and leave it here. We can't move it now—"

Sula heard his approach first, and then the rest heard a rustle of the rattan as Joe appeared. He had brought the bearers, who were waiting nearby.

"Send them away, Joe," Hudson said. "We've got trouble."

Hudson led them out of the rattan, and the cluster of frightened natives disappeared into the bush the moment Joe had finished speaking to them.

The distant baying of dogs.

Hudson waved Joe down the track and started to run. "The swamp," Hudson told them. "It's the only place we've a chance to lose those dogs."

They ran hard for three hundred yards, tripping over roots, stumbling in potholes and slithering through mud patches until they came to a small clearing in the forest. That it had once been a garden was obvious, but the grove of banana and breadfruit trees had been choked by vines; the sweet potatoes and yams were only visible as mounds among the invading *kunai* grass. Hudson halted, unslung his weapon. "Jerry, you and me behind the cedar. Will, take Sula and get in between those bamboos. Joe, over there behind the bananas. Fire when I do, then we take off. We want to stop them, not fight a big deal battle. If there's a couple of dogs, kill them first." He was moving toward cover before the last words were out of his mouth.

Carter shouldered his way into the bamboos, turned and dropped onto the feather mattress of rotting leaves and humus. Sula brushed past him and lay at his shoulder. He turned to glance at her, but she avoided his eye and looked down the track.

Hudson checked his field of fire and wrapped the sling of his Sten gun around his forearm to steady his aim. Beside him Johnson lay on his side, a grenade in hand ready to be thrown. The regular warning-note tick of an unseen bird exploded into a raucous cackle and was swallowed up in a flutter of departing wings. Now all that could be heard above the susurration of the insects was the distant baying of the dogs, getting louder.

Hudson narrowed his eyes, peered across the clearing, waiting for the first hint of movement along the track. When it came he pressed back the safety catch. Johnson hooked his forefinger in the ring of the grenade . . . First to appear were three *kanakas* with dogs on leashes. Behind them, in single file were a party of Japanese marines wearing uniforms of dark-green cloth, camouflaged steel helmets and black canvas boots and gaiters. Each man carried a pack made of hide with the hair on the outside to keep out the rain, a rolled-raincoat groundsheet, ammunition bandoliers and either a snub-nosed submachine gun or a bolt-action Mauser-type rifle. Ordinarily the marines would have been spread out at fifteen-yard intervals and moving warily. Now they were pressing forward in continuous file with no apparent thought of being attacked. The path seemed to be choked with them.

The first men came into the clearing and paused as the dogs broke up to follow the diverging scents. Hudson waited till there was a cluster of fifteen, then turned to Johnson, nodded. Johnson drew the pin, his arm rose straight like a catapult. He'd already ranged in on the spot where he wanted the grenade to land and was reaching for his weapon a split-second after his throwing hand was empty.

Hudson waited until the grenade was in midair, then fired a long burst into the center of the group. Three were going down as the grenade fragments ripped through flesh. A dog was blown halfway across the clearing. Another lost a hind leg. The third dog had survived because its companions had absorbed the main force of the explosion. Hudson shot it.

More Japanese went down as Joe, Johnson and Carter opened fire, but there was no panic. Men who could move dived for the nearest cover, and those further down the track broke out fast to find as much space on the flanks as they could. These were battle-tough veterans who in less than six months had overrun half the Pacific . . . Within thirty seconds the clearing was empty except for the dead, the dying. Two of the native guides were dead. The third was wounded.

Hudson and Johnson withdrew, crawling for twenty yards, then ran stooped along the path to be joined by Joe, Sula, and Carter. Behind them bullets ripped into the position they had just left. Hudson and Carter knew how the Japs would work, they'd fan out sideways in a continuing semicircle searching the target area before them with a moving arc of submachine-gun fire. Once they'd located the enemy firepoints it would only be a question of time before they outflanked each position and overran it. The Japs were methodical but slow to change tactics. Hudson calculated that it would be ten minutes before they started leveling the vegetation and realized that their enemy had withdrawn.

The path narrowed and wound through a grove of bamboo, the

entrance splashed with brilliant sunlight. As the others went through, Carter dropped to one knee and unclipped a grenade wound with fine wire. He quickly unwound the wire and passed it around two palms at ankle level so that it was strung across the path, practically invisible to anyone emerging from jungle darkness into dazzling sunshine. He adjusted a sliding hook on the wire and snapped it onto the firing-pin ring of the grenade, keeping the wire taut. The pressure of a man's ankle against the wire would pull the pin.

A hundred yards behind, bursts of automatic fire ripped through the foliage. Carter started to run after the others. Fifty yards ahead, Joe was waiting to direct him off the track and down a steep bank to where the ground was soft underfoot and the vegetation smelling strongly of decay. The jungle closed in to form a roof overhead, the mosquitoes hung in swarms. Carter slithered and splashed through patches of swamp where the mud sucked hungrily at his boots and small watersnakes weaved like stitching through the stagnant water. The further they went, the worse the smell became from the moribund vegetation—dead trees rotted in the water; others leaned against each other like drunks. Even the creepers hung listless and emaciated, trailing away leafless above the water. A ghostly, gray-green moss clung to everything, muffling noise and life.

Carter had just caught up with the others when he heard the grenade go off. There was a scream that turned into a continuous wail, and sporadic bursts of automatic fire as the Japs took cover. Carter listened to the noise, felt a satisfaction that his booby trap had worked . . . They were, after all, partly in this fix on account of him . . .

Hudson was worried. The Japs had pressed forward much sooner than he'd anticipated. They must have been able to tell there were not many ahead of them by the fire power that had been brought to bear, and gambled on a withdrawal.

As the water got deeper and the jungle gave way to continuous swamp, the sky opened up and reed beds began to cluster around the rotting trees. Streams of bubbles rose from the water as if there were men below still trapped in a graveyard of wrecked ships whose gutted superstructures loomed menacingly above the surface. Narrow channels ran through the reed beds. Carter figured that they were on the fringes of the river delta he had seen from the ocean.

Johnson was looking about him. "Keep your eyes open for crocs," he said. "See that one there . . . ?"

Carter followed the pointed finger but only to see a widening ripple and a cloud of mud.

He looked down at the brackish water now rising nearly to his knees. It was thicker than Turkish coffee and as impenetrable to the eye. A crocodile could glide up to within inches without being seen. He stepped forward and nearly fell as his foot sank in the mud. The stinging sensation from his ankles told him that the leeches were at work. His eyelids were swelling with mosquito bites. "Where are we heading?" he asked.

"There's a fish village around here," Hudson told him. "We'll get hold of a canoe and hide up in the reed till they pull out."

"And then what?" Johnson asked.

"Work back and see if we can pick up the explosive."

"If some kids find it or one of Joe's boys blabs that beach will be staked out waiting for us to come back," Johnson said.

Hudson was looking about him, as if for a landmark. He spoke to Joe, who gestured ahead through the lopsided screen of thinning vegetation toward what looked like a prairie of waving grass. There was no limit to it, no mountain range to say where it ended. It stretched to the horizon like the sea. In the foreground, where the last stunted trees of the forest emerged from the water like the piles of a rotting jetty, was a thickly thatched house built on spindly stilts. A long thin dugout canoe was moored at the foot of a crude ladder.

Hudson approached the canoe and swore softly . . . it was half full of water, rotten and holed beneath the freeboard. How far could it carry five people? Carter heard a noise beside his ear, turned and looked up. A face looked down and then withdrew. It could have been a man or woman—bald, toothless.

Hudson turned to Sula. "Give her some salt and tell her that we need the canoe. It can't be the only one they've got. It hasn't been used since God knows when."

He pushed his finger into the hull as if it were putty.

118

As Johnson started to pull the nose of the canoe from a bed of lilies, a shrill, angry chatter came from above. This time the whole of what was apparently an old woman came into view. Her whole body was patterned with a gridwork of gray, flaking scales that became scabs when they reached her crown; Carter swallowed hard.

Sula gamely climbed the ladder and entered the hut. The angry gabble turned into what sounded like monosyllabic barks of refusal.

Johnson looked at Hudson. "How much longer are we going to wait, skip?"

The question was answered from another quarter—a burst of automatic fire kicked up water and exploded splinters from the piles beside Carter's head. He threw himself full length and floundered behind a tussock of tall grass.

At the outskirts of the jungle soldiers were visible taking up positions behind the trees. They were not hanging back but advancing, calling to each other and splashing forward with their weapons held across their chests. Carter selected a man more ambitious than the others and let him reach the cover of a liana-covered stump. He drew a bead on the stump and fired a short burst the moment that the man had taken two steps from it. The soldier stopped in his tracks as if struck by a thought rather than a bullet, grabbed at a vine and fell backward, still clinging to it. Carter fired another burst and looked around for the others.

Johnson was sprawled across the canoe, and for a moment Carter thought he was dead until he pulled himself up, his hand on his side. It came away bloody. He sank down into the mud so that the patch of red at his waist disappeared below the water. He looked at Carter, his eyes blank. A second rattle of small-arms fire made Carter duck, thinking that the enemy had outflanked them. It was Joe firing out on the left. His shoulders glinted behind a clump of sorghum. Above their heads the old woman was wailing as if this invasion of her world had tipped her into madness.

Bullets were coming now from all directions. Hudson hauled at the prow of the canoe and the slime sucked greedily. Three paddles slapped down from the stilt house, and Sula jumped down after them, disappearing up to her waist in the mud. Her action provoked a long enemy burst that shivered the cane walls of the stilt house to sawdust. The wailing abruptly stopped.

Hudson grunted, heaved, and the canoe started to move. Johnson tried to push and then collapsed face downward in the water. Carter heaved him over the side into the dugout and turned to fire at two Japanese who were less than twenty yards away. One went down, the other veered sideways to find cover and a firing position. A pulled stitch of bullets streaked past Carter's right side and he fired a haphazard burst in the direction of the shots.

The canoe was now maneuverable. Sula was aboard, and Hudson scrambling in. Johnson had pulled himself up and was trying to wield a paddle. Carter saw Joe splashing through the water, and unhooked a grenade. The canoe was moving forward, forward and away from him. The Japanese were shouting and coming forward in clusters. Carter pulled the pin from the grenade and drew back his arm. One-two-three, his arm straightened and he threw himself flat so that the water closed over his head and his face was pressed into the mud. An instantaneous explosion and the mud shuddered with the force of the impact. Carter did not turn to look as he got up and ran, expecting with every pace to feel the bullets shredding his flesh. He caught up with the canoe and slumped across it, not trying to get in out of fear of capsizing it. Five strokes and they had cleared open water and entered a narrow channel between the reeds. Another five and they were enclosed by the reeds.

A reprieve—for Carter most of all.

CHAPTER TWELVE

YUKICHI stayed within the shade of the tunnel mouth and looked across the road to the thin sloping beach dropping away through the coconut palms to the sea. The water sparkled invitingly and the bulk of Matupi smiled benignly in the sunshine. Yukichi glanced at his watch. Two minutes to go. It would be interesting to see if the reputation for punctuality was maintained. He glanced sideways and saw General Koji mopping his brow. He was surrounded by a galaxy of officers from the Rabaul garrison, shifting uneasily in a manner that was not totally attributable to the heat.

In the distance there was a hum of engines and a light type 95 tank crawled through the dust, followed by two vehicles. A member of the tank crew stood in the turret with his goggles pushed up across his forehead and his hands resting on the stock of the 7.7-mm machine gun. His eyes ranged the cliff face.

121

Yukichi concentrated on the second vehicle as it stopped outside the tunnel. Beside the driver sat a man wearing the white dress uniform of an admiral of the fleet in the Japanese Navy. He wore a white-topped short-peaked hat, white shoes and a high-buttoned tunic carrying four rows of medal ribbons.

The man was approaching sixty but looked younger. His expression was benign and open, his mouth sensual but sensitive, his eyes watchful but not suspicious. It was an intelligent, feeling face that might have belonged to a university professor. In fact it belonged to Admiral Isoruku Yamamoto, Commander in Chief of the Japanese Combined Fleet.

Yamamoto waited for the door of his vehicle to be opened and then stepped out to exchange salutes with General Koji and the assembled party. It was noticeable that his salute was not a compromise gesture toward military etiquette. It was brisk and firm, with his stiff fingers quivering against the peak of his cap. There had been no relaxation of protocol since the first meeting at the airfield.

"You are a most honored visitor," Koji said. His salute was not inferior to that of Yamamoto.

"I have heard a great deal about what you have achieved here," Yamamoto said pleasantly. "Six miles of tunnels, I believe?"

"Nearer seven at the moment," Koji said. Japanese diffidence made him qualify this statement in case it sounded like presumptuous boasting. "The pumice stone lava is very easy to tunnel through."

Yamamoto nodded. "I will be most interested to see what you have done." He cast an eye over the officers who had been assembled to receive him and moved into the mouth of the tunnel. He took half a dozen paces and came to a halt before a forty-foot barge incongruously mounted on a low trolley. He looked questioningly at Koji, who turned toward Yukichi. A mode of procedure for the visit had been established between commanding officer and adjutant shortly after it had been announced.

Yukichi said, "We have found that the best method to resist enemy air attacks is to unload supply vessels at sea and maintain the barges in these tunnels. Disembarkation takes place at night and the barges can be swiftly winched to and from the tunnels."

"You mean across the road and down the beach?"

"Precisely, sir," Yukichi replied.

Yamamoto looked about him and then down to the narrow-gauge railway line on which the barge's trolley rested. "And that?"

"If a barge is damaged or requires servicing we can move it to the workshops, which are located further back in the tunnels. The track also facilitates movement of the barges within the tunnels. We normally berth a number of barges in each tunnel."

Yamamoto nodded. "I imagine materials can also be brought direct into the tunnels without going through the docks?"

"When necessary, yes, sir."

Yamamoto moved deeper into the tunnel, past a second barge and a group of men who were working on repairs to the rudder assembly. He was genuinely intrigued by what he could see about him. The twenty-foot-high tunnel with its own lighting and ventilation system sloped away before him. With seven miles of such tunnels the scope for concealing men and armaments was enormous. It was impossible to imagine how the enemy could ever breach them. He paused again, faced with a structure like a small tank on rubber wheels.

"We use these for pulling loads around the tunnels," Yukichi explained. "They are battery-driven floats which are charged every night." He bowed his head respectfully and ushered Yamamoto onto the protected metal platform backed by stacked truck batteries. "There are no gasoline fumes to contaminate the air."

Yamamoto stepped onto the float and again nodded approvingly. "Very simple and effective," he said.

General Koji and Yukichi got onto the platform beside him and the driver pressed the control lever. With a faint whirring noise the float began to glide forward. The other officers moved forward to climb aboard two other floats that were standing by. They felt honored and relieved. The first stage of the visit appeared to be going satisfactorily.

Ten minutes later Yukichi was grasping a wooden pointer and facing a wall chart that showed the layout of the tunnels. In the place of honor among his audience in the large chamber hewn from solid rock sat an attentive Yamamoto, his hat on his lap.

Yukichi cleared his throat and began. "As an introduction to your visit, admiral, I would respectfully wish to show you the structure of the tunnels. You can see how the perimeter of the cliffs follows a semicircle. We have tunneled in from this at six points so that the tunnels are like the spokes of a wheel culminating at what might be termed the hub—where we are currently situated. Barges are berthed in the mouths of five of these tunnels and there are rail tracks leading back into the interior."

He tapped the point where the tunnels met on the chart.

"In the central command area we have administration offices, armories, interrogation cells, a radio station and, of course, the briefing theater where we are now sitting. All communication radiates from the center. Between each tunnel we have constructed other joining tunnels like the crosslinks of a spider's web."

His pointer ranged the chart.

"In these are contained hospital facilities, ammunition and supply dumps, accommodation for the troops and extensive workshops. We can repair damaged equipment and also assemble materiel that is shipped in to us by our brothers in the merchant marine."

"And there is no danger from air attack?"

"None. We are scarcely aware that enemy bombers are overhead."

"All disembarkation of supplies is done at night and that is the only time that our barges can be caught in the open," Koji added. "We have lost only four in the last six months."

Yamamoto studied the chart closely. It was clear that he was impressed. "And the dotted lines going inland from the junction point?"

"Tunnels under construction, sir," Yukichi said.

"We are constantly enlarging the network, as you know," Koji said. "With the increasing buildup of men and materials we need more space. I also wish to initiate a system by which all fuel reserves can be stored within the tunnels. I intend to create a series of reservoirs so that oil and gasoline can be pumped ashore direct rather than brought in by the various methods we are forced to employ at the moment."

Yamamoto listened with increasing satisfaction. As long as this underground fortress maintained its impregnability, it seemed im-

124

possible that the Americans and their allies could take Rabaul. The potential for another leap forward by the Imperial Army remained undiminished.

"I would like to see the excavation that is being done at the moment," he said.

The party left the briefing theater and emerged into the brightly lit area which formed the hollowed-out junction of the six tunnels slanting up to the cliff face. They passed General Koji's office and the radio station and moved on foot into a tunnel showing signs of recent excavation. A temporary lighting system had been erected and a concertina ventilation pipe followed the wall like an endless worm. They passed a side tunnel revealing packing cases stacked to the ceiling and were met by two emaciated Indians pushing a barrow full of rubble. Their tightly stretched skin glistened with sweat and their legs were obscenely thin, the knees standing out like knots in a piece of cord. Behind them came a guard, his nostrils and mouth covered by a lint mask. He responded to Yamamoto as if brought face to face with a ghost and stood stiffly to attention before being told to go on his way.

Despite an attempt at ventilation, the air was difficult to breathe and laden with particles of dust. Yukichi looked at the walls. There were indications that heavy boulders were mixed with the pumice. The excavation could not be easy at this point. Two hundred yards down the tunnel the heat became almost unbearable and the uneven floor strewn with rubble. A generator shuddered and there was a concentration of lights and the rattle of an electric drill. The scene was like an impression of hell. Near-naked skeletons toiled in a crucible of heat, dirt, noise. The guards with their dust-covered masks looked like plump larvae, as if they had fed on the flesh of their emaciated prisoners.

Koji noted that Yamamoto narrowed his eyes as he looked at the Indians. "I am considering transferring all prisoners and internees to work in the tunnels," he said. "We have lost many of the men that we brought from Singapore."

"I am not surprised," Yamamoto said. He looked around the assembled officers who were mopping their brows. "Who is responsible for these men?"

There was a moment's pause and a grizzled colonel stepped

125

forward and bowed. He had lost an eye at Guadalcanal and was known to be a fine soldier. "I am, sir. Colonel Namura. Seventeenth Army. My responsibilities include the prison camp." He spoke the last six words with a slight but perceptible edge of distaste to his voice. It suggested that he did not believe that looking after prisoners was the work of an officer such as himself.

Yamamoto spoke calmly and without emotion. As he did so, he lowered his voice so that only those near him could hear what he was saying. "If you cannot keep your prisoners alive, their work will have to be done by our own men. I am certain you share my belief that our soldiers' energies are best reserved for fighting the enemy. Please bear that in mind."

Namura dropped his head to his chest in acknowledgment of the rebuke and the party retraced their footsteps down the tunnel. The two Indians were returning with the empty barrow. Yukichi looked on them coldly. If they had fought to the death like honorable men they would not be here now. It did not seem fair that Namura should be criticized for his treatment of such creatures.

Koji, too, was annoyed by the admiral's remarks. He had hoped that the short visit would be an unstinted success. It was also difficult to know what to do about Namura. He was a soldier who itched for active service. He involved himself with his duties at the military police headquarters in the town, but rarely visited the prison camp. To relieve him of his duties would be seen as a punishment: too severe a solution. Perhaps he could arrange that Yukichi discreetly took over responsibility for the prison camp.

Koji looked toward his adjutant and saw him being approached by a signalman who had emerged from the radio station. The man appeared highly agitated. Did one small setback preface another more serious?

He saw Yukichi enter the radio station and turned to Yamamoto. "I have prepared a room for you next to my office. Would you care to take some saki while we continue our discussion?"

"I would prefer some tea," Yamamoto said.

He mounted a flight of stone steps and a door was slid open by an armed guard. The remaining officers bowed their heads and were dismissed.

Yamamoto had just settled into a chair when there was an ur-

126

gent tap on the door and Yukichi entered.

"I am sorry to interrupt you," he said, "but we have received a rather disturbing report. A small party of the enemy have apparently come ashore in the Matupi area—"

"Matupi?" Koji said. "But you visited our detachment there this morning—"

"That is correct, sir."

Koji's real anger was not against Yukichi but against fate for having disrupted his plans. He controlled himself and turned to Yamamoto.

"I think that we must be prepared for the possibility that this raiding party is a suicide squad put ashore to assassinate you. I have been expecting something like this."

Yamamoto looked from Koji to Yukichi. "If that is the case, I am surprised that they were able to land."

"I am sorry, sir," Koji said. "We have taken extensive precautions but. . . . I accept full responsibility."

"How many raiders are there?" Yamamoto asked.

"The report states three," said Yukichi. "Also, two natives, one of them a woman."

"I think we can consider that as being five," Yamamoto said drily. "Where are they now?"

"One of our native trackers found them and alerted our marine detachment at Matupi point. There was a skirmish, and the raiding party withdrew into the swamps. I understand that one of them is seriously wounded."

"In other words, they escaped . . . Are they being pursued?"

Yukichi nodded emphatically. "I have ordered a K-boat to proceed to the swamps immediately. I doubt if the raiders will be able to survive the night."

Yamamoto nodded. "Please keep me informed of all developments."

"Of course, sir."

Koji intervened deferentially. "Despite the measures that are being taken, I think we should proceed with great caution in respect to the rest of your visit. May I suggest that a khaki uniform would make you less immediately identifiable—?"

"The purpose of my visit *is* to be immediately identifiable,"

127

Yamamoto said sharply. "I will not let seventy thousand men see me hiding from five." He turned toward the orderly who had arrived with the tea, then, "Come, gentlemen, we must not alarm ourselves, I have confidence in your ability to rectify the situation. I have also seen the swamp." He extended his hands to receive a bowl of tea and smiled grimly. "I have confidence in that too."

Chapter Thirteen

THE sun was sliding down the sky. In half an hour it would be dark. Somewhere in the swamp a crocodile barked. Feather-topped grasses, wild grains and ferns gave way to palisades of eight-foot-high canegrass that crackled like a fire as the prow of the canoe pushed them aside. The humidity was stifling. Narrow passages were carpeted with pink-flowered water lilies and blue nymphae. In open waterholes fish jumped as terrapin dived for the mud three feet below. And always there were birds. Marsh eagles kite-diving above. Egrets, cranes, ducks and geese on the lagoons. They turned in surprise as the canoe approached and then lifted in their hundreds like massed sentinels.

Carter looked down at the water in the bottom of the canoe. It was alive with darting waterfleas and stained red with Johnson's blood. The canoe was sinking. And night was coming.

"Any idea where we're heading?" Carter tried to keep his voice calm. It was only a question of time before the rotten fibrous hull of the canoe became totally waterlogged and slid below the surface. Then they would face the darkness and the marauding crocodiles up to their waists in a limitless swamp.

"Joe says there's a village around here somewhere. We'll be able to get another canoe." Hudson's voice was tense and weary as he caught his paddle in a knot of underwater tubers and the canoe lurched alarmingly.

Johnson swore and moved his hand from his side. The blood that seeped through his shirt was already flecked white with blowfly eggs.

Their position looked hopeless . . . paddling deeper into the swamp to find a canoe that would take them back to Matupi, and if they did not find the village they would be worse off than if they returned toward the jungle—except if they returned, the Japs would be waiting . . .

The canoe emerged into a small lagoon choked with lilies and surrounded by sedge. There was no onward passage in sight. Something disturbed one of the lilies and a stir of mud washed over the leaves. Carter felt that just above the surface eyes were watching him. Waiting. Knowing that he would soon be down there in the water and totally vulnerable.

The canoe scuffed across the lilies and nosed into the cane, which recoiled like a pontoon—the root systems had become so solidly enmeshed they formed a floating raft.

Joe pressed his paddle down flat among the cane and scrambled out of the canoe. The platform sank a few inches and a stream of foul-smelling bubbles rose to the surface. One by one Hudson, Carter and Sula followed. Johnson sat where he was. He could not lie back because his head would have been below the water. He took his hand from his wound and looked at the fresh blood.

"Sodding mosquitoes are still biting me," he said. "Why don't they help themselves to the lot?"

"Just hang on," said Hudson. "We'll take a look at that when we get to the village."

Normally Johnson would have asked "when," but this time his face gave no indication that he'd heard Hudson's remark. He looked very much like he'd had it.

Dragging the canoe through the floating island of cane was like walking on a trampoline. The surface undulated, it was impossible to find any point of purchase. Sudden holes or a thinning of the root cover would cause one to stumble up to his waist. Joe hacked a path with a bush knife but the cane still chafed and the leaves often carried an edge like a razor blade. Worst were the tiny goads that drifted from the leaves of certain canes like a dust of silver needles to set up a violent, itching rash that infected the eye, armpit and groin.

Above their heads the sky turned gray and the light leaked away among the forest canes. Battalions of frogs began to croak and an airforce of flying foxes flapped overhead toward their evening feeding ground. Hudson looked up at them. "Could mean that there's a village fruit garden near here." His voice was flat, held out little hope, and nobody bothered to answer.

Suddenly there was an explosion of wings from a point twenty yards to their left and a flight of magpie geese took to the air. As they shrilled away Joe's bush knife bit into the cane with renewed vigor and he hacked toward the spot where the geese had risen. As abruptly as it had begun, the sedge gave way to an open lagoon, patterned by a mosaic of water weed and clumps of lilies with circular, traylike leaves. Through the water weed was a path of clear water that might have been made by a boat.

The canoe was relaunched, and Carter watched the water begin to flood the bottom as if soaking through a sponge. He climbed in gingerly, and Johnson slumped back against his knees. He could feel the man trembling and leaned forward to touch his forehead. It was feverish. They crossed the lagoon and were entering a narrow waterway when Joe pointed to a cagelike structure built across a narrow passageway into the reeds—a bamboo pen with a dropgate propped open just above the water. Any small crocodile or terrapin entering the cage would dislodge one of the supporting poles and be trapped.

"Thank Christ," Hudson said. "There must be people near here."

Joe was nodding in agreement. He gestured ahead and indicated a wide channel going off to the right.

Driven by new hope, Carter dug his paddle into the dark water.

The canoe jerked forward, making the bilgewater slop against the sides. At the end of the reach the sedge drew back to form the borders of a small lake and a low parcel of land rose abruptly from the swamp, its center crowned by a huddle of rosewood and cedars interlaced with palms.

As the dusk deepened, the distance between canoe and land narrowed and the square outline of huts could be seen against the trees. A single fire flickered weakly and human figures drifted among the shadows like wraiths. It was a gloomy place made welcome only by the sight of half a dozen canoes pulled up on the muddy strand.

Hudson let the canoe ground and stepped ashore. Ordinarily the arrival of a party of strangers would bring small children clustering around the canoe while young girls giggled behind their hands and even the most timid locals watched from the doorways of huts. Here, nobody came forward, so Hudson went up to an old man sitting by a meager fire. His features were ravaged by leprosy. Carter tried to recognize the blackened bones that littered the area about the fire, he'd not seen anything like them before. The old man did not look up and responded with a grunt to Hudson's greeting. Carter felt as he had in the settlement behind Rabaul—that he was being watched, and wondered if the Japs could have got there before them . . .

Figures were emerging from the shadows now. Old men, women, even children, painfully thin and covered with tropical ulcers. No young men *visible* in the village. Were they off hunting, or making war on a neighboring tribe of marshmen? Or waiting in ambush?

Hudson called to Sula who was tending to Johnson in the canoe. She arrived bringing the salt and trade tobacco in her *bilum.* The old man hardly turned his head to look at the "gift" as it was placed at his feet. It was wet, he said. His shoulders were scuffed with whorls of fungus and the lobes of his ears frayed by the weight of ornaments that had torn free over the years. When he used his matchstick arms to make a contemptuous gesture, flakes of skin fluttered to the ground. He seemed to be coming apart before their eyes. Hudson said that the salt and tobacco would soon dry. The old man shrugged. Hudson told him they needed a canoe. He

132

paused for a moment, spat out a stream of betel juice. No mistaking the meaning of the gesture. "We're never going to get anywhere with these people," Hudson said.

He'd begun to talk to the old man again when there was a shout from the canoe. Johnson was wrestling with a native who had tried to grab his weapon. Carter started to run and the man released his hold, fled like a shadow for the huts. Suddenly, the clearing was empty except for the old man. More betel juice at Hudson's feet, more angry gesticulating.

"What's he saying?" Carter asked.

"That if we take one of his canoes, the monster that lives in the swamp will drag us below the surface and eat us," Hudson said. "Maybe so, but I wager it's a better bet than staying here." . . . He spoke again to the old man and pointed toward the darkening horizon. The old man ignored him and muttered into his fire.

Hudson started to walk away. "I asked him if that was the way to the sea. I hope he'll think we're heading that way and tell the Japs . . . Did you see those bones?"

"What about them?"

"They were human." Hudson didn't wait for Carter's reaction. "They're about the cruelest people on earth. When they take a prisoner and they don't want to eat him right away they cut his feet off so that he can't make a run. To stop him bleeding to death they hold the stumps in the fire to seal them. That way they can keep a man alive for days."

"Jesus . . . where are the warriors?"

"I've got a feeling not too far away. I saw a fellow poling off into the weeds as we approached," Hudson said.

When they got to the canoe Johnson was lying back with his head half submerged in water. His face was crawling with insects that he was too weak to brush away. Sula and Joe lifted him into one of the canoes drawn up on the shore. Hudson and Carter faced the huts, weapons ready. Only the old man was visible in the gathering darkness . . . he'd thrown the salt on the fire and his ravaged face showed up in the ghostly yellow-green light like a warning skull. His lips moved ceaselessly, like a magician muttering spells and incantations.

Johnson lay with his head in Sula's lap as Joe pushed the canoe

133

out into the lagoon. Long after the outline of the island had disappeared, the light of the fire winked and wavered like a beacon.

Johnson began to groan, to mutter like a man having a nightmare, as if he were suddenly the mouthpiece for the old man they'd left behind. Incoherent speech was punctuated by references to "Japs" and pursuit, his body twitching as he tried to urge it onward away from the invisible enemy.

Hudson listened grimly. It was what he'd feared. The demons of Rabaul had finally overtaken Jeremiah Johnson. . . .

January 23, 1942, the last resistance to the invasion had ended, and the Japanese were masters of the town. Johnson and the shattered remnants of the 2/22 Australian Battalion had taken to the bush intending to follow the coast around until they could be taken off by boat and ferried back to New Guinea. But it was a Jap boat that came ashore, and 180 exhausted men surrendered at the Tol Plantation on the south coast. They had read leaflets telling them that if they surrendered they would be treated like prisoners of war, and at first the leaflets seemed to tell the truth. They were given food and cigarettes and paraded for a roll call. Then they were stripped of their identity discs and their hands tied behind their backs with fishing line. They were divided into eighteen parties of ten men. The Japanese fixed their bayonets. One by one, files of prisoners were marched into the overgrown plantation. Johnson had turned and saw that the guard at the rear of his file was carrying a pick and shovel . . . They were going to be murdered . . . Men began to weep and curse as the Japanese moved in with rifle butts. Some made a run for it and were shot in the back or beaten back into line . . . Johnson saw his chance, dived into the bush. He heard shots, screams, sounds of men being clubbed and bayoneted. Followed by the orderly sound of pick and shovel digging into earth. Then the noises of the jungle, the hum of flies . . . When it was dark he'd gotten up and gone past the shallow graves of his dead comrades, some of them barely covered by a couple of shovelfuls of earth. His hands had been tied so tightly that it was impossible to free them. For days he'd wandered in the jungle while the flies bit his open sores and the twine cut deeper into his wrists. Leeches, mosquitoes and flies had tortured him while he rubbed his flesh away against the spongy trunks of trees.

He became semiconscious with malaria, could not find a sharp outcrop of rock against which to sever his bonds. When he tried to drink in a shallow muddy rill he overbalanced and nearly drowned in a few inches of water. He'd been kept alive by eating the soft green heads of ferns and burrowing for tapioca roots like a pig. At night the rain drenched him to the skin. He had been found by another party of his own men who could barely bring themselves to look at him as they cut his bonds. . . .

This was the particular hell that Johnson was reliving, that had afflicted his mind too often in the past, always simmering just below the surface, threatening to break out. Now there was another present hell . . .

Carter looked about warily, kept his submachine gun propped against the side of the canoe. It was now almost dark. The reed bed's sinister hedges on either side were crackling with unseen creatures. A cloud of fireflies danced like golden rain and ghostly patches of luminescence hung in the water like the reflections of Chinese lanterns. Mosquitoes arrived in droves, greedily lighting on the hand that brushed them away from the face. The slime slurped and sucked at the paddles. On a mudbank, three shapes loomed up. Two slid noiselessly into the water, the other was a log.

Joe shouted and pointed toward the reeds. There was a sound like that of a flimsy door being kicked open and a long, high-prowed canoe burst into the open, propelled by twelve men grunting in unison as their paddles bit into the water. The canoe was a hundred yards away and moving at them through the water like a whipsnake.

Hudson figured a narrow waterway to the left offered the natural escape route, called to the others to steer for it, then changed his mind. Somehow it was all too fortuitous—a setup.

"Hold off! We'll go in further down!"

The canoe shuddered as the full weight of the paddles was thrown against the water and the bow came round. Immediately, there was an angry bellow from the reeds at the mouth of the channel and something sailed through the air to fall with a splash beside the canoe. A throwing spear. The sedge exploded with shouting men. Some charged into the water to hurl spears. The

135

arrival of the canoe had clearly been timed to drive them into an ambush.

The canoe was closing fast. Three men got up, holding spears. Their arms came back as Carter raked the prow with a burst of automatic fire that splintered wood and jerked one man into the water. One spear fell short, another thudded into the hull inches below the gunwale. The canoe veered away.

Hudson saw a spot where the outline of the reeds dipped against the sky and drove the canoe toward it. The dugout clattered through a screen of canegrass and entered a narrow channel choked with hanging fronds, twisted tubers and festoons of creepers studded with orchids. Giant spiderwebs draped over them like dust sheets and something like a mouse with eight furry legs raced up Carter's arm and across his face before darting into the sedge.

After several minutes of urgent paddling Hudson gave the order to stop. Carter slumped forward and sucked in mouthfuls of hot, clammy air. His savaged arm was beginning to throb and his lungs ached. Plops, splashes, crackles, and squawks gave way to a steady chorus of frogs. No sounds of pursuit.

Hudson turned on his flashlight. Its thin beam probed the darkness ahead, attracting a feather boa of moths, some so large that their wing beats sounded like those of a bird. Tentacles of jungle reached out through the sedge or tried to straddle it. Garlands of closed flowers hung down to trail the water. Where the wild sugarcane met the slime, clusters of glowworms formed chokers around the roots.

"They can find their way around this swamp blindfolded," Hudson said. He produced a prismatic compass and studied it. "At least we're heading in the right direction. We'll press on as far as we can go and then rest up till daybreak." He looked back at Johnson. "How are you doing, Jerry?"

At first no reply, then the voice faint but with increasing determination. "I'm not going to walk, this time, I'm not going to walk—"

"Sure," Hudson said gently.

Sula bathed Johnson's forehead and looked up at Hudson. Johnson was going to die. His lower ribs had been shattered by automatic fire. Fragments of bone had penetrated his stomach. They would never be able to carry him through the jungle, nor be able to leave him behind. They'd have to make the effort, and the effort would no doubt ensure that the Japs caught up with them. If Johnson died by daybreak they had a chance . . . These were thoughts on several minds, thoughts that would never be spoken aloud . . . Joe's back muscles rippled and the canoe nosed its way deeper into the enclosing foliage. Carter brushed the wet creepers from his face and listened to the flat, guttural bark of a hunting crocodile. The swamps abounded with them but he still hadn't seen one close up. Ahead, the channel opened up into a dark waterscape of mudbanks topped by thick clumps of cane and reed. A small red eye gleamed jewel-bright fifty yards away in the center of the stream. Carter craned forward. It must be a crocodile—a large one because it seemed several inches above the surface. Carter watched and the eye flew heavenward.

"A croc-bird," Hudson told him. "They're bad news if you're hunting. Look just like a croc at water level."

"Did you hunt a lot?"

"When I was a young man, yes. Thought I was going to make my fortune. Then it got so there were almost more hunters than crocs." He was silent for a moment. "Amazing bloody thing, the crocodile."

Carter held up his hand. "Wait a minute!"

He had heard something, the soft putt, putt, putt of an outboard engine. A long way off, but getting nearer.

Hudson listened, told them to pull in to the bank. The noise continued to come closer. Carter quietly lay his paddle at his feet and picked up his gun. The natives had no motorboats. It had to be the Japs. The engine note maintained a steady rhythm. Carter guessed that it must be traveling on a stretch of open waterway that lay beyond the mudbanks, perhaps one of the main tributaries of the delta. Johnson smothered a groan, was comforted into silence by Sula—

A crashing from the sedge, the sound of something slithering across the mud, the faintest splash. One of Hudson's crocs, thought Carter. They must love this war. Men were too busy killing each other to hunt them. They would understand . . . crocs ate each other too . . .

On an impulse Carter moved his hand from the side of the canoe and looked down. Two close-set slit eyes glowed up at him. He looked around and there were three other pairs standing off at a respectful distance. Crocodiles, waiting quietly and patiently, no doubt attracted by the scent of Johnson's blood. How long would their patience last? The canoe would of course not be difficult to capsize. The crocs would interpret their enforced immobility as defenselessness. Sooner or later there would be a lunge, the sweep of a powerful tail capable of knocking down a horse and they would be struggling in the water. The nutcracker jaws would snap shut through bone and the victim would be pulled down to the crocodile's larder in the mud . . .

Carter watched the eyes and wished for more speed from the approaching motorboat. It must be close now. He glanced ahead, could see nothing. The engine note diminished in volume and a small wave ran as a ripple along the muddy banks and rustled through the reeds. The red eyes bobbed and the canoe rocked on the wasting swell. Carter was moving to pick up his paddle when a bright, dazzling light shone through the canegrass like a falling sun.

They huddled low in the canoe as the searchlight swept over them again. It was fortunate that the men in the boat had not switched it on a few seconds earlier. Carter listened anxiously for any abrupt change in the engine noise that would indicate discovery but the boat moved steadily on until the searchlight was just a glow in the sky.

"Give them a few minutes in case they come back," Carter said, "then push on?"

Hudson nodded.

Carter settled back, rubbed his eyes, aching from the insect bites, and tension. Stimulants at least to keep him awake. He looked at the eyes glowing in the darkness, now joined by two more pairs—small red lights that warned against sleep. He moved the fingers of his bitten arm to stop them from cramping up.

Seconds turned into minutes. Batteries of frogs opened up to drown out all other sounds. Surely it was safe to move now—

"*Tabanda!*" Joe's voice was low, urgent. "Fire." He was pointing back the way they had come.

Carter could smell nothing beyond the slime and rotting vegeta-

138

tion . . . until the merest whiff of something more pungent than the sweet smell of decay wafted from the grasses. Hudson caught it too and slowly stood up. The canoe wobbled and the semicircle of red eyes closed in expectantly. Where the dark mass of the reeds met the gray of the sky a faint comber of light suffused the horizon. It might have been the first hint of dawn but this glow rose in the north. Hudson listened intently. Barely audible was a distant oven-like roar. "They've fired the grass," he said. "They're trying to flush us out so the Japs can get at us."

Now there was no mistaking the acrid smell of burning vegetation. No mistaking either the sound of the motorboat returning. The searchlight began to sweep through 360 degrees, and it was clear from the angle of descent that the boat was passing nearer to their position. They must be very close to the main channel.

Carter ducked and smelled smoke willowing like a mist almost at water level. It stung his already smarting eyes, made him cough. Thank God there were the small muddy islets in front of them to provide some protection from the probing power of the search-light. The light moved on, and Carter looked toward its source to see the shadow outline of the mast on which it was mounted . . . A cane rat broke from the sedge, slid down the bank and started to swim strongly. Two pairs of red lights detached themselves from the pack and the cane rat disappeared with a screech. A wave slapped against the side of the canoe . . . Now the sky behind them was red as curlicues of flame flared up, smoke billowing from the reeds. An angry, crackling roar urged on the flames and clouds of sparks danced before hissing into the water. The fire was leapfrog-ging toward them at the pace of a running man. Johnson choked and gasped for breath.

A refugee army of snakes, frogs and birds began to burst from the undergrowth. The sky was now streaked with red, yellow and white, a vivid, dancing palette disturbed by brushstrokes of swirl-ing smoke. The air was sucked away to feed the flames, it became painful to breathe. Smoke and hot ash swept over the canoe, burn-ing through clothing to the flesh beneath.

Hudson shouted above the mounting roar and dug his paddle into the water. To stay where they were was impossible. The canoe lurched from the bank and found the middle of the channel in a

139

rain of hot ash. Half a dozen strokes before they could find air to breathe. There was a chance that they could survive here if they could build up enough distance between them and the heat and the suffocating smoke . . .

And then the searchlight found them, swept across the water-scape and caught them in the crenelation between two islets. The light dazzled and numbed, surging past and then immediately jumping back. Carter could see the others before him, white on black, like an undeveloped negative. Within two seconds there was the yammer of automatic fire and the water about them turned into a boiling cauldron. Then they were behind a low mudbank and the bullets churned up the mud. If they continued firing at this rate they would level the mudbank to the water—

Abruptly, the firing stopped and there was only the noise of the advancing fire. An updraft of air had hoisted aloft cinders that illuminated the scene like marker flares. The beam of the search-light splashed over their heads and wavered, darting to each extremity of the mudbank in case they tried to slip away. Carter turned and looked behind him. There was no islet nearby that was not within the searchlight's beam. They were pinned down.

A pit-shelled turtle arrived to rest its flippers on the mud beside the canoe, looked up to see Carter, quivered its bottle-top nose and disappeared in a small whirlpool. Carter wished that it could be so easy for him. The engine note of the motorboat and the position of the searchlight had not changed. From the left, a pall of smoke drifted across the water. Here, perhaps, was a chance. The Japs might find their ruse of firing the reeds rebounding on them. It might in fact provide a smokescreen . . . There was an eerie whistling noise, building up into a screech and terminating in an explosion on the far side of the mudbank. A fountain of mud was hurled into the air and the waters raged. The Japs must have a 70-mm gun mounted on their boat, using it at maximum elevation as a mortar.

"Scatter!" Hudson was over the side, his feet sinking knee-deep into the slime. Smoke rolled over their heads. Carter clutched his weapon and scrambled from the rocking canoe, the mud swallow-ing him like a soft greedy mouth. He struggled to move his legs while the death whistle gained in intensity above his head—a blast knocked him down and he lay still as the mud rained down on him. He staggered upright and began to blunder through the slime, seeking only to put some distance between himself and the next ranging shot of the mortar. With each step the mud tried to suck the boots from his feet and slurped and gurgled obscenely. As the searchlight bobbed and darted he saw Joe and Sula dragging the canoe by its headline. Under cover of the smoke they were heading for a small islet further into the main channel. A burst of machine-gun fire came close, and Carter threw himself down behind a tight-knit clump of reeds. Something bit, scraped or stung his leg from below the surface of the mud. He hardly noticed it.

Another shell plummeted into the mud nearby. Water rushed in to fill the cavity. Lucky that the mud was absorbing most of the impact. On a harder surface they would have been mangled by shrapnel. Carter pulled himself upright again and suddenly felt his legs sinking as if he were dropping into a pit. In an instant the slime was above his waist and still rising. He spread his arms wide and released the Sten gun, pushing its stock first into the mud to give himself greater maneuverability. And then his feet touched something firm—a log buried years before perhaps. He waited until certain that he was no longer sinking, then tried to force himself upward by pressure on his arms. His arms sank into the mud, and he looked about him for something to cling to—and froze. Emerging from the water was the head of a crocodile, two feet of interlocking teeth visible along its jaw. The head turned to survey Carter. The small, bright eye widened and gleamed as two huge, four-toed webbed feet slapped against the mud.

Carter looked at his gun. It was out of reach. He stretched and nearly lost his foothold. The crocodile lumbered from the water, revealing its over twenty feet of length. It surveyed him with head cocked to one side, perhaps wondering what this strange creature was, so different from the fowl, fish, turtles, and terrapins that made up most of its diet. Carter lunged again, and the crocodile swung its tail to fall into line with the rest of its body, skidded across the mud. Carter fought panic, stretched out his arm again. This time his slimy fingers brushed against metal. The gun was settling into the slime. He transferred all his weight to one leg and pressed down. His foothold flinched, and the mud slurped and sucked as it sought to keep hold of him.

The crocodile opened its mouth a few inches, only some twelve feet separated them. Even with the mouth apart there was no gap between the two rows of teeth. The crocodile tilted back its head to show the white underneath of its throat and delivered of itself a short, vexed bark—A mortar shell exploded behind, bringing down a fine rain of mud that splattered along its back. A submachine gun opened up fifty yards away. None of it seemed to disturb the crocodile's concentration. At any second, Carter was sure, it was going to rush him.

He pressed his hand deep into the mud, the tips of his fingers touched something . . . He stretched another inch and his fingers closed about the sling of his gun. He pulled it toward him and the gun came free. As if alerted by the sound, the crocodile rose up on its four legs, arched its tail, and charged, mouth stretched wide. Praying that he'd managed to keep the breech and barrel free of mud, Carter found the safety catch and fired. A jagged lightning flash of yellow flame ripped from the barrel into the open mouth. The animal lurched onto one leg, then turned its head sideways as if diverted by the force of the bullets. Carter fired another burst at its eye, and saw the shape of the head change as lead chewed into it, throwing out a spray of blood. Under the impetus of its weight the crocodile slid across the bank toward him, its head thrashing, its tail lashing the mud. The Sten gun's clip emptied in midburst and Carter thrust it forward to parry the snapping jaws. The crocodile slithered against him and lay still, the weight of its body almost pinning him to the mud. The tail swung twice, then stopped in midswirl. The mouth stayed half open.

Carter could feel his heart thumping. He waited for some reflex action that would make the brute suddenly snap into a last flurry. Nothing. Around them a red light danced in the sky and tongues of flame licked through the smoke. Burning grass drifted through the air to fire clumps of reed on the islets. A crackling roar echoed on all sides. The scene was like the aftermath of an air raid.

Only one way, he decided, for him to escape from the mud. Pull himself out using the dead crocodile for purchase. Gingerly at first, he seized one of the forelegs, more than two hand-breadths wide, and threw his arm over the carcass. A python slithered down the bank and into the water followed by a water rat and a bandicoot. The grasses on the islet were burning. Carter hauled himself upward and the crocodile lurched on the mud, as if it was still living. The foreleg moved slowly of its own accord in the first throes of rigor mortis. Gagging, Carter wondered how much more of this he could take. The mud sucked, and small, unseen creatures writhed and wriggled against his flesh. He heaved and managed to drag his weight across the crocodile's back and paused to recover his breath before drawing up his legs. A slight updraught was carrying the smoke above his head so it was impossible to breathe at water level.

Another burst of automatic fire came from the direction of the center of the channel. Carter guessed that it must be either Joe or Hudson trying to keep off the Japs. The searchlight was now only turned on intermittently and the boat's engines had been cut . . . Sula. Was she still alive? He searched the shadowy outlines of the mudbanks, could see nothing. He had to try and find the others. The shooting had stopped, there was only the sound of the fire. He rolled sideways with one last look at the croc and slithered through the slime as if he had taken on the persona of the slaughtered animal. He was terrified of standing up, of feeling himself sinking into the bottomless pit again. He approached a clump of speargrass in order to have something to cling to if necessary and rose unsteadily to his feet. The mud came no higher than his knees.

The searchlight stabbed again. He could tell that the boat had changed its position . . . it had either been poled or allowed to drift in hopes of catching them unawares from a different angle. The beam swept past him and rested on the dead crocodile and the churned-up mud. Carter lay flat with a cheek pressed into the slime and saw the teeth gleam in what seemed a mocking grin. A brief burst of fire splattered mud around the corpse, a swift gabble of Japanese, and then the light was cut.

Carter rose and splashed through mud and waist-deep water to the next bank. Smoke swirled about him. He flinched as the water parted and a shape glided toward him—a white-tailed rat, the size of a small cat. It chugged past him and scuttled up the bank and into the grass as the light came on again.

Carter dropped. It was like a crazy game. Throw yourself flat when the light comes on or you're dead. And don't forget to mind the nasty animals . . . Jesus . . .

The beam jabbed angrily above his head, then splashed and dappled over the surrounding banks. There was a short burst from a machine gun and the sound of bullets striking armored plating.

Somebody was still alive. He moved again and saw a dark shape lying on a bank. Another crocodile? He approached—the shape spun around and leveled a Sten gun at him. He recognized the weapon's silhouette with its ammo clip thrusting horizontally from its breech as British-made. Sula, with Johnson's gun.

She had almost pulled the trigger before she identified him. Which wasn't easy. Covered in mud, he looked like some monster from the swamp. He slumped down beside her. She touched his arm, then returned to watching the nearby banks.

"Where are the others?" Carter finally asked.

"I think Captain Hudson is over there." She gestured toward an islet further from the reed beds. "Joe I do not know."

Carter looked around him. "Where's the canoe?"

"Johnson has taken it."

"*Taken* it?"

Sula continued to look around her. "When the bombs came we pulled the canoe to a bank. I took Johnson's gun. When we look 'round he is paddling away."

Carter let his head drop forward so that his cheek was resting against the mud. It might have been his grave. Any last vestige of hope drained away. With the canoe gone they had no chance of escaping from the swamp. They were marooned, at the pleasure of the Japs. Johnson had done what he had been threatening to do. He had taken leave of his senses.

Chapter Fourteen

JOHNSON knew he was going to die. When he moved, it was as if his stomach was full of broken glass. But in a way the pain was good—at least it goaded him into action. He had awakened from a fitful sleep into a period of perfect clarity, as a man wracked by fever can suddenly sit up and talk coherently. But there were going to be no words. He knew what he had to do. Nothing needed to be explained.

He dabbed with his paddle and felt the faintest tremble of a current against the side of the canoe. This must be one of the fingers of the delta reaching out to the sea. Above his head were stars. Before him another wilderness of swamp registering as a black hedge or reeds silhouetted against the sky. Smoke swirled about him and patches of mist hung eerily above the water. The searchlight rippled out, laying bars of light as it probed among the banks and flats.

He had paddled back and come out into the main channel, where it began to curve sharply. He had been able to cross to the other side without falling into the path of the searchlight. Now he was drifting down in the lee of the far bank.

He could see his target clearly. A long, shallow-draft vessel with reinforcement above the waterline and a swept-back prow. The searchlight was mounted on a platform halfway up a stubby mast. No armament was visible, but the flashes of light which accompanied random bursts of automatic fire suggested that the machine gun was mounted behind shields in the prow. Johnson moved his hand to his waist and closed slippery fingers around the clip that held the last grenade.

His fingers were jelly, barely capable of exerting pressure. He squeezed and the metal mouth parted and then snapped back again. Pain set fire to the inside of his stomach and a dangerous swoon of nausea came over him. Whatever happened he had to stay in command of his senses. He had to use the pain to stay conscious. He pressed his hand against his side and felt the blood escaping through his fingers, the dressing incapable of staunching the flow. He was weakening. A shower of sparks hissed into the water and clumps of burning grass dropped just short of the bank. If the fire jumped the channel they would surely see him.

He returned his fingers to the grenade clip and suddenly realized that he had let go of the paddle, that it had slipped from his hand and was drifting away. He reached for it, forgetting the pain that any movement caused, and nearly capsized the canoe. There was another paddle in the canoe but he could not reach it. He gritted his teeth and squeezed, making the pain prise the metal apart. The grenade fell into the bottom of the canoe.

Now everything was becoming fuzzy. The fog drifted across the mist and clouded his stinging eyes. Every object was framed in a penumbra of light, its definition suspect. Was it the smoke or was the sight ebbing out of his eyes? Could it be anything other than imagination that made the boat seem to loom up in front of him? He tried to concentrate and found himself slipping until he was lying on his back with his head in three inches of water. Smoke drifted over his head but he could still see the stars. With a start, he also realized that his stomach had stopped hurting . . .

The helmsman was the first to see the drifting canoe. He called out excitedly and the lieutenant peered through one of the slits in the armor-plated screens that protected the sides of the boat. Machine guns were brought to bear. The canoe appeared to be empty. It twisted in the water like a sycamore leaf, barely moving in the listless water. Smoke from the still-burning grassfire hung heavy over the upstream river. The lieutenant ordered the searchlight be swiveled to cut through the swathes of smoke. More excited yells.

A body was lying in the canoe, blood glistening from knee to shoulder, the head tilted to one side. The jungle-green uniform and the western features said clearly that it was one of the raiding party. The lieutenant smiled. Without the canoe there was no chance of the others escaping.

The lieutenant unstrapped his pistol and peered again through the slit. The man was nearly beneath him, and he could see that his eyes were closed. He aimed at the head, then hesitated. The man could not be alive, he must have bled to death an hour before. The lieutenant rested his gun against the edge of the slit and took aim again. A bullet neatly between the eyes. An act of mercy if the man still lived and of personal gratification whether he lived or not.

The canoe tapped softly against the side of the hull as if respectfully announcing its presence. The lieutenant started to pull the trigger and froze. Below him, the eyes had opened. With a ghastly smile the man reached up and thrust something beneath the armored screens and into the motorboat.

The lieutenant looked down as the corporal's machine gun splayed the canoe. A hand grenade was resting against his foot. . . .

Carter heard two explosions almost simultaneously and looked up to see the motorboat blazing from prow to stern. The fuel tanks must have exploded. The screams of burning men were almost drowned by the roar of the flames. The armor-plated sides of the boat had turned it into a casserole in which men were cooking. A blazing rag doll threw itself into the water and was followed by another. There was a flash and a third explosion and Carter instinctively ducked. One of the mortar shells had exploded. The flames licked even higher and the mast toppled over slowly as if melting, spilling the now extinguished searchlight into the water.

147

Another explosion rocked the vessel, and it began to settle. The flames fed hungrily and noisily. The only human sounds came from the water—moans, groans, distorted through burned mouths.

Carter watched the vessel founder. There was a splashing from the water, and the funeral-pyre glow thrown by the boat showed a man trying to swim toward him. He was swimming clumsily and crying out in pain through a burned hole in his black and blistered face. He slapped at the water as if blind. His feet touched the bottom and then he rose clumsily. He was naked. Whatever uniform he had been wearing had been burned from his body. The raw, welted flesh gleamed in the darkness. The man cried out for help and advanced unsteadily, pawing the air in front of him. Carter turned momentarily away from this scorched, hairless apparition heading straight toward him. He glanced sideways at Sula. Her expression seemed to say what he felt. She raised her gun, then lowered it again. The man came on so that in a few more paces he would emerge onto the mudbank and stumble over them —the burst of automatic fire from the right jarred Carter as if awakening him from a nightmare. The man was knocked sideways and sprawled in the shallow water. Hudson came up with Joe behind him, reslung his gun and nodded toward the corpse. "The best we could do for him," he said.

Carter turned away from the small, still body.

"What the hell happened out there?"

"I think Jerry had more idea what was going on than we gave him credit for," Hudson said.

"Jerry?"

Hudson sunk to one knee and peered toward the blazing boat. "Yes, I saw a canoe drifting past on the far side. I think it was him."

Carter shook his head. "So that's why he took it."

"Don't feel guilty, I had doubts too," Hudson said. He turned away. "We'd better find out if there's anything left of that canoe." He started to wade into the water, calling out to Joe. "Stick together. This is the best free feed those damn crocs will ever have had."

Ash was falling like black flaky rain as they entered the water. Creatures, some of them scorched and maimed by the fire, swam

148

past in an irregular convoy. Occasional splashes and flurries suggested the activities of hunting crocodiles or the death struggles of badly wounded animals that could swim no further. All around the fire was dying down, the risk of it leapfrogging to the far bank becoming less. Carter passed a second naked corpse lying half-submerged and face downward in the water. The mud sucked treacherously at their feet, and underwater tubers encircled their legs like restraining fingers.

Carter looked beyond the still-burning boat to see a thin shape lying on the water. He called out to the others and pressed forward. The boat settled deeper into the mud, and there was an angry hissing sound as red-hot metal sizzled like a branding iron into the water. A few paces revealed that the shape was the canoe, but there was also the dark outline of something perching on it. A bird or a possum, thought Carter, until he came close enough to see that it was another Japanese, his head barely above the capsized hull. He looked at his enemy with expressionless eyes and then released his hold and allowed himself to sink below the water. He did not reappear.

Nobody said anything. Joe and Sula quickly righted the canoe. As they did so, the body of Johnson materialized on the surface, as if he had been trapped beneath it. A stitchwork of bullets ran from his cheek to his thigh. The thick dugout construction of the canoe had absorbed the blast without visible damage.

"Put him in the canoe," Hudson said. "We don't want to leave him here."

They lifted Johnson into his original position in the canoe. Joe found a paddle. The flames from the motorboat had sunk to below the level of the hull. The night now glowed rather than blazed. Without another word they climbed into the canoe and steered toward the reeds . . .

They had, almost beyond their belief and comprehension, lived to survive—and fight?—another day. The mission, of course, was infinitely more complicated and dangerous than before, with the Japanese aware of their presence on Rabaul, if not their purpose.

Or so they thought.

CHAPTER FIFTEEN

IT was ten o'clock in the morning and already the sun shone down hot on the corrugated-iron building behind Rabaul harbor. The panels groaned before the onslaught, strained against their rivets and buckled in the heat. Geckos scrabbled across the walls as if frightened of getting their feet burned by resting in one place. An untidy queue of Japanese of all ranks curled away from the locked entrance and quickly found the shelter of the surrounding palm trees. Two guards with the tips of their fixed bayonets rising higher than their heads stood with their backs almost against the door. There was the sound of bolts being drawn, and the front of the queue pressed forward eagerly. Men who had been squatting in the shadow or climbing for coconuts hurried to take up their places. There were arguments and scuffles. Officers and NCO's exerted their authority and order prevailed, usually at the expense of those without rank.

150

The main door opened with a crack, as if it had expanded in the heat, and a small, round-shouldered Japanese girl was revealed. She wore a simple kimono, and her once elaborate hairstyle was now no more than contained on her head. She looked very tired. She spoke a few words of greeting and bowed. The men at the front of the queue bowed in return, and those behind pressed forward. There were sounds of anger and more scuffling. The guards held their rifles across their chests and pressed back those who attempted to slip inside the building. Any possibility of a riot was averted by the appearance of a second woman, plump and middle-aged, her hairstyle no concession to coquetry. Her voice had a hard edge to it, and when she talked it was at a level barely less than a shout. Her gestures made it obvious that if there was any more trouble the door would be shut—permanently. Her words were received in silence. When she had finished and retired inside the building, the first eight men in the queue entered without challenge from the others. Hardly had the door closed on them than the leaves of the palms began to shiver and the ground shake. A powerful tremor lasted for several seconds and the walls of the tin house trembled bringing down a cloud of dust. The men waiting outside cheered and made ribald remarks. The tremors were becoming increasingly more frequent in Rabaul, but this one was particularly well-timed.

Across the dirt road from the House of Contentment and Love, set up by His Majesty the Emperor of Nippon and serviced by the Daughters of the Rising Sun, Major Yukichi digested the scene and frowned. It was clearly necessary that the officers have a separate brothel. The interests of dignity and discipline could not be served when officers and men stood shoulder to shoulder in the same queue and emptied themselves into the same women. If there were not enough Japanese women available—and it was already rumored that Rabaul was ill-served in this respect, compared with other garrisons of the Imperial Army—the men would have to make do with native women. There were enough cases of rape reported to suggest that this should not prove too much of a hardship. Yukichi made a note to express his feelings on this matter to General Koji and ordered his driver to proceed to the morning briefing session.

When he arrived at the command bunker he was surprised to find two light tanks and a detachment of marines in attendance. The troops were dispersing among the trees and beginning to dig trenches. The morning briefing session had been canceled and General Koji wished to see him alone. Yukichi stepped forward uneasily.

The general was alone as Yukichi entered the room. He barely acknowledged Yukichi's salute and promptly handed him a slip of paper. The message had arrived from the radio station and was timed as having come in an hour before. It came from the spotter plane and was very much to the point.

"K-boat burned out west of Pari village. No sign of survivors or enemy. Am continuing search."

"Burned out?" Yukichi repeated the words incredulously. "But our last report stated that the enemy had been located and pinned down. That it was merely a matter of time—"

"That report was ten hours ago," Koji said. "Didn't you experience any anxiety during the intervening silence?"

Yukichi said nothing. It was true, he'd assumed that the five members of the raiding party had been wiped out without problem. "The fire, sir," he said eventually. "Isn't it possible that the fire destroyed everything? Perhaps the K-boat was engulfed? Perhaps the enemy were killed as well—?"

"Perhaps," Koji said. "But we can't *assume* that. I will not be reassured until I see the bodies. To survive as long as they have done, the enemy have shown considerable initiative. If they have escaped again—and I do not consider this to be beyond the realm of possibility—then they constitute an even more serious threat to Admiral Yamamoto than I had feared. We must redouble our efforts to locate and destroy them." He looked at Yukichi. "I am relieving you of all other duties so that you can concentrate on destroying these assassins."

Yukichi bowed his head and hoped that his flash of fear on hearing the words "relieving you of all other duties" had not shown too clearly on his face. It was not unusual in such a situation that a scapegoat should be sought. Certainly, he considered ruefully, his new responsibilities made him an ideal candidate for the role.

"I am honored by your choice, sir," he said.

Koji nodded briskly. "Take as many men as you need. You will have my sympathetic ear should any of your plans meet with opposition from other service commanders in the garrison. I suggest that you begin by reconsidering the contingency plans that we discussed and presenting me with your up-to-date recommendations. Remember—the protection of Admiral Yamamoto is our prime objective."

"Yes, sir."

"And use your initiative, Yukichi. I am *relying* on you."

Major Yukichi saluted and turned on his heels. The implication behind the last words was not lost on him. Failure would be measured by not finding the raiders. Disaster by anything happening to Yamamoto. The weight on his shoulders was considerably heavier than when he had entered the room. He smiled grimly as he went through the door. It had clearly not been the moment to discuss the brothel arrangements for the troops.

Carter awoke and attempted to open his eyes. At first it seemed that there was an adhesive sticking them shut. Then they parted painfully, weighed down by swollen lids and gummed by mucus. A few inches from his nose the thick jungle foliage pressed in, somber in its perpetual gloaming. The mud on his limbs had dried and encased them like a plaster cast. He moved and it cracked. His arms and back ached, he felt feverish. His bitten forearms throbbed. He started to unwind the blood-soaked bandage and when he came to the wound the flesh was soft and weeping. He quickly rewound it.

He glanced at his watch. One o'clock. He had been asleep for nearly seven hours. The escape through the swamp had totally drained him.

With the dawn they'd seen the jungle and the shadow of Matupi behind. At the same instant they had seen the black speck of the spotter plane against the eastern sky. Like a searching vulture it had begun its sweep with a method and diligence that was typically Japanese. As the plane got nearer the jungle became closer. Eventually they had been able to take shelter between the spreading roots of a moss-strewn tree that rose from the water like a huge

153

deformed spider. While they were here the plane passed forty feet above their heads without seeing them. They had watched it lift over the jungle and then wheel to take up a different tack.

It was here, too, that they had left Johnson, sliding the man who had saved their lives into a watery coffin formed by a basketwork of submerged roots.

When the plane had gone they had picked their way through the water forest to the jungle proper, where they had hidden the canoe. The party then had collapsed into sleep . . .

Carter stood up, fighting off a wave of giddiness, and looked about him. Hudson was asleep with his hat over his face. Joe was digging at a rotting stump with his bush knife. He prised deep into the soft, spongy wood and a handful of fat white grubs fell to the ground. He popped three into his mouth like sweets and, sensing that he was being watched, turned to Carter and held out the grubs.

Carter shook his head. "No thanks. I think I'm going to become a vegetarian."

Joe shrugged, finished, and returned to probing the stump in search of more. Suddenly he stiffened and gestured to Carter to take cover. Seconds later there was the sound of someone approaching through the undergrowth. There was only one other creature apart from man that made a noise when it moved through the jungle: the cassowary, a large emu-like bird protected in its blunderings by its ability to eviscerate a wild pig with one sweep of its razor-sharp claws—

Then there was a double birdcall and Joe relaxed as Sula appeared, moving easily through the undergrowth, and distinctly *not* a cassowary bird. She had obviously found somewhere to wash, her flesh gleamed and her wet grass skirt clung to her thighs. She motioned to Carter. "Good bathing place close."

She turned and he followed, almost unable to contemplate the luxury of clean water against his ravaged flesh. Sula led the way through knee-high vegetation studded with tall trees and patches of swamp until they began to ascend a gentle slope bordered by the beginnings of a stream scarcely wider than his shoulders and running through a channel worn in the soft earth to the depth of

154

a hip bath. A fallen log had helped form a waterfall, and it was to the small pool beneath that Sula pointed. A shaft of sunlight fell like a spotlight from the canopy of foliage above and splashed onto the brilliant scarlet flowers of a flame-of-the-forest climber that hung like a hundred-foot streamer from the forest top.

Carter waded into the pool and felt the bottom firm beneath his feet. There was even a clump of moss that came to the water's edge that he placed his weapon on and began to peel off his equipment and uniform. It was only when he was nearly naked that he thought about Sula. He turned and saw her watching him without apparent concern, then go beneath some low-hanging branches. Carter took off the last article of clothing and sat in the pool with his back against the log and a gentle cascade falling about his shoulders. The cool clear water against his skin was, for that moment, the greatest luxury that he could remember. Even the air seemed easier to breathe, as if it had been miraculously transported from the upper reaches of the Mississippi where he had spent so many boyhood vacations on his grandfather's farm.

He closed his eyes and tried not to think about Johnson. He tried not to think about what lay ahead. Just for a few moments he wanted to escape. Above his head came the weird, wheezing cry of a hornbill. The bird flopped from the branches like a half-opened parachute and slowly flapped away, its head drooping as if unable to support the weight of its enormous parrotlike beak. Carter closed his eyes again and lay back. The water was so cool. Even the insects kept their distance. The thought of getting back into his filthy uniform made him stand up and start to rinse his clothes, seeing them quickly turn the clear water a muddy brown. . . .

Through the jagged leaves Sula stared at Carter's body—the broad shoulders tapering down to the narrow waist, the tight flat buttocks, the slack promise of his heavy penis, the thick bars of muscle in the thighs. She felt an unashamed desire for sex on the bed of moss with her legs dangling in the water. She wanted this man inside her. Her feelings as uncomplicated as they were direct. She had felt and understood his gaze in the outrigger canoe. She wanted to walk to the edge of the pool and take off her skirt; step into the water beside him and take the uniform from his hands. She hated the uniform. It was ugly. It disguised his natural shape,

155

which she thought beautiful and should be seen. She could live with this man. Make children with him. The danger that they were both in, the possibility that death might come at any moment, made it more difficult for her to conceal her feelings. To die leaving them unexpressed would be sad. At the same time she knew that the war came first. His war, her war too. If they were to survive all thought and effort had to be concentrated on the mission. Survival was what mattered. . . .

Carter forced his legs into his sodden trousers and felt the familiar chafing pains as the material rubbed against the scratches, insect bites and deepening sores. He pulled on his T-shirt and slipped his dog tags over his head. He sat on the moss and pushed his swollen feet into his boots. What had once been tough leather was now all pulpy. He tightened the laces and reached for the rolled bandage. His arm seemed to be stiffening up. He flexed his fingers and hoped that his imagination was making the situation worse. If the wound became gangrenous . . . better not to think about it.

Sula came out from the trees then and came toward him. She waded into the pool and took the bandage from Carter's fingers. Dropping to her knees she held it under the small waterfall and then began carefully to encircle Carter's forearm. Her head tilted to look at the metal tags against his chest. "Car-ter," she read, laying an equal stress on each syllable, then smiled, well-pleased with herself.

When they returned to the resting place Joe had accumulated a small pile of edible roots and Hudson was awake and cleaning his weapon. He gestured to the ground in front of him and Sula knelt down. Carter sat cross-legged and began to strip his own gun. Joe hovered nearby.

"Right," Hudson said. "Don't know about the rest of you, but I'm a little more determined than ever. Not just for us, Jerry . . . That's all I'm going to say about that. We've got to put the last twenty-four hours behind us. Nothing has changed. We're rested up. Now it's on to phase two. Except we now have two major problems—the recovery of the explosives and the fact that the Japs know we're here."

Carter chewed on a root and spat out the stringy pith. "Maybe

156

they'll think we burned up in the fire."

"Maybe. But they won't take it for granted. When they see us hanging up by our heels, that's the only thing that's going to persuade them we're dead. Right now they'll be combing the brush for us."

"But they do not know why we are here," Sula said.

"I hope you're right. It depends whether they've found the explosives. If we can recover it and get bearers we'll go tonight. As planned, but twenty-four hours late."

"And if they've found the explosives?" Carter asked.

"Then we're cooked," Hudson said. "We'll fall back on our withdrawal procedures." He punched his fist against the palm of his hand. "But I'm not prepared to think about that, not yet. This thing has got to succeed." He paused. "We've been through too bloody much for it not to."

He'd taught Sula how to disassemble Johnson's gun and she was now deftly putting it back together. Carter slotted a full ammo clip into the breach of his gun.

Hudson motioned to Joe. "We'll work back to the beach to retrieve the explosive, then split up, Will and Joe to fetch Green, Sula and me with the bearers. Rendezvous at a spot to be agreed at twenty-two hundred hours—"

Joe had put a finger against his lips and pointed to the bush, then made a "disperse" gesture and drove his clenched fist up and down to indicate the need for speed . . . "hubba-hubba," Carter thought, which was the G.I.'s word for it.

Weapons were snatched up and the party melted into the thick foliage. Seconds passed before there was the sound of a twig cracking, followed by something brushing through the undergrowth.

A cockatoo yelped from the top of a tree, and for a second Carter thought it was a dog barking and felt terrified. Then there was more rustling and the crackle of a radio. No question. Japs.

Carter twisted his head and looked up, hoping not to see anything, wanting even less to be taken by surprise. He didn't dare move in case a sound gave his position away. If a Jap stumbled on him it was a question of which would react faster. All around him were leaves, shots, tubers, roots, creepers, climbers—different shapes, different greens, some solid, some opaque, some translu-

157

cent. Wrapped as he was in their Medusa-like coils it was impossible to see someone standing three feet away.

The crackle dipped as another channel cut into the static and then continued to sizzle. There was no sound of voices. The silence was unnerving. He knew they were listening too. Waiting for the faintest unfamiliar sound.

A minute passed. The crackle became marginally louder. Perhaps the man carrying the radio had turned his back. A few more seconds and the crackling became fainter, eventually to die away altogether.

Carter stayed where he was and listened. No unfamiliar sounds. Only insects, birds, a spasmodic belch of frog-talk from the swamp. He slowly eased his bodyweight from one hip to the other and wondered if the Japs had withdrawn a few yards to take up cover and see if anyone moved. He felt alone. Soldiers were supposed to fight in platoons, companies, brigades, armies. Never be isolated, except in death.

CHAPTER SIXTEEN

YUKICHI squatted on the sand and dangled his fingers in the water. It was warm. Shoals of small minnows pressed in on the shore. They stirred listlessly, barely interested in avoiding his fingers. Some floated on their backs, dead. A cloud of yellow suffused the water. Further out it was the color of stale mustard. Yukichi wondered if it was always like this. Some volcanic leakage, most likely. Perhaps it was not merely the heat of the sun that made the shallow water so warm. The sulphurous smell was most disagreeable. He wrinkled his nostrils and stood up.

To the left was the marine detachment at Matupi Point that he had visited shortly before the raiders were sighted. Behind him was the spot where the native tracker had blundered into the enemy. Why had they landed here? The post at the mouth of the bay had been bombed many times so the enemy must be well aware of its existence. They would hardly choose to put a party ashore near it.

Most probably the strong currents had swept the inflatable dinghies away from their intended landing positions. They would have had to have come ashore by night, but even then it was a miracle that they had not been picked out by the searchlight.

Yukichi looked along the small bay to the five dugout canoes pulled up on the beach. It did not make sense. The raiders could not have landed here, yet they were discovered nearby and close to a heavily fortified defense post they must have known about. What were they doing here? Planning to attack the post? It hardly seemed likely. He began to pace backward and forward along the sand, then paused as a thought occurred . . .

Did the raiders believed that Admiral Yamamoto was going to visit the post and were they preparing an ambush? Not likely. To start with, so far as he knew, there had been no plans for the admiral to make a visit. Secondly, the post was well-fortified from the land as well as from the sea. Whether the Americans believed that the admiral was going to visit the post or not, there could be no special advantage in choosing it as the site of an assassination attempt. Just the opposite.

What else then? Yukichi looked about him. On his right the volcanic mass of Matupi thrust itself into the air, a thin column of smoke drifting from its muzzle. The steep jungle-covered sides began to rise a quarter of a mile away and fell steeply on the side that overlooked the airfield. Yukichi paused in his walking and examined the sharply defined outline of the volcano . . . a possibility was starting to grow in his mind . . .

The fussy putt-putt-putt of a motorcycle made him look past the three marines with submachine guns who stood facing the jungle at the head of the beach. A dispatch rider appeared, his face and goggles thick with dust. He spoke to one of the bodyguards and then slowly steered the heavy machine over the uneven sand, the suspension creaking. He stopped five feet from Yukichi, cut the engine and struggled to pull the bike onto its stand. This done, he removed a glove, saluted and opened one of the dispatch boxes fastened on either side of the back wheel. He removed two sheets of paper and handed them to Yukichi.

They were both radio messages. One came from an amphibious party that had followed the trail taken by the K-boat. It reported

160

that three white men and a black man and woman, all armed, had landed at Pari Village in a waterlogged canoe. One of the white men was injured and remained in the canoe. The spokesman for the party spoke good pidgin and was believed to be an Australian. He had demanded a canoe and when this was refused he had taken one at gunpoint. The villagers had chased him but had been beaten off. They had noted the direction that the invaders had followed and informed the K-boat when it arrived. In agreement with their boat masters they had fired the reed beds so that the invaders might be burned or driven into the hands of the Japanese. In the night they had heard much shooting and a series of explosions. In the morning they had paddled to the area and been surprised to find that the masters' boat was destroyed and the water littered with the corpses of burned men mauled by crocodiles and other predators. The report went on to say that the area of the incident had been visited and the natives' story substantiated. All of the bodies recovered appeared to be Japanese and there was no sign of the raiders.

Yukichi crumpled the piece of paper in his hand. It merely substantiated most of the facts he already knew. He started to read the second message and immediately his interest quickened. Returning after a series of unsuccessful sweeps over the swamp, the spotter plane had noted what appeared to be the body of a white man floating in the area between jungle and swamp. It was being drawn through the water by a crocodile. The pilot had made several dives and succeeded in frightening off the crocodile. He had also made contact with one of the patrols that Yukichi had sent to the area. They in turn had located the corpse and retrieved what remained of it. A swift examination had revealed wounds caused by submachine-gun fire. Also, burns.

Yukichi began to feel better. One of the raiders was clearly dead. Now there were only four. He looked at the map reference on the message and hurried up the beach. The dispatch rider waited for an order, then eased his motorcycle off its stand. By the time he had started it Yukichi was already striding down the pathway that led to the road as his bodyguards jostled each other to keep up. Two hundred yards in the hot sunshine and he arrived in a small clearing with barely enough room for a vehicle to turn around. His driver sat up, with an alacrity that suggested he had been on the point of dozing off, and quickly handed over the map case as ordered.

Yukichi spread it on the hood and checked the spot where the body had been found. As he had expected it was in reasonable striking distance of Matupi. So, it was almost certain that the four survivors had reentered the jungle and were still capable of carrying out their mission. He turned away from the map with a gesture that indicated it could be refolded and replaced in the case and looked thoughtfully toward the truncated summit of the volcano which showed above the trees. He felt the controlled excitement of a man who has found the key to his problem. He knew, he felt, what the raiders were trying to do. And a plan of his own was beginning to take shape in his mind. . . .

Twenty yards into the jungle Joe heard the sound of the vehicle starting up and rose to his feet. He pressed forward and peered through a screen of pendanus leaves just as the armored car was leaving the clearing. The dust began to settle, the clearing was empty. Joe waited until the sound of the vehicles had died away and the noises of the jungle returned to normal. He listened particularly for the sharp, ticking alarm calls of a bird that would tell him that there were still men hiding nearby. Satisfied, he retreated into the bush to the place where Hudson, Carter and Sula had already regrouped, and reported what he had witnessed.

Carter shot a worried look at Hudson. "Do you think they've found something?"

Hudson shrugged. "We'd better find out." He nodded at Joe and they started to move forward cautiously, circling the trees and starting down the path to the beach. Suddenly Joe stopped and flung out his arm in a "go to earth" gesture. They plunged into the undergrowth. Carter controlled his breathing and eased off his safety catch.

Seconds passed, and then came an unfamiliar wheezing, creaking noise accompanied by the sound of human grumbling. Carter peered through the grass and saw a Japanese pushing a heavy motorbike, the underpart of its engine clogged with sand. He was muttering under his breath, and it required no linguistic skill to detect the string of imprecations that were falling on every mechanical part of the machine that had failed him. There was something comically sad about the man and his enormous, cumbersome bike. Something that made it impossible to hate him. He was an enemy. That was all.

When bike and rider were swallowed up by the undergrowth Joe gave the signal that it was safe to continue. They hugged the edge of the path and suddenly saw a wedge of sky and blue sea before them. Joe went forward again. Carter sank to one knee and faced the way they had come, his gun ready. He glanced at Sula, she returned it. Hudson noticed the exchange and kept his eyes on the path.

Joe came back and told them the beach was clear. Hudson hurried forward with Carter close behind him. They reached the last barrier of undergrowth and crawled until they could poke their heads through the leaves and look out onto the beach. Their eyes moved to the same place and their faces fell.

The dugouts were not moored against the rock.

Carter looked along the beach and thought he recognized the canoe he had come ashore in. There was no sign of the dinghy, which was not surprising. The natives would hardly run the risk of becoming implicated with the invaders by leaving the explosives attached to their canoes. Perhaps they had been cut free and sunk beside the rock to await collection.

Carter swiftly shared his thoughts with Hudson. It was agreed that Joe should go forward to investigate by seeming to be making his way to one of the fishing towers that stood offshore. These untidy erections of saplings were lit by burning brands at night, and men waited with spear and bow and arrow for fish to be attracted by the light.

Joe left his gun and moved down the beach. The first thing he noticed was that the yellow tide had spread to cover most of the shoreward end of the bay. Instead of isolated patches there was one large stain like a scum of paint. He had never seen anything like it before. He looked up at Matupi. The old volcano must have stomach pains to be passing that yellow stuff into the sea. He glanced along the deserted beach, then waded into the sea. The water was warm. Too warm to have been heated by the sun. The heat must be coming from the volcano. When he lowered his head

163

to water level he could see the faintest mist of fumes hovering above the surface on the Matupi side of the bay. He moved toward the rocks with the yellow paste swilling against his thighs. It was impossible to see the bottom now. At least the yellow stain would have made it difficult for the Japs to find the explosive. He wondered, though, would lying on the bottom for twenty-four hours and the increasing heat affect it? Something stirred in the yellow tide beside him and he moved away quickly. It was a dying water snake that lunged at him with sluggish malice, then sank slowly in the water, leaving a crust of small bubbles on the yellow surface.

Joe reached the rock and began to circle it, feeling carefully with his toes. He touched nothing but sand and stones. He looked around him at the other rocks. Had he come to the right one? There was no other rock with a flat surface of stone just above water level. He looked toward the shore, wondering how many unseen eyes were watching him, wondering what he was doing out here among the rocks. He decided to provide an answer. He came on a dying catfish and caught it by the tail, taking care to avoid the poisonous spines. Its whiskers drooped dejectedly and it barely found the strength to twitch in his grasp. Another water snake came to hand and he grabbed it and moved among the rocks.

From the top of the beach, Hudson and Carter watched anxiously.

"He hasn't found them," Carter said.

Hudson shrugged. "He's not going to start jumping up and down and wave his arms."

They waited as Joe reappeared from among the rocks and started to wade back toward the shore with his "catch." He walked up the beach, noting the tire marks made by the motorbike, and the footprints of Japanese soldiers. There were no indications, though, that large numbers of the enemy had been there. He entered the jungle—and turned away from the position where he had left the others, a sixth sense warning him he was being watched.

He transferred both fish to his left hand and started to move up the path leading to the clearing. There was a slight bend in the path, and when he had passed it he threw the fish into the bush and ran as hard as he could for twenty yards before diving behind the

164

trunk of a redwood that grew almost across the path. He drew his bush knife and sank to his haunches. Seconds passed, he listened intently for the slightest sound that would tell him someone was coming, a twig snapping or the noise of grass brushing together in a way that could not be caused by the wind. His eyes searched the canopy of foliage above his head for any sign of a bird quietly slipping away as someone approached. His nostrils sifted the thousand jungle scents of blossom and decay for the alien smell of man—

A sharp prick beneath his ear, a firm pressure against his throat that did not diminish as he slowly turned his head. He saw the gleam of a knife blade, tilted his chin.

It was his father.

The man who had glided up behind Joe was an adumbration of his son. A little over five and a half feet in height his body had the appearance of a skeleton over which a skin slightly too small for it had been stretched. His ribs were a counting frame, and there were pockets of recessed flesh behind his collarbones. His arms could have passed through a girl's bracelet up to the shoulder and his legs were scarcely thicker at the thigh than at the calf. A twist of cloth around his waist was carried forward to cover his genitals. When he grinned he revealed four betel-stained teeth. Father and son embraced, and the old man replaced his knife in the waistband of his loincloth. "I did not teach you very well." He chuckled. "Surely you can hear an old man's bones creaking."

"You move like a spirit, old man."

"I will soon be one," he said matter-of-factly. "It is true that you hid in the swamp?"

"Yes. I never want to see it again. We left one of the *tabandas* there."

The old man shook his head. "I have been waiting for your return." There was a note of relief in the voice.

"We have come for the explosives, papa."

The old man laid a clawlike hand on his son's arm. "The sago bags. I have them safely."

Joe smiled.

"The Japs ran through the jungle like litters of wild pig. They

165

searched the shore but never the canoes. When night came we brought the bags ashore. The bladder boats are also hidden."

"You have done well, papa. Come, I will take you to the *tabandas*. They will want to thank you." He led his father back down the path, explaining that carriers would be needed as soon as night fell . . .

Hudson and the others were waiting anxiously, wondering why Joe had not returned. The old man ran forward when he saw Hudson and eagerly shook his hand.

"Baka!" Hudson returned the handshake with interest, asking the old man why he had come.

The old man explained that he had supplied native carriers to his son, but they had returned in a panic, saying that the Japanese were coming and that everyone would be killed. They had refused to go back and it was only with great difficulty and his personal *purri-purri*, his magic, that he had persuaded them to bring the explosives ashore and hide them. He went on to say that although he was the *luluai*, the headman, of his tribe, the Japanese had appointed his *tultul*, second-in-command, in his place because of his widely expressed pro-Japanese feelings. The tribe was now divided into two—the older element siding with their traditional chief, the younger with the *tultul*. With every day that passed it was becoming more difficult to make the people remain loyal to the old regime.

Hudson could believe it. He remembered the amazement of the natives on New Ireland when all powerful white men suddenly ran like startled bandicoots at the first hint of a Japanese invasion. Respect was replaced by contempt overnight. The Japanese were the masters now.

Carter was worried too. The risk of betrayal was even greater than he'd imagined. Which was all the more reason why they would have to carry out the mission this coming night.

Baka beckoned with an arm like a praying mantis, turned and began to move through the jungle at a fast walk. Carter became breathless trying to keep up with him, yet the old man never broke into a run. He seemed to flit from tree to tree. Eventually the ground began to rise and they came to a place where a patch of clinker showed itself through the undergrowth. Carter estimated that they were approaching the volcano and that the stony residue

was left over from some previous eruption. Strange rock forma-
tions began to appear like modern statues abandoned in an overgrown greenhouse. Among them was a narrow gorge, its mouth
choked by prickly vine. This plant, known to the natives as "hold
'im fas'," could shred flesh almost to the bone with its sharp clinging claws.

Baka paused by the gorge and looked around at his followers.
Carter gazed at the hanging creepers and the dark, gloomy
rocks. He waited for the old man to continue, but Baka stood his
ground and reached out for one of the creepers that hung down
like a bell rope. He gestured Joe to do the same and the two old
men pulled in unison. The prickly vine stirred and then lifted into
the air, revealing it to be a camouflage for what lay beneath. The
narrow stone walls of the gorge were piled almost to the brim with
square balelike shapes tightly bound with sago palm leaves. Baka
and Joe released their creepers and the "hold 'im fas'" dropped
back into place. There was nothing to indicate what it concealed.

"You're a genius, Baka," Hudson said.

Carter could only nod in agreement.

The old man half inclined his head.

"Carriers come on time," he said.

Hudson turned to Carter. "Okay. You and Joe might as well get
on your way. You'll probably have to make a lot of detours and the
more notice you can give Green the better. We'll stick to the same
rendezvous spot. The bottom of the middle scar that appears to
overlook the airfield. Both the tracks that go up from the southwest
meet there."

Carter, moving to the shelter of the rocks, suggested Joe go with
Hudson for the heavy bundles of explosives. Which would also
mean that Sula would be with him. Hudson observed as much,
looked hard at Carter. "What you're saying makes sense, unless
you have personal reasons. I think you're fond of the girl, and I
think she's fond of you. If one of you gets captured or wounded
the other may have to make a tough decision. Easier if there are
no emotional feelings."

Carter nodded uncomfortably. "I suppose you're right," he said.

Hudson's expression relaxed. "I take your point, though, about
Joe and the loads. He's got broader shoulders."

"Well—"

"Just be careful, for all our sakes," and before Carter could say anything he'd turned and walked across to the others, spoke a few words to Sula, who came up to Carter.

"Is everything all right?"

Carter bent to pick up his pack. "Fine," he said abruptly. "Just fine."

The two roads that led to the airfield had been closed to all unauthorized traffic and roadblocks set up. Four light tanks were stationed around the perimeter wire and the sandbag walls enclosing the antiaircraft guns had been lowered so that the guns could be brought to bear on the lower slopes of Matupi. Machine-gun positions had been allocated so that every approach to the strip could be covered by interlocking fields of fire.

Beside the control tower, two trucks waited with engines running. Each contained twenty-five marines in full combat dress wearing steel helmets and carrying submachine guns. Other detachments of marines, armed with flame throwers, had infiltrated the dried-up riverbed which lay between the airstrip and the south face of Matupi. They squatted in the shade with a radio channel permanently open to the control tower.

On the runway the two Mitsubishi Betty bombers waited with their entourage of Zeke fighters. The crews of the two bombers were lined up beside their machines, standing at ease and waiting.

On the roof of the control tower an anxious Yukichi swept the side of the volcano with his binoculars. He could see nothing but a thick carpet of green pitted by vertical depressions and giving way to fields of wasted lava on the upper slopes. There was no sudden transition but a series of spurs and re-entrants that formed an irregular pattern of green and black.

The radio crackled and the operator looked up. "He is approaching the roadblock."

"Inform all units," Yukichi ordered.

The operator talked fast into his mouthpiece and within seconds the engines of the Zekes began to roar to life. The propellers spun into a shimmering haze. Yukichi watched the first two taxi down the runway and turned his attention to the approach road.

168

"He has left the roadblock," the radio man informed him.

Two motorcycles with sidecars appeared around the bend. On each sidecar was mounted a 7.7-mm machine gun with a traverse that could cover both sides of the road. In the event of attack the motorcycles would accelerate up the road so that the enemy could be engaged on two fronts and their firepower split. Behind the motorcycles was a light truck with a machine gun mounted on the roof of the driver's cab and two rows of marines sitting back to back and covering each side of the road. Behind them came Admiral Yamamoto's vehicle, with the bodyguards sitting fore and aft of the figure in the familiar white uniform. There was wire mesh across the windshield and along both sides to prevent a bomb or grenade from being lobbed inside. Rearing forward from the hood at an angle of 45 degrees was a sharpened bar of metal which would meet any wire stretched across the road before it decapitated the driver. Last in the procession was a heavy-duty truck on the back of which had been mounted a 37-mm gun. It was an impressive cavalcade.

Yukichi looked across the blackened stretches of *kunai* grass that flanked the road. Some of them were still smoking. He had ordered them burned in case they offered shelter to an attacker prepared to die in an assassination attempt. He had also had the road surface and drainage culverts examined for mines. Every precaution, it seemed to him, had been taken.

Below the tower, the guard of honor came to attention and the Japanese flag swirled proudly. The first two Zekes were in the air and fanning out to circle the airfield. The antiaircraft guns were spinning on their turntables, the gunners checking their elevations.

Yukichi wiped beads of sweat from his forehead. It was not only the heat that made his shirt cling to him. Again he swept his binoculars over Matupi. Nothing.

The procession came to a halt and a cloud of red dust drifted against the white dress trousers as they descended from the vehicle stationed precisely in front of the guard of honor. The guard presented arms, and two buglers blew a shrill undulating call that startled a hornbill out of a breadfruit tree a hundred yards away. Salutes were exchanged and the guard of honor stood in pride as

169

the four rows of medal ribbons made a perfunctory sortie along each line. The inspection over, the buglers sounded a farewell call and Yamamoto's personal pilot saluted smartly and led the way through the sandbag-buttressed control building toward the runway.

Yukichi watched Matupi and waited. Yamamoto's plane was fifty feet from the control tower. The small, stocky figure in the conspicuous white admiral's uniform would be clearly visible to anyone on the side of the volcano. A rifle with telescopic sights, a good eye and steady hands—that was all that was needed. Yukichi began to count the paces between the building and the plane. One-two-three. The figure moved at a steady, unforced pace.

From the window of the second Betty bomber Admiral Matomi Ugaki, Yamamoto's chief of staff, looked down, his face drawn. He knew the danger that threatened his leader and each one of them. His gaze rose unwillingly to the stern face of the volcano and he wished himself airborne.

Yukichi looked down expectantly. The figure in white paused to exchange a few words with the crew and then mounted the steps of the plane with a smart salute. The hatch folded shut. As the Zekes roared overhead, the two Mitsubishi Betties taxied out to the center of the runway and Yamamoto's plane gathered speed and slowly lifted into the air, tilting over to the right of the volcano and setting course for the Solomon Sea and Bougainville. Four Zekes closed in protectively and the second Betty took off and collected the two remaining Zekes.

Yukichi watched the planes until they were specks in the sky, then looked back to the volcano. From the expression on his face it was difficult to know what he was thinking, or feeling.

Chapter Seventeen

Carter knelt in the *kunai* grass and listened to the Japanese calling to each other. They seemed to be everywhere around him. This was the third patrol they had come across since leaving Hudson. Why were they so active around the airfield? Surely they were not expecting an airborne invasion. It seemed incredible but what other reason could there be for the numbers of men moving around the foot of the volcano? More likely, the Japs refused to believe that the raiding party had died in the swamps and were taking no chances.

A hawk dipped low overhead, then sheered away in alarm, leaving the prey that had first attracted its attention to dither among the grasses. Carter looked around for Sula. This was a bad place to hide. The leeches were thick on the ground and waving their heads in the air as they scented blood. The mosquitoes were so thick you could run your fingers across them in the air. There was

171

also a biting insect so small that its presence could only be detected by the ever-spreading profusion of painful red welts on any portion of exposed skin.

Carter tried to calculate how far they still had to go to the prison camp and whether they would get there before nightfall. Whatever happened, there was going to be precious little time to alert Green. He had it worse than any of them. Their suffering could be measured in hours. He had been enduring a living death for over a year. Would he still have the strength to make it up the volcano, where even Joe acknowledged the difficulty of the climb?

A plane flew overhead and cut back its engines as it prepared to land. Carter could see nothing but heard the changing sound. The airfield was over to the left, lying in almost perpetual shadow at the foot of the volcano.

They had decided to take to the grass to save time but had soon been pushed off the narrow pathway by the Japanese. After circling the first group, who had made their presence known by suddenly opening up with a field radio just as Sula was coming around the bend of the track toward them, they had nearly run into a second patrol. The lead soldier of the file had been looking over his shoulder so that Sula saw him before he saw her. By the time he turned around, Sula had gone into the grass. Now they proceeded stop-go, stop-go, tedious and exhausting. Waiting gave aches and pains time to grow and muscles the opportunity to cramp up. The throbbing in Carter's forearm had now spread to the whole arm, creating a hard, aching swelling beneath the armpit. Strength was ebbing away. The sole of his boot had now separated from the welt and was only attached to the heel. Attempts to bind it with lengths of creeper foundered after a few hundred yards' walking.

A rustling in the grass, Sula said nothing, picked up her weapon and motioned him on. The Japanese had either stopped calling or moved on. There was only the sibilant hiss of the grass ends rubbing together in the slight breeze.

After a dozen yards they came to a shallow drainage ditch with a cracked sunbaked bottom patterned like a crocodile's back. Sula stepped down and extended the fingers of her right hand three times to say that they should leave fifteen yards between them.

Carter let her draw ahead, watching her slim body weave

through the undergrowth. They kept walking along the ditch, giant grasshoppers springing up in front of them. The sun was sinking and the grass tops borrowed a flamingo pink from the paintbox of reds that suffused the western sky. It was as if they were witnessing a distant battle, or as if Matupi had already erupted and set fire to the heavens.

Carter came to a place where the ditch crossed open ground and found no sign of Sula. He knelt, and she appeared from the grass. Her pointing arm brushed his cheek as she sank down beside him.

"Ahead there is the road that passes the airfield. The ditch runs beneath it. Once we have crossed the road we will find the river that flows past the prison camp. We can follow the river. It will be easier among the trees." She paused for a second, rose lightly to her feet. In another five minutes they came to the road, which ran on a causeway across what had originally been a swamp. To cross it was to come into full view of the surrounding countryside. As they watched, a truck full of soldiers went past, traveling toward the volcano. The soldiers were wearing packs with rolled-up ground sheets strapped to them. Carter looked at Sula. She jabbed a finger along the ditch, indicating that it would take them safely beneath the road.

She was wrong. When they approached the culvert it was to find that wooden stakes laced with barbed wire had been driven into the ground across the opening to seal it. The stakes were freshly cut, which indicated that the Japanese were always one step ahead. Sula started to move toward the barricade, but Carter stopped her. He'd noticed a thin wire leading away into the foliage along the side of the road—either an alarm signal or a booby trap. He pointed to what he had seen, waved his hand from side to side in a "no go" signal.

Sula waited, listened. A nervous tremble ran through the grass. The sound died away, silence. She climbed the bank and started to walk across the road. She glanced toward the airfield—two hundred yards away a coil of barbed wire was stretched across the road to form a temporary roadblock. A Japanese soldier with his rifle slung across his shoulder was watching her. She kept walking and waited for the challenge. Beyond the roadblock she was vaguely conscious of a truck approaching. Her feet met the bank on the far side, she slithered down it and ran to the end of the culvert, nearly seizing the barbed wire. She whistled twice and eventually Carter's face appeared. She waved her arms across her face and Carter acknowledged with a thumbs-up signal. She drew back into the grass and waited. Now they were in trouble—on separate sides of the road and with no chance of Carter getting across without being seen. Would it be best to wait for nightfall or to fall back along the road until they were out of view of the roadblock? It occurred to her that the truck had not passed. She listened and heard an engine. Stooping low she moved along the bank toward the road-block. When she judged that she was fifty yards away, she wormed up the bank and tilted her head back so that she could look down the road with the minimum risk of being seen. The barbed wire had disappeared, and with it all vestiges of roadblock. The truck that had picked up the men and barbed wire was reversing down the road looking for somewhere to turn. When she looked up again the truck was vanishing in a cloud of dust. Relief.

On the far side of the road Carter waited, fought off the leeches. He felt something drop down the back of his shirt and writhed in distaste. Of all the creatures in the jungle he loathed leeches the most . . . the thought of sharing his blood with these vile, black worms made him sick. He heard the long whistle and scrambled up the bank, a machine gun in each hand. He crossed the road without looking right or left. After the claustrophobic jungle it seemed strange to burst suddenly into the open, even for a few seconds. He leapt down the bank beside Sula. The ditch ran straight for another hundred yards before meeting a swathe of jungle that followed the line of the river. Ahead and to the left was the mountain behind which lay the prison camp. Carter had only seen it from the far side. He estimated the camp to be about a mile away. With any luck they would reach it before nightfall.

Sula moved ahead, and Carter followed until they came to the bank of the river. The water level was as low as when Carter had first seen it but this time there were no rumbles of distant thunder from the hills. They waited and listened for several minutes but the only sound and movement came from screeching swallows diving to snatch up insects that hung in swarms over the shallow pools. Carter tapped his watch. Sula nodded, moved out across the river-

174

bed, skipping from rock to rock. Carter waited for her to reach the far side, then followed with the weapons, choosing a less adventurous route.

He was nearly at the far bank when he felt a sharp twinge of pain, pain that brought with it an awful premonition. He hauled himself up by a tangled mass of roots and quickly sought the shelter of a grove of palms. The numbness in his arm seemed to have spread to the fingers of both hands as he pulled open the front of his pants, looked down. A shock of horror, even though he'd known what he was going to see from the moment of the first sharp razor nick . . . A leech had attached itself to the rounded dome of his penis.

His first impulse was to pluck it off, then he realized that this would not only be excruciatingly painful but increase the risk of infection to a certainty. He wanted to yell out, in rage and fear.

Sula now came inquiringly to his side, looked from his agonized face to his shielding hand and tried to draw it away. Carter shook her off. Her hand returned, and this time he did not resist, allowed her to look while he turned his head.

Almost before he realized what was happening she had dropped to her knees in front of him. She took his penis in her fingers and put her mouth around it. His first reaction was to draw away, but she put out a restraining hand and gripped him tightly by the thigh. Her lips shut off the leech from the air, and after a few seconds it released its hold. The moment that she felt it separate, Sula twisted her head and spat it out into the grass.

By the time he had stopped trembling Sula was on her feet. He tried to say something but she silenced him with a headshake and pointed toward a spot where the mountains dipped toward the *kunai*.

"Less than a mile," she said, and began to pick her way along the riverbank.

175

Chapter Eighteen

THE figure in the white admiral's uniform gazed thoughtfully out of the window of the bomber. Seventeen-thirty hours and the south coast of Bougainville Island was looming up ahead. The two bombers and their escort began their descent to two thousand feet so that they could make full advantage of their camouflage against the shadowy green of the jungle. . . .

Four miles to the south, sixteen P-38 Lockheed Lightnings were on the last leg of their flight from Henderson Field. They had flown 410 miles at thirty feet above the waves, their wings and bellies weighed down by two supplementary fuel tanks with total capacity of 475 gallons. The pilots searched the skies ahead of them and checked their watches. Their interception point was thirty miles west of the Kahili strip, and they were flying as low as they dared to avoid being spotted by any enemy planes or ships patroling in the area. Visibility was good, with flurries of high cloud above twenty thousand feet, and the west coast of the island of Bougainville showed up clearly with thick jungle vegetation crowding down to the water's edge.

"Eleven o'clock." An excited voice broke radio silence, and all eyes scanned the horizon.

A V-formation of planes was approaching along the coast from the northwest—two Betty bombers with an escort of what seemed like six Zekes. The bombers were flying almost wing-tip to wing-tip with two fighters on each side and two above and a little behind. Their altitude was two thousand feet. Immediately four of the Lightnings jettisoned their long-range belly tanks and started to climb toward the bombers. The remaining twelve climbed more steeply to give high-level protection. For the passengers in the two bombers the first warning of attack was given when the P-38's were a mile from their target. Anyone not strapped to his seat was flung across the aircraft as the Betties spun sideways and streaked toward the safety of the jungle. The escorting Zekes sprayed out to meet their challengers and head off pursuit. The first P-38 screeched down at over four hundred miles per hour and the yammer of 22-mm cannon and 13-mm machine guns vied with the scream of 3,000-horsepower engines. The leading Betty side-slipped to safety and continued its dive toward the treetops. As it leveled out its green and brown markings seemed to melt into the jungle and the pursuing P-38 was forced to take evasive action as three Zekes closed in. Turning sharply, the pilot saw a fourth Zeke in his sights and pressed the button. Cannon shells chewed through the fuselage, the plane shuddered and slowly turned over on its back. It started to go down in a gentle curve. Now the first Betty could be seen as a shadow flying almost at treetop height. Two P-38's broke through the cover of the outnumbered Zekes and went after it. With a landscape of uneven green flickering beneath its undercarriage the bomber desperately veered from side to side to throw off its pursuers. A thin column of smoke began to trail like black cotton from one of its wings.

Up at seven thousand feet two more P-38's saw their chance and came down to attack the second bomber—half the tail plane was shot to pieces. The Betty lurched sideways and slid toward the ocean, hit the water, broke up in a cloud of spray.

Over the Bougainville jungle the first Betty hedge-hopped desperately, slipping, skidding and bunting its rudder in an attempt to reach the fighter cover that was screaming off the strip at Kahili like a swarm of avenging hornets. A P-38 sat on its tail, and a long burst ignited the starboard engine. Orange flames began to kick around the cowling and black smoke streamed from the wingtip. The bomber began to shudder and lose speed. Flame ran the length of the wing and enveloped the fuselage. It tried to climb and then slumped so that the trail of black smoke kinked like a painted eyebrow. Another burst and the plane fell out of the sky. Its undamaged wing hit a tree and splintered. The blazing plane bounded twice, cleared a flaming trail through the jungle and exploded. Seen by the farthest-flung of the P-38's, a dense column of thick black smoke began to billow into the air.

A funeral pyre for the architect of Pearl Harbor, thought the pilot. Good riddance.

It was what he, and the world, was supposed to think.

Chapter Nineteen

HUDSON squatted by a rock and watched the last of the bales being brought out of the ravine. The native carriers had one emotion in common—fear. They muttered among themselves, looked suspiciously at Hudson and their loads. Hudson could sympathize with them . . . the weight was double what they had expected to carry and the going would be tough. Only the provision of salt and stick tobacco—one third now, two thirds when the job was done —had clinched a grudging acceptance.

Hudson needed a smoke himself. His nerves were tight, the business with Carter about Sula had not helped . . . One of the carriers tore down a large leaf and rolled it between his hands until it was a malleable wand, folded back the end and continued to wind it tightly until he had made a small thick mat that he placed on his head. He sank to one knee, then two of his comrades lifted a bale and placed it on the mat. With arms outstretched he slowly rose,

179

the veins at his temples bulging, juggled his load to achieve the right balancing point and waited, his head low on his shoulders. The carriers were mostly young but with one barrel-chested fifty-year-old whose bald head had a dent in it where someone had struck him with an ax. He scorned a mat, picked up his load, and fitted it onto the dent without assistance.

Baka appeared across the clearing then, and Hudson repeated his thanks for providing the carriers. Baka took his hand and squeezed it warmly, and Hudson blushed beneath his tan. Not for the first time he wondered how many of Baka's people would survive if they succeeded in making Matupi erupt. These people were carrying what might be the instruments of their own destruction. It was their gardens that would be overrun with lava, their houses that would be burned to ash . . . He returned the pressure on Baka's hand, then turned quickly away and gave the signal to move out.

Joe embraced his father and started to lead the way from the clearing. The old man waited until the last carrier had gone, then looked carefully about to see if they had left any signs that they had been there. Afterward he returned to his village.

Carter looked toward the prison camp, and his heart sank. The swathe of cleared vegetation around the perimeter wire had been widened and the clump of rattan had disappeared, which meant it was going to be impossible to signal to Green that they had arrived. It also meant that there was going to be less cover when they approached the wire.

Sula, beside Carter in the elephant grass, read his expression and listened as he explained the problem.

Carter looked toward the high barbed-wire fences. They were at the opposite corner to the one by which he had first approached the camp, and his field of visibility was limited. Such figures as he could see in the European compound were pitifully thin and dressed in rags. He leaned forward and tried to see what was happening in the rest of the camp. There was no movement in the Chinese compound and the entrance to the Indian compound was padlocked. What might have been the covered heads of sitting Indian women were just visible through the wire. Some of the huts had their entrances boarded up with red planks. He guessed an

180

outbreak of some contagious disease had been isolated there. Cholera? Was that why there seemed to be so few people about? He had better take a closer look. Telling Sula to remain where she was, be began to crawl just inside the lush vegetation that abutted on the open strip of ground around the camp. The sun had now disappeared behind the trees and the tree frogs were beginning to croak.

What followed was a series of little nightmares . . . Opposite the Chinese compound, looking into one of the low thatched huts, he saw people stretched out on the floor like so many bundles of rags, and, as if to demonstrate the degradation for him, a woman captured a rat on a string, dropped it into a simmering pot . . . A new smell came to him, a harsh chemical smell like creosote. Looking through the screen of grass to the barred huts he realized what it was for, that people had started to die from disease. He wondered how many huts were sealed, had the disease spread beyond the Indian area—was Green dead? If he were the mission was over, because he was the only one who could lead them to the cave that led into the volcano . . . A few more yards on naked elbows and he could spy on the guardhouse. The corrugated-iron roof caught the last rays of sun. A square tent was next to it, sides rolled up for cooler sleeping for the guards. Two pairs of putteed legs showed below the tent flap. A third man lounged on a paliasse. A battered truck with red rising sun emblem on the door was also nearby. There were nearly a dozen bedrolls, at Carter's rough count. Carter heard the creek of leather boots as the missing guard walked near, stopped, moved on, and was surprised they'd bother to patrol here during the day—the inmates hardly looked like they had the strength to walk, let alone escape . . . He heard a truck approaching and stop, engine groaning as if it carried a heavy load. It did, ragged skeletons, Europeans and Chinese and a few Indians, some still wearing turbans, a work party. Carter quickly scanned the faces for Green. Not there. The men were manacled at the wrist, beaten if they hesitated a moment after being unloaded. One man, an Indian, did not move from the truck. Perhaps he'd been caught in a cave-in. He was pulled to the ground by his chain, lay on his back. The prisoners were separating into different compounds, out of view of the truck, so they did not see one of the

181

guards plunge a rifle with fixed bayonet up to the barrel into the stomach of the man. The two other guards then lifted the body, tossed it into a small truck . . . Next a loud wailing noise sounded throughout the camp, and two of the soldiers entered a hut, emerged with clipboards, sheets of paper attached. The roll was to be taken, and the pitiful human refuse was herded out to be accounted for . . .

Sula was waiting where he'd left her. He told her nothing of what he'd seen, or feared about Green. A bit of English drifted across the wire, an Australian accent, voice raised and angry but almost immediately submerged by a gabble of Japanese, something about digging tunnels. Shortly afterward he could see the enemy withdrawing down the center aisle between the huts, the prisoners breaking rank. He waited impatiently, not daring to approach the barbed wire while there were still so many inmates about. Any overt response from them would alert the guards. He turned to Sula, pointed to the guardroom. He'd drawn her a map of the camp and selected a range of birdcall signals that she was to use to alert him of sentry movements. She nodded, moved off.

He started through the grass to the place he had preselected for his attempt at the wire. There was a shallow depression in the ground that ought to give enough cover. Gun held between two hands, he emerged from the undergrowth and began to crawl across the open space, feeling horribly naked. He lay on his back, removed the wire-expanding devices. One of them had buckled in a fall and he had to struggle to set it up. He forced his knife around, it slipped out of the socket and his hand was gashed by the barbed wire. He tried again, this time the metal rods opened and the wires strained apart. When the lowest was on the ground he pressed flat and wriggled forward. His uniform snagged twice but he managed to free it, reached the inside of the camp and paused to listen. Nothing except wheezes, snores from the huts.

He was about to move forward when he saw someone, and froze. The figure came toward him, weaving from side to side. Not a Jap. The man was muttering, scratching, obviously a fair ways around the bend. Carter got quickly to his feet, grabbed the man's arm and asked under his breath, "Do you know Harry Green? Where is he? I want you to take me to him . . ." The man shook free just as two sharply defined birdcalls sounded. Carter put a hand over the man's mouth, dragged him toward the shelter of the huts. "Harry Green," Carter repeated, as though talking to a child, and this time the man seemed calmer as he nodded. Carter released his hand and the man opened his mouth to shout. Carter caught him before he could, heard three more birdcalls, the signal that a sentry was out and near. He warned the man that they'd both be killed if he made a noise to draw the sentry. The man muttered, shivered, then took Carter's hand and led him across an open space between two rows of huts, paused in the shadow of a doorway. Boards creaked, someone turned in his sleep. The man entered the hut, pulling Carter in after him. The walls stopped a foot below the roof and moonlight streamed in.

Some two dozen men lay on the floor, most without any covering. Some were curled up in fetal positions with their hands between their legs. Others stretched out as if at the other end of life —corpses on an undertaker's table. They were packed shoulder to shoulder with scarcely room to turn. The hut buzzed with flies and mosquitoes.

Carter let himself be led between the rows of men, searching for Green. One man at the end, with his back to them, looked promising. Carter hurried forward. The pressure on his arm was released and his guide hobbled to the side of the sleeping figure. He bent down and shook his shoulder. After a pause the man grunted and turned around. It was not Green.

Carter dropped to his knees. "I'm looking for Harry Green—"
The man shook his head. "He ain't here anymore."

Chapter Twenty

CARTER felt like he'd been kicked in the stomach.

"The Japs took him away yesterday. They caught him stealing rice." The man shook his head and squinted at Carter. He spoke with an American accent. "Who the hell are you anyway?"

"It doesn't matter," Carter said. "Forget you saw me. Where did they take him?"

"To the pit, in the jungle near here." He jerked a skinny arm over his shoulder. "There's a track, that's where they execute people—"

Carter's heart fell. "He's dead?"

"If he's lucky. They don't always kill you right away. Not if the high crime is stealing. The Japs don't like thieves . . . Hey, get down!"

Carter dropped to one elbow and turned his head. Through the chink in the ill-matched cane wall he could see the bright glare of

184

an approaching flashlight. The disturbed man began to babble and was moving toward the doorway before anybody could stop him. Carter pressed himself into the lines of bodies and lay still, heart thumping. With a quick movement the man he'd been talking to leaned across to pull a tattered blanket over his legs, then turned his body so that he was facing the doorway and lay eyeball to eyeball with Carter, the gun concealed between them.

Carter heard the unhinged man's voice leaving the hut and the immediate challenge, then a guttural explosion of Japanese and the sound of a blow followed by a yelp of pain and the agitated mumble quickly receding into the distance. A short silence and the creak of a board as a rubber-soled boot trod on it. Carter could feel the Japs' presence in the doorway, surveying the interior of the hut. A beam of light traveled up the far side and then splashed over him as it returned down the second row of bodies. He held his breath. The floorboard creaked again and the light withdrew.

Carter lay in silence. Minutes passed, and then his companion raised himself on one elbow and looked around. He rose to move stealthily to the doorway. When he returned he lay down and spoke in a low voice.

"They've gone. What do you want Harry for?"

Carter, of course, had to fudge it . . . "It's too long a story, friend . . . I've got to get going—"

"I'll come with you."

"Hey, I'm sorry, but it just wouldn't work—"

"Listen, damn it, I was shot down over this stinking jungle." There was the pressure of clawlike fingers on Carter's arm. "They're going to start making us dig tunnels in the rock. They've already killed nearly all the Indians . . ."

The man's voice was rising dangerously high, his neighbor stirred in his sleep and told him to shut up.

"I'm sorry," Carter mumbled, and did what he had to do, brought his fist up against the man's jaw, connecting flush and knocking him senseless.

Carter waited for any reaction to the noise and moved swiftly to the doorway. The moon was about to disappear behind a bank of cloud. He figured he had about thirty seconds to reach the wire before it reappeared. Listening carefully for any unusual sound he

185

scanned the surrounding huts, hoping that the deranged man had been discouraged from any further roaming. The moon dimmed and was soon extinguished. Behind him he could hear the pilot begin to groan as he came around. It was time to go.

Carter sprang for the wire, keeping as low as he could, sprawled full length in front of it, listened again, then quickly changed his position and wriggled under the wire. Out with the knife and the extending rods were released as the moon reappeared. He held them against his gun and crawled back across the agonizing stubble of severed stalks to the temporary safety of the undergrowth.

He felt exhausted, empty . . . The news about Green was a body blow. What the hell were they going to do now? He gave the birdcall signal for Sula to return and began to fold the wire expanders before replacing them in his pocket.

Sula appeared through the undergrowth. Her look of anticipation quickly faded when she saw he was alone. He motioned to her to follow him into the bush, out of earshot of the camp.

"Green wasn't there. He may well have been executed. Have you heard of a place called the Pit?"

Sula shook her head. "There are places like that everywhere . . . you remember my father . . ."

Carter nodded, then, "Apparently there's a track over by the corner of camp. We'd better take a look and see if we can find it."

She nodded and started to pick her way. Carter blundered behind, wondering whether she had a different order of eyesight. She ducked and weaved past creepers and obstructing branches while he diverted them with his head. She walked on a carpet, he on a torture bed of seared twigs that exploded like shots with every step he took.

After a quarter of an hour the jungle lightened on either side and he looked up to see a corridor of stars. The ground was soft and pitted. He risked shining his flashlight quickly at ground level and saw the unmistakable prints of heavy-duty tires. They'd come to the track. Now the going was easy, their path illuminated by clumps of glowworms and clouds of fireflies—

Sula paused, Carter strained his senses. There was always a sweet smell of decay in the jungle, but now the air carried a stronger, more bitter odor. Carter pressed forward, and after

186

they'd walked along the track some two hundred yards a faint glow showed ahead, growing in intensity as they approached until a single lantern could be seen hanging among the trees. The odor there was overpowering. When they were within twenty yards of the lantern Sula stopped and motioned toward the ground. Carter sank down on one knee, listened. At first he thought he heard someone moaning in pain, then realized it was a low, tuneless dirge that was coming from a man within a stone's throw of them. Carter started to crawl forward.

The lantern illuminated a small clearing, the ground muddy and churned by turning trucks. At one side was a crude shelter of palm leaves supported by a framework of saplings. In the center of the clearing hung a man trussed with his knees against his chest and his wrists bound round his shins. He was suspended by his ankles, his head lolling down, a splash of blood at the temple. The rope from which he hung was looped over two horizontal poles lashed to facing uprights. The ends of the two poles overlapped slightly so that it required only a slight movement from the man to work himself free from one pole and impose all his weight on the other. The poles were already bent dramatically, and it was clear that one alone would not support him. If he dropped, it would be into the mouth of the pit above which he was now dangling. From Carter's distance the man's face was all but unrecognizable under a mask of flies. At first glance he appeared to be dead but as Carter watched he shook his head to rid himself of the tormenting insects and the rope slipped another half inch toward the end of the pole.

From the pit came a noise like a submerged beehive. A throbbing, reverberating hum. To and from the maw streamed a moving column of insects, spiraling up or spilling over its edge. They in turn attracted bats and small owls so that the air was full of squeaks and screeches and the beating of a myriad of wings.

To Carter, the scene was like an engraving of purgatory . . . he did not know that he was watching a refinement of the *ana-tsurushi* —the hanging-in-the-pit—a method of torture employed by the Japanese to make sixteenth-century Christian martyrs recant their faith . . . Carter shrank back as another figure came into the light, a soldier with a rifle slung over his shoulder. For a moment the long bayonet bisected the light of the lamp, and a kind of des-

187

sicated humming came from the man as he circled the pit.

Carter looked back to the hanging man, and understood the cruel reason for the wound on his temple; a vein had been severed to provide some outlet for the blood and thereby to prevent the victim finding release in unconsciousness and too easy a death. He winced as the man twisted slightly on the rope and the light glistened on the black coils of flies around his nostrils, eyes and mouth.

The soldier was talking to the man now, talking and singing snatches of a tuneless melody. His movements were unsteady and disjointed, and it was now clear to Carter that he was drunk. As if to confirm the fact, he bent down and rose with an earthenware vessel that he raised to his mouth and swilled greedily. So greedily that he lost his balance, staggered backward and nearly dropped his rifle. This act of clumsiness made him furious and he shouted at the figure on the rope as if blaming him. A groan was the man's only reply, which seemed to act as a further goad. The soldier seized his rifle in the port position and passed it threateningly below the man's face.

Carter looked about him, wondered if there were any more of the enemy in the neighborhood . . . by the time they'd checked the man would be dead. Even now the soldier was reaching toward the support poles with the tip of his bayonet.

Carter put down his gun and slid out his knife. The soldier jabbed at one of the poles, missed, and as he did Carter came up behind him. The soldier heard his footfall and started to swing around. He had half turned when Carter caught him 'round the head and pulled him backward. He bit Carter's arm but was held tight against his chest, still clinging to the rifle. The knife went into the side underneath the right arm and glanced off a rib. The soldier gasped, then bit even deeper. Another blow to the chest struck his breastbone. He dropped his rifle and kicked his legs in the air to break Carter's grasp. He was a small man but fighting for his life made him writhe and wriggle like a pinned snake. He parried a third blow with his forearm and dug back viciously with his elbow to the pit of Carter's stomach.

Carter didn't dare loosen his grip around the man's head in case he started yelling. His teeth were deep into Carter's flesh. Carter

188

struck again, and this time the blade went home without hitting bone. The soldier's struggles became a series of weak, fluttering spasms and then ceased altogether. Carter felt the teeth relax their grip and slowly began to lower the deadweight of the man toward the ground. The soldier sprawled backward and suddenly his mouth jerked open. Carter dived to smother the cry with his body. He pressed down with all his weight and slid his hands around the soldier's throat, squeezed, forcing his fingers deep into the windpipe. There was no tremor or movement, but he did not release his grip until he was certain that the man was dead. He rolled to one side and rose unsteadily to his feet, breathless. Carter looked at him. Nobody could equal the Japanese for sadism. Few came near equaling them for raw courage.

Carter listened for any sound that might indicate the struggle had been overheard. The throbbing of insects had been replaced by an eerie silence, but now it began to build up again . . . the ratchety croak of a tree frog rattled out from a nearby cedar and distant cousins in the swamps fluted and belched. From the direction of the prison camp there was no noise. Carter moved swiftly to the side of the pit and shone his torch in the man's face. One eye opened and blinked. Carter twisted his head, and recognized Green, his face a swollen gray in the faint glow of the torch.

"Harry, we've come for you, hang 'n."

"Don't have much fucking alternative, do I?" The rope edged to within a hair's breadth of the end of one of the poles.

Sula slid into the clearing, drew Carter's attention to a long pole leaning against the thatched shelter. They ran toward it and brought it back to the edge of the pit. Carter waved Sula to the opposite side of the pit near one of the uprights and raised the heavy pole to his shoulder. Taking a deep breath, he began to edge it forward. When he got to the stretched triangle of rope he slowly inched the pole through the middle. The balance began to shift as the pole reached out farther and the tip suddenly began to drop, bringing the wood dangerously close to the rope. Carter shifted his stance, Sula clung to the upright and stretched out her hand. Her fingertips brushed the end of the pole, she began to guide it toward her side. It was nearly over her shoulder when Green flinched

189

and the rope slipped the end of one of the transversals and snapped away from the other end with a noise like a bow being released. Carter clung on but Sula's end of the pole was torn from her grasp and bounded on the edge of the pit. Green swung against the side. For a second it seemed he would drop, but the end of the pole came to a rest two inches away from disaster. Sula dropped to her knees and bent down to grab the rope. While she clung on, Carter slowly lowered his end of the pole to the ground. It was now lying across the hole with Green dangling against one wall. Carter ran 'round the pit to Sula, and together, finally, they hauled Green to safety.

Sula got out her knife and moved to cut his bonds—

"*No.*" Carter seized her wrist. "Untie him. We're going to need the rope."

"Thank God you got here," Green said as Sula wiped his face, then set to picking apart the knots that had cut deep into his flesh. When she released his legs Green nearly yelled out in pain as he tried to straighten them.

Carter massaged the ankles hard. "You'll be okay once we get the circulation moving." He spoke with a confidence he did not feel. Green might, in fact, be crippled, and if he was, there was no chance they'd be able to carry him up the side of Matupi in three hours. He began to manipulate Green's legs as Sula started on his wrists. "How long have you been like that, Harry?"

"Since it got dark. You didn't know it but it's the second time you've saved my life today . . . they had me down in the jail, interrogation . . . they'd have killed me. Then some colonel strides in—nasty little one-eyed bastard—and they all start panicking. I didn't understand much but enough to know that a party had been put ashore. They sort of forgot about me after that. Chucked me in a cell till they brought me back here." He groaned again and closed his eyes. "Bloody head's like a sockful of crickets."

"How did you get in trouble?" Carter asked.

"I knew I had to build myself up a bit to be any good to you. I needed some extra grub so I took a few risks when I was working in the docks. Slashing open rice bags, that kind of thing. In the end I helped myself to a guard's dinner." He grimaced with pain as he tried to move his arms. "He took a poor view of it. 'Sabotaging the

190

Japanese war effort.' That's how it was translated to me, can you believe that?"

Carter pulled the rope away from Green's body. "Well, with any luck you're soon going to be doing a lot more sabotaging. Now, can you get your shorts off by yourself?"

"My shorts? *Why?*"

"You're going to change clothes with the Jap."

He did not wait for a reply but began stripping the uniform from the dead soldier.

"I'm not going to wear that filthy little sod's uniform." Green suddenly sounded very British.

Carter did not pause to argue. "Give me your shorts."

Green hesitated, and Carter nodded to Sula. Green's shorts were down to his ankles before he could deliver another protest. Carter pulled off the soldier's boots and looked at Green's bare feet. The boots were going to be a tight fit but the rest seemed all right. Green was smallish even when he wasn't half starved.

Carter pulled the shorts onto the soldier and tied them around his waist. He smeared grime on the body and folded the knees to the chest.

Green was sitting up now, watching him in amazement. Carter started tying the wrist to the shins. The soldier's head was lolling against his shoulder. He called to Sula and told her to keep watch up the track, in case another guard came up to relieve his comrade.

Green waited until Sula had gone, then started to pull on the pants. "Where's Hudson?" he asked.

"Waiting for us on Matupi, I hope."

"Thank God, I thought they might have got him. Damn beautiful girl you've got there. Great asset."

Carter had to smile. "Try to stand up."

Green did, and collapsed immediately.

"Legs?"

"Legs and head. I can't move."

"It'll get better. I'll walk you around in a minute."

Carter took a loop from one of the soldier's ankles and let it out to the length by which Green had been hanging, then secured the rope around both ankles. The corpse was now folded up in a fetal position exactly as Green had been, his head almost resting on his

191

knees. Carter smeared more dirt on his back and stood up. Ever since coming to the pit he'd avoided looking into it. The dense cloud of flies and carpet of beetles that crunched underfoot at its edge was enough.

Taking the flashlight, he approached the pit and looked down. Twenty feet below, the ground seemed to be trembling. A persistent undulation. He was looking at moving pall of maggots. Among them was the wasted face of the Indian, half-submerged in the awful mulch.

Carter turned away, gagging, crossed to the soldier and lifted him up by the loop of rope sprouting from his ankles. He dragged him forward to the edge of the pit, hoisted him up with one hand underneath the bent knees, heaved him head downward into the center of the pit. He checked that the telltale rope trailing away from the ankles was clearly visible and turned away.

Green was struggling with his boots, unable to bend forward. Carter helped him and was heartened to see that his body did appear to have more flesh on it than at the time of the first visit. Perhaps the fattening program had been marginally successful. He finished tying the laces and made the birdcall whistle for Sula to return. Green rose unsteadily to his feet while Carter found the Japanese's cap and rifle. He handed over the cap.

"I'll carry the rifle for a while." Carter clapped him on the shoulder. "Try walking."

Green took a few unsteady paces and started to rub his arms. "I'll be all right after a couple of miles."

Carter grinned. "I believe it."

When Sula came back they replaced the pole and took a last look around. Carter found the jar that the Jap had been drinking from and sniffed it—clearly some local rotgut either bought or stolen from the natives. Carter poured it away behind a tree and left the empty jar clearly visible near the shelter.

"Okay," he said. "Matupi."

They had taken a dozen steps through the jungle when Green stopped and supported himself with his arm against a tree. Carter closed with him anxiously.

"What's that smell?" Green asked.

"Air," Carter told him. "I hope it doesn't kill you."

CHAPTER TWENTY-ONE

HUDSON squatted in the darkness and listened to the rain splashing off the leaves. It had started at about nine. A continuous, heavy tropical downpour turning the pathways into rivulets. That was nearly two hours ago. Carter and Sula were almost an hour late. And Green? Even if they'd somehow managed to get him out of the prison camp it was difficult to imagine worse conditions for a wasted fifty-year-old to travel in. Even the normally sure-footed carriers had been slipping and sliding on the steep glasslike slopes. Sometimes the water coming down had been over their ankles.

Twice it had been necessary to hide from Japanese patrols, and the disruption of the carriers' normal walking rhythm plus their struggling with the heavy loads had begun to sap their strength. They were also terrified of the Japanese, what they knew would be done to them if they were caught carrying loads for the enemy. They were also frightened of the mountain. To them, Matupi was a holy place, and the volcano a god, who sometimes spoke out angrily to the humans that nested in his hair.

Every generation had passed on stories of eruptions to the next. Every movement of the mountain was monitored and interpreted. Joe had reported that the rain was Matupi's tears because the white men were coming to harm it. Such superstition was powerful stuff. Hudson did not know how long he could fight against it. It was useless talking about the evil done by the Japanese and the necessity of overthrowing them. Before the Japanese there had been the Australians, and before them the Germans. They had all been *tabandas*—masters—but Matupi was the king. He never varied his position against the skyline. His whims were far more terrifying than anything perpetrated by the Germans or even the Japanese.

The rain continued to drum down. Hudson shivered from chills and fever. Why were the Japs out in such force? They'd certainly stepped up their activities since the first visit to the prison camp when there'd been no evidence of inland patroling. He worried that Carter and Sula were either dead or captured. A hundred things could have gone wrong on the way to or at the prison camp. He'd give them until midnight, then plant the explosive at a point of his own choosing near the summit, set the fuses and hope.

Joe appeared at his side to say that one of the carriers who had injured his leg in a fall was complaining and demanding to return to his village. He was a bad influence on the others and Joe thought they ought to let him go. He, Joe, could carry the load.

Hudson disagreed. If they let one go the others would want to go too. And there was the danger that another fall or a desertion would force them to jettison a load—a tenth of their explosive potential. Detonating the full thousand pounds might be vital if they couldn't find the tunnel.

Hudson's clothes stuck to his smarting skin, and the cold rain awoke old wounds and memories. It was the rain that had brought on the fever Marjory had died from. He wondered why he'd stayed on after that. He'd never intended to; just long enough to sell out and then it was going to be back home to Australia. But no purchaser had appeared immediately and so he had thrown himself into the store, mostly as an outlet for his grief. As the months passed the wound had begun to heal, and by the time he bought the plantation he knew that he was not going to leave after all. He lived alone but it was a life that suited him. Until the Japs came—

The triple screech of a cockatoo snapped him back to the present. The sound came again, and Joe was at his side. Hudson jerked his head forward, Joe listened for a second, then moved into the shadows. The dark shapes of bushes and creepers swayed and shimmied before the buffeting of the rain. It was impossible to hear any movement further than a few feet away. A patrol could arrive on top of them without being detected—Suddenly the foliage parted, and Joe's glistening body appeared . . . followed by Carter.

Hudson gripped Carter's hand. "What happened? Where are the others?"

"Prepare yourself for a shock." He whistled softly, and Sula appeared, guiding a Japanese soldier who had difficulty in keeping his footing. Hudson peered forward incredulously, and finally recognized Green's face beneath the forage cap.

Green stretched out a hand and sank gratefully onto the muddy ground. "Sorry to hold you up, Andrew, bit out of training."

"Jesus, man, I thought you'd signed on for the Emperor." Hudson said it with a straight face.

The two Japanese soldiers approached the clearing and flashed their hand torches.

"Where is he?" the first asked.

"He's crazy," the second said. "You wait. He'll probably come jumping out at us."

He started waving his flashlight around the trees and calling out. "Show yourself, Soryu! Don't be a fool!"

The first man shone his flashlight toward the pit and up at the empty poles. "The old thief didn't last long." He pinched his nostrils and advanced to look down into the pit. The body lay hunched up in the writhing slime like an embryo tipped out of an eggshell. The rope trailed from its ankles.

The second soldier, moving his flashlight about, hurried toward one of the trees surrounding the clearing and picked up an earthenware jar. He sniffed it and grimaced. "Jungle juice," he said.

The first soldier took the empty jar, sniffed and shook it on the back of his hand. A few drops sprinkled down and turned the skin

195

cold. He sniffed again and recognized the fermented juice of mashed paw paw which had been mixed with sugar and distilled in an oil drum still. The practice was illegal but much indulged in by Japanese soldiers who preferred insensibility to boredom.

He held up the jar and shone his flashlight into it. The recent presence of liquid could be detected to a line just below the rim. He whistled through his teeth. "If he drank all this he may be gone for days."

"Forever," his companion said.

Hudson watched the carriers forming up with their loads, and for the first time felt a genuine sense of excitement. Now they had a real chance. All that was necessary was for Green to find the tunnel. That, and something that had been conspicuously lacking in the operation so far—luck.

The first evidence of a change of fortune came when it stopped raining. Matupi had dried his tears, Hudson thought. Sula rolled the cloak of bark she had prepared for herself and dusted the water from her face and arms.

Carter watched the carriers lifting the explosives onto their heads. Thin shafts of moonlight had been quick to break through the lowering clouds. There was a danger that the carriers would start taking their loads for granted and forget they were carrying something so potent that it could blow them to powder. Joe wove among them. A sharp word here, the condition of a load checked there, a word of encouragement where it was needed. These were his people and he felt doubly responsible for them. Any failure would reflect on him both as a man and as the son of a chief.

Green's eyes probed the darkness. He took a breath of the cold air and shivered. His legs were turning to jelly. He only hoped that they would not suddenly collapse under him. There was nothing he could do about it. Strength was ebbing out of them.

"Okay?" There was an edge of worry in Carter's murmured question.

"Fine . . . we have to follow this track round toward the back of the mountain. We split off to the right when we get our first glimpse of the scree." *If* we get it, he thought to himself as he spoke. How many years had it been since he was last up here?

Certainly a year before the Jap invasion. And he had never seen the volcano at night—except out of a pub window. If he could just lead them to the tunnel he would be satisfied. There had been talk about getting away on a submarine after the explosion but he hadn't really listened. Whether the Japs believed he was dead or not, there was no point in struggling back to the camp. But a submarine? That would be like Christmas, and who believed any-more . . . ?

"We'll lead the way," Carter said. "Tug on my shirt when you want to rest."

Carter and Green moved at the head of the convoy, with Joe in case it was necessary to scout ahead. Then came the ten carriers and Hudson in the rear. If any bearer wanted to desert he had to go past Hudson or Carter or dive run the bush. Sula stayed two hundred yards in the rear in case the enemy came up fast . . . The pace of the convoy had been slow even before Green arrived.

The path began to veer to the right. Green was relieved to look up and see a distant patch of scree where the jungle began to lose its fingerhold on the clinker-strewn slopes of the volcano. A few yards ahead a well-used path plunged over the lip and down the mountainside. Green congratulated himself. So far so good. As they approached the intersection there was a discontented mur-mur from the carriers, one of them began to hobble and said he couldn't go on . . . it was the man with the stoved-in head. Carter stepped forward and gleaned that the man was saying that his village lay down the track and he had a lame foot and couldn't go on. Then more carriers said they wanted to go no further. Carter looked and could see where the village lay by some pinpoints of light on a distant ridge. There was a fierce argument in whispers. Hudson moved in, offering a slight increase in the reward already promised, mingled with threats of what he would persuade Baka to do to any man who reneged. Joe looked at the ringleader as if he'd like to kill him. It was clear by the man's surly look as he took up his load that he was no longer reliable. Clearly, they were sitting on a powder keg, in more ways than one.

After a few hundred yards the path was blocked by the remains of a recent landslide of glistening earth, and the carriers immedi-ately began to murmur. Not only would it be difficult to cross this

197

obstacle but their tracks would be clearly visible to any Jap patrol. Joe promptly waded into the soft earth and began to pick his way around and over obstacles. The carriers watched, apprehensively, until he was swallowed up by the darkness. Hudson looked at Carter, then at his watch. They were behind schedule and falling further behind with every second.

Four minutes later Joe returned. "It gets better," he told Hudson.

"I've heard that before," Carter said.

Hudson detailed Carter and Green to accompany Joe and began to rouse the carriers. Green was sandwiched between Carter and Joe and received help from each as he panted over the obstacles, sometimes up to the waist in wet earth.

"Are you okay?" Carter asked as he sprawled across the trunk of a fallen redwood.

Green nodded grimly. "You need my friend Errol Elynn for this number. On the evidence of the films I've seen he's stood up a bit better than I have."

"You're doing great," Carter said.

"Dawn Patrol," Green said.

"What?" Carter sank down behind the tree, pulling Green with him.

"It was just one of his films. Came out to Rabaul just before the Japs. I thought he was a better actor when he was in New Guinea."

"Save your breath," Carter urged.

"He was a damned good tennis player, though," Green went on. "Mind you, you had to be if you turned up on court in a pair of white jodpurs."

Carter pressed his finger to his lips.

Green remained silent for a few seconds, then leaned forward as Carter started to move. "Did I tell you about the time I knocked him down—?"

"So help me, I'll knock *you* down if you don't shut up," Carter said, and moved on before Green could speak.

Behind the carriers, Hudson watched anxiously as the man struggled to keep a foothold. He felt a buried branch stir beneath his feet and with it a tremor ran through the newly stirred earth. It would need no more than a misplaced foot to start a slide. If

198

Matupi generated a fullscale tremor then the whole party might be swept away.

Sula had now caught up with them, wearing the bark coat she'd made keep off the rain. She reported no action at their rear and went back down the track, Hudson looking after her for a few long moments before starting to scramble through the roots. A few less years, he thought, and he might well give Carter some competition . . .

Now the going became tough enough to silence even Green, who could only groan and wheeze as the mountain reared up before them. The vegetation had become thicker so that bush knives were needed on even established paths. At this altitude mosquitoes ceased to be a problem, but leeches thrived. The thighs of the porters were covered by them, looking like weal marks in the darkness.

"How much farther?" Carter asked.

Green stopped, leaned against his rifle, went into a violent spasm of coughing, and for a moment Carter thought he was going to fall. "We've got a way to go yet. Should be a zigzag path up here on the right. Any chance of a spot of light on the subject? I remember there used to be a rather oddly shaped rock opposite it."

"Wait for the moon," Carter said. He couldn't help being skeptical of Green. Even if Joe had been leading the way he would have been worried. The idea that an old Limey who'd once come up here looking for butterflies should be able to find his way around at night was too much . . .

"Ah, I think this is it." Green parted some grass by the side of the road. "That torch, please."

The three words were uttered with an unexpected firmness. Carter shone his flashlight and saw that there *was* a curiously shaped boulder lunging out of the undergrowth.

"I've a rather remarkable visual memory," Green said. "Don't like to sound conceited, but it's true. If you drove me anywhere in a car I could always find my way back." He crossed the path and started peering into the undergrowth. "Here it is. It gets a bit hairy from now on."

He did not exaggerate. The path went straight up the side of the mountain to become no more than a series of vertical stepping-

199

stones, making it necessary to bring the knee up to chest level at each step. Carter offered to take Green's rifle, but the man refused, saying that he was using it as a staff. Carter wondered how he could keep going. The climb must be pulling his joints out of their sockets. Maybe working on the docks had kept him in some kind of physical condition in spite of the starvation rations . . . A large boulder jutted out from the mountain. Carter stood on its edge and looked up. Just visible by the fitful light of the moon was the rim of the volcano. He felt a start of excitement. They really were almost there. After all they had been through it didn't seem possible there could actually be an end to this purgatory.

Behind, the carriers toiled on, their knotted muscles glistening, their eyes wide with concentration and fear. A misplaced step here could cost them their lives no matter what load they were carrying.

On the path Hudson waited, worried. The moonlight was a two-edged weapon . . . it made it easier for them to see—and be seen. Looking toward the summit he could pick out places where the vegetation was beginning to be divided by outcrops of volcanic rock and shale, which provided less cover than they'd had so far.

The tunnel had to be close.

And there was the noise. Fourteen people and ten heavy loads could not travel silently under these conditions. If the Japs had come this high they'd surely hear them—

Carter had climbed ahead when Green called softly up to him. "Hold on, I think it's around here somewhere."

They were entering a region where a gray-green moss covered every surface like an all-reaching shroud, hung down from trees and creepers and made footholds difficult to judge. What seemed like solid ground could turn out to be a crevasse between two rocks covered by the treacherous lichen. The risk of a fatal error by the carriers was now multiplied . . . Carter called a halt and waited for Green to find his bearings. He looked hopefully at Joe, who shook his head. Apart from the moss, this scoop of vegetation on a steep mountainside had no easily identifiable feature to distinguish it from any other spot they had paused at.

Green obviously thought differently, climbed up to Carter's side and looked down to where he'd been standing. "This is definitely it," he said. "I can see the Birdwing as if it was yesterday—"

"You said it was a Grass Yellow when you first talked to us," Carter said.

Green looked annoyed. "Are you sure?"

"Positive," Carter said, and couldn't resist adding, "I have a rather remarkable verbal memory."

Green ignored it, started to ease himself down the way he had come. Carter followed, helping where he could. On the rocks, the carriers put down their loads and waited in grudging silence.

"It's damn annoying," Green said, as if he had misplaced a collar stud. "I know it's around here." He moved into the waist-high vegetation and prodded at the lichen-hung mountainside with his bayonet. There was the unmistakable sound of steel meeting rock.

Carter scrambled down from the rock and moved to Green's side. "Look, there must be a million places on the mountain that look exactly like this."

And saying it he struck angrily at the moss, and suddenly felt his fist traveling through space. Thrown off balance, he fell forward. The ground disappeared beneath his feet. For what seemed eternity he hung there in space, then met a hard, unyielding surface that drove his knees toward his face and sent him sprawling backward, the wind knocked out of him. He felt around in the pitch darkness, looked up to see Green's face silhouetted against the gray sky.

"Well done, old chap," Green said. "You've found it."

Chapter Twenty-Two

CARTER fumbled for his flashlight, thinking that the most eerie thing about this darkness was that it was warm . . . the inside of caves in his experience had always been cool and clammy. But there was no scent of moisture in this air. It was like standing in front of a freshly opened oven.

He pressed the flashlight's button, and a dim circle of light revealed that he'd fallen onto a table of rain-spattered rock that sloped down to a narrow opening like the mouth of a funnel. The rock rose steeply above his head, and water was still dripping from a recent storm. Where it had formed small pools on the cave floor, the surface was steaming as the heat evaporated it—a sudden shape invaded the air, and a bat with a wingspan like an eagle swooped down and under the rock, delivering an admonishing squeak.

Carter looked at the tunnel. Somehow he'd been expecting something much larger, a hole the size of a subway tunnel that an army might march through. He picked himself up and went forward to shine the light under the rock overhang. The tunnel opened up on the other side but was still not high enough for a man to walk upright in. What was noticeable was the smell that prickled his nostrils—the acrid smell of sulphur.

"You all right? You came rather a cropper."

"I'm fine," he muttered, and started to shine his flashlight at footholds in the rock. "Tell Hudson we've found it and get the boys to start lowering the stuff down.

"Right."

Green's head disappeared and after a few minutes Carter began to wonder where the others were. Impatiently he climbed to the mouth of the cave and found Hudson and Joe involved in a bitter dispute with the carriers, all of whom were refusing to go any further. In particular, the man with the cleft head, who kept pointing to his foot and turning the sole upward as if to indicate that he was carrying a thorn. The other carriers looked warily at the mouth of the cave as if expecting a demon to emerge from it.

Joe was determined that his fellow tribesmen should carry the explosives into the tunnel and fulfill their contract. The carriers were as adamant that they would not. The spirits of the mountain would strike them down if they entered Matupi's belly. Just to walk on his skin was to invite trouble.

Hudson was certain that it was the man with the cleft head who was causing the trouble, a self-appointed spokesman who did most of the talking while the others merely nodded. Now that the loads were outside the cave they could do without him. The longer they stood here, the greater the risk of the Japs stumbling across them. To be caught a few yards from their goal . . .

Hudson took off his pack and removed enough salt and tobacco for one man. He gave it to the troublemaker, thanked him for his efforts and, expressing the wish that his leg would soon be perfectly recovered, sent him on his way. The man departed almost unwillingly, as if suspicious that he was being forced to miss out on something. His followers looked at each other for a new spokesman and then, when none was forthcoming, followed Joe's lead and started moving the explosives to the lip of the cave.

Ropes of liana were cut and several men scrambled down into the cave to receive the loads as they were lowered. Carter watched the bulky shapes coming down toward him and thought back to the transfer operation from submarine to tossing dinghy. Had that really been only two days before? When Jerry Johnson had been alive . . .?

Major Yukichi pulled his waterproof cloak tighter around his shoulders and listened to the spasmodic drip, drip of rain from the leaves. The gap between each sound was becoming longer. The heavy rain had stopped over an hour ago and bright moonlight was fragmented through the undergrowth. Yukichi was beginning to face up to the fact that he had been wrong. The raiding party, it seemed, had not been planning to assassinate Yamamoto when he took off from the airfield. Perhaps they were not even on the mountain. It was conceivable they had died in the swamp. The man whose body they had recovered might have been struggling on by himself after having left his dead comrades. All the planning and deployment of men and materials had been for nothing . . . well, not for nothing. The primary objective of the operation had been achieved.

Yamamoto was alive and safe.

Yukichi yawned. He had now been on the mountain since the admiral's plane took off. There was no point in waiting here in ambush any longer. He would order all units to return to base and place patrols on a pre-alarm footing.

He looked across the trees to the distant mountain rising above banks of serene white cloud, half-closed his eyes and could see his homeland in northern Honshu . . . the forests of pine and sugi, of oaks, maples, and keaki. Those scars on the hillside could have concealed a Buddhist temple or the graceful tower of a pagoda. He looked again at the banks of cloud and made up a poem that he would send with his next letter to his wife.

Now beneath the moon,
Clouds pass like pillow;
I wish my head on one,
My face next to yours.

His creative flight was aborted by a tug on the string attached to his ankle. Someone was approaching down the track. . . .

CHAPTER TWENTY-THREE

AFTER they had crawled beneath the overhang they had to drag the explosives down the passage. The going was hard and the claustrophobic conditions terrified the carriers. The walls of igneous rock were pitted and calloused, and coated in places with a muddy brown deposit. Carter surmised that the shaft must represent the site of an ancient eruption. The rocks up which they had climbed to reach the cave opening could have been spewed out millions of years ago.

"How far in do we want to go?" Carter's voice echoed before him down the dark corridor. He was still speaking in a hushed whisper, although there was no need for it. No need except that imposed by the atmosphere of the place; it encouraged sepulchral whispers, like the inside of a church.

"We might as well go the whole hog," Hudson said. "The nearer we can get to the middle, the better."

Another bat squeaked overhead. The shadows of its wingtips brushing the walls of the corridor. Green shuddered. "Probably a bloody vampire," he said.

"A horseshoe bat," Hudson said. "You're safe if you're not an insect. There must be a cave around here."

"I can't believe we've really done it," Carter said.

"We haven't," Hudson said. "Not until we've set the fuses."

"How about a song?" Green said. "What do you fancy? *Yankee Doodle Dandy, Waltzing Matilda* or *Rule Brittainia?*"

"You're something, Harry," Carter said, this time with no sarcasm. "When I first saw you tonight I thought you were dead."

"It's my indomitable spirit. Stood me in good stead in my battle with Flynn. Did I ever tell you about that? It was after the tennis club dance—"

"Knock it off, Harry," Hudson said. He shined his pocket flashlight forward. "Looks as if it's opening out ahead, we'll take a look." He motioned to Carter to come with him and adjusted his light to full beam. The roof above their heads soon lifted to a cavernous chamber carved by escaping volcanic matter. The floor was covered with bat droppings; hundreds of bright red eyes glinted down from the ceiling where nursing mothers hung with their young folded in their wing membranes. From the air available it seemed another sill might go off from high in the roof of the chamber. In the corner of the cavern was a floor opening and a drop of about ten feet into another stage of the shaft. The acrid smell was more intense, and there was a noise like a magnified beat of a human heart, a rhythmic pumping noise from the bowels of the earth.

Hudson turned off his light. A faint glow was visible at the mouth of the lower tunnel. He weighed the alternatives: to place the explosive in the chamber, or press on further toward the heart of the volcano. He turned to Carter. "Bring the others up, I'm going to take a look."

Carter returned to the rest of the party and told them about the cavern. The carriers were huddled together, trembling with fear in spite of the heat; it was obvious they could not be expected to go much further. They kept glancing toward the tunnel entrance, and only the presence of Joe's broad frame blocking the way dissuaded

207

them from bolting for it, even at the risk of leaving behind their reward.

The last load had been manhandled into the chamber when Hudson's light could be seen wavering along the lower shaft. His face appeared above floor level, and he shook his head.

"It's amazing. There's a lake of boiling basalt. I can't see the far side of it."

"Should we get the stuff down there?" Carter asked. Unspoken but implicit were the words "or is it too dangerous?"

"Yes. The first fifty or so feet are tough but after that we're in the central cone. It's—" he struggled to find the right word—*"fantastic."* Hudson then pulled himself up and addressed the sullen carriers. Their reaction was the opposite of his enthusiasm. More argument followed and they were finally promised categorically that they could return to their village after the next barrier had been passed. Grudgingly, they prepared to carry their loads.

The entrance to the lower shaft was narrow and tortuous, and it took two men to maneuver each load around, one pulling and one pushing and lifting to move it down the undulating corridor. The heat was suffocating, the floor littered with small boulders, some fused into the rock, others free-moving with sharp rasping edges that threatened the bags as they bumped and ground over the floor.

Carter tried to help Joe, who was carrying the load abandoned by the deserting bearer, and was soon reminded that his mauled arm was becoming useless. The pain had subsided to a throbbing ache but there was little strength left in the arm. He could also feel the ache beginning to spread across his shoulders.

Arms aching, eyes watering, legs and sides scraped by rocks, the carriers emerged from the tunnel like corks from a bottle. Carter followed and rubbed his eyes. The sight that met them was truly amazing.

Below a shore of strangely shaped petrified lava was a smooth-sided basin dropping to a lake of molten matter, hissing and steaming like a witch's cauldron. The regular pulsebeat already heard was now much louder, sending an angry ripple churning through the mass of basalt in fusion. The heat was like standing near an open blast furnace. It was difficult not to imagine that any moment

208

a blazing river of lava would be tapped to pour all over them.

The flashlight beams could find no limit to the great space that formed the hollow central cone of Matupi. The jagged teeth of rock stretched away on both sides. The throbbing mass of lava buckled and broke, into infinity, it seemed.

Carter felt truly diminished. A small human presence seemed an anomoly here. The attempt to interfere with one of nature's most awe-inspiring mysteries, a kind of impertinence. They were literally dwarfed by what lay before them. He could understand the carriers who shrank back against the outer wall, their palms pressed flat against it and a look of wonder on their faces that almost bypassed fear. He thought back to all the signs: the tremors, the boiled fish, the sulphur stream, the yellow tide. It was impossible to believe that they had not been right. Matupi was primed for an eruption.

Hudson held up a hand as a shield against the radiant heat and looked about him. The side of the volcano nearest the town and the airfield would be the natural choice for setting the explosive, but it might not be the most easily breached. Probably better to concentrate the force of the explosion at a spot where a previous eruption had occurred: in and around the tunnel they'd entered by. Carter agreed, and orders were given to the carriers. Sensing that deliverance was at hand the men worked at a frantic pace. The loads were tucked contiguously under the rock that loomed forward to form the roof of the vast chamber, knitting into the twisting convolutions as if they were a part of them. The palm leaf covering was beginning to curl and turn brown with the intense heat. The stench of sulphur coated the inside of the mouth. It was no longer possible to swallow.

Carter opened up his pack and took out the detonators, hoping that neither sea nor marsh had penetrated the container and that the heat would not affect the timing mechanism. The detonators had been tested beyond the most demanding natural conditions, but they hardly even approximated those found here in the molten heart of the volcano. Carter began to place the detonators while Sula and Hudson parceled out the salt and tobacco. The carriers clustered around, argued and complained about the apportionment of their fee.

Carter hesitated. He was still not happy about the detonators. They were hot between his fingers, so hot they seemed to melt. It would be best to test one under the worst conditions available. As near to the side of the lava lake as he could get.

Green appeared beside him, his face awash with sweat, as Carter continued to fiddle with the detonator.

"Reminds me of the night of the dance," Green said, "when I knocked out Errol Flynn. He was a different man when he was drunk . . ."

Preoccupied with the detonator, Carter left Green behind and began to edge toward the insufferable heat of the crucible. He walked until his feet were roasting through the soles of his boots and his eyebrows were singed against his forehead. Thirty feet from the brink he bent down and prepared to release the detonator—

And two powerful searchlights shone down as if an electric light had been switched on. Joe spun around with his Sten gun rising to his hip. A brief yammer of automatic fire, and Joe fell backward, blood spouting from his body. His hands scrabbled against the rock and lay still. Japanese voices shouted that no one move, echoed away into a silence broken only by the frenzied pulsing of the lava lake. . . .

Major Yukichi stood behind one of the searchlights and assessed what he saw—the dead native with the gun, the girl on her knees with the gun beside her, the two whites. The cowering local carriers in the background he was less interested in.

When he advanced he saw that one of the whites was wearing a Japanese uniform—no doubt stripped from the man he'd murdered in the swamps. Beheading was too good for this scum. The two men looked at him with exhausted eyes, bitter and ravaged. He was surprised how old they seemed. Perhaps it was the strong light on their haggard, pitted faces. He turned to the girl. She looked toward the light with undisguised loathing.

So, at last he had the four of them. And just when he had been about to call off the search patrol. Damn fortunate that the talkative carrier had strolled into their hands carrying his bag of salt and tobacco. Hardly any inducement had been needed to make him tell them why he was breaking the curfew and where he'd come from.

In fact, he'd seemed rather pleased to lead them back to the cave entrance . . . Yukichi now kicked the gun away from the girl's grasp, watched as it clattered across the rocks. A couple of words and one of the searchlights veered toward the loads. He approached them and spoke again. A soldier stepped forward and swung a bush knife —a gasp from the carriers, and an order to stop from Yukichi, who tore back the leaf covering. The shiny transparent bags seemed to contain white powder. Yukichi was puzzled for a moment, until he found the first detonator. He looked around at the combined bulk of the square bundles and whistled through his teeth. Incredible. The bags contained explosives, and these people had been intending to detonate an explosion inside the volcano . . . trying to start an eruption that would bring a tidal wave of lava down on Rabaul . . . In a way he couldn't help feeling a certain grudging admiration. It was a scheme that showed a bravura imagination, and it had come within a breath of being implemented. If he had called off the ambush five minutes earlier—

A high-flung spatter of lava warned against complacency. The volcano was clearly in a highly volatile condition. Perhaps the Australians had gotten special information during their time at Rabaul and knew when it was likely to erupt. It was probably this knowledge that had led to the formation of the plan . . . If the lava started to expand over the lip of the subcrater, as it was threatening to do, then the explosive would go off without detonators. The volcano might erupt of its own accord at any moment. An expert opinion would be needed but this would take time. Almost certainly somebody would have to be brought from Japan. In the meantime the presence of the explosive anywhere in the vicinity of Matupi was an enormous threat. The capture of these four invaders was hardly the end of the problem.

He began to shout orders. More soldiers had emerged from the tunnel and moving in the confused brilliance of the searchlights began to pressure the carriers once again to take up their loads and drag them from the chamber.

Sula and Hudson were forced to lie on the hot rock. Carter too . . . When the searchlight first came on he'd been stooping by the lava lake forty feet away from the others. He had dived behind some rocks and had lain there, hearing the burst of automatic fire

211

that had killed Joe, the sound of his body falling and the clatter of his weapon hitting the rock. It was unbearably hot but he didn't dare move. With every Jap voice he expected momentary discovery, but no one had come near him. The heat of the lava was enough to drive anyone back, he realized, and the Japs were only looking for *four invaders.* They apparently still didn't know that Green had been taken from the prison camp.

And this was their only hope. He *had* to avoid capture, except how much pain could he take? His feet were toward the lava lake and he could smell the rubber soles of his boots melting; inside them his feet were literally baking. The rocks he lay on were like the hot plates of an oven, lifting the skin from his body. At every point where his flesh touched rock it was blistering. The hairs inside his nostrils were singed, and to breathe the dry sulphur-laden air was terribly painful. He wanted to stand up and fire and a burst into the explosive so that the whole thing went up, Mission accomplished, end of the agony . . . Except he wasn't in the business of sentencing people to death. He stifled the desire to scream. Suddenly one of the searchlights went out. He heard footsteps approaching. His fingers brushed against the hot metal of his weapon. The footsteps had stopped. Was a smiling soldier looking down at him, his finger curling round the trigger of his automatic? He heard a slight expulsion of air as somebody stooped to retrieve something, and the footsteps moved away . . . One of them had been ordered to pick up Sula's gun. Jesus . . . Finally, the number of voices in the chamber began to diminish and he could hear the muffled sounds of movement back up the tunnel. The artificial light began to drain away, then completely disappeared. Silence now, except for the rhythmic pumping of the lava, which seemed to have accelerated.

Carter counted off ten more seconds, then jerked his scorched flesh away from the crucible. He ran a dozen unsteady steps and nearly sprawled over Joe's body. He looked almost majestic in death, the flickering light from the lava playing on his gleaming black chest. The inside of the volcano was a fitting Valhalla.

Carter pressed his flashlight, it did not work. He cursed and looked about him. All the equipment and arms had been taken, including the explosives and detonators. The detonators—he

212

remembered that he'd been testing one when the Japs arrived. Should he bother to try to retrieve it? He hesitated, turned to face the lava. He might need it, if it hadn't melted away or become too unstable to handle. Taking a deep breath he ran back and picked up the detonator in his blistered fingers. It was too hot to hold and he threw it behind him, feeling his hair scorch as the close-range glare of the molten lava threatened to blind him. The heat lanced deep into his eyes. If he breathed in he would burn out his lungs. He picked up the detonator, tried to cool it by spitting on it, but it was impossible to work up any saliva—the inside of his mouth was dry. He got it into one of his pockets. Now, somehow, he had to find his way out in the dark. He must not lose touch with the others. He was, face it, their only hope.

When they came out into the open air from the cave Hudson saw there were about twenty soldiers, all heavily armed and wearing helmets. A force of marines, by the look of them. Showing his teeth in a mocking leer was the carrier who had been sent home and who was obviously responsible for their discovery. Hudson felt sick. He should never have let the man go. He was a troublemaker and there had always been the chance that he would blunder into a Jap patrol. It seemed so obvious, now.

Sula came out, and the man strutted toward her, as if eager to show her that his limp had magically disappeared. Sula let him get near, then lashed out with a kick to his testicles. The pitch of his screech was shattering as he collapsed, knees drawn up against his chest. Someone instantly kicked Sula's feet from beneath her, an automatic was pressed against her temple, and she, Hudson, and Green were manacled.

Yukichi hurried to the radio operator and told him that he wished to speak with General Koji. Urgent.

CHAPTER TWENTY-FOUR

GENERAL Koji was clearly agitated. "You heard what Admiral Yamamoto said during the inspection, Namura. More attention must be paid to the condition of the prisoners. We must consider increasing their rations."

Colonel Namura shifted uneasily. The skin in his eyeless socket was bunched together like a knot. "At the expense of our own men?"

Koji said nothing.

Namura took advantage of the silence. "I am a combat officer, general. For a man in my position to be responsible for prisoners and internees, it is"—he broke off trying to find the right word—"demeaning."

"Nevertheless it must be done. And efficiently. The discipline at the camp is lax. This drunken soldier who has disappeared—"

"A madman, general. Nothing he did would surprise me. Twice

214

he has gone absent without leave. He probably has a still in the jungle. That is another problem I labor under—the quality of the men placed at my disposal. All the units that are asked to supply men for duty at the camp take the opportunity to purge themselves of their most degenerate elements—"

"I am not interested in excuses. I am interested in action," Koji snapped. "You must instill in these men your own tenacity and sense of duty. You have never failed in the field. Give me no cause for complaint now. When the prisoners are brought here to work in the tunnels they require diligent supervision."

"I am trained to command soldiers, not coolies," Namura said stubbornly.

General Koji sighed. Like Yukichi and every other officer in the Imperial Army he found it difficult not to sympathize with Namura's attitude. To him, too, the internees were a nuisance and the prisoners an execration. The thought that men in full possession of their faculties could lay down their arms and surrender was painful to him. Such creatures were so craven as to have forfeited all right to be treated like human beings. To have to associate with them was to be spiritually tainted. Nevertheless, it must be done—

A discreet tap at the door, and Koji's personal radioman appeared. "I have Major Yukichi on the radio, sir. He says it's urgent."

Koji stood up and beckoned Namura to follow him.

"Any word from Bougainville?"

The radioman shook his head as he stood aside and held open the door. "No sir."

"Strange. We will contact them after I have spoken to Yukichi." He strode down the musty corridor and into the small room banked to the ceiling with powerful transmitters. The radioman's pad and headphones lay on a small table surrounded by code books. Koji sat at the table and reached for the headphones. Namura and the operator stood behind him.

"Samurai One. This is Shogun speaking."

"Samurai One to Shogun." Yukichi's voice was clearly audible through the static. He spoke slowly, accentuating each word. "Have intercepted an enemy party. One killed, three captured.

215

Also large quantity of unfamiliar high explosive carried by ten bearers. Enemy was in process of placing explosive inside crater of Matupi—"

Sounds of amazement from the three men in the room. For the moment all rank had disappeared.

"—I believe that volcano is about to erupt. Repeat, about to erupt. If explosive ignites, the outcome could be catastrophic. Have you understood me so far? Over."

Koji swallowed. "Message understood. Take every precaution and move explosive to nearest road. We will organize trucks to transport it to barge for disposal at sea. Report your position and where you estimate you will reach road." He stood up and shoved the headphones into the hands of the operator, who started to take down map references.

"If the volcano erupts," Koji told Namura, "there is serious danger to the tunnel system. Take all available men—including the prisoners—and set them to filling sandbags and blocking the entrance. Find a barge. There's a supply convoy standing off tonight, isn't there?"

"Yes, sir," Namura said. "Nearly all the barges are unloading materiel, but there is one in for servicing that I think we can use."

"Confirm that. If it's out of action we'll have to take a barge off the convoy detail."

"What about the airfield?" Namura asked.

"Red Alert, everything standing by to take off. We'll have only a few minutes if Matupi erupts."

The operator turned toward Koji. "Have you anything more for Major Yukichi, sir?"

Koji leaned toward the mouthpiece. "Shogun to Samurai One. Well done. Return to base immediately, with prisoners . . ."

Yukichi got up from his knees beside the radio and took a deep breath before beginning to issue orders. Away from the suffocating heat of the interior the air seemed cool. Calling over his lieutenant, he told him he and fifteen men were going to be responsible for conducting the carriers and explosives to the road. He indicated the rendezvous point on the map and suggested a route that avoided the landslide. The lieutenant asked him what was to be

216

done with the carriers at the other end. Yukichi told him that when there was no further use for them they were to be taken to the center of the nearest village that could be reached by road and shot. This would provide a warning for the inhabitants.

The lieutenant nodded, saluted, folded his map and returned it to his case as he began to issue his own orders.

Yukichi called up his best sergeant and told him to select the five most trusted men in the party. A length of chain was procured and threaded through the manacled hands of Hudson, Green and Sula, fastening them together in a cumberous line. As soon as it was secured a blow from a rifle butt urged Hudson forward.

On the slab of rock the turncoat carrier rose unsteadily to his feet and was promptly thrust toward the nearest load. The first word of crotch-grasping protest brought the flat of a rifle stock against the side of his jaw and a stream of Japanese that left no doubt about its meaning. He hurried toward a load before the rifle could be raised again.

From behind the screen of moss that hung down over the entrance of the cave Carter watched the scene. The escape from the heart of the volcano in the dark had been terrible. He'd never been sure whether he was taking the right way or diverging into a labyrinth of tunnels there'd be no escape from. He'd not been able to see anything until the gray circle of light at the end of the first tunnel. Now that he had escaped he had to watch Hudson, Sula and Green being led away in chains, and couldn't follow them because the carriers were still loading.

The Japs were dividing into two parties, that much was obvious. The moon was now shining brightly and he could see that seven men were accompanying his people, the rest staying with the explosives. He looked sideways and saw that the moss curtain extended along the side of the mountain. Maybe if he edged along behind it he could bypass the slower-moving carriers. Once they'd joined a track he would never be able to get past them . . .

The rock was still wet. He sank to his blistered knees and pressed his mouth to the rainwater that had gathered in a shallow depression. His split lips stung, but there was a relief in being able to swallow again. He got up and climbed across the rock to the side of the mountain, holding his gun in his fast-weakening right hand. He waited a few seconds, then pressed on until the damp moss was brushing against his face. Hoping that no eyes were turned toward the mountain he continued to edge along until human noises began to fade. Looking down in the moonlight he could see a steep descent to where the path ought to be, picking its way through grass-strewn clinkers and an occasional outcrop of heat-blasted rock. He lowered himself and tested the clinker with his foot. It seemed to have welded into a solid mass. Slowly, he began to make his way down, preselecting each objective on the route and gauging the number of steps and footholds needed to reach it. Pain and exhaustion were draining him. Keep *moving,* he told himself, or pretty soon you won't be able to move at all . . . He managed to reach the path, and was now further 'round the mountain than he had been when they branched off. He had to retrace his steps. He moved carefully, prepared to go into the undergrowth at the slightest warning. After about fifty yards he heard someone descending to his left. A light flashed and a Japanese voice cursed a slight fall of stones.

Carter ducked down the edge of the path and saw the first two marines emerge. And then came Hudson, followed by Sula and Green. The chain that joined them rattled and glinted in the moonlight. Green was staggering, it looked as if his legs would give out at any moment. One of the marines was an officer. He wore a cap instead of a helmet and carried a large pistol. He pushed forward now along the path to station himself behind Sula, and spoke urgently. The party began to move forward at a smart pace that jerked Green along like a reluctant beast of burden.

Carter let them get twenty yards ahead, then followed, feeling as he had when he'd been alone in the ocean seeing the dinghy drifting away from him. He was blindly following Hudson and the others, but what could he achieve against seven heavily armed Japanese marines? He might account for one or two but the others would quickly take cover and flush him out. Further, manacled and chained together as they were, Hudson's group had no chance of breaking loose into the bush; they'd be cut down instantly if they came under fire, and there was no chance of getting far enough ahead of them to try an ambush. He'd just have to continue tagging along . . .

A quarter of a mile down the path the marines suddenly stopped and went for cover. Lights were approaching. Challenges were made and replied to in Japanese and there was an excited round of greetings. Another patrol had arrived. Carter could hear the chain rattling as the prisoners were dragged forward to be shown off. There was the sound of blows and a cry of pain that he recognized as coming from Green.

The new patrol was a large one by the sound of it. His position seemed even more futile. He was powerless by himself. Lights flashed again and men started to move toward him. Carter barely had time to take cover before boots went swishing past, presumably going to reinforce the party accompanying the explosives. He counted ten pairs of feet. If that was half the patrol then there were now *seventeen* men guarding the prisoners.

Clinging to the mountainside below the path, Carter looked about him. There was a large gap in the clouds and the moon shone down, throwing a ghostly gray light over the tight folds of jungle and the razor-back ridges that stretched away to become part of the distant mountains. Paths ran along some of the ridges and zigzagged up their sides through patches of cultivated land hacked from the dense undergrowth. Clinging to the topmost sides of the ridges were clusters of huts positioned to give the best vantage point against attack by neighboring villages.

Carter oriented himself in relation to Rabaul, invisible around the side of the mountain, and realized that he was looking down at the village from which the carriers had come.

Joe's village. In one of those huts was Baka, unaware that his son was dead.

Baka was Hudson's friend. He had hidden the explosives and found them carriers. Now he was their only chance. Could he be persuaded to put together a rescue party?

A good deal would depend on his reaction to his son's death. Would he be eager for revenge or would his mood turn to bitterness and recrimination against the ones who'd put Joe's life in such peril? No use speculating, he had no alternative. He began calculating the distance to the village and the best route to take. He knew it meant abandoning the others but he also knew that he was no use tagging along behind them.

The far side of the valley leading to the ridge showed a steeply dropping path, the actual course of which could not be seen because of the convex swelling of the mountainside and the vegetation. Down to the right was a ragged line running through the grass. Carter did not waste time but lunged down the mountainside. He knew that he was making a noise, but hoped the Japs would think it came from a cassowary or a litter of wild pigs. There was no time for careful movement. Blisters rubbed off against the rocks, and he began to wonder if he had a square inch of skin left on his body.

He paused to look back and could see isolated pinpoints of light on the mountainside. Fortunately they seemed to be moving horizontally, the carriers had only just got down the staircase of giant rocks. He struggled on and fell into the path, a deep furrow almost overgrown with grass. The descent was so slippery and precipitous that Carter could not keep his feet and was constantly forced to cling to the razor-sharp grass to stay upright. His hands were wet with blood and his injured arm ached with a pain that ricocheted through the whole of the right side of his body. When he reached the bottom he slipped and fell ten feet to land in a narrow stream swollen with the water that had run down from the mountains.

Now began the ascent and with it the agony of driving exhausted limbs beyond the pain barrier. Waves of dizziness clouded his eyes, already half-closed by insect bites. After five minutes' climbing he was above the dense thicket of trees that crowded in around the stream and could see across to Matupi and the route he'd taken. He wiped the sweat from his forehead and looked below the looming black outline of the volcano. A file of lights was descending the mountainside and coming toward him. He saw the lights bob and waver as the men holding them hesitated before selecting a foothold. Then they came on, dropping relentlessly. Had the Japs seen him? Unlikely. They must be planning a punitive expedition against the carriers' village. The soldiers on the mountain path had seemed voluble and excited, hot for action.

Carter resumed his scramble up the ridge, and now he had another incentive to reach the village . . . to warn its inhabitants of what was coming down on them.

He stumbled and fell awkwardly, jarring his injured arm, dragged himself up, gasping, and watched his knee rise toward his face as he sought the next slippery foothold. For fifteen minutes he hardly raised his head, trying to preserve a dogged rhythm that would keep one foot rising in front of the other. When he looked up it was to find himself in a grove of bamboos, their leaves rustling in the slight breeze. The path took a long diagonal turn along the side of the ridge and he was able to straighten and rub his aching back as he walked. Ahead of him he could see the top of the ridge silhouetted against the sky and estimated that the village must be above him.

He glanced up into the trees and started back. A man was looking down at him. A man hunched on an untidy throne of stakes and twigs like a shored-up bird's nest. The man did not move but leaned forward showing all his teeth in a wide, mocking grin. He was withered, wasted, his skin was pocked. His eyes were black holes and he had no nose, only a scrap of material thrust like a wedge into the nasal orifice. His flesh was hollow parchment, wrinkled and split by time. One hand leaned forward across a knee, the bony finger pointing admonishingly.

The man was dead.

Carter looked around the grove and saw that the trees were full of such men, each propped in a sitting position on an untidy scaffold, each long since killed. The bodies had been preserved, probably by smoking. The grove was apparently some kind of burial ground. The rows of white teeth grinned in the moonlight, and Carter shivered. If he had need of omens this was distinctly not the place to find them.

He willed himself forward, heard a dog barking as he came around a bend where the path rose steeply. He must be near the village now. Soon he saw a glimpse of thatch among the palms and a rattan fence interwoven with spiky palm leaves. More dogs started to bark. He started toward a hut and was met by a wild-eyed man grasping a spear that he was clearly prepared to throw. The man crouched at the doorway of his hut and jerked back his arm threateningly. Carter decided that it was advisable to stop in his tracks.

"Chief Place?" he said, trying to introduce a question mark into his voice. *"Luluai?"* He pointed over his shoulder. "Japan 'e come. *Raus!"*

The last words were more successfully interpreted than the first. The native looked in the direction Carter had pointed and lowered his spear, listened a moment and could obviously hear something beyond the range of Carter's ears. He stared once more into Carter's face, clearly puzzled by the sudden arrival of an exhausted white man in the middle of the night, and pointed further up the hillside. The barking of dogs now sounded from a different side of the village and Carter guessed that the Japs had taken a shortcut through the burial ground. They must know the village from their patroling activities. He ran across open ground slippery with rain and heard the first shots without knowing whether they were aimed at him. A semicircle of huts loomed up behind an ornamental stockade and he hurdled it as men, women and children began to spill into the open. The second man he blundered into was Baka, clutching a bow and long arrows.

"Japan 'e come!" he repeated.

The old man seized his arm in a grip of steel. "Joe?"

Carter shook his head.

Baka did not release his hand but tightened his grip.

Carter saw the ash daubed on the man's face. It was a sign of mourning. How had he known that his son was dead? Two long bursts of automatic fire came through the flimsy walls of the huts. The Japanese were firing to kill anyone inside them. Sago fronds splintered into chaff. A child screamed.

Carter's first instinct was to return the fire but he restrained himself. At the moment the soldiers did not know he existed. They soon would if a machine gun opened up.

The clearing was full of shouting people. A woman went down, her hands clasping her thigh. Baka was calling to men as they ran past, but panic had taken over and Carter knew that if he stayed where he was he would quickly be killed. He ran hard for the far side of the village, Baka after him. A man in front of them was hit and spun over and over like a rabbit picked off in full flight. Carter veered, threw himself down behind a hut as bullets sprayed the air above his head. He turned and saw that Baka and two warriors

222

were lying beside him. Beneath the hut a pig calmly continued to nose among the human excrement, which formed the mainstay of its diet.

Carter now sniffed smoke and heard the crackle of flames. They had to keep moving. He wriggled backward to where the ground began to fall away and had just slid behind a huge ficus tree when he saw his first Japanese soldier. The man was moving quietly up the slope, his weapon ready. He was clearly waiting for anyone who ran from the huts. Carter heard Baka moving beside him and saw the chief drawing back his bow. A twang and a thump and the soldier placed his hand against his neck as if stung by an insect. If he still possessed a sense of touch at that moment he must have felt the shaft of the arrow that had transfixed his neck. His fingers were still at his neck as his knees buckled and he slumped forward, legs twitching. After a few seconds the legs stopped.

More huts were burning, and a fresh breeze fanned smoke down the hillside. Flames roared skyward and turned walls of interwoven sago palm into blazing banners. The Japanese were moving through the village, shooting and bayoneting anyone that moved. They obviously intended that their reprisal should be complete, that the word should spread through the whole peninsula about what happened to those who went against them.

Carter hesitated. Two more soldiers were approaching up the hillside. He moved back behind the tree, wondering if he'd been seen. There was a warning call as the body of the dead soldier was found. Immediately, bullets started kicking up earth around the ficus tree. The soldiers were firing blind at the point where they assumed the arrow had come from. Carter huddled behind the tree with Baka and the two warriors, knowing that he had split-seconds to come to a decision . . . If he used his weapon he would give himself away. If he did not, he would die. Abruptly the Japs stopped firing. One of them was probably crawling out among the trees. There was a great whoosh and a hut collapsed in a cloud of sparks. At the same instant half a dozen terrified women and children ran from the burning village, and were silhouetted against the flames.

Carter saw a chance that the troops' attention would be diverted and ran straight ahead, trying to keep the ficus tree between himself and them. There was a cane fence surrounding a garden, and he dropped his shoulder and went through it as if it was a paper hoop. It was only then that bullets whistled around his head and he heard someone call out. He did not stop. Cassava and sweet potato crunched underfoot as he slithered and slipped in the soft cultivated earth. Then there was another wall and he went through that too, feeling nothing beneath his feet. The ground opened up, and he fell, pitching forward with a force that jerked his gun from his grasp. He rolled over several times and came to rest with the wind knocked out of him.

Head whirling, he clawed his way to a kneeling position to find that he'd plunged over the far side of the ridge. The fence he'd crashed through marked the border of the village gardens. Above his head a red glow lit up the sky and he could still hear the crackling flames and sounds of the dying.

Baka managed to scramble down beside him with another man who got his weapon for him. There was no sign of the other warrior.

The three of them lay still for a few moments, then when there were no sounds of pursuit Baka led the way down into the shelter of the thick jungle. Carter was barely able to stand upright. He had come for help and was leaving with an old man and a so-called warrior who was hardly more than a boy.

The night was half over, and everything they had so nearly achieved lay in ruins.

Chapter Twenty-Five

HUDSON sprawled in the back of the truck, his shoulders against the driver's cab. Green lay at his feet, occasionally twitching convulsively. He was nearer death than life now and the pendulum was not going to swing back. Sula sat erect against the side of the lorry, the look of defiance she'd managed since their capture was still there.

They were going through the dock area devastated by American bombing, no fixed installation remained standing. Gutted warehouses and cranes were twisted beyond recognition to look like fire-scorched trees. There were heaps of rubble, some of it still smoking. But this did not mean that the port was out of action.

Everywhere he looked Hudson could see groups of men working. Some were manhandling a truck that had been burned out in an earlier raid and was half blocking an approaching road to the wharves. Others were working on the wharves themselves, unload-

225

ing the flat-bottomed barges packed to the gunwales with ammunition cases and gasoline cans, then loading the contents onto trucks that waited with engines revving. Mobile cranes bumped over the quays. The operation was geared to speed and instant dispersal in the event of an air raid.

Hudson saw to his amazement that some of the wharves were made from the hulls of bombed vessels that had been towed to the side of the dock and filled in with cement. As he watched, a man emerged from the belowdeck area, which could clearly be used as a shelter during an air attack. Hudson looked out to sea but could only detect the shielded red lights of the barges, which would not be visible from the air. The ships they were plying to were obviously dispersed outside the harbor to minimize the risk of air attack.

The truck slowed down to allow a fully laden truck to pull out, and Hudson looked past the barrel of the submachine gun that rested almost against his temple and saw something in the water that puzzled him. At first he thought it was a submerged submarine being towed by a barge but then realized that the long cigar shape, its outline barely breaking the water, must itself be a submersible barge that could be used for transporting gasoline or oil without being spotted from the air. A few minutes' firsthand observation was making it clear how these people were able to outwit all the Americans' long-range attempts to prevent them from building up supplies of men, arms and provisions, and, once entrenched, how difficult it would be to budge them. To remove a limpet from a rock was hard enough, but to remove a limpet from *inside* a rock . . .

The truck started up again and Hudson looked at the scene of devastation and frenetic activity about him and thought back to the town he had known . . . orderly lines of red- and green-roofed bungalows with wide verandas set behind avenues of shady trees, each street named after a different species of tree, Yara Avenue lined with tall casuarina trees, Mango Avenue with its rows of mangoes, Malaguna Avenue with its line of huge rain trees planted in the middle of the wide road . . . There'd been well-kept lawns, pathways of white coral, hedges of coleus, croton, hibiscus and frangipani, bright colors dozing under a tropical sun . . . Now the colors were dust-gray and mud-brown. Most of the bungalows had been swept away and the trees blasted down to their roots. The sleepy tropical town had been bombed flat.

The truck left the harbor area and with its escort vehicle passed through a roadblock, then entered the road that curved between the narrow strip of coconut palms abutting on the sea and the cliff face. At every tunnel entrance they passed, gangs of men were feverishly filling sandbags and building walls across the opening. The Japs had not lost any time.

Ahead, a light waved them down. The truck slowed to a halt. The guard standing up in the opening beside the driver pressed the muzzle of his machine gun into Hudson's neck. If anything happened, Hudson knew, he was going to be the first to go. In his present mood the thought did not really bother him all that much.

Almost contemptuously he twisted his hand to push the barrel aside and peer through the opening in the back of the cab. To his amazement he saw that the stern of a barge was emerging from one of the tunnels. It rested on a trolley of rough-hewn logs, which in turn glided on a pair of rails which sloped down through the palms toward the sea. The short stubby funnel emerged, barely clearing the tunnel root, and then the prow, pushed by three sweating Japanese soldiers, their faces glistening in the moonlight. A wire hawser was attached to the prow and stretched tight as the barge began to slide backward. Hudson could hear the sound of winches creaking as it jerked toward the sea.

So, the barges were kept *inside* the tunnels as well. Which explained why air reconnaissance around the area of the bay had never shown where they were moored. Hudson cursed himself again. What a prize they'd had, and lost.

The hawser went slack now as the barge entered the water, and Hudson's truck started to move forward. As it gathered speed he glanced at the men who were filling sandbags outside the next tunnel entrance—skinny, emaciated Europeans working under the surveillance of Japanese guards. They must have been brought from the camp. The Japs were clearly treating the possible eruption of Matupi as an emergency. Some of the prisoners could hardly lift a bag.

Hudson caught Sula's eye and tried to smile. Her face remained sullen. What was she thinking of? Joe? Carter? The failure of the mission? Who could blame her?

A gap opened up in the palms and Hudson could see across the bay to the outline of Matupi. Dawn was less than a couple of hours away and already a faint gray light was beginning to define the horizon. What had happened to Carter? Had he ever managed to get out of the volcano? He literally prayed that somehow Carter would escape, that somehow one of them would be salvaged from the operation.

There was no hope for the rest.

The six heavy trucks were lined up in a clearing from which stone had once been quarried. The jungle finished abruptly on the semicircular rim, and the ground was patterned with tire marks. Some of the Japanese were smoking when the first bearers arrived, but they conscientiously ground out their cigarettes and nervously straightened their forage caps. Nobody knew what type the explosive was, which gave the imagination much to feed on. Two light tanks were parked strategically and discreetly across the other side of the clearing where it opened onto the track which led to the road.

When the carriers had assembled it was confirmed there were indeed ten loads of explosive. Yukichi's lieutenant responded to the captain in charge of the convoy, and it was agreed that the loads should be allocated two in a truck and a gap of three hundred yards left between each vehicle. The route taken to the embarkation point had been signposted and would avoid passing close to the airfield for security reasons. Each vehicle would carry two armed guards and would proceed no faster than ten miles per hour. The carriers would travel in the sixth truck. Yukichi's lieutenant armed himself with details of the circuitous route and started to give orders for the explosives to be loaded onto the trucks. . . .

Behind a screen of foliage at the top of the quarry, Carter looked down on the scene with an increasing sense of helplessness. He, Baka and the warrior whose name was Tuka had worked their way around from the burning village and had at last caught up with the train of carriers and their guards as they wended their way down the mountain. They were still as powerless to do anything. Worse,

228

the prize was being driven away from them.

There were now forty Japanese below, not including the crews of the two tanks. The tailgate was raised on the first truck and the driver eased forward as if carrying a load of eggshells. An officer watched it pass out of the quarry and down the track, then dropped his arm for the second to follow. The minutes passed with Carter waiting for something—anything—to happen that would give him an opening. One of the tanks had left after the second truck, but its companion remained, the stubby 37-mm gun pointing banefully toward Carter's position, as if daring him to move.

With one load of explosives left, three heavily armed marines started shepherding the carriers toward the final truck. There were some murmurs of protest and suddenly one of the natives broke from the group and ran for the side of the quarry, climbed like a spider and, for a moment Carter thought, was going to escape. Except a stitchwork of bullets climbed faster and he fell backward, landing heavily in an untidy heap. One of the marines walked toward him and fired again. The other carriers climbed silently into the back of the truck.

The last explosives truck received the signal and began to pull out. The carriers were made to lie down in the bottom of their truck in case any of them still had an appetite for escape, and the guards climbed in. Seconds ticked away and the tank still watched, waited. The carrier's truck pulled away and started to bump over the ruts. It slowed down at the entrance to the quarry and the officer climbed in. The tank jerked forward. Soon the quarry was empty and the drone of the vehicles had died away.

Carter stood up and started to follow Baka down to the man who'd been shot. Blood was spreading out beneath his back, some of the bullets had passed through his body. Flies were already abundantly in evidence. Despite the wounds a tremble of life still passed through the man's limbs. One eye stared wide, uncomprehending. Baka dropped to his knees and spoke urgently into the man's ear. At first there was no reply. Then the lips started to move, soundlessly. Baka spoke again in a tone that was almost an order. The eye closed in a wince. Another pause. Then a mumble of words. Baka listened till the man was silent and placed a hand on his shoulder as if in thanks, benediction, then turned to Carter and explained in halting English that the convoy was going to the sea. He picked up a stick and drew a rough map on the ground. Carter saw Matupi, the airfield and the bays. Baka jabbed at a spot to mark their position and then pointed to the side of the main bay beneath the volcano.

Carter looked at the map. They must be going to dump the explosives out at sea. Unless they were planning to take them somewhere by water. Either way, the embarkation point would remain the same. It did not seem far by Baka's rough map, but they had no vehicle . . .

Baka started to draw again with his stick . . . long lines, forming three sides of a rectangle from where they were to the sea. The chief was saying that they could soon reach the sea if they took the path over the hill. Carter looked at the carrier, flies clustered over his eyes and mouth, turned away and dragged himself to his feet. Perhaps the carrier was the lucky one. He was out of it.

Hudson walked down the tunnel, marveling at its length. They must have covered almost four hundred yards already and passed half a dozen intersections with other tunnels that could accommodate an automobile. There were subdued lights strung along the roof at thirty-foot intervals, and a thick concertina tube that must pump air into the interior. One of the side tunnels was obviously used as a hospital. It contained a row of strangely assorted beds, doubtless looted from the houses in the town. In the beds were sick and wounded men being tended by uniformed Japanese nurses. Another tunnel running diagonally across the one they were in had contained forty-eight-inch rubber pipes, smelling of gas and fuel oil which rainbowed in splashes across the rough stone floor. It seemed as if the Japs were also storing fuel in the tunnel.

They passed another tunnel where extractor fans roared and in the foreground men worked with welding equipment on a damaged antiaircraft gun. As far as the eye could see there were mechanics renovating and assembling equipment. It was an impressive sight, not unlike a production line in a modern factory.

Hudson looked at the major who was accompanying them and read the expression in the man's eyes as he glanced about him and looked back. *This* place will never be taken, said the glance. We have done wonders here and we will not give them up . . . Another hundred yards down the slightly sloping tunnel and they came to a brightly lit open space in which several tunnels converged. Looking back, Hudson could see that all but one of them contained rails like the ones on which the barge had been moving. Presumably they were used to transport goods and materiel into the center of the tunnel network.

On one side of the open space was a shelf of rock with a guardrail in front of it. Behind the rail were three doors, one with two armed marines on guard outside it. They snapped to attention as Yukichi approached, the sound of their boots echoing down the long corridors. Yukichi ordered the accompanying guards to hold the prisoners, tapped on the door and slid it open when a voice told him to enter. The door slid shut behind him.

Hudson looked at Sula. She didn't flinch. Green shivered so that the chain rattled, but it was due to fever and exhaustion, not fear. Hudson moved to support him but one of the guards jabbed him away roughly with the muzzle of his rifle.

The door opened and Yukichi reappeared. He said something to the guards and they pushed their prisoners forward.

Hudson blinked as he entered the room. His eyes were still not accustomed to the bright light after the semidarkness of the tunnels. An officer wearing general's insignia and a small mustache rose to his feet.

"Lieutenant General Koji," he said in near-perfect English. "Commander of the Imperial Seventeenth Army. We have been expecting you." He turned toward a figure sitting beside the desk. "May I present Admiral Yamamoto."

Chapter Twenty-Six

HUDSON looked down in disbelief at the short, stocky figure. Yamamoto looked up at him, his aesthetic face a mask. He was wearing a white uniform with epaulettes, four rows of ribbons, and white shoes. He held his white-topped hat on his lap. In this position he seemed withdrawn, almost deferential, somehow not the most feared, and famous, admiral in the Pacific. When he spoke it was with a faint trace of an American accent.

"I am sad," he said. "Yesterday I lost nine friends, but my life was saved—by you." His smile was a bitter one. "Can you tell me a greater irony?"

Hudson said nothing. Yamamoto saw that he was confused and continued.

"When your presence on the island was discovered it was thought that you had found out about my visit to the garrison.

General Koji here believed you had been put ashore to assassinate me."

So that was it, thought Hudson. That explained the patrols, their implacable determination to hunt them down.

"Nobody could understand what you were doing in the area of Matupi. It was heavily defended yet not a place I was likely to visit. Then Major Yukichi—" Yamamoto nodded toward the man—"the tenacious Major Yukichi had an idea. The airfield. As I boarded the plane I would be vulnerable, exposed, an easy target for a sniper aiming from the side of the volcano. He estimated you would be waiting for me when I left for my next destination. I believe my white uniform does tend to make me rather distinctive."

"There are other reasons for your distinction," said Hudson. His tone was double-edged.

Yamamoto ignored it. "I will finish my story. Believing that you intended to kill me at the moment that I boarded the plane it was decided to set a trap for you. Units took up ambush positions on the side of Matupi and around the airfield. They waited to intercept you or to attack you at the moment you opened fire and revealed your position." He paused. "It was a double—the uniform really is more significant than the face—who drove to the airport and boarded the plane with my senior staff." He looked at Koji.

Koji spoke like a man reading a funeral address. "We have recently learned that the plane that would have been carrying Admiral Yamamoto was shot down by American fighters. Up to now, there is no news of any survivors."

"You see why I speak of irony," Yamamoto said. "You would have been delighted to kill me but you have ended up saving my life. Now it appears likely that *you,* at least, had no inkling that I was at Rabaul. You were here solely to make your assault on Matupi." He waved a hand. "Speaking as one soldier to another, I must congratulate you."

"I wish I could find a reason to congratulate you," Hudson said.

There was an angry murmur from Koji that Yamamoto silenced with a gesture. His voice lost none of its measured calm. "I can understand your attitude," he said. "However, I have only one statement to make about my decision to attack Pearl Harbor. When a man is choking the life out of you, you drive your knee into his groin."

Yamamoto then rose to his feet and put on his hat. General Koji got up with him.

"I will go to my room and do some work until it is time for my plane to leave." Yamamoto turned to Yukichi. "Have you any more news?"

"The explosive should be nearly at the dockside now, sir. I will check on the wireless and let you know. After that, another half-hour and it will be outside the harbor. As soon as we receive word that it has been sunk we will leave for the airfield. I calculate that you should be able to take off by dawn."

Yamamoto nodded. "A sample of the explosive is being kept for analysis?"

"Yes, sir."

"And the vulcanologist?"

"We have two arriving at fourteen hundred hours tomorrow."

"Good. I think one of them had better stay here."

"Yes, sir."

Yamamoto turned to the three prisoners. "It is unlikely that we will ever meet again. I salute you."

His hand snapped to his forehead, and he went out.

Barefoot, Carter slipped, slithered and fell down the last twenty feet to the beach. An untidy snaggle of driftwood trapped in the rocks shifted in a tangled mass as the sea rushed through it. Carter took up a position behind it and looked down the narrow strip of beach. Fifty yards ahead a makeshift pontoon jetty stretched out to sea with a concrete bunker behind it. A strip of jungle had been cleared to make a track and a turning area. Some battered oil drums were in evidence.

Carter guessed that the area had once been used as a fuel dump, probably before the tunnel network had been developed. A barge was moored against the jetty, rolling slightly on the swell. There were lights moving on the jetty, and Carter strained to make out how many men were there . . . it looked like three, most likely the crew of the barge waiting for the trucks.

They did not have long to wait. As Baka and Tuka crept up to him the sidelights of the first truck could be glimpsed approaching slowly down the track. What in hell was he going to do? The lights swung round and faced inland as the truck prepared to reverse toward the jetty. Well, get off your ass and make something happen, Carter told himself.

He made a sign to Baka and Tuka and ducked back toward the boulders at the rear of the beach. A colony of tiny crabs scattered. The sharp stones took bits out of Carter's bare blistered feet, but he no longer noticed pain. As he approached the barge at the jetty, he could make out its truncated smokestack and the wheelhouse amidships.

A pinpoint of light showed somebody was smoking at the wheel. That meant four men, or maybe still only three. Two men were walking down the jetty toward the truck. From where he was crouched Carter could not see what was happening but he heard the tailgate going down and soon two figures reappeared, carrying one of the familiar loads. The sky had lightened in the east, and the moon was a luminous ball hanging against a backdrop of white steel. The palm leaf covering had fallen away, and the shiny bags glinted in the moonlight.

The truck revved noisily, simultaneous with the sound of the tailgate slamming, and the driver ground his gears in his eagerness to get away. On the jetty, the two men walked carefully while the pontoon structure undulated between them.

Carter hesitated. Were there any guards left on shore? Was there a chance of seizing the barge and one of the loads before the second truck arrived?

He started forward, then shrank back immediately. Another vehicle was approaching, but it was not a truck. The lights were set much closer together, and the engine note was different. It was the first tank which had overtaken the second truck.

Carter stumbled back beneath the roots and foliage that hung down from the cliff like a screen. He looked toward the barge, his heart hammering. The men had just lifted the first load aboard.

Nine more to come. The minutes ticked away, he was achieving nothing.

General Koji moved around his desk and advanced toward Hudson. His face was angry. "Your tone toward Admiral Yamamoto was impertinent."

Hudson said nothing. He knew that there was no point in trading insults. Anything he said would only make things worse for all of them.

Koji glared at him and turned to Yukichi. "These are the three survivors?"

"Yes, sir. There was also the man who died in the swamp, and we killed a man in the volcano, as I reported over the wireless. These are the other three."

"Two old men and a native woman. It does not say much for Allied resources."

Hudson smiled. "If two old men and a native woman could get so far, perhaps it doesn't say much for your defenses."

Koji studied him. "You appreciate that I would be quite justified in treating you as spies and having you executed." He turned back to his desk. "Your chances of survival depend on the amount of cooperation you give us."

Hudson said nothing. He did not believe that he would ever set foot outside the tunnels alive unless it was to be taken for execution. Every coast-watcher who had been captured had been beheaded, usually after torture. He knew well enough from Jerry Johnson how the Japs behaved. No matter what happened you always ended up the same way. Dead.

"There are some questions that intrigue us," Koji continued. "How did you know about the condition of the volcano?"

Hudson did not look at Green, though he sensed the old man's defiance. Hudson selected a corner of the room and stared at it without speaking.

"How did you bring the explosives to the island?" Koji's voice droned on. "Who were your contacts among the natives?" Silence. "Were you working with your so-called coast-watchers? What were your plans for withdrawal?" He broke off for a few seconds. "It is no good avoiding my eyes. Believe me, my questions *will* receive answers. There is no doubt of it."

The last six words were spoken with a chilling intensity.

Green started to cough and Hudson looked at Sula. Her expression said they must not weaken, she would not . . .

Koji turned to Yukichi. "Where is Colonel Namura?"

"He is sealing the tunnels, sir."

"Ask him to come immediately."

Yukichi bowed and went out.

General Koji sat behind his desk. His eyes moved from Hudson to Sula to Green and back again. One of the guards standing against the wall quickly scratched the end of his nose. He, too, was included in Koji's scrutiny and did not relish seeing the cold snake-eyes rolling over him looking for signs of fear and weakness. Koji believed that with men of a certain caliber, silence was more effective than threats and bluster. Their imagination could furnish better images of terror than he could describe. Until the real pain came.

The door opened and Namura came in, the sides of his cap dark with sweat where it rested against the temples. His empty eye socket gaped intimidatingly. Yukichi was behind him. Both men saluted.

Koji turned to Hudson and said offhandedly, "Your prisoners, colonel."

Namura turned his eye on Hudson, then Sula, then Green. Green's head had fallen on his chest, his chin tucked in close to his body. The expression on Namura's face changed. He advanced to Green, seized his chin and twisted it into the light.

"That man was in the prison camp!"

"What?" Koji came to his feet.

Yukichi stepped forward. "Are you sure?"

"Positive."

"When did you last see him?"

Namura hesitated. "Yesterday. Yes, yesterday. He was in the jail for interrogation."

Koji, Yukichi and Namura looked at each other. It was almost possible to hear their minds working. Sifting, resifting the facts. Making sure that what they were forced to believe was actually true.

237

"Then there is *another* man still free . . ."

Nobody said anything. Hudson looked at their faces, started to smile. Koji slapped him hard across the face.

Yukichi spoke urgently. "I am going to check that the explosives are all right. May I recommend that Admiral Yamamoto does not move from here until I return?"

"Agreed," Koji said. "I will inform all units and issue a Red Alert."

Yukichi saluted and ran out of the room.

Koji turned to Namura. "I am handing over the prisoners for questioning, colonel. You will find out everything they know— *quickly.*"

The air raid siren coincided with the arrival of the last truck. At first Carter thought it was an alarm signal in some way connected with him. Then within seconds he heard the drone of the Liberators and saw the flashes from the antiaircraft gun emplacements ranging 'round the twin horns of the harbor. There was the crackle of exploding shells and puffs of smoke hung in the clear sky, small and concentrated at first, then drifting away like blobs of cloud. Now he could see the planes, flying in a diamond pattern, spread out in clusters of five. Searchlights raked the sky, but the planes were already as visible as a flight of geese. The first sticks of bombs fell, and there was a vicious *crump, crump,* like heavy blows sinking into the pit of a stomach. The sky was suddenly full of cotton wool and spurts of flame. A Liberator was hit and caught fire immediately, as if made of tissue paper. It screamed down, leaving a trail of smoke, and exploded on impact with the sea.

Carter pressed his hands against his ears. The hammer of pounding guns, the shrill whistle of falling bombs, the dull thud of the explosions shook the whole of the wharf area. The bombers were coming nearer. Their bomb run was from one end of the docks to the other. On the jetty men were scattering for the shelter of the concrete bunker. The last load of explosives lay alone and isolated beside the barge. Two of the crew leapt aboard. The third was in the wheelhouse. The last man dived inside the bunker. Inland there was the sound of diesel engines as the two tanks and the truck dispersed into the jungle.

238

And suddenly the barge was defenseless. The realization came on Carter as a bomb fell five hundred yards from the beach, sending timber flailing a hundred feet into the air. He tugged Baka by the arm and started to run down the beach toward the jetty without waiting to see if he was being followed. At any moment he thought something in the flashing, exploding night must hit him. He clawed himself up onto the jetty and started to run. Behind him he heard the thump of bare feet that told him he was not alone.

A stick of bombs fell in the sea a hundred yards away, a fountain of water soared up. The blast also knocked him sideways, and the spray fell in a hissing shower. Beneath him the pontoons slapped the water and the jetty reared like a bucking horse, making it impossible to stand upright.

Carter pulled himself up as the first wave died away. He saw that the last load of explosive was being edged toward the side of the jetty. Every wave-induced tremor that undulated through the floating structure was jogging it nearer to the sea.

As he ran forward a soldier jumped onto the jetty and moved toward the stern line, then looked up in surprise as he saw the figure running toward him. Another bomb screeched down. The man sank to his knees and tried to protect his head with his hands. The bomb exploded in the jungle, bringing a hail of debris clattering down on the wooden planks. Carter shouldered the bale back into the middle of the jetty as the Japanese soldier got to his feet. For a moment, comprehension and a new fear came on his face, until Carter clubbed him into a heap with a blow from his gun, and kept running for the wheelhouse.

A second crewman appeared looking over the side and just had time to call out before Carter hit him. He fell back, clutching his head. Carter ran along the jetty until he was level with the wheelhouse. He saw a man reaching to unhook an automatic and fired a short burst through the glass. The glass shattered and the man slid from view, leaving the automatic swinging gently where his finger had brushed against it.

Carter jumped aboard and made sure that the man in the wheelhouse was dead, turned and nearly fell over the man on deck who was having his throat cut by Tuka. Baka had already dealt with the man by the stern line.

Another bomb fell further along the coast. Carter looked back anxiously down the jetty. No sign of movement from the block-house. The barge was throbbing, the motor running. How the hell did you drive it? It couldn't be too complicated.

He called to Baka and Tuka to cast off the lines and bring the dead Japanese and the explosives aboard. He tried to breathe normally and looked at the dials, gauges, and levers with considerably less confidence. A quick glance told him that everybody was aboard. Then he turned a lever to the left. The noise of the engine increased but there was no indication that power was being transmitted to the propeller. Then the nose of the barge started to swing around toward the shore. He could feel Baka and Tuka's eyes on him. Unless he did something fast the barge would drift gently onto the beach.

"*Tabanda!*" Tuka grabbed at Carter's arm and pointed along the shore.

Along the coast the headlights of two vehicles could be seen approaching the jetty.

Yukichi cursed his driver and told him to go faster. He knew that he was being unreasonable but he needed to shout at someone. The driver made a token gesture of hunching over the wheel and checking in the mirror to see that the accompanying truck was keeping up with them. He could not go any faster without losing it, and in these conditions excessive speed was madness . . . they'd already nearly driven into a bomb crater in the center of the town.

Above their heads the aerial battle was still going on. The Zekes and Zeroes waiting on call from Matupi had been quickly launched into the air, and were trying to smash through the fighter cover of the F-6F Hellcats to get at the Liberators. The airfield itself was getting heavy bombing.

Yukichi wondered why the Americans had changed the pattern of their attacks and were coming in just before dawn. Perhaps they hoped for an element of surprise as well as the advantage in accuracy that the light would give them. Maybe they were trying to get the last of the barges as they returned to the tunnels. Whatever the reason, they were taking a big risk. Without cloud cover the cumbersome Liberators were sitting ducks for the veteran crews of the anti-air guns and any fighter that could get past the Hellcats.

As he watched, two pinpoint lines of tracer intersected at the tail of a bomber and flames started to pour from it. Slowly but inexorably the nose dipped, and the plane dived toward the sea, leaving a trail of black smoke. Yukichi's view was interrupted by a clump of trees. When he next looked there was only a scatter of burning wreckage on the surface of the water.

The vehicle bumped over a pothole and Yukichi's head hit the roof. He swore at his driver and the road, and strained his eyes into the darkness. They must be nearly there now. The headlights picked up a truck pulled onto the side of the road. Yukichi swore again as his driver had to slow down and edge around the obstacle in four-wheel drive, the vehicle sideslipping crazily in the soft earth. Now he could see the concrete bunker ahead and figures emerging from it. The driver found the road again and within seconds Yukichi was jumping out and running to the jetty.

It was empty. The outline of the barge could just be seen pulling away from the shore.

Yukichi turned to the men who had come from the bunker, who told him they had nearly finished loading the barge when the raid began. They had taken cover, they admitted slightly shamefacedly. The barge captain must have taken the decision to proceed with his instructions and dump the explosives out at sea without further delay.

Yukichi nodded, the men had made the right decision. If the barge was hit the further away from shore it happened, the better. The man had shown courage and initiative. Yukichi would see that he was recommended for a decoration when he returned. *If* he returned. The danger was not yet over. Nevertheless Yukichi felt relieved as he turned away from the jetty. Now he could concentrate on finding the missing raider.

Chapter Twenty-Seven

HUDSON sat in the cell and waited. It was dark but he could see light through the grille in the door and hear the sounds of feet and orders being shouted. The Japanese seemed to have a lot on their plates at the moment. They had taken his watch but he calculated it was half an hour since they'd been thrown into the cell. Green appeared to be in a coma. Sula was sitting with her back to a wall and her long legs drawn up almost to her breasts. A hand rested against Green's temple as if she was caressing a pet. They were still manacled and chained to each other.

Hudson looked at his two companions and thought of the torture, certain death, waiting for them. He closed his eyes. If only he hadn't let that carrier go . . .

It was Green who broke the silence, his voice faint but under control. "Andrew? There's something that's been worrying me."

Hudson looked at Sula. Her eyes met his and she shook her head. "What is it, Harry?"

"I didn't tell you the truth about Errol Flynn."

"Doesn't matter, Harry." There were probably a hundred old-timers in the islands who had Errol Flynn stories. Damn few ever met him.

"I didn't knock him out, fellow hit me with a bottle before I could get my guard up—"

"Don't worry, Harry." Hudson laid a hand on Green's shoulder. "When I tell it, you knocked him cold. A straight left to the point of the jaw."

Green made a contented noise at the back of his throat as if savoring the image. "I could have done it too, if he'd fought like a gentleman." A pause. "Andrew?" The voice was fainter.

"Yes, Harry?"

"Do you remember why I wanted to get out of the camp?"

"Something about a hundred thousand quid, wasn't it?"

"Yes. Chap who'd made a strike up at Edie Creek. He hid his cache when he came out here to see his brother. The Japs got him the same time they got me. When he was dying he drew me a map." Green raised his hands and tapped the breast pocket of his tattered Jap tunic. "Help yourself."

"You want me to take care of it for you?"

Green made a wheezing noise. "You're very diplomatic for an Australian, Andrew. I'm not going to have any use for it. Take it!"

Hudson saw that there was no point in arguing, and managed to retrieve a wrinkled piece of paper which he thrust into one of his own pockets. "Thanks, Harry. Remember, I'm just holding it for you."

"See that our girl friend gets a cut." He lowered his voice to a whisper. "And Will, when you see him . . . a good boy . . . Do you remember the old days, Andrew? When the only Jap we knew was Jap River fever. Do you remember the cure? A handful of quinine tablets and a bottle of whiskey. It was a toss-up which killed you —the fever or the Scotch." He started a laugh which ended in a spasm of coughing.

"Don't talk, save your strength."

"We didn't do badly, did we?" Green said.

"Did great," Hudson said.

"The Japs may have this place, but . . ." his accent became very British . . . "they're like monkeys climbing up a tree, the higher they get the more you see their arses."

The cell door crashed open as if an eavesdropper had heard the last remark. Framed in it was the squat menace of Namura with a guard behind him. His eyeless socket was a black hole in his face. He looked from Hudson to the recumbent Green. Green's mouth was open, but his eyes were closed.

"He's dead," Hudson said.

If Namura understood he gave no sign of it. His eye fixed on Sula and a finger advanced in a beckoning gesture. The guard stepped forward and unlocked the padlock on the chain. Sula was pulled to her feet and the padlock relocked. She turned to Hudson and for the first time her composure began to weaken. Now she was face to face with the reality.

"The girl doesn't know anything," Hudson said.

Namura paused in the act of leaving the cell and glanced sharply at the guard. Instantly a boot thudded into Hudson's kidneys. Sula was pulled from the cell as she tried to protest, and the door slammed shut.

Hudson was alone in the darkness, chained to Green's corpse.

Carter spun the wheel to port and felt the barge respond. His first relief after feeling the barge move through the water had been the lack of pursuing shots from the jetty. He took this to mean the Japs had assumed it was the captain taking the vessel out to sea.

He looked toward the main dock area. A second wave of bombers was coming in, puffs of smoke and fountains of spray showed the path the bombs were taking. As far as he could see there were no barges still at the wharves and only one gutted truck propped on its end against a pile of rubble and burning brightly. The barges seemed to be taking shelter in the lea of the cliffs. As he watched, a Hellcat came in low over the water and started strafing one of them. A Zero came sweeping down on its tail, and the F-6F pilot pulled back his stick and climbed for safety.

Carter peered through the shattered window of the wheelhouse.

A stray bomb was one thing. He hadn't figured on being singled out for a personal attack by one of his own side. The pilot could well get the surprise of his foreshortened life. Along the shore the antiaircraft gun emplacements were blazing away, and Carter could see the men and the patterns on the camouflage netting illuminated in the flash each time they fired. Out to sea there were other flashes as Japanese ships opened up at the attackers. Beside him Baka and Tuka crouched . . . nothing in their most haunted dreams could have ever prepared them for what was going on now.

The prow of the barge struck something. When Carter looked down at the wreckage floating in the water he saw a seat with a man strapped in it—he was burnt dead. There were two other bodies wearing flying helmets and a piece of fuselage with a saucy painting of a Varga-type bathing cutie on it. The name scrawled in bold italic letters beneath it was unreadable below the waves. It was the remains of a downed Liberator, no survivors.

Carter left the corpses behind. Without the raid he would still be pinned down on the beach. Now he had a weapon. How was he going to deliver it? He looked toward the cliff face which hid the main entrances to the caves and felt his top pocket. He still had the detonator he had been about to test in the volcano. He pulled it out and examined it. It seemed to be in decent condition. He could take the barge in close, set the detonator and jump with Baka and Tuka.

But what about Sula, Hudson and Green? Was he going to abandon them?

He thought of Sula and the possibility of never seeing her again. Not a possibility—it was a near certainty. His eyes were drawn to the cliffs again. She must be in there somewhere. They must all be.

As he looked he saw a bright red light flashing from the cliffs just above sea level. And then another, slightly to starboard. The lights were obviously signals. But to whom? Then he saw one of the barges near the beach give a quick answering flash. It threw up a small rooster tail in the water and steered in on the light.

Carter was puzzled. Surely the skipper was not going to run his craft up on the beach and abandon it. For a few seconds it seemed that this must be what was happening . . . the barge nosed in against the shore, its prow almost touching the steeply shelving

245

beach. Then, as Carter watched in amazement, the barge started to move slowly up the beach like some prehistoric reptile emerging from the sea.

He looked again and realized what must be happening. The light was being flashed from inside one of the tunnels and was invisible from the air. It was a guide light for the skipper and a signal that the tunnel team was ready to receive his craft. The barges were winched up the beach and berthed in the tunnels. The red light Carter had been watching went out and another started flashing beside it. Another barge flashed and moved in.

Inside the cliff the barges would be perfectly protected yet accessible to the docks. They could pop in and out like mice from the wall . . .

Inside the cliffs.

The words repeated themselves in his brain, and the fingers of his injured arm gripped the wheel with a new vigor. Was it possible? Could this floating bomb become a Trojan horse that the Japs winched into their stronghold? He began to steer toward the cliffs almost oblivious to the hell that was still breaking out all around him.

Oblivion did not last long. Alerted by the warning shriek of a 1,700-horsepower engine hurtling out of the sky, Carter looked to port and saw a TBF-1 Avenger swooping in low toward him. A trail of machine-gun bullets accelerated toward him, and a silver cigar dropped from the plane's belly. A torpedo. As the Avenger zipped overhead Carter spun the wheel and flung Baka and Tuka across the wheelhouse. The bales of explosives slewed across the deck and slammed against the side with a nerve-jarring thud. The stubby little craft keeled over at such an angle that it shipped water. The bales tumbled down and nearly vanished over the side.

Carter clung to the wheel and saw the seascape blur past. At any second he expected to feel himself being torn apart by the force of a gigantic explosion, but the vessel began to right itself on its new course. He scanned the water. Gliding serenely toward him as if drawn by a magnet was a silver shape trailing a long line of bubbles. The prow was still coming round and as Carter braced himself, the torpedo missed by only a foot and continued toward the shore. A sigh of relief cut short when another menacing shape swooped toward him—a Zeke fighter. His instinctive reaction was to duck, then realized the Zeke was on his side. It swept overhead in pursuit of the climbing Avenger. Tracers started carving up the sky. The torpedo exploded harmlessly against a wharf. Carter brought the vessel round and resumed his course toward the cliffs. Two barges were moving up the beach simultaneously and another light beckoned. Carter looked about him. On the starboard side of the wheelhouse hung a signal lantern. What was he waiting for? There was only one other barge visible that was still at sea.

Calling to Tuka to hold the wheel steady, Carter switched on the lamp. It glowed red, illuminating Baka's perplexed face. Carter switched off the lamp and began to explain what he was going to try to do. He told the two men that there was no obligation to come with him. They could be dropped off to swim ashore. Baka looked at Tuka and both men shook their heads, they'd stay, though Tuka admitted that his decision was helped by the fact that he could not swim.

The shore was now two hundred yards away. Carter could see the palms hanging over the water and the dark shadow that was the mouth of the tunnel. The red light kept blinking. Two figures were waiting knee-deep in the water, and there was a dark shape between them, which Carter thought must be a platform or trolley on which the barge would be winched into the tunnel. He hoped that the men would be so conditioned by what was to them an everyday task that they would not pay too much attention to the crew of the barge they were berthing. Looking back, he saw that the bales were scattered all over the open hold. He told Baka and Tuka to place them together near the funnel and below the level of the gunwales.

The air attack appeared to be over, although the antiaircraft guns around the airfield were still hammering away. A few fires burned among the wharves and there was a dense column of smoke rising from the hillside above the town where a Liberator had come down. Men were calling to each other and flashing torches among the bomb craters. Searchlights combed the sky. The smell of burning men and machines drifted across the water.

Less than a hundred yards now. Eighty . . . fifty. Baka and Tuka crouched at his feet, gripping their bush knives. Carter could see the faces of the Japanese clearly now. One of them wore a cap pulled low over his eyes, the other had a white handkerchief knotted 'round his head. Their hands came up to receive the prow of the barge. Carter cut power, sensing that he had left it too late. There was an angry shout from the shore. The barge crunched against something and scraped to a halt. Palm fronds were brushing against the side of the wheelhouse.

Carter was nearly frozen with tension. There was the sound of something cranking against the prow. He shrank back into the shadows, his heart ticking like a bomb. Another shout.

He stooped toward the gun that lay at his feet, there was a cranking noise and the sound of a hawser stretched tight. The barge trembled, lurched and began its journey up the beach.

The Trojan horse was on the move.

CHAPTER TWENTY-EIGHT

YUKICHI paced impatiently as he watched the gang of men filling in the bomb crater. From where he was standing he could see the cliffs. Admiral Yamamoto would have to take this road to the airport. The crater would have to be filled in before he could move.

He looked out to sea toward the east. Dawn was breaking. The first fingers of light were reaching over the horizon. The sun would soon rise, showing itself gloriously as the emblem that adorned the national flag, reanimating in each soldier that looked on it a sense of faith in his country's destiny.

Yukichi filled his lungs with the scents of battle and turned away from the men repairing the damage to the road. He walked along a line of splintered tree stumps and past bungalows smashed almost out of recognition by bombs and looting. A dog ran past him with something in its mouth. Yukichi watched it disappear into one

249

of the houses. No matter what the Americans threw at them they would never retake Rabaul. They could dig a moonscape of craters six feet deep with their bombs and never really harm the tunnels.

Yukichi came to an intersection and looked up toward what remained of the corrugated-iron building. The events of the last forty-eight hours had driven all thoughts of the House of Contentment and Love from his mind. Now the problem had been resolved by an American bomb. Except for one wall which abutted on the hillside, and part of a steeply shelving floor, there was nothing left except a heap of twisted metal. Scraps of scorched clothing flapped among the rubble as an ambulance truck was taking away the bodies and other men picked through the smoking ruins looking for survivors.

Yukichi turned on his heels and started walking back the way he had come. The girls in the brothel should have been housed in the tunnels . . . if they were indispensable to the welfare of the troops they should have been considered worthy of sharing their accommodations. . . . He noticed that fresh earth spattered the road and crossed to find a deep hole in one of the overgrown lawns. Projecting from it was the tailfin of an enormous thousand-pound bomb that had not exploded. Either the firing mechanism had failed or the bomb was on a delayed-action time fuse. The Americans had dropped several delayed-action bombs in recent weeks, taking a heavy toll of men brought in to clear up damage. He turned his back and hurried away, thinking what a disaster it would be if the bomb went off when the admiral was passing. He would have the street sealed off for twenty-four hours.

Yukichi had barely reached the end of the road and was in sight of his vehicle—when the bomb went off. The blast hurled him forward. He felt as if a battering ram had smashed his backbone. His ears sang and his nose was bleeding. Earth half covered his body and spattered down like rain on the surrounding foliage. He tried to pull himself to his knees, and fell forward on his face.

Carter heard the explosion as the barge shuddered awkwardly across the road but he hardly noticed it. He had more immediate problems. Pulling back into the shadow of the wheelhouse he looked down to see a group of men parting as the barge approached the tunnel entrance. They were holding sandbags. Carter saw the emaciated bodies in the tattered shorts and thought he recognized faces he had seen at the prison camp. What were they doing here? His question was soon answered. As the barge entered the tunnel, its funnel nearly scraping the roof, the men stepped forward and started laying lines of sandbags across the entrance behind it. They were making a wall three sandbags thick, presumably to keep out the ash and lava if Matupi erupted. Two guards supervised, rifles slung over their shoulders, and they carried canes which they were quick to wield if a bag was misplaced or not positioned fast enough.

Carter swiveled around to look in front of him. Two unarmed soldiers operated the winch which was set in the side of the tunnel, with the hawser taking a couple of turns round a movable capstan set in a slot in the middle of two rails. Other slots receded into the tunnel suggesting that the capstan could be moved to accommodate more than one barge. At the moment there were no barges ahead.

Carter's barge rocked on its trolley and came to rest with its prow nudging against the capstan. The tunnel sloped slightly into the interior so that the capstan acted as a stop. Take it away and unhook the hawser and the barge would only need a slight push to glide into the interior of the mountain . . . Baka and Tuka could take care of the two men on the winch. That left the two guards for him. He whispered to the two natives and dropped to his hands and knees to crawl from the wheelhouse. He reached the narrow gangway and moved past the smokestack to the open hold. He looked down at his gun, prayed that it would not choose this moment to jam.

The mouth of the cave was just beyond the stern, and he could hear the whining orders of the Japanese and the swishing of their canes. When he arrived at the stern he would be right above them. He eased off the safety catch and crept past the bales of explosive to take up a position beside the rudder mechanism. Looking forward he could see Baka waiting for the signal beside the wheelhouse. He extended an upraised thumb and got to his feet.

The first soldier had his arm raised in the act of striking a prisoner as Carter shot him through the head from point-blank range.

The second ducked and turned, and a short burst clipped the sandbags before hitting him in the back. He crumpled up beneath the punctured bags, the sand covering him. The prisoners, startled, couldn't take in what was happening. Carter vaulted from the barge to find himself face to face with the man he'd knocked out in the prison hut.

"Christ," the man said. The expression on his face suggested that even the appearance of the real article could not have prompted a stronger reaction.

Carter snatched off one of the guard's caps and shoved it on the head of the smallest man. "Pick up that rifle and look as if you're guarding us. The rest of you keep working and listen."

Sula lay on the table, her body spread-eagled, leather straps cutting into her wrists and ankles. Above her a bright light shone from a low ceiling. The dimensions of the room would have been claustrophobic in any circumstance. Carved out of the rock it was like a tomb.

Namura stood near the door. He felt ill at ease although he did his best not show it. To be present at an interrogation was something he detested. Not because he had any repugnance for bloodshed but because he believed that it was beneath his dignity. However, General Koji had ordered him to attend . . . He dabbed at the sweat that had been running into his eyeless socket and nodded at the interrogator to continue.

The interrogator, a squat man with nails bitten down to the quick, spoke slowly. "I am going to repeat a simple question. Where were you meeting the submarine?"

Sula closed her eyes tight. "I know nothing about a submarine."

Namura shifted impatiently, and the interrogator rightly interpreted this as a sign that his slowness in getting information was meeting with disapproval. He decided to change his approach. Perhaps humiliation would be the answer. He moved closer to the table so that his thigh brushed against one of Sula's spread-eagled legs.

"You have two choices. I can be gentle with you . . ." He let his words trail away and raised his hand in the air before letting it fall on Sula's breasts. He massaged them slowly, then lowered his

252

fingertips so that they trailed across her belly and fell between her legs. Sula jerked her head from the table and spat in the man's face.

There was a moment's pause, then a sharp crack as his fist came down to shatter her nose.

The interrogator's voice took on a chilling edge. ". . . or I can be very hard."

Sula fought to breathe. Blood was flowing into her mouth. She felt she was suffocating.

Namura stepped forward and spoke in Japanese. "We have no time for subtlety or finesse. You are a woman and we will find the simplest way to cut the truth out of you."

He nodded to the interrogator, who translated his words, then turned to the guard. "Give me your bayonet."

General Koji sat in his office and looked at his watch. Yukichi ought to have been back by now. There had been no word since his report that the barge had picked up the explosives and put out to sea. Perhaps the wireless room was too busy with messages relating to the bombing raid. First reports suggested that the Americans had paid heavily—seven bombers and three fighters shot down, three bombers so badly damaged it was highly doubtful they ever returned to base. In return, only three Zeroes and a Zeke had been lost, although considerable damage had been done to the runway at the airfield, making it difficult for the returning planes to land. The harbor area had received its usual battering but with minimal damage to installation, materiel and personnel: two mobile cranes and an ammunition truck destroyed, one barge and a submersible barge—thankfully empty—damaged. Thirteen men dead, forty-five injured . . .

Koji looked at the telephone on his desk, anticipating that at any moment it would ring and he would hear Yamamoto's voice patiently asking why it was still impossible to leave for the airfield. He knew that the admiral mourned the loss of his friends and aides in the American ambush of his plane and wished to finish his tour and start reorganizing his staff with the least possible delay.

Koji stood up and walked to the door. He would visit the communications center himself and see what was happening. He was eager for the latest details of how his well-prepared soldiers had driven back the enemy, as well as news of Yukichi.

The two guards outside the room came to attention as he passed and started to move across the open space toward the communications center. A familiar whirring noise made him look to his right, and he saw one of the battery-driven floats approaching with two soldiers on board. He frowned. It was clearly set down in brigade regulations that the floats would only be used for towing materiel. Ordinary soldiers were expected to walk in the tunnels.

General Koji looked around for an officer or non-commissioned soldier. It was not his place to reprimand ordinary soldiers.

The two soldiers saw the general standing in the middle of the open space and stopped the float immediately, jumped from it as if it was white-hot and stood with heads bowed.

Koji asked their names and what they thought they were doing. They told him that they had been on guard duty and were returning their weapons to the armory. Koji told the men to complete their business and then report to their sergeant. They were to inform him that they had been riding on a float without good cause and ask for punishment. The men saluted and hurried the last few yards to the armory.

Koji went on his way and entered the radio vault, telling the men not to stand up but get on with what they were doing. He asked for the latest details of the raid and learned that a Zeke had been badly damaged on landing and the pilot killed. Planes could take off from the airfield but they would need another hour to get it fully operational. The corrected figure for enemy losses was now six bombers and three fighters destroyed.

Maintenance units were going all out in the middle of the town to repair the main road, which had been straddled by bombs and made impassable. Trucks looking for a detour had become bogged down, and there was now a traffic jam. Only tracked vehicles would get through. There was still no word from Yukichi. Did the general wish to contact him by wireless?

Koji considered and declined. Yukichi must be held up by the roadworks. He would be back within the hour and by that time the airfield would be fully operational and Yamamoto could take off in safety. There was no need to cling to his adjutant . . . Yukichi had proved that he was shrewd, resourceful and more than capable of looking after himself.

General Koji left the communications center and climbed the stairs to his office. He paused outside the room he had placed at Yamamoto's disposal and listened. There was no sound. For a moment he thought of knocking and giving the admiral the latest news, then decided against it. Yamamoto would be working, planning, perhaps even getting some much-needed sleep. It would be best to leave him alone. In truth, Koji acknowledged to himself, he was grateful to find reasons for not appearing before the admiral. He was too much in awe of him ever to feel completely at ease in his presence.

General Koji entered his office and slid the door shut behind him.

The two guards stood at ease and looked across the open space toward the abandoned float standing at the mouth of one of the tunnels.

Hudson sat in the darkness and instinctively glanced at the wrist where his watch should have been. How long since they'd taken Sula away? Twenty minutes? Half an hour? He strained for sounds he didn't want to hear. Actually there was little she could tell them even if she'd wanted to . . .

He got up to move to the door and found himself checked by the chain that attached him to Green's lifeless body. He half-carried the corpse to a spot beside the door and laid it down gently. Poor old Greeny. Looking at that wasted body it was impossible to believe that the man had been capable of driving himself up the side of Matupi . . . Hudson thrust his fingers into his breast pocket and retrieved the crumpled piece of paper that Green had given him. He unfolded it and held it up to the grille. By the faint light he could make out a map reference and two maps drawn to different scales, one showing an area of Edie Creek and the other, larger scale, indicating exactly where the cache was buried in relation to a building. The drawing was done with the shaky hand of a dying man. The writing was almost indecipherable. It seemed genuine enough, but who was ever going to benefit from it? Certainly not the poor devil who had originally worked the claim. Or Harry

Green. On reflection, it seemed like a very unlucky piece of paper to be stuck with . . .

The guard's face loomed up at the grille, and Hudson dropped his manacled hands. The guard stared at him, turned away. Hudson stayed where he was, straining for any breath of fresh air that penetrated the tunnels from the outside world, listening to every sound.

The four Japanese left the armory and started to walk up one of the tunnels used for berthing the barges. Each carried a submachine gun. They were going to relieve the crew of one of the antiaircraft guns positioned on top of the cliffs. None of them was sorry to be leaving the stifling atmosphere of the tunnels. There was always a breeze on the cliffs, and they'd be able to light a fire and smoke out the lice that infested their uniforms.

As they walked, a party of prisoners approached, accompanied by two guards. Some of the men carried spades. The soldiers did not pay much attention. They certainly did not notice the stooped figure in jungle green concealing a Sten gun in the center rank. To the soldiers these were just prisoners being marched to extend the tunnels. They would not be passing this way often.

The prisoners stumbled along in ragged columns and pressed in against the wall to let the soldiers pass. They waited humbly, spades on shoulders. The first soldier turned his head to speak to a comrade and saw the warning signal ignite in the man's eyes. He spun round and received the cutting edge of a spade in his neck. The three other soldiers were engulfed before they could call out as a flurry of arms dragged them down and the life was choked or beaten out of them. Their weapons were reallocated and their bodies dragged on down the tunnel and thrown behind ammunition crates piled in a hewn-out alcove. There was the sound of heavy, nervous breathing as men looked at each other, knowing that they'd committed themselves, that, literally, there was no turning back. The untidy columns formed up again, and the men in the soldiers' uniforms pulled their caps low over their faces and held tight to the slings of their rifles, aware that they might have to use them at any moment. The other weapons stayed with the men in the center column. Now they had four automatics, including Carter's gun.

256

Ahead, light splashed into the corridor and there was the grinding noise of a machine. Carter urged his men to close up and keep marching. So far they had been walking in semidarkness and the men in the center ranks with the weapons could be easily concealed.

The light came from a workshop area in which a man with a protective mask worked at a motorized lathe. A shower of sparks spilled across the stone floor. Other men were working at benches or overhauling an aircraft engine suspended by a chain hoist from the ceiling. None of the mechanics gave the prisoners more than a passing glance as they passed on their way to the interior.

Carter looked anxiously ahead. Each step was taking them closer to trouble, further away from the explosive. Whatever happened somebody had to get back to that. Where the hell were the others? With tunnels going off to left and right it would take hours to find them. And it was impossible to march around with forty men, two of them dressed as Japanese guards and failing miserably to look the part if seen in anything stronger than candlelight, for more than a few minutes without arousing suspicion.

Ahead, the tunnel leveled out and opened up. A glare of bright lights cut through the gloom. Carter was wondering what to do when he heard the scream—long and rising and piercing new layers of pain as it went on, and he was running before the scream had entered its dying fall. He knew Sula's voice as if it were his own.

He burst into an open space and saw two marines staring in amazement at his ragged, barefoot body. The scream started again, and he was running before they had unslung their weapons. Up another corridor, past a blaze of lights. One of the marines came to his senses and dropped on one knee to take aim. As he raised his gun, a burst of bullets from the tunnel mouth cut him down and sent him pitching forward, his face hanging over the ledge. The second guard swung around to return the fire and went down as bullets pockmarked the wall behind him. Men began to flood into the open space.

Carter found himself outside a door with the scream filling his ears. There was a madness in him that could have kicked down a brick wall. His foot lashed out and the door burst open.

He glimpsed Sula pegged out on a table and three Japs, one of them almost on top of her. Namura's eyeless socket was nearest the door. In front of him he saw the guard's look of surprise as he fought to unsling his rifle. Namura started to turn round, grabbing for his pistol, and as he did so Carter shot him through the head, then opened up on the guard, who jerked backward, then he slid to the floor, leaving a red trail on the wall. Now there was only the interrogator, standing with the bloody bayonet in his hand. Carter shot him through the heart. He fell backward on top of the guard. The air was full of smoke and cordite.

Carter stepped over Namura's body and advanced to the table. Sula's bloody nose was swollen across her face like a humpback bridge. More blood was between her thighs. She began to cry again, this time in unbelieving joy at seeing him. He drew out his knife and slashed through the bonds at her wrists and ankles. He could see what she had endured from the depth of the weals.

"Can you move?"

She moved her legs from the table and cried out as she put her weight on them. Blood was running down to her knees. She closed her eyes momentarily and gripped his arm, then managed to stoop and take up the guard's rifle. She said nothing but looked at Carter and nodded.

From outside came automatic fire and a volley of shouts. Carter watched Sula take two steps and moved quickly to the door with her at his elbow.

"Where are the others?" he asked. Sliding back the door and peering out at floor level, he could see men firing from the mouths of the tunnels. The air was thick with smoke. In the confined atmosphere of the tunnels the noise was deafening. Sula's eyes took in the corridor. She was clearly confused. "I think . . ." she pointed uncertainly away from the central junction.

Carter got to his feet. "You wait here."

He started in the direction she had pointed.

Sula came after him.

Hudson heard the sound of shots and craned his head to see out of the grille. Who was doing the shooting? Some Japs must have gone crazy, group hara-kiri . . .

And then there was the sound of more shots and a small battle breaking out. Hudson began to believe in the impossible.

Outside the cell his guard was clearly uncertain whether to search out the action or stay with his prisoner. He ran a short way down the tunnel, then returned. The sight of Hudson's staring face infuriated him, and he jabbed his bayonet through the grille.

"Better pack it in while you've got the chance, mate," Hudson said.

The Jap yelled threats at him and withdrew his bayonet.

There was the sound of more firing. Then a voice . . . calling out his name? He must be crazy, except then he heard it clearly. "Hudson, Hudson . . ." It was Carter's voice, no mistake.

He threw himself against the grille and started to call out, "Over here, over here . . ."

The Japanese guard promptly turned and drove his bayonet straight at Hudson's face. It was only diverted by one of the bars of the grille, narrowly missing his cheek as it started backward. He tripped over his chain and fell. The guard opened fire and bullets passed just above his head. Carter was still shouting. He scrambled for the corner of the cell farthest from the door and nearest the wall of the tunnel. The bayonet swung round with him until the bars of the grille stopped it from moving any further. Bullets chewed chunks out of the soft pumice stone. Hudson dragged Green's corpse behind him and pressed himself flat against the wall. The guard fired again, the bullet thumping into the wall. Hudson was now within the angle of safety . . . the guard would have to come into the cell to get him—

A burst of fire from the tunnel and the bayonet tilted up crazily toward the ceiling and eventually slid from sight. The cell door opened, and Carter and Sula were, unbelievably, there.

"What took you so long?"

The chatter of a Nambu-92 machine gun cut short any smart reply.

Hudson rattled his chain. "The guard has a key."

Sula was at the door keeping watch. She dragged the body into the cell and searched the pockets, tossing the key to Carter, who went to catch it and suddenly found that his right arm would not move. The key dropped to the ground. Hudson retrieved it, grabbed and unhooked the padlock, and threw it across the cell. His manacled hands tore at the chain.

"*Right.* Now show me the way out of here."

Carter gripped his gun with his left hand and moved for the door. He paused and looked over his shoulder at the others. "Okay, follow me."

General Koji had heard the opening burst of fire with the same sense of astonishment as Hudson. It sounded so close as to be right outside his door. His first reaction was for Yamamoto's safety. Drawing his revolver he had run for the door and tried to pull it open. As more shots sounded he found the door difficult to budge. The reason was soon obvious . . . as the door slid open a few inches the body of one of his guards was revealed wedged against it. Koji squinted through the gap and saw that the mouth of the tunnel opposite was full of men—ragged men whom he recognized as part of Colonel Namura's work force. They must have overpowered their guards and seized their weapons. Incredible. Another burst of fire sprayed the front of the offices and he scrambled back to his desk and snatched up the telephone. It was dead.

At any moment, he realized, the men might burst through the door, or worse—through Yamamoto's a few yards away. He ran back to the door to hold them off until reinforcements arrived. He was taking aim with his pistol when he glimpsed the sling of the dead guard's submachine gun an arm's length away. Lying flat against the floor and using the body as a shield, he stretched out an arm and plucked at the air until his fingers closed around the sling and he could pull the weapon to him. Scrambling to his knees he squinted down the barrel and felt for the safety catch. It was not where he expected it to be. After a moment's surprise he realized the model must have changed since he'd last fired it. He examined the weapon quickly and discovered what modifications had been made.

From the mouth of the tunnel opposite, three men made a rush toward him. He aimed at their knees and fired a long burst, waving the muzzle slightly, as if shaking drops of water from it. The first man fell forward, losing his weapon, and the man to his right tried to pick it up. He too went down. The third man lost his nerve and ran for the shelter of the nearest tunnel. A belated burst of covering fire splintered the door above Koji's head, and then silence. Koji risked a glance at the tunnel mouth and saw only the two bodies of the men he had shot. He'd managed a temporary respite. But how temporary? And what had happened to Yamamoto? There was another sign of movement in the tunnel mouth and he fired a burst. If he could just keep them away for a few more moments reinforcements must arrive . . .

Yamamoto was sleeping when the shooting started. It was his habit to take short, restorative catnaps whenever a suitable occasion presented itself. In this way he found the hours which other men devoted to sleeping could be more profitably employed. Quickly identifying the noise of automatic fire he swung his legs from the low bed and moved toward the door. He had taken two steps when a sharp pain stung him just below the left collarbone. His hand instinctively moved to the spot, and he was surprised to feel something damp and see a patch of red spreading out from beneath his fingers and staining his white uniform. He realized with a shock that he had been hit by a bullet. A neat, round hole was visible in one of the door panels.

The pain was not as great as his sense of surprise. Had his life been spared one day only to be taken the next? It occurred to him that he was unarmed, apart from his ceremonial sword which lay on a small table. He drew it with difficulty and looked down at the shining steel. The act was a symbolic one. The thought of defending himself in a physical sense did not enter his mind. He was thinking of a poem he had written a few days before:

> *I am still the sword*
> *of my Emperor;*
> *I will not be sheathed*
> *Until I die.*

The blood had now spread to his ribbons and he crossed the room and lay on the bed. Looking up, the ceiling was bathed in gray light and he remembered how it had been as a child, when the icy wind blew across the Sea of Japan from Russia and the snows

261

came. Even in October the snow had fallen to a depth of twelve or fourteen feet in the village and the small thatched house had been buried until spring. Planks had been propped on poles underneath the eaves and these kept the snow away to form passages by which the people of the village could move from house to house, burrowing through tunnels dug at the street corners. He had lain on the *tatami* with a blanket over him and gazed through the oiled-paper window at the imprisoning walls of snow that cut him off from the outside world. It was almost the same now. He could even feel the cold creeping into his bones.

He closed his eyes. The noise of battle seemed a long way away. . . .

When Carter emerged from Hudson's cell it took him only seconds to realize that the odds were stacking against them. The sound of automatic fire was drowned by the rattle of the Nambu machine gun that was spraying the open space. He guessed that the prisoners had been held up at the junction of the tunnel—those of them that were left. It was only a question of time before they were overrun. Somehow, Carter knew, they had to get back across the brightly lit intersection. Fast.

A party of soldiers ran out of a side tunnel, and Carter pressed back against the wall. Clearly they were only interested in the area the shots were converging on. They began firing indiscriminately, with no idea what was happening. If they'd known what they were up against—or, rather, *not* up against—they would have been on their feet and charging. Parties of defenders were opening up from several different tunnels, which helped confuse them about the real strength of the insurgents.

Carter waved the others back, then ducked into a side tunnel piled to the ceiling with giant spools of signal wire. He looked about him quickly but there was nothing else. No convenient box of flares or hand grenades. Hudson plucked at his arm and pointed ahead with his manacled wrists. At the intersection of the tunnel with another of the main arterial tunnels was the square black bulk of one of the battery floats. Carter ran toward it and threw himself down against the wall. The noise of the machine gun was now deafening. He extended his head into the main tunnel and saw that the two-man team was tucked in against the wall with the gun mounted on three speedily arranged sandbags to stop the tripod from sliding to the floor. They were shooting into the open space. A dozen Japanese armed with carbines and submachine guns were edging down the opposite wall, about to attack.

Carter turned to the float. There was room for four people on the narrow driving platform. The steel shields on each side were intended more as protection for the battery than for anyone riding on the float. Carter fitted his last magazine and looked at the others. Time was running out.

He ran forward and jumped onto the float. There was a driving wheel, a hand brake and an upright lever for engaging the power. Sula came up at his left side and rested her rifle on the battery. Hudson was on the right of the platform. Carter took off the brake with his left hand and tried to press the lever. His arm let him down again. Hudson thrust forward with his manacled hands and there was a low whirring noise, virtually imperceptible amid the rattle of gunfire. It sounded as if there was still somebody firing from the barge tunnel. The float began to glide forward and close the distance to the unsuspecting men manning the Nambu. Carter held his gun in his left hand and tried to take steady aim at the machine-gun team.

The float was now building up speed as Hudson hunched himself on the platform and pressed his shoulder against the lever. Carter squinted down the waivering barrel, pressed the trigger. The machine-gunner jerked forward, the barrel of his weapon slewed up toward the ceiling, still firing. The second man rolled aside and found himself directly in the path of the float. He twisted again as one of the protective shields caught him a glancing blow on the head, which stretched him out senseless. The float charged on down the corridor. Sula shot two men point-blank, clubbed a third who jumped at her before she could take aim. Carter was firing behind them now as Hudson tried to steer with his manacled hands.

The float burst into the open space. There was a blaze of lights and the acrid smell of smoke. Bullets ricocheted off the steel plating and the float lurched as it bounded over the outstretched arm of one of the dead prisoners who had tried to rush the offices.

Carter turned to see the choice of two tunnels and nearly hit a second float before swinging the wheel over and skimming through the litter of broken glass and spent cartridge cases into welcome darkness.

Around them, those not dead or dying and still able to move were retreating up the tunnel, shooting out the lights as they went. They tried to run as the float went past and then relapsed into a stumbling walk as they cursed their wasted limbs. Carter steered the float into the alcove where they had hidden the bodies of the Japanese and led the others toward the tunnel mouth, hoping that they would not meet any soldiers flooding in over the sandbagged barrier. He saw the outline of the barge against the lightening sky, a sight that gave him the strength to drive his exhausted legs forward. All he needed was a couple of minutes . . .

Behind them there came a violent glare of light and heat, and a volley of screams. Carter turned to see that fifty yards back the tunnel was a mass of flames. The Japanese were using a flame-thrower, anybody in its path was being incinerated.

Carter reached the barge and was met by Baka and Tuka, who told him that trucks were letting men off outside the nearest tunnel entrance. He told them to help him over the side of the barge, then urged Sula and Hudson to remove the capstan. He tossed his weapon into the barge and jumped to grab at the gunwale with his good hand. Baka and Tuka pushed him upward. He landed in a heap on top of the explosives.

Beneath him Carter could feel the barge trembling. Hudson was calling for help with the capstan. The roar of the flame-thrower sounded again, the screams of burning men seemed only a few yards away. Carter fumbled in his pocket and withdrew the detonator between two fingertips. Unable to use his right arm, he immediately dropped it between the bales. Shots began to ricochet off the hull. His face pressed against the bags, Carter forced his good arm between the loads and stretched out his fingers. There was a warning shout from below. The barge was beginning to slide forward. Carter pulled out the detonator, pressed the minimum setting. He could feel the barge moving. He thrust the thin tube beneath the rough twine and rolled over the side as the barge gathered speed, falling clumsily, and laying half-stunned, as bullets spattered

264

around him and the terrible heat of the flame-thrower scorched his face.

Then the firing stopped, leaving shouts of warning mixed with the sounds of pain.

Carter made for the tunnel entrance with every bit of strength left in his body. Baka and Tuka had run off. Hudson and Sula were in front of him. He could already see the palms and smell fresh air. He dived over the sandbags and glimpsed a row of trucks a hundred yards down the road. Shouts, and a machine gun opened up. With Sula and Hudson by his side he raced across the road, and into the coconut palms.

Koji came out of Yamamoto's room with tears in his eyes. He looked about, saw a medical orderly kneeling by one of the guards. He started to call to him, and then looked up. There was a strange noise approaching down one of the tunnels. A shaking, shuddering, grating roar, it sounded like a tank out of control. Koji saw a shower of sparks and realized what it was, seconds before the prow of the barge burst into the open area with its smokestack scraping the tunnel roof. The trolley disintegrated, the barge spun 'round, slithering broadside against the ledge to stop with a thunderous crash. There was a pause in which the dust began to settle and men began to scramble to their feet.

And then the barge exploded.

As seen from the outside, the explosion lifted the cliffs five feet into the air and then dropped them in an untidy heap. A column of orange and yellow flame burst from the ground as if an enormous gas jet had been turned up. The tunnel exits spewed men, machines. Trees that stood in the way were blasted into pieces. A mushroom cloud of thick black smoke climbed high into the sky and layers of cliff collapsed into the road, burying men and trucks, spilling rocks almost to the water's edge. Long after the first explosion the ground shook repeatedly with secondary detonations as subterranean fuel and ammunition dumps were touched off by the intense heat. Still, no subsequent noise compared with that of the first bang, a full-blooded clout to the eardrums that left the hearer dizzy and giddy, the inhabitant of a twilight world where all the senses were turned down to the wattage of flickering candles.

Carter lay on his face in the sand and felt the hurricane roar over his head. He could sense the palms straining before the blast, their trunks bending to within an inch of snapping, their roots desperately clinging to the ground. He could hear the avalanche of stone crashing down on the road, the splash of rocks dropping like mortar shells into the sea. With every second he expected to be engulfed or smashed to pieces. There seemed to be no end to the enormous weight of earth that had been belched into the air. It was only when the roar had become a rumble and the rumble a trickle that he opened his eyes and looked around.

The palms were torn out of the ground, the road had disappeared. The cliffs were now rubble wreathed in thick clouds of red dust. Flames danced above the turned earth.

Carter rose unsteadily to his feet, his ears ringing. He gazed about him through the blasted palms and suddenly remembered the two Japanese who had guided his barge onto the trolley. There was no sign of them. He took half a dozen painful steps and leaned against a palm. The truck was the same color as the sand and the sky and the sea. Everything was gray. He closed his eyes and opened them to see movement in the trees ahead. He dropped to his knees, felt dizziness and nausea. Then he started to crawl for cover and toppled over on his side. With a start, he realized that his strength had given out. This was it. He could not go any further.

"Will? Are you all right?" Hudson's voice sounded against his ear. The manacled hands were gripping his shoulder.

"We've found the canoe. Come *on.*"

Carter allowed himself to be hauled to his feet and accepted Hudson's support through the palms.

"Baka and the other guy," he asked, "did they—?"

"They're okay, I told them to beat it." Before them was the sea. Thousands of ivory-white fragments of coral lay like an unending carpet along the water's edge. The canoe straddled them—a dugout with an outrigger and three paddles.

Sula, who had been collecting palm fronds for shade and coconuts for food, ran up the beach, stopped, silently put her arms

266

around him. For a few moments he could feel her heart beating against his.

Hudson moved to the canoe and started pushing it into the water. There was hardly a ripple to disturb the surface.

Carter looked down at Sula, allowed himself to stroke the back of her head. Out to sea, the sun was beginning to rise as they started for the canoe.

Yukichi braced the barrel of his pistol against the palm and tried to hold it steady. The pain in his back was excruciating but he fought to maintain control of his senses. The tall man was holding the prow of the canoe. The girl was climbing into it. Now came the man he wanted most—the man whose existence he'd only learned about a few hours before, the man who'd outwitted him until this, the very last turn of the cards. Yukichi closed one eye and squinted down the barrel. A fresh wave of pain broke over him. The sight waivered over the center of his target. Yukichi's finger tightened. At that instant the first rays of sun broke over the horizon and the picture before Yukichi's eyes disappeared into a dazzle of orange. His pressure on the trigger slackened. It was no good. He would have to run forward and fire from point-blank range. He lowered his pistol to waist level so that he could hold it steady between two hands. Now he was ready. At least he would die with honor.

Carter looked at what had once been the cliffs. Fires were still burning but the eerie silence was now broken by the calls of men clambering over the rubble. He took a step toward the canoe and looked up at Matupi. The eastern face of the volcano was painted a soft pink by the first rays of the sun. It looked almost benign in the early morning light.

He turned back to the canoe. Sula sat in the prow, Hudson stood behind her, gripping a Japanese submachine gun in his manacled hands.

Carter began to walk toward them—

"Banzai."

Carter turned 'round as a Japanese soldier staggered from the palms with a pistol in his outstretched arms.

267

"Get *down,*" Hudson called out. As Carter threw himself to the sand, he fired one long continuous burst at the soldier, shredding the front of his dirty uniform, knocking him back into the brush.

The last thing Major Yukichi saw as the pistol flew from his fingers was the rising sun. After that he saw nothing at all.

Chapter Twenty-Nine

THE PT boat had been searching for survivors from the two Liberators that came down after the big raid on Rabaul. After twenty-four hours of diligent sweeping that took it within sight of the coast of New Britain it had found nothing and the sea was getting rough. The captain was about to return to base when the youngest and newest member of the crew swallowed his nerves and shouted that he saw something on the starboard bow. Older hands followed his pointing arm and saw what might have been a scrap of wreckage or driftwood lifting above the waves. Closer inspection showed that it was a dugout canoe with outrigger containing three half-naked bodies lying side by side under a crude shelter of palm fronds and articles of clothing. They looked like corpses laid out on a funeral pyre. It was only when the noise of the engines came deafeningly close that they began to show signs of still being alive. The canoe was held steady with boat hooks and a party

269

scrambled over the side to recover the bodies.

"Jeez!" a sailor whispered, watching the swollen, sun-blistered bodies come over the side. "Are they going to live?"

"Sure," another one said. "They're in great shape compared to some of the guys we've fished out."

"But his arm, it's hanging like a piece of string."

"I've seen worse—"

"And they lived?"

"Some of them." He stepped aside as Hudson's bush jacket was thrown onto the deck from the canoe.

A sailor scrambled over the side and the men with the boat hooks released their hold. The engines of the PT boat fluffed the water and the empty canoe started drifting away.

A sailor looked down at Hudson's jacket disapprovingly, hooked his toe under the torn bloodstained cloth and flicked it into the ocean. The map to half a million dollars' worth of gold was still in the breast pocket as it skipped jauntily on the long, white wake and then disappeared beneath the waves. . . .

In the tiny cabin Carter lay on a bunk and looked at the rivets a few inches above his head. The captain had visited, informing them that he had radioed his base with news of the rescue. He would get them back as quickly as possible.

Sula was asleep in another bunk. She'd lain close to Carter while they'd been adrift. He missed her, and looked forward to her . . .

Carter's stomach ached, his arm throbbed. In the cramped surroundings he remembered the waiting to go ashore from the submarine. And now so many were dead . . . Johnson and Joe, the innocent women and children of Baka's village, the inmates of the prison camp they'd set out to protect and ended up by sacrificing. Human beings had suffered and died but Matupi had not erupted. Carter turned his head and saw that Hudson was watching him.

"What a mess we've made of everything."

"You mean the volcano?"

"Everything."

Hudson shook his head.

"Yeah, we survived, and if we'd stayed at Moresby we'd have survived and so would've a lot of other people."

Hudson pulled himself onto an elbow and drank some water.

"Listen, boy"—his voice was uneven but he spoke with an intensity Carter hadn't heard from him before. "Maybe we could have done it different or done it better but what we did was right. I believe that. I also happen to have a stake in this country. What we did was for that too." His head fell back against the pillow.

Carter listened to the creaking whirr of the fan. "I know what you mean but—" He slowly spread the fingers of his left hand as he tried to find the words.

Hudson turned his head again. "You don't think we *achieved* anything? You know who was in that tunnel network when it went up?"

Carter did not have time to answer before a sailor appeared in the doorway of the stifling cabin. He held a pack of Camels with two cigarettes protruding. At a closer look at the swollen, cracked lips he tapped the cigarettes back into the pack.

"Hi," he said uneasily, "I don't know what outfit you guys are from . . ." He stopped as he saw Sula. "Anyway, we just got some news that might make you feel a little better. Three Thirty-nine Squadron out of Guadalcanal shot down Yamamoto. The little bastard's dead. Confirmed."

He waited for sounds of pleasure and approval. There was a silence punctuated by a short laugh from the older man. "Thanks."

The sailor was nonplussed. He shifted uncomfortably for a moment and then picked up a jug. "I'll get you some more water," he said.

There was no reply so he went out.

Carter stared at the ceiling and thought about Yamamoto. It was difficult to single out a response to the news of one more death, no matter how important the individual. His flesh would rot, his wife weep, his children ask why he did not come home. Pearl Harbor was a long time ago.

Of course, he might have felt somewhat differently, more personally, if he had known the truth of the admiral's demise—and his very special part in it.

The mounting roar of the engines blessedly wiped out all possibility of further thought. For the moment, at least, the war, and all its ironies, was the stuff of dreams.

271

POSTSCRIPT

A war historian with an appetite for statistics has recorded that 20,959 tons of bombs were dropped on Rabaul by Allied aircraft and 388 tons of projectiles fired at it from naval vessels. Despite this relentless bombardment, Rabaul was never successfully reinvaded once the Japanese had installed themselves after their invasion on January 23, 1942. It was bypassed in General MacArthur's island-hopping strategy and it was not until September 6, 1945, in the post-Hiroshima and Nagasaki era, that the then commander, Lieutenant General Hitoshi Imamura, surrendered his 57,368 men to General Sturdee of the Australian Army on board H.M.S. *Glory* off Rabaul.

Not all the tunnel network was destroyed. A few tunnels are still penetrable. There are even the rusted hulks of barges that the Japanese used to bring their supplies ashore. Other equipment rusts and rots. It may be that there are tunnels which hold secrets

272

so far undiscovered. The Japanese naval radio station, hidden in a tunnel only a few hundred yards from the main street of the town, escaped attention for more than twenty years after the end of the war.

Although an eruption was recorded in 1969, Matupi has not seriously erupted since 1937. However, another Papua New Guinea volcano, Mount Lamington, exploded on January 21, 1951, with the destructive force of an atomic bomb, devastating 68 square miles and killing nearly 3,000 people with a "burning cloud" of fragmented lava. A volcano observatory now exists at Rabaul and regular soundings of Matupi are taken so that advance warnings may be given before it next erupts.

Lieutenant John F. Kennedy, later to become president of the United States of America, commanded PT Boat 109 in the South Pacific. When his ship was wrecked on a reef, Lieutenant Kennedy was saved from the Japanese by loyal natives and Coast-watcher Reg Evans operating from Kolombangara in the Solomon Islands.

General Douglas MacArthur was fifty-five years old and already retired from the U.S. Army when, in 1935, he agreed to undertake the reorganization of the Philippines Army, to all intents and purposes a dead-end job. When the Japanese attacked the Philippines in December 1941 he led a spirited but unsuccessful resistance which culminated in his being ordered to Australia to become Supreme Commander of Allied Forces of all services in the Southwest Pacific. In this post he proved himself to be one of the greatest logistic commanders the world has known and a man whose flamboyant egotism insured that his enemies were not limited to those in the armies he fought against. After victory in the Pacific MacArthur became a much respected Supreme Commander in occupied Japan and, in 1950, when he was seventy years old, a brilliant but controversial commander of the UN forces in Korea. He was recalled by President Truman in 1951 for disobeying his commander-in-chief's orders.

Errol Flynn arrived in New Guinea on a yacht from Australia in 1925. He spent seven years there as a cadet patrol officer, planter,

273

labor recruiter and gold prospector. None of the careers he embraced ever yielded him anything. Most of the ladies he embraced yielded him everything. Jealous husbands queued up to aim punches at him, but there is no recorded evidence of his ever having been bested in a fight. Harry Green's recollection of being laid out by a bottle was unusual. Flynn normally needed only his fists. He left suddenly in the direction of Hong Kong—and, of course, eventually Hollywood—leaving a number of broken hearts and jaws and an even larger number of debts. Shortly after his departure, the owner of a local hotel where Flynn had been staying opened a trunk that the future movie star had left behind. It was full of the hotel's sheets and towels.

As recorded by the Americans and Japanese, the death of Admiral Yamamoto poses several interesting questions, few of which have been satisfactorily answered.

When his plane was shot down in the Bougainville jungle, none of the rescue parties sent to the spot was able to penetrate the thick jungle before a Japanese lieutenant on a routine patrol in the area was led to the wreckage by a native. He was apparently qualified to identify a charred body that had been thrown clear of the plane as that of Yamamoto. The body was taken by bearer and boat to the town of Buin. There, a shallow grave was hastily dug on the top of a nearby mountain and the body placed in it and covered with bundles of palm leaves and branches. Gasoline was poured on and ignited, and the resulting ashes were taken to Japan by destroyer.

It was not until a month after the arrival of the ashes that a Japanese radio broadcast announced to the Empire that "Admiral Yamamoto, while directing general strategy in the front line in April of this year, engaged in combat with the enemy and met gallant death in a war plane." The announcer then choked and burst into tears. The announcement on Radio Tokyo caused a great deal of speculation in the United States. The New York *Times* commented: "This indicates that he had not been killed outright but died later from his injuries." The mystery remained because there had been no major activity in the Pacific during April. There were rumors that Yamamoto had committed suicide.

The American press did not have all the details. The American forces were strangely reticent about revealing just how the admiral had died. Despite the presumed morale-boosting possibilities of the coup against Yamamoto's plane, news of the exploit did not come out until *after the war.*

Today, the reasons given seem not altogether convincing. The first was that details of the raid would have alerted the Japanese to the fact that their code had been broken. Since three of the Zekes escorting Yamamoto's bomber survived the American attack, it must be assumed that they were in a position to give firsthand information of their battle with a force numerically twice the size of their own that had suddenly loomed up from the Solomon Sea. Such information must have made the Japanese suspicious. How saying nothing might allay Japanese suspicions is not clear.

The second reason, rather long in coming, for not informing a revenge-hungry American public that Yamamoto had been shot down was that the brother of one of the pilots taking part in the raid was held as a Japanese prisoner of war and there was a fear of reprisals. This risk could have been obviated, one would think, by mentioning neither the unit nor the pilots responsible for the attack in any bulletin that was released.

The attitude of both the Japanese and the Americans to Yamamoto's death does invite conjecture. Was it in fact his body that was identified amidst the burnt-out wreckage in the Bougainville jungle? Perhaps it does not matter. Admiral Yamamoto did die, somewhere, in April 1943, and with his death Japan lost its premiere military strategist. The manner and place of his death pale into relative insignificance beside this fact—whether in the Bougainville jungle, or on a rude cot in the tunnels of Rabaul. . . .